Formally known as
Hope's Chance (2012)
By: Jennifer Foor

This book is dedicated to all of my readers.
Thank you so much for the continued support.

To my beta readers. And their countless hours of time they give me. I am forever indebted to you.

1

Hope

The last day of my senior year in high school was coming to an end. After I fluffed my long ponytail of brown locks, reminding myself that I'd spent no time on my appearance this morning, I looked around at all of the classmates I'd most likely never see again. The large second hand on the black and white clock seemed to move slower than normal. As it made its way to the twelve, I gently obtained my bag off the floor and wrapped it around my shoulder. It was about to get chaotic.

With a short glance across the room I spotted my ex. He had this smirk on his face that I wished I could smack off. Had it not been for the struggles of my past few years, I never would have given him the time of day. He'd taken advantage of my weaknesses, and used me for his own personal punching bag, not physically, but mentally. I couldn't wait to rid him from my life.

When the bell rang loudly I flipped him the finger, bidding him a goodbye he'd never forget.

The halls were crowded as my peers ran around like maniacs. Papers were flying in the air, like kids had just tossed them as they exited the building. It was funny how on the last day of school the halls became empty within seconds. I however, lingered around, knowing I wouldn't be returning. Technically, I was graduating early, on account of my birthday being later in the year. Since I had doubled up on classes and spent the last two summers enrolled with the misfit kids who couldn't pass during the normal school year, just to be able to do it.

You're probably thinking that I loved school, or that I was somehow extraordinarily studious. That couldn't be further from the truth. What pushed me into making the decision were my parents. They used to have such a great relationship, but two years ago my father started having an affair with his secretary. I won't get into the details of how it was discovered, or what it did to me emotionally. I certainly won't bore you with the details of my mother losing her self-worth and falling into an enormous bout of depression.

Shortly after it was revealed, he declared that his new whore wasn't enough for him. He didn't ask to return home, or try to at least make amends with me. Instead he went out and found someone even more disturbingly young to spend his time with. Now the bastard was entertaining the notion of remarrying again. The woman was just five years older than me, and to make matters worse, he didn't see that there was anything wrong with his actions. His mid-life crisis only made me realize how much I loathed him for what he'd done to my life.

When my parents first separated, my father moved all the way to Pennsylvania, to apparently start over, or whatever you call it when you sign up for dating services and creep online to get laid. He left my mother with a steep mortgage she couldn't afford, and eventually we had to move in with my grandparents. According to my mother, which was usually not a good source of information, he hadn't paid child support for nearly a year now.

My dad had worked in real estate and seemed to move somewhere new when the market went dry. To my astonishment he'd called me last month to inform me that he and Buffy, (yes, that's her name) were moving back to Virginia. My mother wasn't thrilled, but even through her animosity toward him, she seemed happy he wanted to make another go at having a relationship with me. I think what was difficult was living in a small town, and seeing families interacting. Once you've become the talk of the town's gossip, it's hard to break away from judgment. I longed for normalcy.

The next morning was my visit with my father. Though reluctant, I did my best to lay out a nice outfit, and planned to do something remotely decent with my hair. It had gotten extremely long, and I wasn't sure if I wanted to take a chance and cut it all off, or deal with it for another blazing hot summer.

I looked down at the clothes. *Would he care what I wore? Did I need to make a good impression around his new girl-toy?* I was overwhelmed with anxiety over this whole ordeal. Finally, after a few hours, and an empty closet, I decided on a light blue sun dress. It would make my olive complexion pop, and my indigo eyes sparkle.

After fighting to get out of bed, I started on the task of getting ready. I was going to curl my entire head of long hair, but noticed the time and settled to throw my frizzy mess up in a subtle pony tail, with an azure bow that matched my dress. I had to grimace when I took one final look in the mirror. For someone that had a high-school diploma, I'd managed to make myself look around the age of twelve.

After giving me an inquisitive stare regarding my outfit of choice, my mother reluctantly handed me the directions to my father's new house. She gave me a million pointers before kissing me goodbye. I could tell she hated the idea of him being happy, and it was easy to admit that I loathed it too.

When I pulled into the community I noticed how large the houses were. Long private driveways separated every yard. A double check on the piece of paper let me know that the address I was sitting in front of was in fact my father's. When I saw the matching numbers on a stone pillar leading down a matching concrete driveway, I figured it had to be wrong. My little Volkswagen Jetta putted its way down the paved entrance until I came to a stop behind a Land Rover SUV. The house had a stoned front with ivy growing up either of its sides. The windows and doors were trimmed in large white wood with black shutters.

I stepped out of the car, making sure the wind wasn't blowing my dress up above my ass, before heading toward the door. It surprisingly flew open, alarming me. A young girl, who resembled a plastic Barbie doll, came skipping toward me. She was wearing a form-fitting dress that could have been made from only spandex. It was bright pink with giant yellow flowers scattered over it. Her platinum blonde hair was curled as if she were going to model in the next issue of Playboy. In fact, she kind of looked like maybe he'd picked her up at the Playboy mansion, or maybe he'd stolen her away from Heff. "Ohhh yay! I'm so glad you're here." She actually squeaked. "Come here; let me get a good look at you."

Oh my God, this was a terrible idea!

I stood like a statue while this large breasted bimbo

tugged and pinched every part of me that I'd assumed was deemed private. When I finally thought she was finished being amused, I began to forge forward. That's when she reached over and grabbed both of my breasts.

"Oh my, what the-?" She'd shocked me. Frantic to get away from her, I swatted her hands.

"Your breasts are so perky and natural. I told the doctor that's how I wanted mine, but nothing's as good as the real things," she proclaimed with a giggle.

"Um, I don't know what to say to that." This female in front of me seemed so made up. I couldn't understand how my dad had gone from my average looking mother, to this hot-mess.

I suppose what made it worse for me was the fact that I never put any effort into dolling myself up for anyone. My hair and skin gave me enough decent features to allow me to get away with walking out the door looking natural. I never saw an interest in becoming something that I wasn't. It was obvious this person in front of me struggled with her appearance. I almost felt sorry for her, because I was certain that somewhere in there she was probably very beautiful.

She seemed to act offended, but shortly after put on another million-dollar smile. "Oh, sweetie, I'm just paying you a compliment. Come on inside. Your father's going to be so happy you're finally here. He's been talking about you non-stop." Before I could say yes, or even hell-to-the-no, she grabbed me by the arm and tugged me into the house.

The woman never let go of me as she lead us through a large foyer, into a family room. My father was sitting in a leather recliner watching a golf match on the television. He didn't even turn in our direction, even with the volume level of his Barbie up higher than the surround sound. "Baby, look who I found outside," she said, as she let go of me and bounced herself onto his lap. Before he could even turn in my direction, she was slapping him with a kiss that may or may not have contained her entire tongue.

I cringed at the sight, but quickly gained my composure as my father shoved her to the side, standing up to finally give me his attention.

"Well, look at my little girl, all grown up." He took my hands into his and gave me a once over. "You look very pretty, honey. It's been so long." He leaned over to kiss me on the forehead. "I see you've met Buffy already. Isn't she a keeper?" He gazed back at her as if she was some prize. Once again I fought the bile rising in my throat. I put on my best casual smile, but in the back of my mind all I could think of was belting out that song from the eighties "*Angel is a Centerfold*".

"We met outside, dad." It wasn't like I needed to explain. I'm sure it was a rhetorical statement.

"Why don't you come on in and make yourself at home. We haven't had time to furnish the whole house yet, but the kitchen is stocked, and Buffy's made a nice spread for us to feast on." I stared at my father, who hadn't really aged much. His hair has some gray on the sides, but still was thick and a dark brown in color. To say that I favored his side of the family would have been an understatement. There was no denying that I was his child.

Out of nowhere, the chick grabbed my arm again, dragging me through the house. She took me upstairs and showed me the four large bedrooms, which each had their own bathroom. Two of them looked out into the backyard. I saw the pool and fell in love instantly, before Buffy pulled me along to show off more of her and my father's ginormous crib.

When we'd finally made it back down to the kitchen, the food was ready to eat. "We have to take a break from the tour for a bit, so we can eat before all of this food gets cold. Do you like fresh tea?" She asked.

"Um, sure." I watched as she opened the refrigerator and pulled out a large pitcher.

"Great. Here." She poured me a glass before continuing. "You go on and sit yourself down over there and we'll join you in a sec." Buffy pointed in the direction of the morning room. It faced the pool, which I couldn't take my eyes off of.

My grandparent's house was small, to say the least. They never expected to have my mom and I move in when we lost our home. A small den had been converted into a bedroom for me, but it didn't even have a real closet. I had to use one we bought at a store that took up half the room.

Brunch tasted fantastic, but my father barely spoke. He left the conversation up to his new squeeze. She tried to talk to me about fashion, music and finally television, claiming her favorite show was that horrible reality one on MTV with the young mothers. She made a point to mention the age at which my mother had been when she got pregnant with me. I thought I was going to choke on a piece of French toast as she offered that bit of information, as if they'd been long-lost friends. My father seemed mesmerized with everything that came out of her pretty little mouth. She could have talked about a shit fetish and had his undivided attention. It was absurd, and got under my skin.

I wasn't sure if it was an instantaneous decision, but I was fully aware that I had lost my appetite.

"So tell me, Hope, what's there to do in this town?

Your father and I need to get out there and meet some people. We have this big house and no one to entertain." Buffy flipped her hair as she questioned me. It was as if everything she did was annoying me. I was coming to the realization that it probably wasn't her that was annoying me so much as the fact that my father was being a tool.

I cleared my throat and looked directly at him, hoping in some way he could read my mind and snap out of whatever spell he was under.

"Do you know of any bars or places that Buff and I could go dancing? I know about the country club, we've already joined that." I'd been to the country club with my ex, and didn't care for the snooty people that hung out there.

Had my dad turned into one of those people?
Was this a bad dream?

"I don't know of any clubs or bars, dad. They aren't my thing, and besides I'm only seventeen. I'm not even allowed to enter into any of those types of establishments until I'm twenty one." He clearly should have known that. Wasn't the parent supposed to be protective about their daughters running around late at night, where they had no business being in the first place?

"Well I guess things have changed a lot since I was a teenager." He laughed it off, as if he'd gone out as a kid and did whatever he wanted. "I'm just teasing you, kiddo. I wanted to make sure your mother was doing a good job keeping you under lock and key. Lord knows she'd let you run around just to spite me."

It was impossible for me to not be offended. While trying to grasp what he'd just said to me, I caught him watching Buffy as she leaned over to clear his plate from the table. The vomit began to surface in my mouth, and I needed some air, pronto. "Do you mind if I check out the back yard?"

"Sure, make yourself at home." My father was too busy admiring his piece of ass to give a damn about what I was doing.

Fat chance! This was the last place that I'd ever call home.

He remained seated when I got up and ambled toward the French doors leading to the pool yard. When I shut them behind me, I couldn't help but close my eyes and take a deep breath, thankful I'd made it through the meal without stabbing either one of them with a fork.

The yard was landscaped with tall grasses and lots of unique rocks. Several lounge chairs sat around the pool, and the entire perimeter was privacy-fenced in. Attached to the far end was a building. Since my father had given me the go-ahead to look around, I took it upon myself to venture inside. Assuming that it was just a pool house to change and store chemicals, I barged right inside.

I'd been very wrong.

The most handsome piece of man that I'd ever seen was bent over, pulling off a pair of wet swimming trunks. The beads of water glistened over his skin. Like slow motion, I watched as one left a trail while sliding down to his crack. When the door shut behind me, he turned around. His eyes widened and my presence was definitely made known. I didn't know what to say, as I stood there taking in his rock-hard physique.

I-COULD-NOT-STOP-LOOKING.

He had a tattoo on his arm that I couldn't quite make out. Both of his ears were pierced and I was certain that those eyes were a shade of brown. His tan skin kept beckoning me to peek, and it was with much regret that I began to actually

13

lick my lips and bite down on the bottom one.

I'd never reacted like this before in the presence of a man. It was both highly embarrassing, and way out of character. After my last relationship, I'd come to feel as if guys only wanted one thing. I knew it wasn't right to judge one personal experience on all of them, but it was what I knew.

Still, something about this man in front of me was so beautiful that it intrigued my curiosity. I wanted to know who he was, and what he was doing there.

2

Chance

It was hard for me to believe that in the last year I'd ruined my life, and possibly my future. My full ride to Penn State University had been revoked. If my mother were still alive she'd be kicking my ass, still after six months had gone by. What happened was a horrible tragedy, and the dean of schools did what he had to do, due to the drastic circumstances surrounding it. In one night I'd managed to destroy everything I'd worked so hard for.

I'd once strived for greatness, excelling in every aspect of my existence. Now I lived with my sister, in a pool house in her back yard at that.

We were always close and she never questioned me when I'd confessed to her what happened that night. I couldn't lie about something so horrendous, but making someone believe me wasn't that easy. Not when it was on every television station and in all of the local newspapers.

After I'd been kicked out of school, lost my job, and left without a penny to my name, Buffy saved me, like she

15

always seemed to do while we were kids. My sister set me up with a place to live, and a job that would last me at least a year. Her new sugar daddy had bought an old fixer upper and they had big plans for what they wanted the house to become, inside and out.

I hadn't held a hammer since high school, but thankfully it ended up being like riding a bike. After a few days work, I got the hang of things. When I wasn't sure about something, I'd watch how-to videos until I felt confident to get the work done appropriately. It wasn't like they were entrusting me with big jobs. The contractors had been in and out of the place since before they even moved in. I was more or less the go-to for small repairs.

Working by myself gave me time to think about the mistakes I'd made to get me in this very predicament. At times I considered running away from it by ending my life, but knew that was the pussy way out. The damage was done. I had nowhere to hide, and even in death I think it would haunt me.

All my friends had disowned me, insisting that they couldn't be associated with someone like me; someone that could do such heinous things and get away with it for so long. It was a devastating blow. In the long run, I guess they were never really my friends. If they were, then they would have known I wasn't capable of becoming the monster they all thought me to be.

Even my girlfriend who I'd dated since my freshman year at college dumped me, claiming the pressure of being involved was too much, and yada yada. I'd heard the same crap before. The truth was that her parents forbid her from having anything to do with me. They had the nerve to call me a street thug and a common criminal on several attempts that

I'd made to visit her at their place of residence. She finally wrote me a letter asking me to never contact her again or they'd be forced to get a restraining order against me.

For the first few months after the trial, I secluded myself in my sister's apartment. It was over top of the bar where she danced. After work she'd always bring bottles of liquor upstairs to bury my pain with. As short-lived as it was, it took the edge off, and at least made me think that I didn't care. It was the only real time I was able to sleep while still living in Pennsylvania.

After my sister met Mark Ryan things changed. She stopped working, and soon spent all of her time with him. Within six months they were shacking up and planning on the big move to Virginia; and because of them, I was given a fresh start in a new state. Eventually, maybe I could make new friends and have a future that my mother would have been proud of, instead of the one that had put her into an early grave. Maybe I'd be able to play baseball again. I knew a career doing what I loved was far-fetched, but I at least wanted something to hold on to.

For the past two weeks I'd been working on the inside of the house. It'd been vacant for almost a year before Mark had gotten it as a foreclosure. He said it was a steal, but I just took his word for it. Anything over five grand was too expensive for me. I'd blown my mother's entire life insurance on lawyers, trying to keep myself out of jail. I hated that; the fact that my mother had worked so hard for us to be independent. She only wanted us to be successful and never hurt for anything. All of it made me feel like such a failure.

Like everything in my life so far, I was trying to make my new situation work. I got the most important rooms in livable shape, and even assisted with getting the cabinets installed in the kitchen before the granite countertops were delivered. There was still much to do, but I didn't have a deadline, which was nice since most of what I was doing was foreign to me. It was a good thing that the internet had evolved into a place where you could learn how to do anything.

I'd planned on fixing some shingles that were missing on the roof, but my sister and Mark asked me to take the day off. They claimed that they had someone "very special" coming over, and that they didn't want to be disturbed with the sound of the hammer slamming against the roof. It was fine. I never really relaxed on the weekends. Sitting in the small pool house just made me think of what my life could have been. As much as I appreciated having my own space, I got lonely easily. I'd gone from being sociable to having nothing at all. That kind of adjustment wasn't simple. On most nights I would drink myself to a stupor and eventually pass out. My sister feared that one evening I was going to get so drunk I would fall into the pool and drown.

Even though I had the rest of the day off, I still woke up at the crack of dawn. I weeded the front garden next to the driveway and painted the mailbox. While I had the can of paint out, I decided to touch up the white parts of the fence around the pool. The sun was warm, even early this particular morning, and I found myself sweating profusely as I finished touching up the fence. For a while I sat on a lounge chair and soaked up the rays, telling myself it was too early to crack open a beer. Somewhere I'd been taught that a person waits until at least noon to have their first drink.

When I felt like my balls were literally sticking to the side of my legs, I decided to grab a pair of swimming trunks and hop into the pool. Even if the company was already there, I wouldn't be bothering them. I avoided jumping in and causing big splash sounds. Instead, I just floated around for a while in pure silence watching the clouds in the sky, and wondering if my mother was up there somewhere looking down on me.

When my hands started to prune up, I climbed out. Realizing all of the towels were in the pool house, I hurried to get inside. The morning breeze hit me right away, making me shiver even with the sun shining down. I made it inside within seconds and immediately began to strip out of my wet bathing suit that clung to my skin. I didn't bother going into my bedroom, since I knew I was all alone. After all, it was my place.

When I first heard the creak of the door, I thought it was just my sister. Then I turned around and discovered that I'd been wrong. This little brunette stared at me with wide eyes, and I was fully aware of what she couldn't take her gaze away from.

"What the hell? Who're you and what're you doing in here?" I'd raised my voice out of shock, knowing I had every right to be stern. She'd come into my home without even knocking.

The petite brunette threw her hands over her face, pretending to be embarrassed, even though I knew what I'd witnessed. She hadn't been very ashamed just seconds before. "Oh my God, I am so sorry! I didn't know somebody was in here. My father said I could look wherever I wanted. Seriously I had no idea."

She turned her entire body around even though her hands were already covering her face. I finished pulling on a pair of boxers while trying to come to grips with who this chick could be. "You can turn around now, I'm decent." I was still slipping on some basketball shorts, but at least I was covered. "So who's your dad?"

She looked almost angry. Her eyes widened, and I could tell that she felt I was the one in the wrong. "Why? Who the hell are you?" With her hands on her hips she appeared to think she was in control of the situation. I, however, begged to differ.

"I'm Chance, Chance Avery."

"And?" Her right eyebrow angled up, as did her chin. She was like a teacher, waiting for a child to tell the truth.

It was obvious that I wasn't a child, and also a fact that she was invading *my* space. "And what?"

"And why are you in my father's pool house? Does he know you're in here or do I need to call the cops?" *She was threatening me. This was getting interesting.*

The last thing I needed was trouble with the law my first month here. "No, no! I'm Buffy's brother. I'm doing work for Mark. How was I supposed to know he had a daughter? It's not like he ever mentioned it to me before."

She exhaled heavily and looked down at the floor. I literally watched her body start to sag. "Figures, considering he hasn't been a part of my life for a while now."

I wanted nothing more than to tell this chick to get lost, but after seeing the change in her, I couldn't help but feel sorry for the girl. She was apparently having a shitty day. "Why don't you come sit down for a minute? I'm sure after seeing my bare ass you could use a drink. So what'll it be?" While I waited for her response, I thought about what she'd actually seen. I was no flasher, but I did get a rise knowing how intrigued she seemed as she stared at my package.

"What do you have?" Her head popped up, like I'd said something that interested her.

"Bourbon and Coke." The surprise on her face let me know that she expected me to say something non-alcoholic. I was certainly rusty with my people skills.

It wasn't as if I was expecting company. Had I known that I'd be barged in on, I wouldn't have come in from the pool with goose bumps, leaving me losing inches by the second. From the look on her face I'd say she was still impressed.

"Wow, that's some variety. I've never had bourbon. Anything stiff would be good right now. This day couldn't get any worse. Surprise me!"

I gave her a half-smile and headed to the tiny kitchen area. Mark was pretty positive that the people who lived here before rented out this pool house. It had one bedroom, a kitchen, a small bathroom and living room, but it was perfect for me. It wasn't like I entertained, or even had friends at all to come hang out.

I decided to get her a bottle of water that I found in the door of the fridge. I wasn't about to send her back to them with liquor on her breath. My sister had bought the water insisting that if I drank soda all day after working in the sun I'd get heat exhaustion. Usually I just sipped water straight from the hose, after dousing my body in it to cool off. While heading back in her direction, I wondered if she would have liked seeing me do that as well. *Women and their fantasies.*

When I returned to the living room, I sat in the chair facing her.

"Hope," she said.

"Huh?" Was she asking me for something?

"My name is Hope. Hope Ryan," she explained as she took the bottle of water. "Thanks for this. I actually didn't know if I could handle the bourbon after the meal I just had to eat."

"That bad, huh?"

"No offense, but your sister isn't much older than me. I guess I just wasn't prepared ya know?" The girl named Hope seemed offended by my sister's presence. I watched her drink down half of the bottle, considering what I should say next. I knew I had to be careful. She was obviously having a terrible time dealing with the age situation.

I'd managed to pour myself half a glass of bourbon and had already taken two sips. The ice clattered in the bottom of the cup, while I swiveled it around watching it. "Nah, it's cool. My sister can be hard to handle at first. She has a good heart though."

She smirked but refused to reply. I was intrigued.

"What?"

"Nothing! Well, I was going to say something, but you'll just get pissed off."

"Didn't anyone ever tell you it wasn't nice to start something and not finish it? If you're going to assume something, the least you could do is share." She looked up at me. Her eyes were like blue sparkles, and they glowed against her dark complexion. Summer had just begun, but she was already tanned. Her hair had streaks of different browns, but it didn't look like it came from a box, it appeared to be natural highlights. She was strikingly beautiful.

No wonder Mark hadn't mentioned her to me.

"Fine, I was going to say that she really likes the color pink. No, not likes, LOVES the color pink." Her spontaneous assumption caused her to giggle, as if a color could determine one's personality.

I wanted to defend my sister, but something about

22

this girl made me feel like she was just trying to break the ice. I hadn't had a friend in a long time. I couldn't bring myself to act like an asshole; I needed this. "I never noticed. I suppose she likes a whole array of colors. So what about you? What colors do you favor?"

Did I really just ask that? How lame could I be?

I was surprised when she answered abruptly. "Not pink. Anything but pink." Hope had a problem with Buffy. In some ways I could even understand why. They were opposites, not to mention that my sister had her claws in the girl's father. It made sense.

"Okay. Are you always like this, or do you only have an attitude on the weekends?"

"Like what?" She asked innocently, while folding her hands.

"I don't know. Flip. Sarcastic."

"How would you feel if you hadn't seen or talked to your father in over a year? How would you act if he invited you over and ignored you because he was busy staring at his new eye-candy's fake tits?" I was halfway into a large gulp of bourbon when the word "tits" came out of her pretty little mouth. The liquor went soaring everywhere. Once I stopped gagging from the utter shock, I turned back to face her. She'd stood up from the sofa and placed her hands on her hips. "Look, I'm really sorry that I barged in on you getting changed. Had I been told that someone was living out here, I never would've bothered you. It was nice meeting you, Chance. I'm going to get going before I lose my shit or my brunch. Have a nice life." She stomped out of the pool house with attitude. There was no reason for me to run after her. From the way she was acting, I'd never see her again anyway.

I got up and walked to the window, watching her

23

head back toward the house, while I finished my drink. It was a damn shame that we hadn't met under different circumstances. There was a lot about her that I would have liked to explore.

I'd start with that killer body, and work my way right into her heart.

3

Hope

After I'd come barging back into the main house from my unexpected meeting with Chance, all I was focused on doing was going home. My father was in his recliner watching golf again, while Buffy filed her nails with her feet draped over the end of the couch. I had to laugh at that. My father and mother used to yell at me over and over for sitting that same way on a couch. How could he have changed so much? Furthermore, why hadn't he come looking for me after brunch was cleaned up? Was this visit all some ploy to earn brownie points with his little honey?

I didn't hesitate as I made my way into the family room and announced that I was leaving. My father turned and gave me a smile, while Buffy came racing over, planting a big hug on me. I patted her a few times on the back and pulled away from her embrace. "Thanks for brunch. It was nice meeting you."

Not really!

As soon as I made it out of the driveway, I began to sob. The sheer emotions that were running through my mind were enough to cause me to hyperventilate. I couldn't have held back the anguish even if I wanted to. Once I'd gotten a few miles away I finally had to pull over to the side of the road, because I couldn't see through the tears that had filled my eyes.

It was inconceivable for me to understand why he'd moved back here. It certainly hadn't been because of me. *Was I just dreaming or had that really been the catastrophe that I saw it as?* While I sat on the side of the road I felt my stomach knotting up. In just enough time I managed to unbuckle my seat belt, get out, and run toward the grass, where I vomited all of the food I'd eaten. I leaned against my car trying to gain some composure, and make sure I was completely finished hurling.

All the times I'd wished I had my father back in my life, and when I got him it was nothing like I pictured it would be. I wanted to crawl into a hole and die. There was no way I could drive home like this and explain what happened to my mother. She hated the guy. She'd go out, buy a gun, and then later be on the news for murdering him. *Okay, maybe that was going overboard.* I had to get myself calmed down first. It was my only option.

While still trying to feel better, I noticed a truck pulling to the side of the road. A male driver got out and began to approach me. I always carried pepper spray on my key ring, but it was still stuck in the ignition of the car. My heart started to beat faster while I began to panic. I wasn't on a heavily driven road. In fact, while I was puking there hadn't been any cars that passed going in either direction.

The man's voice startled me, signaling he'd approached me at a faster rate than I expected. "Are ya alright, miss? Do you need some help?"

He wore a baseball cap that covered his face. While giving him a once over, I noticed a long scar across his cheek. I'm not usually one to stereotype, but he gave me the creeps like he was straight out of a horror movie. He got about a foot away from me and reached for my arm. "Did you hear me, hun? I can take you wherever you want to go. Why don't you come get into my truck? It's got a bed in the back." His long hair stuck out of the rear of his cap. I noticed right away how greasy it was, and how the odor of his body was pungent.

The moment he got a hold of my arm, I froze in place. I couldn't speak, and I surely couldn't scream, not that anyone would be able to hear me on this part of the highway anyway.

The man had managed to pull me another four feet away from my car before a motorcycle came driving toward us. At first I feared it would keep going, but the driver skidded in between our vehicles and immediately got his bike into a sitting position. The strange man had released his hold on me as the other person approached rapidly.

"Are you okay?" He asked while still wearing his helmet. For some reason I felt safe answering his question.

I couldn't look in the direction of the creep as I replied. I shook my head frantically. "NO!" I took off to the opposite side of the vehicle, hoping to be free of danger.

The men had words, but I couldn't hear what they were saying. Their conversation was jumbled as my body continued shaking. I was losing control fast, and knew I needed to get back inside of my car and lock the door.

I watched the motorcycle guy shoving the trucker in

the direction of the rig. While standing there quietly, I saw the first man pulling away in his truck, and the other one heading in my direction. That's when everything became black, and then I felt myself fall.

After my encounter with Mark's daughter, I needed a pack of cigarettes. I decided to hop on my motorcycle and head to the nearest convenience store. The weather was so nice, even beginning to get hot. The leaves on the trees had long been green, and it finally felt like summer outside. There was nothing like jumping on my bike and driving fast, feeling the wind hitting my body as I coasted down the road. It was invigorating.

When I got about three miles from the house I spotted two vehicles pulled over on the shoulder, and one of the cars happened to be the same one that had been in the driveway earlier in the day. As I got closer I noticed that a man had his hands on her, and I didn't even think about my next actions. My bike came to a halt and I immediately approached Hope and the stranger. "Are you okay?" I asked, simply wondering how she'd gotten herself into such a predicament.

This chick was having a terrible day.

When she answered with those desperate eyes, I knew she was in trouble. "What the fuck do you think you're doing? Get your hands off of her," I screamed at the trucker.

Hope moved over to the side, holding her hands over

29

her face while she wept. I advanced toward the guy, but not close enough to hit him. For all he knew I was her brother, or maybe even a boyfriend. At any rate, he was making it obvious that he was a stranger. "I was just offering the girl a ride."

"I bet you were." The guy was disgusting, and from the look of him he hadn't bathed in days. "You need to get back on the road, man. You've got no business being here."

"I don't want no trouble." He put his hands in the air, offering some kind of motion that he meant no harm to her, which was obviously a lie.

"If you know what's good for you, you'll leave now." I didn't have to raise my voice to get my point across. He'd been caught, and he knew he had to get out of there.

I watched him back up until he reached the door to his rig. There was no way this guy was pulling her against her will to offer her assistance. No, he wanted to lure her into the back of that truck and have his way with her. I wasn't about to let that happen.

When he left without incident, I figured he was absolutely shady. I'd obviously arrived at just the right moment. He was most likely some type of criminal who didn't want to get involved with the police.

I knew how that felt.

As soon as I watched that truck disappear down the road I turned my attention to Hope. She was still crying heavily with her hands covering her face. In almost slow motion I watched her body start to fall to the ground. My hands caught her before she was able to hit the hard asphalt, and all I could do was stand there on the side of the road wondering what to do next.

I thought about taking her back to her father's, but

when I carried her to the passenger side of the car I noticed the vomit in the grass. When she darted out of the pool house I assumed she was frustrated and upset, but seeing that she was sick to her stomach confirmed she was having an incomprehensible time. I managed to get her reclined in the seat, and decided to wait it out on the driver's side. There was no way I was abandoning her there all alone on this strip of the highway, and I wasn't about to leave my bike either. It was the only thing I had left to my name.

After making sure she was okay I found a good station on the radio, and turned the air on to blow on Hope's skin. I knew she'd wake up and freak out, so I sat there mentally preparing myself for the shock.

I couldn't believe I'd gotten myself into this situation. My head found a semi-comfortable position on the steering wheel while I stared at the girl beside me. Her arms were covered in goose bumps from the cool air, and her hair was blowing in small strands across her face. Her breathing had calmed, and her cleavage protruded from the low cut sundress when her chest inhaled and exhaled. I tried so hard not to look, but I hadn't been this close to another girl other than my sister in a very long time, and it made me feel uncomfortable. I was an adult, albeit I had no idea how old this girl was sitting next to me. I assumed she was close to my sister's age, but the bow in her hair made her look like a teenager. The last thing I needed was for someone to get the wrong idea about why we were in this car alone on the side of the road.

As much as I knew I shouldn't want to do it, I leaned over and gently rubbed on Hope's cheek. She was so beautiful, so vulnerable.

"Hope? Hey wake up, Hope."

31

As soon as her lids began to open the screaming started. I imagine it derived from not realizing where she was or what was going on. I held my hands up and placed them on the ceiling of the car. "Whoa, wait a minute. You were approached by a stranger. I pulled over and got him to leave. I swear, that's all."

She paused from screaming and fighting to get out of the vehicle and looked at me, finally remembering all that had happened.

"You passed out. All I did was carry you to the car. I couldn't leave you alone, so I stayed to make sure you were all right," I explained.

She looked down at her clothes, out the rear window of her car, and then back at her arms. "Did anything else happen?" I had no idea what she was implying.

"With what? You mean did I touch you inappropriately?" If her father got word of her accusations I'd be homeless. It felt like she'd kicked me in the balls. I didn't want to be accused of hurting another person again. I put my head down and frowned. "I promise you that I would never do that. If you're okay, I think it would be best if I just got going, seeing as you seem to be fine now."

As I went to climb out of the car she reached for me, grabbing my arm and preventing me from exiting. "Wait. Please."

I sat back down and looked directly into those cobalt eyes. "What?"

"If you hadn't come, I don't know what would have happened today. You may have just saved my life." She was still holding my arm.

I grabbed her by the hand and removed her hold on me. "I don't know about saving lives, but I'm glad you're out of danger, Hope. I guess maybe I'll see you around."

When I climbed onto my bike I noticed Hope hopping over the seat to get to the driver's side. She started her car and readjusted her mirror. I spotted her looking at me, but chose to ignore it. Maybe it was just a coincidence, or perhaps she was only thankful for me being there at the right time. It would have been a shame if something happened to her on the way home from such a problematic morning already.

I decided to wait until Hope pulled away before I left, and when she finally did I realized that I'd forgotten all about wanting that pack of cigarettes.

4

Hope

My mother hounded me from the moment I stepped in the door. I swear she must have made a list of questions to ask when I came through it.

"How big is the house?

What does the slut look like?

Does your father have any gray hair?

Has he gained any weight?

What kind of car does he drive?

How old is the new girl?

Was she nice to you?

Are you going back there?

Did he ask you to move in with him?"

After a while I couldn't take it anymore, and locked myself in my room. The last thing I wanted to do was rehash the *great* morning that I *didn't* have with my father. All of her other questions were completely irrelevant anyway.

Once inside the confines of my room, I inserted my ear buds and cranked up my music. My body plopped down on the bed while I stared at the ceiling. My day had started out horrible and eventually turned to shit. Within a matter of hours I was certain it had become one of the worst of my life. The only thing that made it more bearable was meeting Chance Avery.

It would have been nice to have been formally introduced with his clothes on, but seeing his naked backside left me with good visuals to focus on during my current bout of depression. He was so muscular and I was certain he must be athletic. When he finally turned around I saw his face, and was amazed how handsome he was. A part of me just assumed he couldn't be a whole package, but instead his brown eyes accented his dark hair. When he grinned behind that glass of liquor, I noticed how white and perfect his teeth were. That smile could melt a girl's heart, and probably did quite often.

I felt so bad about how I'd been around him. It was embarrassing to think back on how I reacted. The way I talked about his sister was uncalled for. How could he have sat there and listened to me making fun of her like that? Clearly he had more patience than I did.

He must have pegged me as such a spoiled little bitch. It didn't help that I had a stupid bow in my hair. The idea of him just assuming I was some little girl was disturbing. I'd worked so hard to become a woman, and failed to display it when it really counted. At least he knew I had to be sixteen to drive a car; not that seventeen was much better. I hated that my birthday was on the last day of the year.

In my defense, I thought that when I pulled away from the house it would be the last time I ever saw him, but when he showed up on that motorcycle and saved me from that creepy man, I was flabbergasted. *Talk about a knight in shining armor.* Maybe he'd just been in the right place at the perfect time.

Then my mind went on a swooning frenzy.

I wondered how old he was. Did he have a girlfriend? Did he want a girlfriend? Maybe he was engaged? Maybe he was gay? He was definitely hot enough to be. Whoever was kissing him was lucky to feel lips like his touching them. I licked over mine just imagining it.

I was so jealous, and I didn't even know this guy. *What was wrong with me?*

The thing was, I wanted to know him, but doing so would require me to go back to that house. I cringed at the thought.

I had the whole summer ahead of me, and that was the last place I planned on spending my time. My father had been such a jerk neglecting to spend one single moment getting to know the daughter that he'd basically left behind. He lacked personality and compassion, at least where it counted.

I promised myself that I wasn't going to get upset over him anymore, but as the tension of today's events overwhelmed me, I knew it was going to be impossible.

I wasn't ready to tell my mother the truth about the visit. My father hadn't given me the attention or the emotional connection I assumed he would. What had happened to the man that used to pick me up and swing me around every night he came home from work? How could he not have missed me at all? She would be appalled by his actions, and it would open up a can of worms that I didn't want to be involved in.

Right now I wanted to scream. He broke my heart again and he probably hadn't even noticed.

I started crying into my pillow, because the walls

were thin and I didn't want my mother hearing me. The last thing I needed was her trying to start a war with my father. I wasn't ready to see him yet, but I couldn't bear to have him leave the state again.

When I finally closed my eyes, I dreamed of nothing but Chance Avery. His tan skin and his big muscles wouldn't leave my mind. I wasn't sure that I even wanted them to. It was just a fantasy, but I appreciated the distraction.

I could feel his eyes on me as we strolled through the green grass. His shirt was off, while he sported a pair of black swimming trunks. I looked down and noticed that I was in a skimpy bikini, although I didn't feel embarrassed. He pulled me close, sheltering my view from the sun with his tall body. From the moment our eyes met I couldn't stop staring. Chance took his fingers and brushed them over my lips, causing me to inhale deeply as I accepted his warm touch. I could feel parts of me beginning to react to such an affectionate gesture. His breath was closer, instigating me to hold my gaze and watch his face approaching, slowly, as his lips brushed over mine. Suddenly everything around us became silent.

The wind had ceased.

The birds stopped singing.

There was nothing, but us.

I woke up to my alarm clock buzzing. I'd forgotten to turn it off again. My hands finally made contact with the little bugger and the sirens stopped sounding in my ears. I couldn't believe that stupid thing had kept me from feeling a kiss that I knew would take me to new heights. Sure, it was an adolescent dream, but it was as close as I'd ever get to the real thing.

Just from habit, I reached over and picked up my phone. I'd already gotten six messages either late the night before or early in the morning.

The first few were from my best friend Rylee.

Hey Bitch, call me. We have plans for 2moro.

Call me hoe!

Where are you?

One text was from my mother, asking if I got to my father's safe.

Everything Okay? Did you find the address?

The last two were from my ex, Trevor. I'd ended our one-year relationship over six months ago, but he refused to take a hint. He was leaving for college and I couldn't wait to have a huge distance between us. He was rich, coming from money his whole life. During our relationship I'd most always felt like a charity case, and he made sure to remind me when I didn't. He'd pushed me into losing my virginity, even though I wasn't ready, and then ended up cheating on me, because I apparently wasn't good enough. That night was horrible, and I'd regretted it every day since then. Of course, after that I opened up a bit about my sexuality, knowing that I wasn't the problem, but my partner most certainly was. Towards the end of the relationship when I was beginning to basically wonder why we were together in the first place, he'd become violent, scaring me a few times with his temper. Maybe my mother and I had some kind of hereditary gene that caused men to cheat on us and treat us horribly. At any rate, I couldn't stand the guy, who in turn was convinced that he was put on this planet to be worshipped by women. Sure, he was handsome, but his attitude lacked compassion, and his brain was even smaller than his dick.

Trevor clearly had issues about our breakup. It was

obvious that his ego had taken a hit, and he'd made it some mission to get me back just to prove he could. I was too smart to believe he would change. He'd be an asshole for the rest of his life, and if I never saw him again it would be too soon.

His first texts were the same thing he'd sent almost every day.

I miss you, hot stuff. Please call me.

His second was not what I had wanted to wake up to.

I'll see you tonight whether you like or not. Nobody stands me up!

Wow! It seemed like a threat. I could have responded getting him all worked up so that he would hound me for the rest of the day, or I could pretend like his texts never even happened.

I turned my attention back to Rylee before getting ready to shower. I was giving her free reign, which was never a good idea.

Surprise me. Call me in a few hours.

Rylee was wild, with no filter. She was the exact definition of crazy, and she loved every minute of it. I should have known she'd get us into in trouble.

Chance

It had been a very interesting day, to say the least. Considering the last month of my life consisted of being around my sister and her father-figure boyfriend, it was definitely one I wouldn't soon forget. In fact, I couldn't stop thinking about Hope. Was I nice enough? Could I have come off as a douche? Would I ever see her again? Would she even consider talking to me if she knew the truth?

The questions burned through my mind, as if something was forcing me to give a damn about something other than all of my problems. I had to say that it was a pleasurable distraction from my solitary life.

When I'd arrived home all I could think about was her sweet smile and how petrified she looked on the side of that road. I didn't even want to think about what could have happened to her if I hadn't been there. We may have been strangers, but I'd never want a woman to be the victim of a heinous crime, especially after what I'd been through.

She needed to be more careful. Just because there were a lot of country back roads, didn't mean it was a safer place to be. She could be lying dead in a ditch. I'd saved her, which was probably why I couldn't shake thoughts of the girl.

She'd distracted me, causing me to smile for at least a few moments. No one could understand what something like that felt like after so long. They couldn't know the hardships that I faced to carry on every day, living with such a dreadful past. My life may have been ruined, but a simple smile at least calmed my soul.

I turned on the local baseball game and plopped down on the couch. I'd finished off the bourbon three hours ago, and all that was left in the fridge was a can of cola and two more bottles of water. I would have to go into town tomorrow and grab some groceries. We'd been there long enough for me to start being independent. I couldn't continue to rely on my sister for everything.

I needed to get it through my head that my past was buried two states away from here. Nobody knew me, and I could possibly start over fresh, finally again after so long.

Just knowing that scared and excited me at the same time. I hoped that this would be the opportunity that I needed, God knows I'd waited long enough for it.

I don't know how long I stayed awake after cozying up on that old couch. One minute I was watching the game, and the next I was driving on my motorcycle with a very sexy lady on the back. We pulled over to what looked like the same patch of woods that she'd been at earlier, except this time we were all alone. Once her helmet was removed she attempted to straighten out her hair. I broke the distance between us, and reached up grabbing the edge of the ribbon and pulling it out of the bow she'd tied. Her hair fell down over her shoulders, while our eyes remained fixed on each other. Hope opened her lips to speak, but I didn't let her. I had to taste her, to feel what it was like to kiss someone again, after so long.

When I woke the next morning, I felt unrested. The majority of the night had been filled with dreams of Hope. Before I became some pedophile, I needed to find out everything my sister knew about her. I couldn't believe she'd been holding out on me. Why hadn't she mentioned that Mark had this smoking hot daughter? She obviously knew that she was coming over yesterday, but insisted on calling her "an important person". I had to wonder if my dear sister was purposely keeping her away from me. It was probably because she was a minor. I didn't know any girl my age that wore ribbons in their hair.

I hadn't seen any pictures of her hanging around the house, though most weren't hung yet. Buffy said they still had a huge storage unit that they needed to unload, so perhaps they were in there, but it was still strange. Why keep it a secret? Did they really think it was necessary to hide her from me?

I started feeling like they didn't trust me at all. Normally I wouldn't have cared, but after everything that had happened, I couldn't help but feel a little bent out of shape about it.

When I heard the door open and close I sat up, realizing I was still on the couch instead of in my bed. I picked up my cell phone and noticed it was near ten in the morning. My sister came prancing in like she'd been up for hours. "Good morning, sleepy head. Time to get up. Mark and I have big plans for us tonight."

She handed me a cup of coffee, and I could tell from the color of it she'd added cream and sugar just how I liked. "Thanks for this," I said, as I took my first sip.

She sat down beside me and put her hands on her

42

knees. I had to let out a chuckle when I noticed her entire outfit was pink.

"What's so funny, little brother?"

"Oh, it's nothing really. I was just thinking about something that happened yesterday. On television." I added the last part so she would let it go.

"So, anyway...Mark and I found this great little place across town. It's a restaurant that has a bar side with dancing. We decided that we're going to go check it out tonight. I'm so excited."

"Well that's good, sis. I know how much you want to get out and meet new people here."

"Oh, that's the best part. Mark insisted that you come with us. Eeeek! I can't wait. We talked about it last night, but I didn't want to come outside and wake you. Plus, I wasn't wearing any clothes at the time."

I set my coffee down on the table. "Ugh! Really? I don't need that morning visual, Buff. Damn! Keep that shit to yourself."

She smacked me on my leg. "Shut up, Chance. You wouldn't be complaining if you were in my shoes."

"Sometimes I think that platinum hair of yours has caused you permanent brain damage." I liked to tease my sister whenever I had the opportunity.

She rolled her eyes and started running her hands through her hair. "Whatever!" She then stood up and headed toward the door. "We're leaving at eight. You better be ready, because if you aren't we're coming in here and dragging your ass with us."

"Oh, I'm scared of that threat. You do realize that you're half the size of me. You haven't been able to take me since you were ten."

43

"Seriously, Chance, do it for me at least. Try! For one night pretend that you want to hang out with your big sister. I do a lot for you."

"Fine, Buff. Whatever. I don't have a choice anyway. I live under your roof and have to abide by the rules. You're the boss."

She leaned her head back in the door. "Just be ready when I said." She ambled away and I picked up the coffee again, but as soon as the door closed it re-opened. "Oh, and Chance, no drinking today. I can't have your ass all incoherent before we even leave for dinner."

I shook my head once I knew she was gone. The last thing I wanted to do was go out with my sister and her boyfriend dancing. I hated to dance, and more importantly watch how my sister did it. Every guy in that bar would be mind-fucking her. It was disturbing as all hell.

5

Hope

When Rylee finally called me, she said she had a way for us to have a "real good time" tonight. I rolled my eyes while talking on the phone, but made her promise it had nothing to do with Trevor. He was getting on my nerves and I couldn't shake the way his last message made me feel. Maybe I was just interpreting it wrong, but I was leery still.

Rylee finally arrived at my house around six p.m. She was wearing a regular looking sundress. It was close to the blue one I'd worn the day before. Once she made it into the boundaries of my room she slipped it down revealing the tightest, skimpiest thing I'd ever seen. It was black and platinum and opened up on the sides from her rib cage down to her hips. Large metal buckles were holding it together. I watched as she adjusted it while looking in the long mirror attached to my door. "That's what I'm talking about," she spoke to herself.

Rylee was a gorgeous girl. She had dark hair, an ebony in color, and almost black eyes. Her father was from Pakistan and she'd gotten his chocolate complexion. Our friends hated being around the both of us, because we were so much darker than all of them. I was always thankful that I got that trait from my mother, although I favored my father in appearance. Her mom was of Cherokee descent and she had passed down the creamiest brown skin a girl could ask for. We didn't have to go tan for the prom, like all of our other friends did. Instead, Rylee and I would go to the ice cream shop and get milkshakes while we waited on them.

"So, what do you think?" Rylee inquired, while smoothing out the tight dress.

"You look hot, but I don't have anything resembling that. Where did you even get something like that?"

"At my mother's shop. Girl, you'd be surprised what people turn in at the second hand store. Anyway, I was working for my mom last weekend in the back. A bunch of bags had come in, and I collected as many as these babies as I could, and shoved them in my purse." Her mother owned a consignment shop inside of the little town we resided. Being the traditional woman that she was, I couldn't imagine what she would say to her daughter for stealing such items.

"There's more? You've got to be joking?"

"Oh no, I'm not! There was an entire bag full of dresses, and several more with other things. A few of them I wouldn't even wear. I was thinking they came from a transvestite. Wouldn't that be hysterical?"

I didn't know if I wanted to picture that, or what else was in the bags. Considering what this one looked like, I was afraid to visualize what the others must have compared to. "So where are we going anyway, because I can't imagine wearing that to the big five."

The big five was a group of fast food places all in the same block of each other in the middle of our small hicktown. They made no sense, but seemed to remain open anyway. All of the teenagers would hang out with their big trucks in the parking lots at all hours of the day and night.

"Silly girl, it's a secret." She threw some bunched up fabric at me. "Now pick which one you're going to hide under your clothes, so I can start on your hair and makeup."

I held the fabric in my hand. "You've got to be kidding. There is no way in hell I'm wearing either of these."

"Trust me," she exclaimed, while primping in the mirror. "You're going to fit right in where we're going."

I stretched out the two dresses across my bed. For me to even be considering either of them was against my religion, and I didn't mean that in any biblical way. These dresses, if that's what they'd even be classified as, should have been against the law to wear.

The lime green dress was tight and short, but draped down in the front. I wasn't sure I had a bra that I could wear, and I was too big to be without one. "This is a no!"

"Fine, then it's settled. You're wearing the pink and black one," she declared, while holding it up.

"You know I hate pink," I slammed. She must have lost her mind from being stuffed into that tiny dress.

"Too late. Now, hurry up and get it on so we can get ready." She wasn't taking 'no' for an answer.

I shook my head, cursed under my breath, and clenched the small fabric into my fist before heading to the bathroom. Once inside I held it up against my body. It looked too small, but once I got it on, it fit every curve of my body. I wasn't modest, but there was a whole different level of confidence needed to pull off wearing something in this magnitude. When I peered in the mirror, I noticed how the pink wasn't as much as I'd originally suspected. The center of

47

the spaghetti strapped dress front and back were black, but on each of the sides were bright pink. I guess it was made to accent a woman's curves, in which it was clearly doing. From the way it draped down in the front, it made my breasts almost double in size. Finally, before I put another dress over it, so that my mother wouldn't see, I bent over to do the ass check. Of course, in doing so, as I feared, I could see my panties.

It took me a little while longer to come to grips with what I was about to do. Rylee had terrible ideas, and the fact that I was letting her go along with one, said a lot about my judgment in character.

I still had no idea where we were going. There was nothing to do in this town and we were way too young to get into either of the bars here.

This couldn't be good.

When I stepped out of the bathroom I was wearing a normal summer dress. It was yellow with white daisies all over it. I headed into the bedroom and saw Rylee rolling her eyes. "What?"

"You weren't even going to let me see it?"

"I didn't want to get caught. My mother would kill me if she saw me wearing something like that. Are you going to tell me where we're going?" I questioned.

She sat me down in front of my mirror and started messing with my hair. "No, it's a surprise. Just be quiet and let me do my magic."

"Fine, but my mother will suspect something if you cover my face in makeup." There was no way I could go out of the house with as much as Rylee wore on a normal basis. My mother would have had a heart attack.

"I'll do your makeup once we leave, stupid. Geesh,

give me some credit. I got a diploma too, ya know."

I rolled my eyes and sat back in the chair while Rylee curled my hair. When it was all said and done I looked like I was headed to a photo shoot. Rylee was pleased with her work; I could see it on her face.

I slipped on a pair of sandals and she rolled her eyes again. She reached into her giant purse and pulled out a pair of black high heels. "You'll be wearing these once we get out of this church house." She was referring to my mother, who at times could be very over-protective of me.

"Shut up. She isn't that bad."

"Oh, yes she is."

My mother was taking a nap when we headed out of the house. She barely opened her eyes to kiss me goodbye. I told her I'd be staying at Rylee's house overnight, and made it out of there without any extra questions, which was a first.

Chance

My sister had barged in my place three times during the day. A few of the occurrences I just wanted to get on my bike and leave, but I really had no place to go. She knew how I was feeling about going out in public. I hadn't done it in so long, and could only assume she thought I would break down and go completely crazy. If she paid more attention to me in the past she would have known that I used to be an easy person to be around. There was probably even a time when I was the life of some parties. That was all before everything came crashing down on me.

To be honest, I didn't really enjoy being around people anymore. After what happened to me, I couldn't trust anyone. My so-called friends had showed me that.

I looked through my closet, realizing I hadn't even unpacked any of my nice clothes. Before everything happened, I had lots of fun events to attend while at Penn State. My rich girlfriend had taken me shopping and left me with a closet of designer clothes. I located one of the boxes out of the back and began scavenging through it. Inside, I found a few V-neck t-shirts that were still folded nicely.

I chose the light blue one with a pair of dark gray

shorts. They were made from linen. I remembered because Veronica, my ex, made a big deal about owning a pair. I never would have bought them for myself, but once I tried them on I understood the hype they got. They were comfortable and light. I wasn't into dancing, but bars could get ungodly hot, and I didn't feel like sweating my ass off all night. My sister came in as I was putting my white Nike's on.

"Oh, hell no! You are not wearing those shoes with that outfit. I would have thought Veronica taught you better than that."

"For someone that wants me to go with her, you aren't being very nice. What's wrong with my shoes?"

"Chance, you can't wear those expensive shorts with a pair of sneakers. Here." She tossed me a pair of boat shoes. I know they had some fancy name, but I always thought they looked like something our granddad had worn. "Wear these instead."

"Yeah, I was going for the old-man look tonight anyway."

"Shut up and get them on. Mark and I are ready to go."

I slipped the shoes on my feet and followed her out the door. When she turned around to stop me, I slammed into the back of her. "Damn it, Buffy, watch where you're going."

"You forgot your hair. Good thing I carry gel in my purse. Come on, Mark's in the car. I'll deal with your hair situation as he drives us there."

"Wait! I think I want to drive myself."

My sister turned around to face me. She was wearing a short leather skirt and a pink top that left her belly hanging out. The bright glare from her belly ring shined in my face. I covered my eyes before I could even talk to her. "Damn girl, you trying to blind me?"

"You're not driving that motorcycle." She pointed toward me as she spoke.

"Yes, I am. Listen, I promised you I would go, but I can't guarantee that I'll have a great time. In fact, I'm counting on it being horrible. With that being said...I think I want to have my own ride. I'm not trying to spoil your and Mark's time. I'll follow you there, and I assure you that I'll have no more than two beers. If I get too drunk we can leave the motorcycle there."

She seemed to be considering my idea, but when the horn honked she knew Mark was growing impatient. "Fine. Don't do anything stupid tonight, Chance. We want to make friends, not lose them."

"Okay, I won't do anything *you* wouldn't do." She turned around and gave me a smile before heading to the car. There had been a time where there wasn't anything she wouldn't have done. The new and improved Buffy had morals, and an image to live up to.

Thankfully she'd forgotten about my hair. I put on my helmet and followed them out of the large driveway on my bike. I'd already decided that shortly after dinner I was going to head home. I'd never been to a bar where something good came out of it, and knew this was going to have the same result. I wasn't going to meet the woman of my dreams in that type of establishment; not after everything that happened to me.

6

Hope

Rylee waited until we were a few miles away from my house to apply makeup. As the foundation filled my pores I started to feel uncomfortable. It was hot outside and the last thing I wanted was something else to make me sweat. The two dresses were bad enough as it was, during the ten minute ride.

I hated having someone else put makeup on me, especially mascara. I couldn't help blinking, which made it even harder for Rylee. After at least fifteen minutes being on the side of the road, she told me I could look in the mirror.

I didn't even recognize myself at first. Between the hair and now makeup I looked so much older.

"Wow! I look different."

"Do you like it?"

"It's a big change," was all I could stammer out.

Rylee rolled her eyes. "Whatever! You look totally hot. I would do you if I were a guy or a lesbian. Shit, if you get enough drinks in me I may do you tonight."

"Oh my God! Shut up. I am not doing anybody tonight or anytime soon." She was crazy. Not only was I in no way interested in women, but I had zero desire to sleep with a stranger.

"You never know what could happen. You might want to be the next re-born Virgin Mary, but I want something new, something strange to start off my summer."

I interrupted her. "Don't talk like that, Rylee. You sound like a whore." I didn't mean it rudely and she knew I didn't. She'd only been with two people that I knew of, and the last relationship ended this past month. Since then, all she could talk about was being single this summer to "experience new things".

We drove in silence for a few more minutes before pulling over to a local bar that was in the middle of nowhere. If you didn't live in the area, you'd never find it.

The Cedar Shack Bar sat off the road. It was a popular local hangout. During the day it was a restaurant, but at night it converted to a bar. I grabbed Rylee by the arm, before she could climb out of her car. "Wait! We can't get in there. It's after eight."

"Do you really think I wouldn't come prepared?" She asked, as she handed a small card that resembled a drivers license. I looked down and noticed the picture sort of looked like me. We definitely had similar features. "Where did you get this?"

"Duh, Hope, sometimes I wonder where your head is. My sister's home from college for the summer, and I gave her money on spring break to buy one of her friends I.D.'s. It's yours. Consider it a graduation present."

I looked down at the Maryland driver's license again. "It says my name is Julie Stanton."

"Well you better be taking that dress off, Jules, so we can get our groove on." She giggled at her apparent sarcasm. "Oh, if anyone asks, my name is Kara."

Kara was her older sister, only by three years, but she was twenty-one.

While slipping out of the top dress, I immediately felt my cheeks becoming red. I had no clue how I was going to make it in this place. Rylee handed me the heels and I watched as she double-checked her lip-gloss in the mirror.

I stood up and gripped my small clutch purse. "So, how do I look?"

"I already told you, totally do-able."

I rolled my eyes and followed behind her as we headed toward the door. I'd never walked in heels, and found it very difficult on a gravel-filled parking lot. By the time we'd made it to the front door I was surprised I hadn't broken an ankle. I straightened out my dress and handed the bouncer my fake I.D.

He looked at it for only a second before turning all of his attention to my dress. He started at my face, but made a beeline for my tits and finally my legs. "Where have you been all my life, gorgeous?"

"Maryland!" I blurted out, just as Rylee pulled me inside.

"Holy shit, Hope, he was totally hitting on you."

I looked around the bar. It was filled with people both young and old. The D.J. was already playing some kind of hip hop music, but nobody was dancing yet. It was still light outside, and I'd heard that bars didn't get busy until later on.

"Come on, let's get drinks." Rylee pulled me toward the bar. We found a corner where nobody was sitting, and she waved down a bartender.

"Hey, ladies, what can I get ya?" He asked. The guy was nice looking, and probably in his early twenties. I could tell right away that he liked what he was seeing. He gave Rylee a big grin when she leaned in to give him her order. "We'll take four shots of Jaeger."

I smacked her on the side. "I wanted a soda."

"Lighten up, princess. If you want to puss out, I'll drink them all myself."

She stuck a twenty on the bar while she watched him making them. Another man gave him an order while he was still filling ours. When he slid the shots in our direction he pushed the twenty back to Rylee. "These are taken care of already," he announced while nudging his head toward the man who'd spoken to him just seconds ago.

I watched Rylee looking the guy over. She stared right into his eyes while downing the first shot. "He's kind of cute, don't you think?"

"I guess. How old do you think he is?"

She grabbed the second shot and licked her lips before she swallowed it. "He can't be older than twenty five. Are you going to drink those?" She pointed to the last two shots.

I rolled my eyes and snatched one. When that awful taste hit my mouth I wanted to gag. Knowing we were in a bar full of adults, I managed to regain composure quickly. Rylee had a big smile on her face. "Now do the other one, and follow me."

I hated the first one, but the second wasn't as horrible. Possibly the shock of the taste was over with. As I gulped the last shot, I watched as she made her way over to the guy that had paid for our drinks. The dude seemed normal enough. He was wearing a black t-shirt and a pair of khakis. He smiled as we approached and pulled out a chair for her to sit. I looked around and spotted the ladies room, finally hoping for a quiet moment to reassess what the hell I was doing here in the first place.

I signaled to Rylee where I was going, and she smiled at me before giving the new guy all of her attention. I pushed past a group of people mingling and made my way to the bathroom. When I got inside, the liquor was already burning in my chest. I leaned over the sink and looked at myself in the mirror.

It'd felt like Rylee put all kinds of makeup on me, but I really wasn't wearing much. She'd made my eyes look more enhanced and my hair had settled down from the heat, making it appear relaxed. It was the dress that I couldn't stand. It was so tight against my skin, and I never thought of myself as fat, but my curves were very apparent. I was used to wearing free flowing summer dresses that did nothing for a physique.

By the time I made it out of the bathroom, the dance floor had filled up. I looked in the center and noticed Rylee grinding all over her new friend. While rolling my eyes I made my way through the people dancing. Since she was my ride home, I had to at least appease her. The guy handed me a beer, and I noticed they each had one for themselves. I hated the taste, but after the two shots, I managed to down half the bottle before the first song finished. All I wanted to do was forget how uncomfortable I was in this environment, and high heels.

It had, at least, become so crowded that my dress

issue wasn't as worrisome. We were surrounded by a large cluster of people, and there wasn't exactly room for anyone to stare.

Rylee and I had been dancing around together for years. We would do it in our pajamas until we literally passed out from exhaustion. As we got older, our practice paid off. We were always admired at the school dances and our boyfriends loved it. This new guy could be added to Rylee's list of admirers. He was clearly into her, as she grinded her ass against his groin.

I started to relax and just let the music take over my senses. I could handle this. It wasn't as terrible as I had feared it would be. If I could just go with the flow for a couple of hours, I may just have a decent enough time to get through it.

I followed Mark and Buffy to the bar on my motorcycle. The drive sucked because Mark drove his SUV slow as hell. If I had known where I was going, I would have passed them once we got out of the development.

I was surprised how packed the little establishment was. Maybe everyone in the entire town had come on this particular evening. I pulled out my driver's license even before it was my turn. I'd just turned twenty-one a few months back, and it made me proud that I didn't need a fake I.D. to get in anywhere. The bouncer at the door looked at it twice until he noticed my sister. She gave one of her million-dollar smiles and he forgot about little me. Once inside, we found a table in the back and started looking at menus. We probably should have arrived sooner if we wanted to eat without loud music.

After ordering something small, we watched everyone dancing. I was surprised how much my sister's dress choice fit in. It seemed all of the women were looking pretty hot. I'd stopped being so protective of her a long time ago, but still didn't like the fact that she wore such provocative attire.

One night a guy followed her out of the club. Before she could even scream, he'd managed to corner her in an alley. She said it only took her a few seconds to realize what was about to happen. He lifted her dress and started forcing himself on her. By the time she'd had the chance to scream, the dude was on the ground. She'd kicked him so hard in the balls that he fell to the pavement. Once he was down she used her stilettos as a weapon and beat him to a pulp.

When she'd threatened to call the police, he begged her not to press charges, claiming he was married and it would ruin his life. She told him if she ever saw him again she'd rip out his balls and nail them to his front door.

She never saw him again.

After that, I stopped worrying.

She'd always been able to handle herself. Guys had been coming on to her since kindergarten. For as long as I could remember my sister always had a boyfriend. In high school Buffy dated older guys, and it was clear that she still carried that preference. I couldn't complain, she was in a happy place, and Mark adored her.

When we'd finished eating my sister yanked us both out to the dance floor. She and Mark immediately began grinding, while I was left to shake around alone. After a few minutes Mark held up his hand and we were brought another round of beers by a roaming barmaid. She smiled as she handed me my bottle.

I took my first sip and stopped dancing. In the center of the floor was something that caught my eye; something familiar. Two girls were bumping and dry humping all over this one dude, and they were wearing my sister's dresses that Mark and I had secretly thrown away when she wasn't home. They were the ones she wore when she'd been working as a dancer, and Mark wanted them gone. I'd gathered them up and taken them to a second hand store in town, figuring my sister would never know the difference.

Thankfully, Mark and Buffy were so caught up in each other neither of them noticed. As I finished my beer I found myself watching the two girls occasionally. They both filled them out, one of them even better than my sister had. They clearly had rhythm, and it reminded me of a couple wild parties I'd attended back at school.

When the song ended, and a slow one came on the couples started grouping together. I stood there alone while Mark and Buffy, as well as everyone else on the dance floor seized their partners and began to slow dance.

That's when I realized the girl with the awesome body

making her way toward the bar. I followed the back of her with my eyes, not realizing I was unconsciously heading in her direction.

I leaned in behind her. "Hey beautiful, can I get you something to drink?" There was no harm in asking. She didn't know who I was, so it was all in fun.

What did I have to lose?

She never turned around. "Sure. I guess I'll have a Bud Light."

I slipped a ten over to the bartender. "Two Bud Lights please."

When the server handed us the beers, she finally turned around to hand me mine. We both froze.

"What are you doing here?" We asked at the same time.

I took a big swig before responding. She wouldn't stop looking at me, making me wonder what in the hell she was expecting me to say. I couldn't believe she was standing in front of me. I'd dreamed about Hope since I'd met her, and now I didn't know how to act.

"I came here with a friend. Please don't tell my father?" That could only mean one thing.

She was under age.

I gave her a quick smile and got closer as I spoke. "I don't have to tell him anything if he sees you for himself."

The color left from her face. "Oh, God!" She pointed to the floor. "He's here?"

"Yeah, he and Buff are out there dancing. I'm sure he didn't see you. What's the big deal anyway?" I needed her to admit that she was a minor.

I watched her down the entire beer. She took the bottle and sat it back on the bar. It was completely empty. "I

61

need to get out of here."

"Why, what's wrong?" I asked.

She ignored me. "Do you see my friend anywhere? She's wearing a platinum dress."

"I know that dress well." I whispered in her ear.

"I bet you do," she said in a flip way. I had to laugh. She thought I had been checking out her friend.

"I recognize the dress because it used to be my sister's, not because of who is wearing it."

Her beautiful light blue eyes stared into mine. "Chance, you have to help me find my friend. I can't be here. He can't see me."

I grasped her by the arm gently. "Stay here. I'll be right back. Don't leave."

I headed toward the dance floor and found her accomplice. I had no idea what the girl's name was. "Hey, um, your friend said she needs to go home."

She never stopped dancing or leaning on the guy she was with. "I'm not ready to leave. Tell her she has to wait."

"She needs to leave now."

"Look, I don't know who you are, but I'm in the middle of having a great time. Tell her to go out to the car if she wants to pout and act like a baby."

Hearing her talk like that when her friend needed her really pissed me off. As I strode away from her I yelled, "Bitch!"

I found Mark and Buffy in a slow embrace. I kissed my sister on the cheek. "Thanks for dinner, but I think I'm going to call it an early night."

She pulled away from Mark. "No! Why? Did something happen? We weren't ignoring you. What's wrong?"

"It's nothing, really I'm fine. I'll see you in the morning. Thanks again." I tottered off the dance floor, and headed over where Hope was hiding. Just to be safe, I looked back to make sure they weren't watching me before I captured her by the hand and led her out of the bar.

Once we made it outside we stood in front of my bike and I handed her my only helmet. "Put this on."

"I can't get on that thing. I hate motorcycles," she adamantly announced.

I climbed on my bike and put the key into the ignition. "You can get on, or go ask your father for a ride. You choose."

I watched as she pulled her skirt up in order to climb behind me on my bike. After getting a glimpse of her panties as she lifted her leg over the seat, I obtained her hands and wrapped them around my waist. "Hold on tight."

7
Hope

I couldn't believe this was happening to me. I was going to kill Rylee in the morning. Well, that was if I made it off of this bike alive.

Chance managed to drive us a few miles away before pulling over at a gas station. He lifted the tinted shield away from my helmet. "Do you want anything inside?"

I shook my head, realizing how stupid I must look with the large thing on my head. He gave me a quick smile before heading into the store. I nervously sat on the bike. My body was shaking even though I knew I was tipsy. The alcohol was supposed to calm my nerves, but they must have been on overdrive, because I couldn't relax to save my life. I'd just had my arms around Chance, the hottest guy I'd ever laid eyes on.

When Chance came back he had a brown bag in his hand. "Scoot off for a second, so I can put this under my seat. I was shocked that the whole bag fit in the small compartment on his motorcycle, but he obviously knew it would, since this was his method of transportation.

"So, where do you live?" He asked.

"Um, I can't go home."

"What do you mean? Why can't you?"

"I told my mother I was staying at Rylee's house. She's super strict, and if she found out I wasn't where I was supposed to be I'll be punished all summer."

"Where the hell am I supposed to take you?" He questioned.

This was horrible. I didn't want to tell this sexy man that I'd just graduated high school. I knew it was a long shot for someone like him to want me, but I'd like to think that with the way I was dressed he'd at least find me attractive. Telling him my age would put that idea to a halt. He'd drop me off at my front door and haul ass out of my neighborhood if he knew what was good for him.

I had to act like I was in control, because I couldn't go home.

There was also this lingering feeling like I didn't even want to.

"Well, can we just go back to your place?" I was fully aware how that sounded, and what it could have implied. "Wait. Before you say it's a terrible idea, let me explain. I promise I just need a place to crash. In the morning I'll have someone pick me up, and you won't have to even see me. Please, Chance. I know that we don't know each other very well, but you know my father, and he would want me to be safe." I hated throwing the dad card in there, but I was panicking. There was no way I could talk my way out of this to my mother, or my father.

Not in these clothes...

Since my other dress was locked in Rylee's car, I was shit out of luck.

"I don't think your father would approve of you staying the night with me, Hope."

"Would you rather I hitchhiked my way somewhere else?" I started handing him the helmet, almost threatening that I was actually going to attempt to walk down the street wearing such an outfit.

This had to work. Please work. I just can't go home.

"I'm telling you, it ain't happening." Why was he being so mean to me? It made no sense at all, especially after he'd come to my rescue before.

"Please. You won't even know I'm there. I promise."

I watched as he seemed to be thinking about it. While he contemplated with his decision, I sat there silently taking in how sexy he looked in what he was wearing. Unlike my ex Trevor, I found myself attracted to him in a way I'd never been with anyone else. Most of it was probably from the way he'd repeatedly come to my rescue, but there was something else about him; something that intrigued me. I wanted to know why I felt drawn to him, and why I couldn't stop picturing my dream where he'd kissed me.

"Fine, but you need to be gone before your father wakes up. I can't afford to be kicked out, because I was trying to be a good person. He won't see it that way. I have too much history for him to be okay with me helping you."

We both climbed on the motorcycle, and once I wrapped my arms back around Chance's waist, we took off. I couldn't understand what he meant, but I knew shortly I could relax and be safe for the night.

The fifteen minute ride to my father's community seemed to fly by. The night air felt good, even though I had a problem admitting to myself that I actually enjoyed being on the back of a bike. Maybe it was that I felt safe with Chance, even though I knew nothing about him.

When we finally pulled up to the house he helped me climb off, and removed my helmet. He reached in the hidden compartment and got the brown bag, then led me to the pool house. When the door opened he headed in first, and started cleaning a large pile of laundry off of the couch. "Sit here."

He went in the kitchen and began turning on a bunch of lights. "Want a beer?"

I smiled and folded my hands in my lap. "Sure."

I heard the caps hitting the countertop before I saw him approaching. He handed me the drink and sat down on the chair across from where I sat.

"Thanks for saving me tonight. Sorry if I ruined your evening. I didn't mean to be a cock-block or anything."

He smiled before taking a long swig of beer. I watched as his lips made contact with the bottle. When he pulled it away he licked them. I started licking mine, like it was some kind of chain reaction. I wanted to taste the beer on my lips and imagine that it came from his.

"Did you hear me?" He asked.

Of course not. I'd been too busy pretending we were making out.

"No, sorry. What did you say?"

"So, I can only assume that you aren't twenty-one yet. It's cool. I snuck into a lot of bars when I was at college. I'm not judging you. It just blows that your dad was in the same bar tonight."

"Yeah, I'm not legal yet. It sucks. Tonight was my friend's idea. She even forced me to wear this dress. Look at me." I stood and looked down at the little number I had on. "I feel so stupid."

He took another long gulp of beer and held the bottle

on his lips. His eyes were burning a hole in my dress. "You don't look stupid. It's quite the opposite actually." The intent in his eyes gave me chills. Right away I could feel my palms becoming clammy.

I started to blush and sat back down quickly. "Thanks. So, um, why don't you have a girlfriend, or do you?"

"I did. Things didn't work out," he said as he snatched the remote. I could tell he didn't want to talk about it, which only made me more curious.

I looked at the large pile of clothes. "Can I borrow something to change in to? This dress is really uncomfortable."

The sudden smirk on his face made it obvious that he certainly liked what he was staring at. Chance gave me another once over before looking through the pile. He handed me a t-shirt and a pair of boxers. They smelled good, and I wondered if he did his own laundry. "Thanks."

"The bathroom's right down the hall if you want to change in there." *Was this guy expecting me to strip in front of him? Of course I wanted privacy.*

While I headed in that direction I looked behind me and caught him checking me out again. I have no idea why I did it, but I couldn't control what came out of my mouth next. "Do you like what you see?"

Chance

I just wanted tonight to be a new start. I didn't intend on making friends, or bringing someone home with me. This was my boss's daughter, and although it was wrong in so many ways, I couldn't help but stare at her perfect ass as she staggered in the direction of my bathroom.

I was shocked when she'd caught me, but instead of getting mad, she smiled and asked, "Do you like what you see?"

This was so bad.

"Maybe." This battle with myself wasn't going as planned.

It had been a while since I touched someone. Part of me was afraid what would happen if I did. I'd managed to keep out of trouble since I moved here, but this was torture.

This girl was stacked like someone in Maxim magazine. To make matters worse, she seemed to want to be around me. If she only knew the truth; I had to tell her. She had to know that being around me was a dangerous mistake, and all I would do is bring her pain.

When she came out of the bathroom, I literally gasped. I'd already grabbed another beer, but not even the cold brew could hide my reaction. She looked so sexy in my clothes. I wanted to close my eyes and beg her to leave, but I couldn't do it.

Hope sat back down on the couch and stretched her tanned legs out on the table rubbing them with her hands. "Thanks again for the clothes, and the beer."

"Sure."

"I feel so good right now. I usually don't drink this much. In fact, the last time I got drunk I was sick all night and swore I'd never do it again." I could tell she was a little buzzed. She was too damn happy to be in this situation and act so relaxed.

I had to keep my composure. *This was not a booty-call.* I was doing her a favor. "It happens. I've had a bunch of those nights, but for some reason it always calls me back."

"Can I smell you?" She asked.

Okay that was weird. "Come again?"

"Well, your clothes smell so amazing. I'm just wondering what they smell like on you?" *Yeah, she was definitely drunk.*

I knew the clothes I was wearing came out of a box, but I had on cologne so they didn't stink. "It's kind of a weird request though. I don't think you should be getting that close to me tonight. We've both had a lot to drink." I knew I hadn't had that much. I could feel a slight buzz, but I didn't want her to know that. I needed to keep at a distance. She couldn't get involved with someone like me. I didn't deserve to have a relationship. It would never work.

She shocked me when she sat her beer down and

pranced over to the large chair I sat in. Her face came so close to my neck that I could feel her breathing. When she spoke I got chills all over my body. "I knew you'd smell even better than your clothes."

I went to push her away, but she lost her balance and fell into my lap. Her giggles filled the room. Before I could react she sat up and placed her forehead against mine. "Am I pretty?"

If she only knew how irresistible she was; I closed my eyes, refusing to look in hers. "Yes. You. Are." I spoke in a whisper, as if it made some kind of difference.

Her lips brushed against mine slowly, and then I felt her warm tongue stroking my bottom lip. I wanted to resist it, to push her away and lock myself in my room, but it felt so good. My mind told me this couldn't happen, but my body wouldn't let me stop her.

I wrapped my hands around Hope's small waist and pulled her into the kiss. By the time my tongue brushed against hers, she'd put her hands up my shirt and ran them over my chest. She pulled away and licked her lips. "Take off your shirt. I want to touch you."

"We shouldn't do this." I suggested, while I held the edge of my shirt to prevent her from moving it.

She took my hand and shoved it away. "Yes we should. Unless you don't want to?" She asked as she backed away from my face.

We stared at each other for a minute. Her lips were already puffy from our kisses while her eyes were burning with such desire. She appeared to be searching for what to say. "Don't you want me, Chance? I saw the way you've been looking at me. You admitted that you liked my body. I'm not very experienced, and my last boyfriend was an asshole. I probably won't be the best but..." She sucked on her bottom lip before continuing. "I'm so hot for you. I've never wanted someone so much before."

I pushed her away enough to pull off my shirt. I would face the repercussions in the morning. This was something that I needed, that I longed for.

I couldn't stop myself.

She was begging.

Her hands were on my bare chest. She had an eager smile on her face as she leaned down and licked the skin on my stomach. I pulled her back up into my arms, grabbing her hair and leading her into another kiss. Her tongue was like heaven. I'd deprived myself of affection like this for far too long that I was burning up inside.

She gripped the t-shirt of mine that she was wearing and pulled it over her head. I stared at the white laced, strapless bra. She took my hands and guided them to cup each breast. I couldn't believe this was happening. The hunger inside of me wanted this while I knew it was a terrible idea.

"Hope, we should stop. You don't want this. It's just the alcohol." I pleaded with her to stop me, because I knew I didn't have the will to do it myself.

"It's not just the alcohol." I watched her body language shift from sexy to very unsure. It was as if she didn't want to give up, but worried it was going to come to that. She was absolutely adorable like this. "Fine. If that's how you feel. Tell me you don't want me, and I'll leave you alone."

"I can't tell you that." I may have been a lot of things, but a liar wasn't one of them.

"Why not?"

I sighed as I watched my hands brushing over the

sides of her hips. She was using her own to control mine, but I was the one feeling everything. I licked my lips before responding to her. "Because, I do."

"You do what, Chance?" She took one of her hands and let go of mine. Before I could protest, she let it glide over the hard lump between my legs. She already knew how much I wanted her. The proof was suddenly obvious.

"Ah, oh God, I want you so bad." I kissed her ravenously before stopping and putting my hand over hers to prevent her from moving. "This isn't going to happen. I'm sorry. I can't do it. I won't."

I had to get up and leave the room before I changed my mind, and ended up taking her to my bed. It wasn't just the fact that I was attracted to her, or that we were all alone. It was the feeling of being wanted by someone after such a long time. I'd imagined this night in my head, but never been so conflicted before. I couldn't have sex with Hope, and be able to enjoy myself when I knew she was intoxicated. It would eat me up inside if I went through with it.

Hope said nothing when I left the room, and all I could assume was that she felt rejected enough to give me space. I had to push her away. It was the right decision.

I'd been sleeping for quite some time before I felt my mattress moving. I sat straight up in bed, forgetting for a moment that I wasn't alone in my apartment. She sat on top of my legs and leaned forward to kiss me before I could protest. I didn't reach up to hold her, but instead kept my hands flat at my sides.

When she finally pulled away to see how I would react, I turned to look at the clock. Noticing that it was near three, I knew this wasn't about any alcohol. This chick was coming on to me all by herself. She wanted this, and I was cornered into making a fast decision. "Hope, please. You're killing me here."

She jumped off the bed and headed for the direction of the door. "I'm so stupid."

For a few minutes I laid there contemplating with myself on what I should do.

I found her sitting on the couch. She didn't say anything as I dropped down to my knees in front of her. My hands were shaking, knowing this was such an intense moment. "I need to know that if I take you back to my bed it's because you want to be there. I can't have you saying that it was a mistake."

She shook her head. "I won't say that. I won't tell anyone this happened. I swear."

Hearing her words made my choice easy. I picked her up into my arms, kissing her the whole way I carried her to my room. I sat her gently on the bed and watched as she backed up onto it, never taking her eyes off of mine.

While crouching down on the mattress, I ran my hands up her legs, taking my time. She watched me pull down her boxers, the whole time licking those sexy lips, which made me want her even more. When the shorts hit the floor I stared at her lying on my bed. I kissed her hip bone and then her stomach. Once I made it to her chest, I slowly used my hands to pull down one side of her bra. Hope remained quiet, letting me take control.

As I succumbed to her hot kisses, I reached my hand inside of her underwear to feel her silky skin. She was so ready, the proof cupped within my hand. While shaking, she unbuttoned my shorts and kicked them off with her feet.

There was no time to think. No time to rationalize that this had gone too far; that it never should be happening. She pulled me into position with her legs, and for a moment, I thought I'd died and gone to heaven.

"We need protection first." I said worrying how incredibly stupid I'd almost been. Just imagining getting this chick pregnant made me cringe.

"I'm on the pill. Stop talking." Her lips covered mine, momentarily making me forget our predicament.

I should have never taken her word for it, but I had. Our hips moved systematically together, first slowly but then at a more rapid pace. I was captivated by her body and when she touched me with those lips, anywhere, I got chills deep inside. Her tongue teased me on my neck and ears, and then finally my mouth. I felt her body arching underneath mine and I couldn't hold out any longer.

I collapsed on top of her, while she stroked my back and stared into my eyes, before finally falling asleep. I closed mine shortly after flipping us around, while keeping our bodies tangled together.

8

Hope

I woke up wondering where I was, until I noticed Chance's body strewn across mine. I lay there for a few minutes taking in just how beautiful he was. How could someone like him be single? A smile crossed my face when I felt his strong arms holding me. I kissed his shoulder and sat up. My head was throbbing as I eased my way out of his bed. When I got into the bathroom I closed the door and emptied my bladder. I opened the medicine cabinet and looked for some kind of pain killer, because it felt like I could throw up, and knew it would only get worse if I didn't find something to relieve it.

When I was unsuccessful, I headed out into the kitchen. As I was walking I heard the front door opening. I ran back into the bathroom and hid behind the shower curtain. If this was my father, I was so dead.

A female voice filled the small pool house. "Chance? Where are you? Wake up sil...oh my God, you're naked!" Buffy screamed.

"So, get out of here. Damn!" I heard him yell.

"Well, I came to check on you. Why were you sleeping naked? You never sleep naked."

I heard the bathroom door move and closed my eyes. I don't know why I thought that if I had them shut I wouldn't get caught, but I did it anyway. When I heard the toilet seat lift up and a loud strand of pee hitting the water, I knew it was Chance. I kept as quiet as I could. "I guess I passed out when I got out of the shower. I don't remember," he confessed.

"Weird, Chance. You are so weird."

He didn't remember? How could he not remember? It was so perfect.

"Whatever. Are you done, or can I get a shower without you hounding me?" He asked as he reached in and turned on the faucet. I couldn't say anything as the frigid water hit my skin. I put my hand over my mouth and held it in.

"I made breakfast. When you're done getting yet another shower, you should come eat. Who gets that many showers anyway? You need to get laid so you can start acting normal. I don't even want to know how many times you're using showers as an excuse to rub one off. Just make sure you continue washing your own clothes. If I touch one cum rag, I'll freaking kill you," she announced as she left. I heard the door slam when the water started getting warm. I almost wanted to laugh at what she'd said.

When I started to relax my body, the shower curtain flew open and Chance came climbing in. "Hope? Oh shit."

I was crouched down in the bottom of the tub, soaking wet and naked, and he was too.

"Sorry, I heard her coming in, and had to hide," I confessed.

We were both still frozen in place. He didn't seem to notice that I was naked. I stood up and faced him, but when I reached my hand out to touch him, he backed away. "What's wrong, Chance?"

"You need to leave. You can't be here."

"But last night?"

"Was a big mistake."

His words crushed me.

Last night had been the best night of my life and those four words destroyed me. I hugged my chest and climbed out of the shower. "Let me just grab some clothes and I'll call my friend to meet me down the street." I headed out of the bathroom, trying desperately to hold back my emotions.

Within seconds he was standing behind me in nothing but a towel. "Hope, please understand. We can't do this. We should have never done anything."

"I understand perfectly. I'm so sorry that I threw myself at you. I thought we liked each other." I wanted to be sick. This couldn't have gone any more differently than I'd imagined. Yet again I'd slept with another guy who clearly couldn't respect me. It was nauseating.

"I'm sorry." Was all he said, and it was enough to break my heart.

I threw on clothes I found on the floor and went running out of the back of the pool house. When I made it into the neighbor's yard behind my father's, I kept running. I didn't want anyone to stop me. I pulled the cell phone out of my small clutch purse and started dialing Rylee.

By the time she picked up I was a mess. I couldn't even get the words out.

"Slow down, Hope. I can't understand you."

78

"I need you... to come... get me."

"What happened to you last night? Who was that guy?"

"I'll... explain... everything when... you get here."

"Where?"

I gave her directions to the entrance of my father's community while I started walking in that direction. If I ever came back here again, it would be too soon.

I felt like it took forever for Rylee to pick me up. When she did, she couldn't believe what she saw. I was soaking wet, and in someone else's clothes, without a bra. I wasn't as wet as before, but since I hadn't had time to towel off, things were pretty see through.

She had a million questions, but once I climbed inside the car, all I could do was cry. I had never felt so humiliated before.

I should have never agreed to her stupid plan last night.

"Where did you go, Hope?" She asked when I'd finally calmed down.

I looked at her. "Obviously I ended up going home with someone."

"Holy crap. Are you serious? I had no idea. Some hot guy came up and said you needed to leave. I told him to tell you to wait in the car if you were unhappy. The next thing I knew the bar was closing and you were nowhere to be found."

I couldn't believe she was turning this around on me. "It was around ten. The bar didn't close for hours. Did you really expect me to wait outside alone that long?"

"I should have just given you my keys. Kyle would

have dropped me off later."

I cringed. "You hooked up with that strange guy?"

"Don't you dare go preaching to me, Hope. You obviously did just as much as I did last night," she said as she continued driving.

"He wasn't a stranger."

Rylee pulled the car onto the shoulder of the road. "What do you mean he wasn't a stranger? Who the hell was he?"

"It doesn't matter," I mumbled.

"You better spill. I am not moving this car until you do," she threatened.

I told her all about Chance.

How we met.

How he saved me.

How he took me home.

She didn't ask for details about what happened once we got there, because the answer was written across my shame-filled face.

Last night had been one of the best nights of my life, but I couldn't let Hope know that. I wouldn't give her any reason to want to start a real relationship with me. If she knew what I'd done, and what everyone thought I'd done, she never would've been with me.

I couldn't stop myself. She was so beautiful. Her skin smelled like honey and I hadn't gotten enough of it. When I woke up and found her gone, I felt sad and alone again. I never expected to talk to her like I had. I saw it in her eyes that I'd crushed her.

How could I be such an insensitive bastard to her, of all people?

I tried to get my mind off of her. I took another cold shower, and started folding clothes, but when I found the dress on the floor, I lost it.

I had to call and apologize. I couldn't live with myself knowing I'd hurt her. Even if she didn't want to ever see me again, she deserved to know the truth. I put the clothes away and walked into the house. My plate was in the microwave like always. My sister and Mark were in the family room glued to the television.

"Hey guys, what's up?"

They both turned to face me. "Chance, where did you go when you left the bar?"

"I came home." I took a bite of bacon. "Why?"

"You know that bar we were at last night?" Mark asked.

"Yeah, what about it?"

"Someone went missing," Buffy stated.

I dropped the bacon on the plate. "You're kidding?"

"Just tell us that you did in fact come straight home, Chance." Of course Mark would want to know.

"I swear to you."

"Did anyone see you driving alone? Did you stop anywhere that may have caught you on camera?"

Shit!

"No, I was alone. I swear to you that I wasn't involved. I came straight home."

Buffy looked over at Mark and then back to me. "The police are running surveillance. If they see your picture…"

I interrupted, "Okay, I get it, Buff. I won't go anywhere or leave town. Trust me, I know the drill."

"Chance, we aren't accusing you of anything. It has to be a coincidence. A terrible coincidence at that," Buffy said. I knew what she was thinking. She was starting to second guess her faith in me. I was alone. I had no friends and now my own sister doubted my innocence.

I'd suddenly lost my appetite, so I stuck my plate in the dishwasher and headed back to my apartment. I hated that everyone just assumed I was guilty. There was only one person that could prove my innocence, but I'd already burned that bridge. The last thing I wanted to do was get her into trouble after I'd crushed her spirits. I would get through this alone, like I always did.

I waited all day and night for the police to put my face to the mug shot in the data base that they had of me. I watched the clock, wondering what was taking them so long. Finally when I had exhausted myself with anticipation, I fell asleep on my couch.

Loud knocking woke me up.

I stood up and stretched before heading to open the door. Two uniformed officers stood on the stoop. "Good evening, Mr. Avery. We were wondering if we could have a word with you."

I held my hand up and pointed inside. "Sure come on in."

The officers sat down on the couch that thankfully was laundry free. "We're sorry to bother you tonight." He slid a picture in my direction. "Our system got a hit on you being at this bar last night. Since you're in the national database we were wondering if you could confirm that you were in fact there."

"That's right. I had dinner with my sister and her boyfriend. When it got late, I headed home."

"Were you alone, Mr. Avery?"

Damn.

"Yes." I lied.

"Sir, we have you on the outside surveillance cameras leaving with someone. The footage is not very good, but it was clearly a woman. Would you like to tell us what really happened?"

"A girl asked me for a ride home. I dropped her off outside of her community. It was around ten-thirty."

They looked at each other and began writing down information. "Where was this community you dropped her off located?"

"It was off the main highway. I can't be certain. She told me where to turn." The lies kept on pouring out of my mouth. I was burying myself again.

"I see." He snatched something out of his uniform pocket. "Is there anything else you can tell me?"

"No. Am I being charged with something?"

"A local woman went missing last night. Just keep the card, kid. We'll be in touch." He said as he laid his card on the table in front of me. "Here is my number in case you remember exactly where the girl lives."

I saw the cops out, and watched my sister approaching me. "The officers said you left with someone. I knew you didn't sleep naked. Why couldn't you just tell us? Who was she?"

"Sorry, Buff, I need to get some sleep. It's been a long day. Goodnight." I said as I closed and locked the door on her.

I ran my hands over my face. I was in a heap of trouble just like last time. This couldn't be happening to me again. *Could it?*

9

Hope

I hadn't gotten much sleep, so when the alarm clock started blaring in my ear I picked it up and threw it against the wall. Immediately my mother came rushing into the room.

"Hope? Your grandmother is trying to rest. What was that noise?" She asked.

"Sorry, mom. It was nothing." I covered my head with my pillow after answering. Once I heard my door close I lifted it away and stared at the ceiling.

I felt my phone vibrating and picked it up.

"Hope. Are you awake?"

"Obviously. What do you want, Rylee?" I was still pissed at her.

"When I got up this morning, while eating my cereal, I saw something I couldn't believe. You're going to shit your panties if I'm right."

"This better be important."

"Someone went missing at the same time we were in that bar. Can you believe it?"

"That's horrible. It doesn't really involve me though. I left early."

"That's why I'm calling you. The paper had an image of the guy they are questioning."

"Is it the guy that you left with?" I wouldn't have been surprised if he was some criminal.

"No, it's the guy YOU left with."

"WHAT?" *How was that even possible?*

"Yep, they don't have a name, but I remember a hot guy when I see one."

"It has to be a misunderstanding. He left with me. We were together until yesterday morning."

"Do you think he returned once you fell asleep?"

"Um, no."

"How can you be sure? You can sleep through a train wreck." That was true, but not in this case. I was well aware of how close he was to me.

I decided that I had to give it to her straight. "Ry, he fell asleep inside of me. There isn't any way he left me to go back and kidnap anyone."

"Oh shit, girl! Sorry. Well I think you need to talk to him at least."

"Forget it. He doesn't want to ever see me again. He made that clear." It was still hard to admit out loud. Rejection never felt good, no matter how I tried to spin it.

"Well, it would suck for a fine specimen like that to be locked away for something he didn't do."

"Whatever, Rylee. I'll call you later."

After I hung up with her I got on my lap top and read the article online. It didn't give many more details than Rylee had already told me, but she was right about the picture. It was Chance.

My mother came into my room and I closed my computer. "Are you going to get up and help out around here, or mope in your bed all day?" She asked.

"Like I have a choice!" I announced sarcastically.

My mother wasn't having my flip comment. She got right up in my face like she always did when she lost her temper. "Listen here, young lady. As long as you live in this house you will pitch in. I am sick of your attitude every day. I worked my ass off to give you a good life. We didn't have much, but we made it work."

I tried to grab her arm but she pulled away. "Don't, Hope. You have your diploma now. It's time for you to be responsible. What are your plans?"

"I...I have no idea, right now."

"Well after the conversation I had with your asshole of a father yesterday, I would say you better decide fast."

"What do you mean? Why did he call?" I started worrying Chance had spilled the beans about our night together. Or worse, maybe someone had told my father he saw me running down the road.

"I had a bad day at work. I got laid off last night. When I got home I called your father and gave him a piece of my mind. He's living in that fancy community, but has never made an effort to pay me a cent in child support."

"Oh, so what happened?"

"He thinks it would be a good idea for you to move in there for a while."

"What? No way, mom! No way."

She sat down on the bed beside me. "Honey, your grandmother is not doing well. She needs to go into a home; and in order for me to afford for her to do that, I will have to sell the house. I don't have a choice."

"There has to be another way," I begged. "Please, mom. Don't make me do this. Don't make me leave. I hate it there. I don't want to go."

"Hope, your father has a huge house. I've been in the neighborhood. He has plenty of room for you. He seemed excited about you coming to live with him."

I started crying. The first reason was about my grandmother. The second was the fact that my mother had no job, and the third...well that was the fact that I would have to see Chance again.

"Please don't do this." I fell into her lap.

She stroked my hair. "When you turn eighteen you can live wherever you want, honey. It is just until the end of the year."

"Where will you go?"

"While the house is for sale, I'll stay here. Once the sale is finalized, I'll find a place to rent. I'll find another job, even if it's cleaning hotel rooms."

My mother held me while we both cried. This was so sudden. It had to be a nightmare.

"Chance, wake up." I heard my sister say as I looked around the living room.

"What?"

She threw me a pack of cigarettes. "Here, I know you want one."

"Thanks."

I started opening the wrapper while she sat down in front of me. Instead of the chair she sat on the table.

"Tables are made for glasses not asses, Buff."

"Shut up and listen to me, Chance. I need to talk to you about something really important."

This was it; Mark was making her kick me out. He didn't want a suspected felon living on his property. I would be homeless and jobless.

I lit up the cigarette in the house, which was something I never did then I took in the biggest drag.

"Mark's daughter is coming to live with us."

The smoke attacked my lungs and I began gagging. I hunched over trying to get myself to breathe. "What did you say?"

"His daughter. I should have told you about her sooner. Her mother is having financial difficulties. She and Mark discussed it last night. It's best for her. We have plenty of room here at the house. She just graduated high school, and she's such a nice girl. Maybe she even has some older friends you could get to know."

"Did you just say high school?" *This couldn't get worse.*

"Yeah, Mark said she'll need to stay with us at least until she turns eighteen."

I froze in place. *It just got worse.*

"If you're worried about the police... don't. Her mother has no idea what happened to you. Everything will be fine," she assured me.

"Maybe I should just start making my own meals out here, and keep to myself," I suggested.

"Don't be ridiculous. We can all eat together, as a family."

Buffy leaned over and gave me a kiss before walking out of the pool house.

I was in deeper shit than I ever could have imagined. Hope was only seventeen. I didn't need to worry about going to jail. Her father was going to murder me.

I slept with a seventeen year old girl. *How could I have been so careless?* We didn't even use protection.

I didn't know what to do. I was panicking. I even considered turning myself into the authorities, confessing to something that I hadn't even done. It would have been better than Mark finding out I had slept with his underage daughter.

I'd dug myself in so deep that there was no escape. I couldn't live with Hope. I couldn't be near her. I'd been horrible to her. She hated me.

90

I was probably the biggest regret of her life, besides the fact that she was a MINOR.

I snatched my keys and helmet and headed out of the house. Even if my sister started chasing me down the driveway, I wasn't going to stop.

10

Hope

For the next week I begged my mother to reconsider her arrangement with my father. I could tell that it was the hardest decision she had ever made, but she wouldn't budge on the outcome. I'd even asked Rylee's parents if I could live with them, but my mother refused the offer when they made it, claiming I needed this time with my father.

I attended my high school graduation with my head held high, even though the world was crumbling amongst me. My life was about to become a disaster, and I wasn't even sure how in the world I was going to manage to get by.

Once my vehicle was filled to the brim with all of my belongings, I hugged my mom a final time. We'd shed enough tears in the last week to fill a river. When I got into the car and pulled away, she waved until I could no longer see her in the rear view mirror. She was only a phone call away. I could visit her whenever I wanted.

Why did this feel like forever?

I couldn't be mad at her. My grandmother's Alzheimer's had gotten so bad that she didn't know us anymore. She needed to be under full-time supervised care.

My mother had managed to get a job at the front desk of the nursing home. She said the hours were crappy, but the pay was good. She would be able to easily afford a one bedroom apartment on her own. That put my mind at ease for the time being.

When I finally arrived at my dad's house, the welcoming committee had come out to greet me. Buffy and my father stood in the driveway.

"Eeeek! I am so excited about you staying with us," Buffy exclaimed.

My father, surprisingly, took me in for a hug. "You're going to love it here, honey. I promise."

I started grabbing my things out of the car when I felt someone standing behind me. I didn't have to turn around to know who it was. I could feel his eyes burning into my back.

"Hope, I want you to meet my brother, Chance. Chance, this is Hope," Buffy said as she stood between the both of us.

I had no choice but to look at him. If I didn't they would suspect something. I knew he didn't want to see me as much as I loathed the idea of seeing him, but we had no choice in the matter. I turned my attention to his welcoming (fake) smile. He brought his hand into mine. "Nice to meet you, Hope." That half-smile and those gorgeous eyes were irresistible.

I tried so hard not to feel something as we touched. "You too!"

Chance acted like we'd never met before, and as much as I wanted him to be that way, it made me angry. How could he be so comfortable around me after what had happened between us? *Was he born without a heart?*

I had to be cordial. I wasn't eighteen, and my parents had the final say in where I lived, whether I liked it or not. I had to make the best of things. It wasn't like I would see him all the time. I could stay in my room and he could stay out back. It would work. It was only until the end of the year.

When the vehicle was almost unpacked, Buffy and my dad went back into the house. They said they were going to cook on the grill to celebrate me moving in. That left Chance and I to grab the last two boxes from the back of the car.

He leaned in and obtained one of them. "Here, this one seems lighter." He placed it into my arms. I started walking away before he grabbed the last box and managed to close the trunk. Once we made it upstairs I sat the box down and stared at the walls. They were white, just plain white. Chance started to say something to me, but Buffy came rushing in. "Before you get upset, your father and I decided you could choose what color you wanted to paint the room. Maybe tomorrow we can head to the hardware store and pick it up together. I think you should paint it bright pink." She said as she strolled back out of the room.

Chance didn't speak at first, but instead he let out a heavy laugh. "I am sure you'll love a pink room."

I rolled my eyes. "Asshole."

"Look, about the other night..."

I put my hand up. "Forget it. We obviously have to live here together, so let's just pretend it never happened." I hated saying it out loud. There was no way I could ever forget how he'd made me feel. I'd never wanted anyone like I did him, and now I was being punished having to see him constantly.

"Fine by me." He marched out without saying anything else. It was difficult to fathom being around him when all I wanted to do was be back in his bed, in his arms again.

I had to get out of that room. That girl should have been named Trouble, not Hope. There was no *hope* for me when she was around. I kept telling myself that she was a minor, but the truth was, we were only a few years apart in age. It was just another excuse I was telling myself to get past what we'd done. Things were different now. We had to act like it never happened. She must have understood, because she went along with the introduction like she'd rehearsed it. The night we spent together had been amazing. Maybe she didn't think so, or maybe she hated me now for the way I had acted that morning.

When I got downstairs, Mark and Buffy were out on the patio. He had the grill fired up and started cooking the steaks. "Need any help?" I offered.

"Actually, Buffy can you give us a minute alone? Guy

talk."

"What's up, Mark?"

"I wanted to talk to you about my daughter."

Stay calm. He doesn't know anything.

"Sure."

"I just wanted to remind you that she is my only child, and I expect you to be on your best behavior when you're around her. I know you've experienced a lot in college, and I just don't want her to be influenced into frat life."

I had to smile at how he'd put it. I understood, but that part of my life was over. I was content with sitting home, drinking a beer and relaxing. "No problem, man."

"And, Chance...you can look, but don't you dare take it any further. She's off limits."

"Alright, no problem." *Too late!*

After he said that, he turned back to his normal laid back self. I headed to the pool house to grab a cigarette while I waited for dinner to be ready.

There wasn't any way around it. I had to ignore Hope. Just thinking about her made me crazy.

When I saw her walking out of the main house, I noticed she had changed into her bathing suit. I took a drag of my cigarette as I ducked back behind something so she couldn't see me. She was stunning. I stood there remembering how every inch of her body felt against my skin. I closed my eyes and found myself visioning our time together.

The outdoor kitchen faced the main house, which meant that Mark's back was turned to me. Hope looked down at her chest and readjusted her two piece bikini before diving right into the pool. It was like slow motion when her body lifted out of the water. Her skin glistened from the combination of the sun and the water as she ran her hands though her long wet hair.

The last time I'd seen her hair wet like that was when I found her in my shower hiding from Buffy. I couldn't believe she was here. How was I going to keep pretending our night meant nothing? How could I be around her when she was almost naked?

Buffy started calling me. I took another drag of my cigarette and came out of my hiding spot. "What's up, sis?"

"Get your suit on," she requested. I noticed her bright pink, two piece. I shook my head and sauntered into the pool house to change, trying to come up with all of the reasons that this was a terrible idea.

Once I got in the pool, I noticed my sister and Hope were having a conversation that I didn't want to be included in. I started doing laps, pretending that Hope didn't get to me. Keeping my distance was the only way that I saw things could work out.

When we finally sat down to eat, Buffy had taken the spot next to Mark, which left me to sit next to Hope. This couldn't get any harder. It was like teasing a dog with a T-bone. Not that I was comparing Hope to a piece of meat, but she definitely made my mouth water. Being next to her wet body was so intense. I wanted to look at her, to peek one time, but I couldn't risk that my sister or Mark would see me. I'd just promised him I wouldn't touch his daughter. If he only knew she was all I could think about, and had been thinking about for over a week, he would have me shot.

Buffy did most of the talking at dinner. I smiled when I saw Hope get up and run to the kitchen, only to bring back a bottle of ketchup, which she covered her steak with. Her dad looked like she killed a puppy.

"Do you want some meat with that ketchup?" I asked.

Our first words to each other in front of her father were about a condiment. *We were both pathetic.*

She gave me a dirty look and began eating her red covered meat. "Don't knock it until you try it. I've always put this stuff on my steak."

"I was just kidding with you anyway," I said, but nobody seemed to care. They kept eating.

When dinner was over we all hung out by the pool. Mark and I were discussing plans for the house, while Buffy and Hope talked about different ideas for decorating her new room. Knowing that she was so close to me was burning a hole into my mind. I wanted to look at her, but there was never a safe moment to do it.

When the mosquitoes started to bite, I thanked Mark for the meal and retired to the pool house. I couldn't stand being that close to her anymore. I was about to explode. A cold shower would be the only remedy for this fellow.

11

Hope

I did everything I could to avoid Chance Avery. One of the things included joining a father-daughter golf tournament with my dad. It was a few towns over so we spent the night there. It was actually nice being able to hang out with him, without Buffy. She was growing on me though, and I found myself enjoying her company more and more every day.

Rylee had been consumed with the new guy she'd met at the bar. She even told him that she was only eighteen and he was okay with it. I invited her over a few times, but between work and Kyle, she was always busy.

As the days went by, Chance and I refused to speak to each other unless we were around my dad and Buffy. I'd managed to avoid him for a whole week between going away and unpacking my room.

The moment we got home from our trip Buffy was on him like peanut butter to jelly. That night at dinner they gave each other googly eyes and looked like they were going to come across the table and start banging right in front of us.

As disturbing as it was, my mind was in other places, like being left in a room with just Chance.

Later that night they came downstairs and announced they were going away for the entire upcoming three-day weekend. Before I could grab my cell phone and make plans with Rylee, Buffy got one of her great ideas. "Oh, I know what you could do this weekend. You could get your room painted."

My father smiled. "I can leave you a credit card to buy whatever you needed, sweetie. Maybe you could have a friend over. No parties of course."

"And Chance can help," Buffy added.

I could tell that it was the last thing Chance wanted to do, but he put on a smile and agreed anyway.

I wanted to tell my father that it was a bad idea; that leaving was a terrible decision, but then I would have to give him a reason why. That was never going to happen.

I helped Buffy pack for the trip with my father, but I wished that I hadn't. Her choice of clothing was not something I wanted to imagine my father being into. She may as well have been walking around topless.

For the past two weeks I'd been forced to watch countless hours of MTV with Buffy. We would sit in the kitchen and talk for hours. She told me about how she and Chance fought as kids, and what it was like growing up in Pennsylvania. She talked about her old boyfriends and being a cheerleader in high school. I tried to avoid talking about Chance, but since he was her brother, the topic always came up.

I learned that he hated grape jelly. Riding on anything that spins made him throw up, and he was afraid of the doll Chucky from the movie *Child's Play*.

Even if Chance and I weren't on speaking terms, or any terms at that, I found comfort in hearing about him. I couldn't explain it. It was like the more I tried to stay away from him, and avoid thinking about him, the more I had to do it. I thought about Chance from the time I woke up, until the time I went to sleep. When I closed my eyes at night, the time we spent together replayed in my mind until I woke up gasping for air, feeling hot and bothered.

Being close to him was torturing me, but the thought of not seeing him made me even more upset. I didn't know what to do, and I feared that this weekend would be even worse. Chance had made it abundantly obvious that we were not friends. I suspected that he'd found out I wasn't yet eighteen. He'd never asked when we were together, and I hadn't thought it would matter. I made the choice to be with him. I'd initiated it that night.

I still had about six whole months to be tortured by his cold shoulder and humiliating stares. Six months wasn't long when I looked at the big picture. I could do this. I could avoid him as much as possible while they were gone.

It would be okay.

Chance

Leave it to my sister to plan a weekend away from the house. I was doing my damndest to stay away from Hope, and avoid her stares. After all this time I was certain she hated me. I couldn't blame her. I hadn't even begun to apologize for what I'd said to her after the night we spent together.

Living here with her was becoming unbearable. It would be better if she had a job or went somewhere, but she didn't. Instead she lay out by the pool day after day in her skimpy bikinis, taunting me with her hot ass body. I found that I had to take several cold showers during the week to keep from going completely insane. One day I'd climbed on the roof to fix more missing shingles. She set a lounge chair up directly under me and started rubbing oil all over herself. I got so caught up in watching her, that I almost lost my balance and fell to my death.

Yesterday she went for a run in the community. I had washed my bike around the side of the house and put it in the garage so it didn't get dusty. She thought nobody was home, but I was in the pool house having lunch. The next thing I knew she was stripping down to her bra and panties, swimming laps in the pool. When she climbed out I could see her hard nipples through her white bra.

Day after day something would happen and I would see it firsthand. It was torture. I was back to smoking almost a pack of cigarettes a day just to relieve some of the stress I was undergoing.

My sister and Mark were due to leave in the morning. They decided to have a nice family dinner before they left. My sister had cooked Italian, which was my favorite. She made homemade bread and the house was filled with the scent of yeast and garlic. The formal dining room had finally been painted and the new furniture was delivered. Buffy had set out candles and lit them around the table. She looked on the internet to find how a fancy place setting should look and did her best to mimic it.

Per her request, we all dressed up and met in the dining room at a quarter to six. I decided on wearing what I had worn to the bar the night Hope had come home with me. Part of it was because I still hadn't unpacked the boxes in my closet, but the other reason was because I knew it would drive her insane to see me wearing it again. The last time I had these clothes on; she had been the one to remove them.

When we got to the table I noticed that Hope's seat was empty. She finally came running down the stairs and around the corner entering the dining room. Buffy had a huge smile on her face as Hope tottered in. She must have lent her one of her outfits. She was wearing a light gray skirt and a thin silk shirt that was see through, revealing a lace tank underneath.

I noticed her father's face from the corner of my eye, and quickly turned my head so that he couldn't see me admiring his daughter. Once again it took everything I had for me not to look at Hope. The table was a large rectangle. Buffy and Mark were at both ends and Hope and I on either side. I stared down at my plate as we ate our salads. When Hope passed the bread around, she reached the tray across the table to me. For just a moment our hands touched. I felt a jolt of electricity running from my fingers all the way down my legs. For that instant our eyes met and I could feel the same heated passion between us that I'd felt that night.

As quickly as it started, it had vanished. Hope looked toward her father and started talking about his cholesterol, and what he should and should not eat while they were away. He gave her a hard time, but promised he would try to pay attention to what he consumed.

Buffy talked about how long the bread took to knead. When Mark praised her good cooking, she blushed. I could tell she was beside herself with happiness. She'd dated such losers for as long as I could remember, but Mark was different. I knew he admired her, and I never got the pervert vibe from him like I had with all the ones in the past.

Mark treated her like a princess. He'd picked her up when she'd hit rock bottom and given her a new life. The day he and I went through those clothes and got rid of them, I knew he cared more about her than how she looked. Even when he gave her the money for the boob job, he specifically told her to do whatever made her feel happy with herself, and that if she didn't do anything at all, he would be fine with it.

She was so happy, which in turn made me happy. Our mother had died at such a young age. We had each other now, and I would do my darndest to stick around and make her proud of me.

When dinner was all finished Mark and Buffy started

clearing the table. I jumped up from my seat and grabbed the plates from their hands. "I think that Hope and I can take care of cleaning up dinner tonight. Right, Hope?"

She gave me a dirty look, but put on a fake-smile when she turned to face her father. "Sure, it's a great idea."

"Oh. Thank you, guys. I still have so much to pack," Buffy admitted.

"Thank you both for helping. She really out did herself tonight didn't she?" Mark said before he followed my sister upstairs, leaving me alone with his daughter.

As soon as they were on the steps I felt Hope burning a hole through me with her stare. "What?"

"Don't ever make decisions for me without asking first." She was pissed. Admittedly, she was cute when she was angry.

"Excuse me. I thought it was the least we could do. Did you not enjoy the meal my sister spent all day on?"

"The meal was great. It was the company that made my stomach hurt."

I lifted a couple more dishes off the table. "Can you be civil for half an hour, so we can get this mess cleaned up?"

"Whatever, Chance."

I couldn't take her attitude. "What is your problem? What have I done to you since you've moved in that's so horrible?"

She gave me a dirty look, and part of me thought that a bowl of marinara sauce was going to be flung at my head. "Obviously, whatever you touch turns to shit. Isn't that why you live in a pool house? You're an asshole, and I wish we never met."

I felt like I was going to throw up, but instead I held my ground. I swallowed my pride and headed into the kitchen where I immediately started filling the dishwasher. I wasn't going to let her see that her words had affected me. She was acting like a bitch.

Hope came in from the dining room, and instead of her lips being scrunched up in anger they were relaxed. She had a sorrowful look in her eyes when she sat the rest of the dishes on the counter. I watched her attempt to touch my arm. "Chance, I.."

I pulled away from her touch. "Don't touch me, Hope. Don't you ever fucking touch me again. I take it you can handle the rest of this." I motioned to the pile of dirty plates. "I'm out of here." I marched out toward the pool house, determined not to look back and see her face. I knew she was pissed, but it couldn't have been anything like the way her words were destroying me.

12
Hope

I'd made a terrible mess of things. How could those words have come out of my mouth? Never in my entire life had I said something so hurtful to another human being. There was no way Chance would ever forgive me. I didn't know if I could even forgive myself.

If he disliked me before, this was the nail in the coffin.

I took my time finishing the dishes, crying the entire time, hoping that my father wouldn't come downstairs and ask why. When I finally turned on the dishwasher and threw the table cloth in the laundry room, I peeked outside. Chance was standing with his back against the pool house door smoking a cigarette. He had his hand covering his face. I held on to the door while considering going out there and apologizing, but I heard someone approaching from behind me.

I turned around to see my father walking to the refrigerator. "Hey, sweetie. Did you finish cleaning up already?"

I pretended to yawn so he would think my watery eyes were caused from that instead of tears. "Yeah, I just finished. I was thinking about swimming, but I can't stop yawning. I think I'm just going to call it an early night."

"Well give me a hug. We're probably going to head out before you wake up tomorrow." He reached over and pulled me into his chest. "Promise to behave yourself while we're gone. If you need anything you just call. I won't be too far."

"Please tell Buffy that dinner was amazing," I proclaimed.

"I will. She really likes you, Hope. You being around is good for us." My father stated, before he headed back upstairs with a tall glass of milk.

I turned off all of the lights and followed behind him. All I wanted to do was bury my head in my pillow and forget how I'd made things ten times worse than they already were with Chance. He hated me, and now I wondered how we were going to coexist without him wanting to cringe each time we were close.

When I got to my room, sulking, I noticed my cell phone blinking. There were three missed calls from Rylee. I called her back as soon as my body hit my bed.

"Hey Ry, Did you call me?" That question was almost something I feared asking her. She was such a trouble maker.

"Yes. I have some amazing news."

"What is it?" In the back of my mind I was hoping she somehow inherited a house that we could live in together.

"Kyle is taking me to the beach to meet his family. Isn't that awesome?"

"Yeah, I guess." I was jealous that she was so happy, while I continued to live with someone that loathed me so much. "Did you tell your parents about it?"

"Hell no! Are you kidding me right now? They would

108

flip out if they even knew I was dating him."

"You're crazy, Rylee. How are you going to get away for an entire weekend without them knowing?"

"Well, that's why I called my best friend. I figured you could cover for me."

"Oh!" I should have considered that before questioning her. Of course she'd want to use me as an excuse.

"So will you?"

"I guess. I mean my dad is going away for the weekend anyway." I went to tell her about Chance, but she cut in before I could.

"Yay! I can't wait to tell Kyle. Thanks, Hope. I owe you big time. Bye!"

Before I could even reply to her goodbye I noticed she'd hung up. *Talk about feeling worthless.* Even my own best friend would rather do something else than hang out with me.

At least I hadn't pissed her off so bad that she wished I was dead, which I had with Chance. In the morning I was supposed to go to the hardware store to look at paint colors. Instead of Chance going with me, like I'd wanted, he would probably tell me to 'go to hell'.

I located some pajamas then headed into the bathroom. Luckily this place came with great benefits. The large soaking tub had been calling my name for over a week and tonight was as good as any to put it to use.

The window that sat against the back of the house didn't have curtains. The neighbors behind us were way too far for someone to see inside, but the pool house wasn't. I climbed over toward the edge of the corner tub and looked down. Chance had turned out all of his lights. He probably went out, or to bed. Both would be my fault.

I considered trying to hang towels over the windows, but there wasn't anyone outside that could see me. The water in the tub started to get warm so I poured in some bubbles and started to take off my clothes. I located a hair tie and got my hair high above my head, then slowly stepped in the hot-soapy water. At first it burned, so I had to stand there until I could cool it down. Finally, it was perfect. I sat down and closed my eyes, trying to forget all about tonight, and Chance Avery.

I'd never experienced this kind of animosity about another human being, until now. I know I'd been a total dick to Hope for weeks, but she didn't have to go there. She didn't have to escalate it to that level. Hope had no clue how hard my life had been in the past year. I was lucky to not be in jail. The pool house was fine with me, and I kind of liked it. I didn't need a big fancy house to make me happy. I needed my family, my sister, who was all I had left in the world.

I knew I had to get out of that house before more was said that I wouldn't be able to take back. My father had been such a nasty bastard, and for a second I felt like I'd sounded exactly like him. The thought made me cringe. I'd gone into the pool house long enough to grab my smokes. When I came back outside I turned off the lights in case she got a hair up her ass and tried to speak to me. Hopefully she would think I was sleeping.

I was standing outside my place leaning against the wall when I happened to see a light upstairs come on. It was pitch black outside and the brightness caught my eye immediately. Within a moment's time I saw her looking out. For a second I thought she saw me too, but she just kept moving around.

My mouth dropped when I saw her disappear and come back with nothing on. I took another drag on my cigarette and watched her standing there topless. I couldn't see past her waist, but the top was fine enough for me. She wasn't doing anything erotic, just standing there. Finally she ducked down and disappeared. I had hoped she'd make another appearance, but after ten minutes I gave up and went back inside.

Was she taunting me again? Was this some sort of game she was playing with my mind? I wished I could say that it wasn't getting to me, but it was. I needed to blow off some steam; to get out of here for a few hours and unwind.

I grabbed my keys off the counter and headed out.

There was nothing more relaxing than being on my bike. It was loud and prevented me from hearing people talking about me or yelling at me. I was free when I was on it. I drove all around those long dark roads, until finally I ended up a few towns over at a local dive bar.

The front lot was filled with motorcycles and people outside smoking cigarettes. I removed my helmet and immediately lit up. The music wasn't what I normally listen to. They were playing country, and as I entered inside I noticed people line dancing in the center. I headed straight to the bar and ordered a beer.

I never turned around to watch the people dancing. I didn't talk to anyone, including the bartender, unless it was for another drink.

After I had ordered my third beverage, a woman approached me. "I haven't seen you around, honey. Are you just passing through?"

The woman was about forty. Years of alcohol had caused wear and tear on her body, and I was certain at one point she was probably a great time. "Just passing through, yeah."

"That's too bad. I could have used the company tonight."

I gave a quick laugh. "I'm giving up on women."

"Well that would be a damn shame. You're quite the looker. Someone must have really done you wrong."

"Yeah, you could say that," I said as I took another sip of beer.

She grasped my arm. "If you want to talk about it, I'm a good listener."

I let her keep her hand there. I wasn't into her, but I didn't want to hurt her feelings. She was obviously just trying to be nice. "Thanks for the offer. I just don't feel like talking. I came here to forget, ya know?"

"Honey, we're all here to forget something," she admitted.

"Well cheers to that." I said as I held my bottle up and clanked it against hers.

I ended up buying the woman a drink before I decided to hit the road. I had already pissed off enough people in my life. I didn't need to make any more enemies.

When I finally arrived back home it was after two. The lights in the main house were all out. I was quiet as I made my way to the pool house. Once inside, I stripped down to my boxers and got in bed. As much as I tried not to think about it, Hope flooded my mind. When I succumbed to sleep I dreamed of her all night long, again.

13

Hope

I didn't hear my father and Buffy leave, but after I looked at the clock, I knew they had. I stayed in bed as long as I could until I heard noises coming from downstairs. I managed to get myself up and dressed before deciding to take a trip to the hardware store, alone.

My father had left me his credit card, as well as fifty bucks in case I wanted to have friends over and order pizza. He knew I wasn't into having parties, so there was never a question of trust there, even though he'd teased me about it.

During that long bath I'd finally relaxed; and when I started to drift off while still in the tub, I climbed out and went straight to bed. I worried that I would be restless after my confrontation with Chance, but I slept through the night without waking up.

Once I was dressed and pulled my hair up in a ponytail I headed downstairs to grab some fruit to eat before I headed out. I found Chance in the kitchen reading the newspaper while eating an apple. At first, I ignored him, while I looked in the fridge for something to take with me. When I realized he was eating the last apple I was frustrated.

"Thanks for eating *my* breakfast." I announced.

He looked down at the half eaten apple and tossed it across the counter. "Help yourself, princess. I lost my appetite." His eyes were filled with hostility as he turned and marched outside.

I stood there shocked. Did he really throw an apple at me? Furthermore, did he just call me princess?

The blood was boiling in my body. I rushed out behind him leaving the door wide open. "What did you call me?"

"You heard me."

"Say it again, Chance. I dare you!"

He turned around and laughed at me. "You dare me? What are you going to tell your daddy? I'm so scared." He threw his hands up in the air. "I don't have time for this shit today."

"Wait! How dare you talk to me like that."

He walked up to me, his eyes never leaving mine. When he seized my arm I tried to pull away, but he wouldn't let go. "Talk to you like that? What about you, talking to me like that. It goes both ways, Hope. Maybe you should practice what you preach."

Tears filled my eyes when I remembered what I had said to him only hours before. "Chance, wait!" He kept walking away from me. "Chance!"

After I waited at least two minutes and he didn't come back, I headed into the house and located my keys. I cried all the way to the hardware store. It took me about three seconds to pick a color for my room, and I didn't even care if I hated it. I waited as the guy mixed it for me and then paid for it. I then took my time getting home, stopping by a drive-thru to grab a milkshake to try and settle my nerves.

I wasn't in a rush to go home, or to paint. My best friend was away with some strange new boyfriend, and I was stuck home alone with the douche-bag, who hated my guts.

Perfect.

When I pulled up at the house I noticed Chance on a ladder. He had removed his shirt and sweat glistened all over his back. Even as mad as I was at him I couldn't help but stare at his perfectly sculpted ass. Every muscle in his shoulders was well-defined. I tilted my glasses down to get a better look, but as I did he turned to look my way.

I clutched my purse and the paint stuff, pretending like it never happened.

When I reached the front door he'd already gotten back to hammering away at something. I headed into my room and started covering everything with plastic. Once I got the paint out and began working on the corners, I lost track of time. I had my IPod hooked up to speakers and sang along to the music as I focused on my task.

A few hours had passed and I was already done with all of the cutting in. The edges and the corners were all painted with two coats. I'd chosen a grayish-blue color and it went perfectly with my black and white comforter set. I didn't want my father to have to buy me a new one when mine was in fine shape.

I poured more paint into the pan and started rolling the walls. A song that I loved came on and I began singing it, belting out the lyrics. I was facing the window when I heard someone laughing. I jumped so high before I turned around and saw Chance leaning against my doorway. He had his arms folded against his chest and a smile on his face. I ran toward the IPod and turned off the music.

"You should think about trying out for American Idol,"

he cackled.

"What are you doing in here, Chance?"

"Well, I came inside to make a sandwich, but when I heard you singing I had to check it out. I didn't know it was actual singing. It kind of sounded like you were in excruciating pain. God knows I was after hearing it."

I picked up a paint brush and threw it straight at his face. Before he could duck, blue paint slapped against his cheek. He took his hand and ran it across the wet paint on his face. "You little bitch. Did you just throw a paintbrush at my face?" He ambled toward me, and had me cornered. I couldn't run. I was pressed up against the wall.

"Chance, I'm sorry. Really, I am. I swear, I didn't mean to-." To be honest I wasn't sure if he was going to hurt me, or torture me. Neither sounded pleasing.

Chance kept my body pressed against the wall. His teeth were tight together and he looked so pissed. He gripped my wrist and squeezed until I let go of the roller I had in my hand. Once he was holding it, he held me tight with one hand and rolled the paint from the top of my head down to my chest.

I closed my eyes and screamed, but nobody could hear me. Once he was satisfied, he let his guard down and I stole the roller out of his hand, flinging the paint toward him. He didn't bother wiping it off, but instead came running at me knocking me down onto my plastic covered bed.

I expected him to hold me down and torture me, but instead he just stared. With one hand he moved a piece of hair out of my face, while keeping his eyes on mine. We were both breathing pretty heavy from the chase and him being this close to me made me forget why I was mad at him in the first place.

When he brushed his lips against mine I let out a quiet moan. Our faces were covered in paint, but our mouths didn't care. Chance's bare chest was pressed against me and once his tongue found mine, I couldn't keep myself from reacting. He started to pull away, but I wrapped my arms around his neck and held him back.

I couldn't stop kissing him.

I didn't want to stop kissing him.

He tasted like salt and heaven, and I wanted more.

I'd thought about him so many times, longing to be with him again.

Chance reached down and lifted the bottom of my shirt. I helped him get it off, and even unhooked my bra before he made the attempt. When his hands cupped my breasts I threw my head back and let out another moan. He stared into my eyes while he licked each of my nipples slowly, like he was savoring them. Before he backed away he kissed each of them again. I pulled him up to my mouth and stroked my tongue against his. When he stuck out his tongue for me to take, I sucked on it before releasing it and savoring those lips again.

My mouth made its way down his neck and this time he was making the sounds.

His hands were on my pants. They didn't have buttons so he kneeled down next to the bed and pulled them off of me.

I must be dreaming.

This couldn't be happening, not after everything.

I'd denied myself this for too long. All of those cold showers led me right back into her arms. I couldn't help myself. I had to touch her, to feel her lips against mine. I wanted to taste her again. I kissed her stomach and then each of her thighs. She knew what I was going for and she spread her legs wider for me. As my mouth touched her sweet spot she arched her body back in pleasure.

I didn't give a shit about the paint, or the fact that five minutes before I wanted to strangle her for how mad she'd made me. This hunger that I had for her had been growing for weeks. I yearned for her touch, and to have her hands all over me again.

I entered her with such passion, and immediately knew that this wasn't what I was used to. Hope wasn't my girlfriend. Hell, I didn't know if we were even friends at all. The only thing I was sure of was that I couldn't deny how much I wanted to be close to her. All of the fighting had only intensified this encounter, making it very powerful.

Hope clung to me as I flipped us all around, making use of her whole room. She held me close while I savored her lips and satiated my own needs. We were too caught up to consider the repercussions. In this moment only she and I existed.

When I finally finished she held me tight against her body. I looked up into her eyes as she stared back at me. We kissed slowly, savoring our experience. *God, had I missed those lips.*

"Chance."

"Yeah?"

"I missed you."

I wanted to tell her that I missed her. Hell, I wanted to say a lot more than that, but I couldn't let myself feel that way again. I promised her father I wouldn't do this. I was going to be a dead man.

"I can't, Hope." She started to pull me back against her. "It isn't that I don't want to. I promised your father that I wouldn't. I can't lose the only family I have left. I'm sorry." I said as I stood and pulled up my shorts.

"He doesn't have to know. Please don't go." She was begging me. I had to get out of there before I did something we'd both regret.

"Hope, there are things that you don't know about me. You wouldn't want me if you knew the truth. I can't change the past. We can't keep doing this. You know it isn't right." I tried to explain.

"I don't care about your past. Don't you get that? I just want to be with you. It's all I think about. All of these weeks trying to avoid you have made me crazy. I thought you hated me. How could you sleep with me again if you knew it would amount to nothing?"

Her eyes were starting to fill with tears. My heart was so cold. I hated hurting her. "Please don't cry."

"Are you still mad at me for what I said last night? I didn't mean it. I have no idea why I said it. I just wanted you so bad and you wouldn't even look at me. It was making me furious. That night we spent together was wonderful, and then you were horrible to me. I don't understand you, Chance. Was I just a fuck to you?"

"I did look at you. I looked at you so many times. All I thought about was that night. It's been driving me crazy since you walked out that morning. You think I wanted to wake up and make you leave? I was afraid of what would happen if you stayed."

She captured me and twisted her hands into mine. "Tell me why you don't want me then. Why can't we just sneak around and be like? What happened to you? What could be so bad that it makes you not willing to let me in?"

"I told you that I promised your dad. I would be homeless if he found out, Hope. Is that what you really want?"

"Of course not, but there has to be a way for us to be together. I like you, and I'm pretty sure you like me, too."

If I told her how many times I'd thought about ways we could be together she'd think I was a stalker. "I've considered every option. Maybe if you were eighteen it would be different."

I tried to look away but she caught my attention. I could tell she was in one of her determined moods. I'd seen her using this same strategy to get something out of Mark. The girl was relentless when she wanted something. "So it's because I'm not eighteen? Jesus, technically I am. I graduated high school. I'm independent. What more can I do?"

"That's just it. You can't do anything. I made a promise to Mark that I wouldn't touch you. Please, can you

121

just understand and leave it alone?" I couldn't argue about it anymore. I leaned over and kissed her forehead, leaving my lips there for a longer time before walking out of her room, and heading back downstairs.

Fighting about it was hopeless. It wouldn't get us what we wanted, which was apparently each other.

14

Hope

I stayed in my room for the next few hours, bawling my eyes out. I truly believed that at any minute Chance would come back into the house and say he'd changed his mind, but he never did. When I finally realized he wasn't coming back in, I got redressed and finished painting my room.

I kept myself occupied, but never belted out a tune again. After another hour's worth of work, I managed to get everything cleaned up, except for myself. I mostly had paint on my face and in my hair. There was still some on my arms, but it was peeling right off.

I thought about taking another bath, in hopes that it would make me tired and I could go to sleep. I needed to eat, but the last thing I wanted to do was see someone who did not even want me, someone I was never allowed to have.

I had to do something. There had to be a way for us to be together. I couldn't stand living in this house another moment and knowing he was just outside my door. My mind was a cesspool of knowledge, and I couldn't find a loophole. There was no way my father would ever let me be with Chance, and he wasn't willing to go against my dad's wishes. It was almost as if my dad had something on him.

He kept talking about things from his past, and his sister even hinted about something bad that happened. I felt horrible for saying those things about him living in a pool house. I don't know why I'd done that. The worst part is that I thought the pool house was great. If he could only see the shack that we had to live in at my grandmother's he would have been appalled.

It was Saturday night and I was hiding out in my room from someone I didn't want to hide from at all. I need to feel him. I just wanted to be close to him.

Then it hit me. I knew exactly what I had to do, but getting the nerve to do it was going to be another story. Modesty was never a downfall, but being with a guy was. Somehow, when I was with Chance, I never felt embarrassed. He made me feel so desirable. Just thinking about the things he did with his tongue gave me goose bumps. I was standing in the middle of my room running my hand over my lips with my eyes closed. I must have looked ridiculous.

With a plan mapped out, I knew what needed to be done. Instead of getting in the shower, I headed down to the pool.

I had no idea where Chance had gone, but once I got outside I made it my mission to hunt him down. I didn't have to walk far. He was sitting at the picnic table smoking a cigarette. "You know those things will kill you?" I hated the smell of them.

He smirked. "Yeah? So will your father when he finds out I fucked his daughter, for the second time."

I watched the smoke exit his lips. It made me think about what he had done with that same mouth earlier. The way he said the word "fuck" gave me butterflies between my legs and I was already so turned on just being this close to him.

I bit my lip and approached him.

"Do you care if I go swimming?" I asked in my sexiest voice.

"Nope, you don't have to ask permission." He answered, while never taking his eyes off my mouth.

I ran my hand over my neck and down the fabric of my shirt, taking my time once I got to my chest. My lips were parted just enough where he could see my tongue licking across my top teeth as I watched my own hand sliding down. I took my shirt into my hands and pulled it over my head slowly, while I faced him. When I looked at him again, he was sitting at the table with his mouth wide open. He was even more shocked to notice I wasn't wearing a bra.

To be honest I was shaking like crazy. If he thought this show was at all easy for me he was insane. Had it not been for us already having sex, I wouldn't be doing it at all. It was my last desperate attempt at getting him to want me.

Was it pathetic? Probably, but I was still going through with it.

He caught my eyes with his and snapped his attention to being serious. I was afraid he would be mad. "What are you trying to do, Hope? Are you teasing me on purpose?"

I watched as I ran my hands up my smooth skin. Without looking over to see his expression, I answered him. "I was kind of hoping you would want to watch."

I didn't wait to see his reaction. I turned my back to him. Slowly, with even more courage than it took for the

125

shirt, I slid my pants down off my feet and dove into the pool. I surfaced in the shallow end, making sure my breasts came out of the water enough for him to see. I played around splashing in front of me, while I looked directly at him.

"Come on. What are you waiting for?" I said quietly again, while I rubbed my hands from my neck to the back of my hair.

"Please don't do this to me. I'm trying so hard to do the right thing here." He put his face into his hands. "I know I screwed up twice already, but this has to stop. I'm making an adult decision. You've got to respect that."

"I'm not even near you. You don't have to touch me, if you don't want to," I taunted him. His mouth was saying one thing, but his eyes were in a different place. I could tell he was already fucking me in his mind and it made me want to keep it up. His hands may not have been touching me, but it felt like they were. I was in a pool of cool water and felt like I was burning up.

"You're killing me." He put his head between his legs and tried to gain composure. "Please stop fighting me on this."

I was determined to keep at it. He had to give in. There was no way he was going to walk away with me doing this.

"What if I had a solution?"

He crossed his arms, like my idea wasn't going to be a good one. I couldn't help notice his muscular biceps flexing as he did it. "Just one weekend. Be with me for one weekend. By Monday you can go back to ignoring me like you normally do."

He observed me with pain in his eyes. When he stood up I got excited, but then I watched him shake his head and walk into the pool house.

I stayed in the shallow end sulking for a few more minutes until I realized I'd made a complete fool out of myself. I should have just stayed in my room. There was nothing more humiliating than what I'd just done. My eyes filled with more tears and I knew I would never be able to face him again.

Just as I started to climb out of the pool I heard a splash coming from the other end. Before I was able to turn I felt his hands around my waist.

His lips found my shoulder and he kissed it with his tongue.

Chance turned me to face him. His hands cupped both sides of my face. "Do you have any idea how crazy you make me?"

I closed my eyes. "Please kiss me. Just kiss me."

Our lips connected, and then he slowly pulled away. "One weekend, Hope. That's all I can give you. You've got to promise me that you won't push for more."

He brought his lips to mine and I realized why he'd gone inside. I pulled away from him. "You brushed your teeth?"

He shrugged. "I didn't want you to have to kiss an ashtray."

"Kiss me again. Don't stop." I pleaded.

His lips were on mine again.

I couldn't help myself. It was bad enough that I'd left her for a second time after sleeping with her, but I couldn't say no when she stood in front of me naked begging me to spend time with her. I cared about her, and I didn't want her sitting in the house crying thinking I didn't want her the way she wanted me.

She had to know if I could change things I would. I tried to rationalize this with myself every day since that night and the same conclusion kept coming up.

I wanted her.

It wasn't just for the sex either. I was crazy about this girl in every way. Day after day I let myself feel again. She was the reason, and I wanted to be able to at least experience what it would be like if things were different.

From the moment she stripped down in front of me I could feel myself weakening. I should have told her that when I went inside it was only to wash the cigarette taste out of my mouth. I didn't want her to have to smell something that dirty. I think she was shocked when I jumped in the pool and reached my arms around her. Her skin felt smooth to touch with the water all around us.

When I reached down and kissed her soft lips I knew that there wasn't any other place I needed to be. I may have broken a promise to Mark, but was it right to break a promise to myself? There was something about this girl that made me feel like I couldn't be without her, something that kept me wanting more. Not just for the purpose of physical interaction, but also the idea of connecting with another person again.

As we continued to kiss, I felt her hands reaching down to my waist. She pulled away when she realized I wasn't wearing any shorts. Hope moved back looking both shocked, with a sense of excitement.

"What?" I asked, wondering why her lips were that far away.

"Nothing. I'm just happy, that's all. I was starting to come to grips that you weren't going to change your mind."

While our tongues mingled around together I floated us over to the steps that were built into the pool. I managed to sit myself on one of them, while I pulled her on top of me without breaking our embrace. My hands reached up and grabbed a chunk of her wet hair and I gently tugged her head back. She reached for my mouth again, presumably to give me more of that sweet tongue. I let her think that our lips were close enough to touch before pulling back again. When she repeated the attempt for the third time I watched her stick out her tongue. I stuck mine out and slid it against hers before finally giving in to her unspoken request.

Our kissing became more aggressive, even going as far as our teeth touching a few times. Her body began rocking up and down on top of me and I knew she could feel how rock hard I was underneath her.

Since we were in the water she was able to arch her back in a certain way and remain floating. This gave me an excellent view of her perfect tits. She wrapped her legs around my waist which enabled me to free my hands. I slid them from her waist to the underneath of her breasts. The water made it easy to maneuver. With one hand still holding the skin just beneath her breast, I pulled her toward me again so that I was able to lick over her right nipple. She moaned as I drug my tongue roughly against it then bit the tip. I latched onto it and repeated the process, knowing damn well that this was the attention she craved.

"Oh, God, yes!" She called out, falling back and letting me have free reign.

She started grinding her ass against my obvious erection. Next I reached down with both hands and guided her to do it harder. I could tell she was ready for me, even under the water. My finger slid right into her slick opening and I began to move it in and out. I used my thumb to rub her soft spot above it and she moaned into the dark of the night. I could feel her muscles tightening around my fingers, while her lips found mine again. Even though I was aware that she hadn't been a virgin our first time, for obvious reasons, I could tell that in some ways she was inexperienced. There was no way with just the little effort I was making that she'd be so consumed. I appreciated that she found it to be satisfying, considering it had been a long time since I'd felt the touch of a woman.

It was easy to slide inside of her again, after just having done it earlier. Our emotions were in sync, and for the time being nothing mattered except the two of us.

The friction from the water allowed it to somehow

feel even tighter, making it difficult for me to be able to keep control. As much as I wanted it to last longer, I knew it was going to be impossible. Like our first time together, I was too captivated by her beauty to be able to focus on anything else. "Please don't stop, Hope," I whispered near her ear. I could feel the heat rising to the tip of my shaft, and she could tell from the sounds that I was close.

I captured her by the waist and flipped her around. She gasped as we became unattached, but I quickly filled the void when I slid in from behind. I thought that if I couldn't see her face that I'd be able to last longer. My attempt was short lived when I peered down at her fine ass. My head rested against her shoulder, and I held her body tight against mine as I began to lose control.

I kept her close to me on the steps while we both regained steady breaths. I could tell she was just as exhausted as I was.

Holding her, feeling her hot body so close to mine, only reminded me of one thing.

One weekend was never going to be enough for me.

15
Hope

When Chance and I finally decided to get out of the pool he rushed over and grabbed two towels, wrapping one around me before doing the same for himself. He then pulled me back into his arms. I let mine reach around his back while my head fell against his hard chest.

"I'm sorry for calling you a princess," he whispered into my hair. "I don't think of you that way, Hope. I've never thought that about you. I was just so mad at what you said to me. I thought of the first thing that would piss you off the most and used it as a weapon."

I squeezed him tighter. "I'm sorry too, Chance. I hated that you wouldn't talk to me. I only wanted your attention. I would've deserved for you to call me much worse. I know I acted like a spoiled little bitch. The thing is, what I said was uncalled for."

"God, I don't want to hurt you."

I moved my head away, allowing me to look up at his face. "So don't."

He studied my expression and I could tell my words

caused him frustration. He closed his eyes and furrowed his brows like he always seemed to do when he became stressed. "It isn't that easy. You understand, right?"

I'd always thought that when you liked someone you pursued them. In this case there was much more to factor.

"Why can't I be with you? Tell me why." At this point I needed to hear him say it. I wanted it to come from his mouth now that I knew for sure our feelings were mutual.

"I told you this already. I promised your dad."

"That's not a good enough reason for me. Who actually lets someone else make decisions like this for them? This is about us."

"You're right. It's not just about your dad. I wish I could talk about it, but it's not going to happen."

I had to look away for a second to hide my disappointment. Once again he was shutting me out. I didn't know what else to do to get his attention, aside from throwing myself in front of a moving vehicle. I'd taken off my clothes and practically begged. It was embarrassing. "Sorry. I just don't understand."

"Please, don't ruin tonight. I promise that when the time is right I'll tell you. I just can't talk about it now."

I had two choices. I could keep pushing until I pissed him off, or I could let it go and be content with the time he was willing to give me. He spoke before I could venture with my own response.

"Will you just drop it?"

I wanted the truth, but I longed to be with Chance more. I couldn't risk ruining this weekend by pushing him away. He needed to know I trusted him, even if knowing the truth could possibly hurt us. Obviously whatever it could be was bad enough that he refused to openly talk about it.

"Okay."

He smiled and traced the edge of my towel. "Since we've got that worked out, do you want to maybe come inside with me?"

I reached down and tangled my fingers into his. Without saying another word, he led me to the pool house.

He pulled me through the small apartment before we came to a stop in front of his bed. My towel fell to the floor, and I watched Chance back away to take in my body. I felt uneasy until he began to speak. "You're so beautiful, Hope. I've never seen anything so perfect."

I looked at Chance. His hair was wet and appeared almost black. Beads of water still sat on his shoulders. He was taking me in with his deep brown eyes. He lifted his hands to the back of his head, causing his biceps to flex. I paid close attention to the tattoo on his skin, and how it somehow made him seem tough.

As he continued looking at me I backed myself up on the bed. He didn't say a word when the towel dropped and climbed beside me. We lay side by side staring into each other's eyes. "I don't deserve you," he whispered.

"Don't say that. Everyone deserves to be happy," I answered, never taking my eyes off of him.

"You don't understand what I've done; what I've been through. I wish I could explain. I know you want the truth. I just can't."

"It's okay. We don't need to talk about it tonight. I promise I won't ask. Chance, my ex was a total douche. He cheated on me, and lied. I get that people make mistakes. We all have a past, but you've saved me twice so far, and I can't accept that you're as bad as you say you are."

He let out a sigh and turned to lie on his back. His

hands came up to his face, and he held them there. Worried, I leaned up and tried to pull them away, but he refused.

Then I heard him chuckle. Realizing he was turning this into a game, I tried with both hands.

"Stop! Stop! I don't want you to see my face," he teased.

Finally he gave in, letting me remove them. I leaned in and kiss him gently on the lips. He clenched the back of my head and wouldn't let me up.

I reached to both sides of his stomach and started tickling him. Before I knew what was happening, he'd flipped me over so he was on top. His fingers rubbed over my mouth and I parted my lips as he did it. He kept moving them from my neck, down to the skin between my breasts. Chance leaned in and kissed me there on my naked flesh.

I figured that he would keep teasing me, but instead he laid his head down and closed his eyes. I ran my hands through his hair, and took in how amazing it felt being with him this way.

We were silent for a while. I honestly thought he'd fallen asleep, but just as I let my eyes close, I heard him speak. "Will you go to the beach with me tomorrow?"

"I'd love that," I answered, before finally allowing myself to fall asleep in Chance's bed, with his arms wrapped around me.

When I attended college my mother kept telling me not to get tied down to one girl. She said there was so much out there for me to learn before I settled down. Of course, at the time I didn't believe her. I ended up getting into a serious relationship and thinking that she was the person I would marry, and have a future with.

Back then I was hoping to study law, so that once my baseball future was over, I'd have something to fall back on. My full ride derived from my love of the game, and before my life was ruined I was pretty sure that I had an opportunity to play in the minors, if not the majors.

My girlfriend's father was a prominently, well-known lawyer and he'd always said he was going to take me under his arm, and eventually get me into his firm. I looked up to the man, and found myself wanting to make him proud of me. My father was never a big part of my life so I always felt like he was the closest thing I had. I never realized that my ex was just a way into a lifestyle that I never knew. She'd been a backup plan.

I thought I knew what love was. I believed that I truly felt that way for her. Even after losing the relationship and the support of her family, I thought I hurt so much because it had really been love.

Now I knew better, because it was nothing compared to the way I felt when I was with Hope. I'm not saying that after being around her for over a month that's what it was, but it was definitely something spectacular. Her touch was electrifying and I craved her energy. The way she looked into my eyes made me feel like she saw through my fears. She didn't care what was standing in our way, as long as we were together. That meant so much to me, even when I knew it was forbidden.

The problem was that I couldn't tell her. If she knew the truth, she wouldn't stop trying. There was no way her father would change his mind about me; especially now that the police were breathing down my back again. There was certainly no way in hell I could tell him that I was with Hope that night. She would never forgive me and he would kick me out, or blame my sister.

I wanted her to understand, but it was easier said than done. Hope had gone to extremes and I felt really bad about it. Don't get me wrong, I loved the show, but she didn't have to do that. She should have never doubted my feelings. I wanted to tell her so badly. I'd practiced it in my head a million times. It just seemed like telling her the truth would only hurt her in the end. I promised her this weekend and after that we'd have to stop.

There was no way she could find out she was that important to me. Too many lives were at stake. My happiness had to wait, so others could have theirs. As much as it hurt, I knew it was how it had to be.

I'd give Hope a great weekend, tell her the truth about my past, and then wait for her to push me away. She would know everything, and that could only lead to one conclusion.

Our relationship would never be.

I tried to sleep, but it was impossible with my bare skin against hers. I just wanted to savor every moment that we had, knowing at any moment it could be our last. It hurt to even think about.

I held my head up and watched her lying there. She seemed so peaceful, and if she'd been feeling half as bad as me, she hadn't been sleeping very well lately. I could never seem to close my eyes at night knowing she was so near.

It was difficult knowing that we couldn't have this. We'd have to go back to pretending nothing ever happened. After having her so close, it was going to prove to be damn near impossible.

I tried not to wake Hope, but I couldn't keep myself from kissing her. Her naturally tanned skin was stunning; she had no idea how perfect she was. I ran my lips over her stomach, kissing every few inches. My mouth kept wandering down to her hip, making her stir. "Sorry," I whispered.

While still half asleep she moaned, "Don't stop."

I lowered the sheet that covered her out of the way and began kissing her inner thigh. I watched as I did it again and saw her responding. She licked her lips. I kissed between Hope's legs, fulfilling a desire that I knew I'd never want to deny her of.

The taste of her sent me into a frenzy. I'd never wanted to do this to anyone I'd been with in my past. For so long I'd refused to even try it, but even on our first night together I found myself craving her in ways that I'd never experienced.

At first I chalked it up to the alcohol, but as the days passed I still felt the same.

She began to convulse uncontrollably, physically motioning she was pleased that I'd woke her. She gripped me by my hair and pulled me up to her face. Her kiss was so powerful, so hungry. I was eager to satiate her every desire.

We switched positions, easily she straddled me while in a sitting position. Hope's flawless breasts were in arms reach and I couldn't stop myself from touching them. Her skin was silky smooth, her nipples hardening when my fingers coursed over them.

Hope began kissing me on my chest, and then my stomach. She licked my belly button then blew cold air on it. It gave me chills, causing my skin to raise. She did it again, this time dragging her tongue over the hair that led down to my cock. Her soft breasts kept rubbing against it. It was almost too much to handle.

She took me in her mouth without hesitation. The sheer fact that she'd done it without being asked turned me on. It felt like heaven, and any man would admit that watching was an instant high. She'd asked for a weekend, and as the seconds on the clock ticked, it was becoming impossible to imagine saying goodbye to all of this.

"Oh shit, Hope. Please slow down. I don't want to go yet." I was begging for it to last.

She did it harder, almost insinuating she wanted it more than I did. As hard as it was to do, I pulled away from her and took a second to catch my breath. She looked at me with hungry eyes, so I did the first thing that came to mind. I held her close, kissing her slowly, while maneuvering myself inside of her again. I knew she had to be sore, so I took my time. We weren't in a hurry; in fact we had all night to do this.

It didn't take long for me to lose it. Once again she'd gotten to me.

I switched positions with Hope so that I could hold her against my chest, not wanting the weight of my body to make her uncomfortable as we slept. Once I had her nestled in my arms we were both able to find peace.

16

Hope

I woke up in exactly the position that I'd wanted to be for so long. Chance's arms were still wrapped around me, and even though I could see that the sun was out, there was no way I was getting out of this bed. Every time we'd been together, something had stopped this from happening.

Chance promised me a weekend and I was determined to hold him to his word. I convinced myself that I wasn't going to think of what was to come. To say that I was excited would have been an understatement. It was going to feel wonderful to lie on the beach next to him, and hold his hand as we strolled along the water's edge. *Maybe it was a bit corny, but a girl can only dream.*

My father and Buffy weren't due back until Monday morning. That meant that Chance and I would have a whole two days and nights together. Even though the beach sounded like a fantastic idea, I didn't really care where we spent it, as long as we were together.

I wanted to savor every single minute of this day, with the reality of it ending hidden in the back of my mind.

I set my chin on Chance's chest and watched as it

rose and fell. His little nipples were so cute and I found myself kissing them, before I even realized I was doing it. His physique was chiseled, and I loved the way it felt against my palms. He had this cute inny belly button with a little patch of hair under it that I played with. There were so many things about Chance that made me swoon. It wasn't because he was older, obviously that meant nothing to me. The most important thing was his heart. He could try to hide his feelings all he wanted, but last night confirmed that he felt something. It was true that I'd seduced him, but what happened after that wasn't just about the sex. I knew that if the circumstances were different, we could have a real shot at being together. Unfortunately, he had to worry about my father finding out, which would turn out to be a literal disaster.

If that was our only hurdle maybe we could find a way around it, but Chance had too much to lose. He loved his sister. I could see it when they were together, and I also knew how happy he was to be able to live so close to her. If we tried to make things work he would have to move. This wasn't just his home. With my father being his only means of money, Chance didn't have a lot of options. Moving to another state had to have been a hard choice for him, considering he was doing it to be close to Buffy. Why else would he have done it?

There was also the fact that I didn't turn eighteen for months. I wasn't allowed to make my own decisions yet, which meant if my father found out about our little secret, he could get Chance in a bunch of trouble. I really didn't know much about statutory laws in my state, and probably needed to find out more so I could be prepared.

After realizing that I was dwelling on the negative, I pushed past my feelings of anxiousness regarding our fate, and wrapped my arms tighter around Chance. When I felt his own sliding over mine, I looked up to see him smiling at me.

"Good morning, beautiful."

With nothing but a sheet lingering between us, I moved it aside and straddled my legs in the middle of his. "Hey."

"If we stay in bed all day we won't ever make it to the beach, and I was really hoping to rub lotion all over your hot ass body in front of every guy there."

I laughed. "Really?" I ran my hand down his chest, reaching between us to gently hold him in my hands. It was so weird for me to be this comfortable with such actions. When I'd been with Trevor I was too modest to let him see me naked. Though I'd had no problem taking everything off in front of Chance. As I sat on top of him I felt beautiful, because that's how he treated me. "I was thinking the same thing about you."

"I bet you weren't picturing it like I was," he teased.

"What do you mean?"

He snickered and started playing with my hair. "Well, I imagined you in shiny oil. All the dudes were staring at you with their mouths open and drool pouring out, while I got to touch every inch of you. I made sure to stop halfway through and give them all a big thumbs up."

"Sounds like you have too much thinking time on your hands, Chance."

"Or I don't want to share you," he said as he hugged me tighter.

I knew he regretted admitting that, because when I looked up at him he had tightened his lips and seemed disappointed with himself.

"Chance..."

"Don't, Hope. Let's just enjoy our day. Okay?"

I laid my head back against his chest. "Of course."

It didn't matter if he wanted to take it back, he'd already said it, and I'd heard it loud and clear.

I can't believe that came out of my mouth. I was trying to be so careful. Some things just couldn't be avoided forever. Besides, I didn't want her to ever think that I was using her. If I had the opportunity to be with her, but to never have sex, I would be fine with it. Just holding her in my arms made me feel happy again; it was something that I hadn't experienced in quite some time.

"We better start getting our things together for the beach," I suggested.

She stayed nestled in between my arm and my chest. "Okay. I'll get up when you do."

"Well, since you're half on top of me it isn't going to be easy."

"I'm comfortable," she whined.

I leaned my head down and kissed her forehead.

"Wanna hop in the shower with me?"

"I've never done that before."

I had to laugh. It was hard for me to remember that she was only seventeen sometimes. When I factored that in it helped me understand that at her age I was just experiencing things for the first time. "If you don't want to, it's fine."

"No. It's not that. I do." Just hearing that made me smile again. She couldn't understand how good it felt to feel wanted again. "Technically we've already been naked in a shower together anyway, so let's go for it.

"I was hoping you'd say that."

Her head lifted up. "Really?"

I mimicked her voice. "Really." When she gave me a certain look I added. "Just a shower though. No funny stuff on your end, missy." I liked teasing her, causing her to give me those looks that I enjoyed seeing.

Hope sighed before following me into the bathroom. While she started the water I faced the toilet and began peeing.

"Oh. My. God. Chance, what are you doing?"

"What does it look like I'm doing? You can't run water and expect me to hold it. Would you rather I pee on your leg once we're in the shower together? Besides, I know you have to go. You didn't get up all night."

She turned her head.

I leaned down and kissed her on the cheek before I climbed in the shower. I heard the seat on the toilet being closed and knew she was going to the bathroom, so I stuck my head out. "What are you doing?" I asked sarcastically.

She took the curtain and covered my face. "Quit it, Chance. I can't concentrate with you in here."

"You're no fun." I pouted. "You do know that I've

been outside of the bathroom in the house when you've been in there. Everybody poops, Hope. It's not a secret."

When I peeked out the second time she had her hands over her face like she was embarrassed. I thought it was funny. I guess it was easier for a guy.

I let the water run down my head while leaning against the shower wall. I felt her arms wrapping around me as I stood there. I loved that she was with me, and wanted the day to be perfect. I needed her to know what she meant to me; even if it was the only time I would ever be able to show it.

My attention was fixed on Hope. "See. Two people can totally get a shower and not be weirded out."

"I wasn't weirded out." She bit down on her lip before continuing. "I'm just a little sore from yesterday. The idea of maneuvering around in this shower just sounded uncomfortable, at least this morning."

"It's cool. Next time I need to be more gentle." I spoke while she began to wash my back. "I was thinking that after we hang out on the beach for a while we could have a nice dinner somewhere."

"I'll do whatever you want. As long as you're with me."

I took my hands and wiped the water from her face. "I can assure you that I won't be leaving your side for the next two days."

She got a big smile on her face. "What happens if the lifeguard is a smoking hot chick and she throws herself at you?"

"There is no way in hell I would even notice her; not when I'm laying next to you. Do you have any idea of the affect you have on me? I can promise you that there won't be

146

one person on that beach that makes me feel the way that you can when you walk into a room, or when I hear you singing, or even when you're throwing paintbrushes at my head." As the water ran down her face, she stared at me speechless. "Hope, I made a decision that today I was going to give it all to you. I'm not going to hold back. This may be temporary, but I want you to know exactly where I stand, because when we aren't together, I don't ever want you questioning it."

She put her hand up and placed it on my cheek. I seized it and kissed the palm. "Turn around and let me finish washing your hair," I requested.

"Chance."

"Yes?"

"Thank you."

"For washing your hair?" I questioned.

"No. For everything else. Just when I think I know you completely, you turn around and surprise me. You're such a special person."

"Keep that in mind when you're checking out all the dudes on the beach today," I said, as I turned off the water, leaned out and located a towel, so that I could wrap it around her.

I started brushing my teeth while she stood there watching me. "What?"

"I need to go in the house to get dressed."

"Okay. I'll be in there in a few minutes. I want to get my trunks on and pack a few things." I watched her walk out of the room and heard the door shut as she left.

Determined to not let her out of my sight, I gathered everything and threw it in a book bag. Once I located my cell phone and wallet I headed toward the main house. On the way there I managed to locate Hope's clothes she'd removed the night before and I picked them up. It didn't look good to see her things on the ground. That could be construed in many ways, and the worst part about that is it was the truth. If Mark and Buffy came home early they'd know what had transpired between us.

When I got into the house I heard her calling my name, so I followed the voice and headed upstairs. I noticed she'd finished painting and putting her room back together. "I like the new color. It's nice," I mentioned.

Being there, looking at her bed, reminded me of the sex we'd had in it. For a few seconds I relived it in my mind.

"Should I bring a change of clothes for later?" She asked, breaking the moment.

"Yeah. Hey do you still have that fake I.D.?"

"Why? I thought you said we were going to be alone?" She inquired.

I shrugged. "I just want to have all of our options open. I'd rather be prepared than not. And, for your information, I plan on us being alone a lot today. Don't get your panties in a bunch," I promised as I sat on her bed.

She came over and put her arms around me. She'd changed into a little green sundress. "I'm not wearing any panties," she whispered in my ear before biting on the lobe.

"We could stay here all day, you know?" I wouldn't have been opposed.

She grabbed her bag and a pair of sunglasses, and proceeded to walk out of her room. "If you want to be the first person I pick to apply my lotion, you better get your ass moving, Chance."

I hurried behind her down the steps and out the front door.

148

I took one of the bags, put it under the seat, and let her keep the other one on her back while we traveled. She offered to take her car, but I loved the feel of driving to the beach on a motorcycle, besides I was dying to being able to have her clinging to the back of me for everyone to see.

Hope didn't hesitate to get on this time. She lifted her leg and climbed right on. I'd found the other helmet out of the garage and made sure hers was secure before putting mine on. Instead of just holding on like normal, she reached her hands under my shirt and clung to my bare chest.

We set off to make the forty minute drive to the ocean. I had a smile on my face the entire time feeling her hands clinging to my body. I knew her dress was blowing up, but today she was all mine and there wasn't anyone going to take her away. Thankfully, she'd put on some panties, at least.

17

Hope

Being on the back of Chance's bike used to make me scared out of my mind, but I knew he wouldn't do anything to hurt me. It gave me a sense of freedom and I was actually enjoying myself. When we arrived at the beach and began driving down the main road, groups of people were looking our way. Chance had stopped halfway and removed his shirt, after the sun was beating down on us, reflecting off the asphalt. I loved leaning my head against his bare back as he drove, even if it was sticky-hot.

We were hearing a lot of whistling as we passed people, but I wasn't sure if it was because Chance had his shirt off, or that my entire thighs were exposed from straddling the bike. My guess was both, but Chance didn't seem to even notice. He found a spot close to the beach and parked his motorcycle. I noticed it was on the boardwalk, which meant we could walk around and get something to eat or drink without having to drive anywhere.

Chance grabbed the bag from under the seat and we started walking through the sand to find a good spot. I couldn't get over how sexy he looked in his board shorts. They hung perfectly on his hips and made me think about the wonderful package he was hiding beneath them.

I felt like such a pervert when it came to Chance, but to be honest I knew it was because I was infatuated with him.

I was following him like a little puppy dog when he suddenly turned around. "Are you checking out my ass?"

"Maybe," I said as I kept moving toward him.

He spun back around and yelled, "Carry on!"

I had to smile. Chance always did that. He could find something sarcastic to say even when things were serious. It was just another quirk about him that I admired.

He found us a perfect spot in the sand. It was close enough to the water that we could see everything, but far enough back so we didn't get our blanket wet.

Chance had one of his naughty leers on his face after we got it spread out and were starting to go through our bags. He reached inside of his and pulled out a bottle of suntan oil. It said that it was SPF ten, which was plenty enough for my dark complexion. He held it up and smiled like he was advertising it for a commercial, showing off his perfect teeth.

I rolled my eyes and tried to ignore him, while he stuck out his lip and gave me a sad face.

In that moment I stood up off the blanket and pulled my sun dress over my head, and when I did, I saw Chance do a double take. I didn't think my bathing suit was bad. It did happen to be a string bikini, and it also was held together with silver metal rings. One was hooked between the breasts, and another on either of the sides. The bottoms were kind of small and had two rings on each hip, leaving the sides open to only bare skin. The suit itself was red and I thought it went great with my skin color. Chance continued to stare.

"What's wrong with you?" I finally asked.

"What are you wearing, Hope?"

"It's my bathing suit. I borrowed it from Buffy a couple weeks ago."

"That does not have enough fabric to constitute as clothing. Holy shit!"

I shrugged and kneeled down beside him, grabbing the bottle from his hands and pouring it on my chest. When I began to rub it in, he threw a towel over me. "Oh my God. What the hell are you thinking?" He was freaking out.

"Jesus, Chance. I'm applying sunscreen to my body. What is your problem?"

He looked around us, and I tried to act like I didn't know what he was looking for. "They are my problem. I wanted you to myself today, but I can see them mind-fucking you already, and I can't beat all of their asses at the same time."

I started laughing. "Did you just say mind-fucking?"

"Yes, and that is also my job."

"Chance, take this." I handed him the bottle. "Put some in your hands and show them who I came here with, and who I'll be leaving with. Oh, and by the way..." I pulled his face toward mine and seized his bottom lip between my teeth. As I pulled away I licked it. My hands were all over his chest and I only stopped when I heard a woman close to us gasp.

I was kind of embarrassed, but Chance pulled me into a hug as we both laughed it off.

He took his time applying the oil to my body, and the more he rubbed the more I wished we were alone. It was making me so hot for him that I could hardly control my breathing. When he got to my thighs I wanted to scream out in pleasure. He could feel me tensing up, and when I looked up at him he had a huge grimace on his face, like he knew what it was doing to me.

After he finished, he laid his body beside mine and whispered in my ear. "That was only the front. Just wait until it is time for the back, baby."

I purred. "Oh, I love it when you call me that."

"Well I love it when you talk like that," he admitted.

I batted my eyes and leaned into his kiss. "You're so lucky that you're gorgeous."

"If you're trying to threaten me with compliments, it's working. I'm very scared right now." He held his fingers up like he was pretending to bite his nails.

Chance finally settled down beside me after he'd applied a generous amount of sunscreen to his face and chest. He kept making me laugh and I loved it. As we lay there, I felt his fingers sliding in between mine and he kept his hand there until we were ready to flip over.

I couldn't believe how perfect it was being out with him. I tried not to think about Monday, but when something is so great, you just can't help it.

Chance

Being on this beach with Hope was amazing. I joked about the other guys checking her out, but it didn't bother me, because I knew she was mine, at least for the time being. That bathing suit she was wearing revealed too much though. I was half worried that when we got into the water she would lose it, then I got kind of excited about that as well.

Hope's smile was back in full-force and it was contagious. When she laughed I found myself mimicking her. When she brushed against me, I wanted to do the same. I loved being obnoxious around her, because it drove her crazy.

When she rubbed that oil on her body, I imagined actually busting a load in my shorts like I was twelve again and seeing my first hot vixen walking across the beach. Except today, Hope was *my* hot vixen. It was funny, she had confidence, but she really had no idea how beautiful she was.

She had her hair pinned up so it bounced around in the air. I know she did it so the breeze didn't blow it in her face. I couldn't help but remove the clip. She jumped up and dove over top of me trying to get it out of my hands.

"Chance, give it back," she demanded.

I stood up and ran toward the water, looking back to make sure she was following. Once I had jumped in to my knees, I noticed she'd stopped at her ankles. "Come and get it."

"It's freezing," she whined.

"If you want it back, you have to come get it. Come on, sissy," I taunted her, taking the hair accessory and clipping it to my shorts, then immediately began splashing her with the freezing cold ocean water.

Finally, she decided she couldn't take it anymore, and came running toward me full speed. We both went crashing down into the water just as a wave came in. When I rose above the water I saw Hope running her hands through her now wet hair. "Jerk," she said as she splashed some in my direction.

I gave her a smile and went under the water. In Virginia the water is dark so there was no way she could tell exactly where I'd gone. I pinched her ass before rising above the water again. Once I was close enough that I could see her legs,

She jumped up and lunged at me, but I quickly grabbed her body and pulled her closer to me first. I loved the way her skin felt when it was wet. It was already smooth and the salty water made it even more desirable.

"I got you now." I said, as we were only inches apart from each other.

She reached her arms behind my neck and her legs around my waist as the waves came crashing down just past where I was standing. Children were at the water's edge screaming as each one broke and turned white. Hope looked at me with those beautiful crystal blue eyes.

"Thank you for today, Chance."

I smiled and kissed her gently on the lips. "There is really no place I'd rather be, Hope."

She leaned her forehead against mine and closed her eyes. While she held on to my neck, I freed my hands and ran them up the outside of her thighs, and then under the back of her bikini bottoms.

She looked around. "Chance? What are you doing?"

I started laughing. "It's fine. Nobody can see us."

She seemed to not believe me.

"Hope, trust me," I said as I grabbed both of her ass cheeks and pulled her closer.

"I do." She leaned in and kissed me again, this time slipping her tongue into my mouth. When she pulled away she looked right into my eyes. "I've never felt safer than when I'm in your arms."

I let out a sigh. "You don't know how much that means to me."

I pulled my hands away from her butt and hugged her. Her mouth tasted salty from being under the water. My lips found the nape of her neck and then her shoulder, and as I kissed them she moaned. She kept her legs around me, but let the rest of her body hover. I held onto her back as she fell back in the water. My eyes focused her chest popping out of that suit. Her breasts were the only part of her floating above water, and the air was causing her nipples to harden.

"Mmm, you're just teasing me now," I groaned.

I took one of my hands and ran it across her wet stomach, stopping right before I got to her floating devices. She gave me a smile and sat back up against my body. "If there weren't all these people around I would suggest we get busy out here."

"They wouldn't know anyway. You know I'm game." I

gave an eager nod.

"Chance! There's no way. They would see our faces. I can't keep a straight expression when you're doing that to me."

"You have got to stop saying shit like that. I'm getting hard as we speak," I confessed.

She pushed herself away from me and began backstroking. I swam toward her and watched as she caught a wave and made her way into shore, only turning back to give me that tantalizing smile she knew made me crazy.

I had to stay in the water for a few extra minutes to get myself calmed down, but finally met her on the beach. She was holding the tanning oil, waiting for me to apply it. "Do you want to put this on me, or will it make you hard in front of all these people?" She teased, looking around to add to her game.

"Touching you in anyway makes me hard, Hope. But, you already know that," I confessed as I took the oil.

She lay on her stomach allowing me to pour it over her back and massage it into her skin. I could tell it felt good because she relaxed her shoulders and let me work my magic. I was able to maintain a calm stature within my shorts, but it wasn't without effort.

When I was finished, she insisted on applying it to my back as well. Hope and I both laid on our stomachs, facing each other. We talked for hours, only taking breaks to turn over or cool off in the water. Being with her was like being in an enchanted place. She was so thoughtful and I found myself hanging onto every word she said. I wanted to know more about her, and I knew it would take a lot longer than just two days.

18
Hope

The hot sun beat down on Chance and I, but neither of us seemed to care. We were too caught up in one another to notice anything else. When we finally agreed we were both hungry, we stood up and realized that we were two of the only few people still on the beach.

Chance had asked me so many questions, starting with what it was like when I was a child, and then on to how I was affected when my parents decided to separate. I told him all about my past relationship and how my previous boyfriend still had hopes of us getting back together. When I assured him it was never going to happen, he just smiled and seemed to be happy about it.

Explaining the breakup of my parents had always been a hard topic for me to deal with. I'd just become a teenager, and with that came all of the physical and emotional changes someone goes through at that age. My parents had been so wrapped up in hating each other that I was left to fend for myself.

I started hanging around the wrong people and eventually my grades began to fall. Thankfully, Rylee had moved closer to where we lived and I started spending more time with her family. Her mother treated me like I was her own. When I got my first period she took me out and bought me feminine products, explaining how everything worked.

My mother never even noticed I'd gotten my period until six months later. I remember it vividly. We were sitting at the dinner table with my grandparents and they'd made beets. I hated the way they tasted, and made your mouth turn red. When my mother put them on my plate and demanded I eat them, I freaked out. I started getting all emotional at the table and my mother, being the last to notice, yelled out. "You act like a woman on her period!" When I yelled back and confirmed that I actually was, she was so shocked. She took me in my room and cried for half the night admitting she had been a bad mother for not being there when I needed her.

After that she seemed to always be one step ahead of my decisions. She was my number one supporter, and as my relationship with my father drifted to non-existent, she was there to pick up the pieces. I admired her so much for that.

When I explained all of that to Chance, he just lay there holding my hand taking it all in with a smile on his face. I could tell that he liked hearing about my mother, and since I knew his mother had died unexpectedly, I felt it wasn't the right moment to ask him about it. If he wanted to tell me he could at anytime.

Chance and I converted our dry and sand free items to one bag, and put all of the beach exposed things in another one. He snatched my bag and carried my flip-flops with one hand, while he held mine with his other as we walked off the beach.

Every time I looked in his direction he was beaming at me, and each time he would give my hand a tighter squeeze. I couldn't help but smile back at him, showing just how fascinated I was.

Once we reached the boardwalk we sauntered around looking for a place to eat. Chance became secretive and began to walk into a parking garage right off the boardwalk. We ducked past a couple cars before reaching an outdoor shower that had a little privacy to it. It was still out in the open, but he pulled out our beach blanket and tucked it into the ceiling so that it made a makeshift curtain. He got me situated inside of it and stood guard on the outside so I could strip out of my bathing suit, and change into something dry, without being sandy.

The water had one temperature, and it wasn't warm. The freezing cold beads sent a shock to my body, making me work on getting rinsed off quicker.

As soon as I turned off the water, he was handing me my sundress and a pair of underwear. For some reason I found it more sweet than embarrassing. I came out from behind the privacy blanket and let him zip up the dress in the back. The one I had brought with me had a built in bra that thankfully supported my breasts enough to wear without me looking ridiculous. When Chance got to the top of my zipper he kissed the back of my neck. "All done, beautiful"

"Thank you!" I said, smiling.

I turned as he slipped in past me and took his turn getting rinsed off. Just as he'd done for me, I reached into the bag and located his clean clothes. When the water turned off I handed him the items, and waited for him to change.

He whipped around the blanket in a baby blue polo

shirt and plaid shorts, leaving me to gasp at the sight of him. He was so handsome. His tan skin and brown eyes stood out with the light shirt, and I admired the way it fit against his chest.

"Wow, you clean up nice," I teased.

"I try."

Chance carried my bags while leading us to a little restaurant off the beaten path. It was in the basement underneath a surf shop. The smell of marinara sauce filled my nose and I knew it was an Italian place right away. Little tables were situated around the small room, and few people filled the seats. Chance led me to a quiet corner table away from everyone else.

He pulled out a chair for me and helped me scoot it back in. "A chair for my lady."

As he took the seat across from me I smiled, watching as he handed me a menu. "So, have you been here before?"

"Buffy brought me here a couple times the first week we were here. The pizzas are the best."

I looked over the menu and then set it back down on the table. "How about we share one?" I suggested.

"Sounds great to me." He reached over and captured my hand. Do you like anchovies?"

I cocked my brow. "Are you being serious? I was thinking olives and pineapple."

His face contorted. "Eww, that sounds horrible."

"So does the fish. Maybe we should just order pepperoni."

He smiled. "With onions. I know you like them at home."

I nodded. "It's nice that you pay attention to little details."

161

"I pay attention to anything that has to do with you, Hope. I want you to know that. When you think I'm not listening, I am."

While keeping my eyes on my hands I smiled. My infatuation for Chance was becoming something else, and I didn't know how I was going to handle it.

"Are you having a good day, Hope?"

"It's been the best." It was so refreshing to be with someone who cared about my feelings. Our day was perfect, and although I worried how I'd be when the weekend was over, I felt content knowing that for the moment he was with me.

He squeezed my hand again before letting go. "I agree."

The waiter came and Chance ordered us a pizza with two iced teas. In all the times I thought he wasn't paying attention to me, he seemed to have picked up on everything. He knew my favorite topping was onions and that I liked my tea plain.

After our drinks and food came, we continued to stare in each other's eyes. His smile did things to me; it made me feel like I was the only person in the room, and I loved it.

Even when we'd finished eating, we sat there talking. He shared stories about when he and his sister were children. He told me about a tree house that all the neighborhood kids hung out in, that you needed a secret word to be able to get inside. He said it was there that he experienced his first kiss. To hear him telling me the story was enchanting. I leaned into his words, hanging onto to every single thing that came from his mouth.

Chance talked about his favorite dog, Buttons, who bit all of his neighbors on their butts, but never hurt him. He said he'd take the dog for walks, purposely getting close to the people he disliked. On several occasions he got into trouble when the dog became aggressive. He said his mother had to replace three pair of pants that he'd destroyed.

After paying our check, Chance led me outside. The crisp air hit me immediately, blowing my dress around. We walked around the boardwalk, holding hands and sharing more stories. At one point we stopped to play a couple games. He won me a stuffed frog by throwing rings onto the top of a small jug. I refused to let him put it in the book bag, since I wanted to walk around with the reminder of his hard work. Chance even persuaded me to go on the Ferris wheel with him. I looked down at the people as it circled around. He held me close and kissed me on top of my head. At one point we both closed our eyes when we were stopped at the very top of the ride.

When we began walking back to where he'd parked his bike, he bought me an ice cream cone that I ended up sharing with him. He kept taking it from me and touching my nose with it, leaving some sitting there, so that he could kiss it back off.

Chance made me laugh and I couldn't remember the last time I'd felt so happy for that amount of time. When we got to the block of the boardwalk where the motorcycle was parked, he pulled me onto the beach. We removed our shoes and held hands as we toddled down toward the water. The waves crashed in the distance before they would come in and reach our feet as we continued on.

We came upon a lifeguard stand and he climbed up inside of it, urging me to follow him. I dropped my things and forged behind him. With little effort he situated me on his lap so we could both look out at the ocean's never ending skyline. We stayed there watching the sunset, while the cool ocean breeze blew across the beach.

Chance kept taking my hand and pulling it to his lips. He wrapped his arms around me and laced his fingers in with mine. I pulled his arms around me more, wishing we could stay in this very moment forever.

"This is so perfect," I admitted.

"So are you," he whispered in my ear.

I closed my eyes and took in the scent of the ocean. It was important to memorize every detail for when all of this was just a memory.

I never imagined I'd find her. It'd never occurred to me that she was what I'd always needed. Today had been effortless; being around her came natural to me. As she pulled my arms around her tighter, I finally felt like I wasn't alone. She had filled a void that I thought would never be satisfied; one I never really wanted to fill again. Until now.

As the night sky fell upon us, I wished for more time. I didn't know how I could do it, how I could let her slip away from me. She knew that my attempts to ignore her in the past month were only to hide my true feelings. She knew now how much I wanted her, but, what she didn't understand was that I needed her. I needed her to listen when I had a bad day, to hold me when I was upset, and to accept me for everything that had happened in my past.

She didn't know that as we sat in the lifeguard chair I held her close because I physically didn't want to let her go. If I could have stayed there forever I would have.

A bar on the boardwalk had a band playing and the music filled the air with a beautiful sound.

Before I could stop myself or consider where it would lead, I made an announcement. "Hope, I think this has been the best day of my life."

She turned around and looked at me. Her eyes glistened from the bright moon above. She slowly pressed her lips against mine. The moment only intensified when I felt her tongue dragging. I opened my mouth greedily and accepted her. Hope brought her legs around and straddled me. I slid my hands beneath her dress, and stuck them inside the elastic of her panties on each cheek. As she kissed me deeper I squeezed, causing her to begin rocking against me.

I sucked on the side of her chin and then her ear lobe, finally licking down her neck. Her hands reached up my shirt. It was easy to push her panties to the side and slide right in. The dark night allowed us privacy as my girlfriend slowly moved above me. I don't think either of us took a breather as continued kisses motivated the pace at which we were moving. When I felt like I was close I lifted her off of me, making sure she wasn't left with a mess on our long ride home.

Afterwards I held her again. She leaned her forehead into mine, letting her lips linger so close to my own. "Chance, I need to ask you something."

I could feel her hot breath against my face, making it obvious that at any moment I could tease her with my tongue. "Anything." I looked directly into her eyes when I answered.

"Take me home and be with me. As much as I love being here like this with you, I'd rather be in your bed, making love."

I pulled her closer, kissing her deeply. Without another word, I climbed down and waited to feel her jump in my arms. We gathered our things and walked hand in hand to the motorcycle.

She held me so tight on the way home that I thought she was trying to squeeze me to death. I welcomed it though, in fact I didn't want her to ever let go. I felt like driving us far away so that we never had to be apart again.

The ride home seemed like it took forever, but I knew it was because of her request. There was nothing on this earth that I wanted to do more than make love to her. I wanted to kiss every inch of her body, to hold her in my arms, and to give her unending satisfaction until we collapsed in a pool of combined sweat.

I wanted to give her all of me, everything I could give her, and then more.

19

I had a hundred thousand words that I wanted to say to Chance. A hundred thousand reasons why I couldn't bear to be without him, but for tonight I would have to settle for this.

Once we got home we bypassed the main house altogether. He never let go of my hand as he led me across the patio and inside his place. He retrieved me a bottle of water out of the kitchen and led me straight into his bedroom, saying nothing.

My bag dropped to the floor, and I was immediately spun around to face him. Chance held my constant gaze as he took my hand and placed it on his shoulder. He started at my fingers and ran his hand all the way up my arm slowly then back down again. He leaned into my neck and opened his mouth to kiss me. I could feel his warm tongue sliding against my skin. He stepped behind me and lightly traced his fingers from my shoulders down to my elbows.

I had goose bumps, feeling as if I was floating in bliss.

He slid the strap of my dress to the side and kissed my bare skin. My head started to drop back when I felt his tongue there. As the second strap lowered I prepared for what was to come. His lips found the center of my back right above where my dress had sat. He kept his mouth there while he slowly unzipped it. I could feel it loosening, but he didn't let it fall. Instead, he reached around while kissing my shoulder again and lightly brushed the skin above my chest.

My breathing became more rapid, and each time he touched me I could feel the heat growing between my legs.

"How can I stand here in this room and not feel moved by you? I can't stop myself from wanting this." He whispered in my ear, while grabbing my dress from the front and slowly shoving it down. Chance held onto the fabric the entire time he removed it from my body. He started at my ankles with his hands slowly sliding up my calves, and then my thighs, until he cupped my backside.

His hands skimmed up past my waist, and just before he reached my breasts he turned me around. I opened my eyes to see him looking directly into mine.

His lips were so close to my mouth, but he didn't stop to kiss me. Instead they fluttered against my own making me gasp. He buried his face into my hair and nudged his nose inside. I tried to reach for his shirt, but he captured both of my hands, kissing the back of my knuckles before putting them down gently.

I watched him then reach behind his head and pull his shirt off. I licked my lips as I stared straight ahead at his perfect physique. He marched me backward until I was sitting on his bed. Chance moved in between my legs and pressed me down to lay with my feet still hanging off. He brought his lips to mine and held them there. My breathing was heavy as we parted. Chance then stood up staring deeply. I licked my lips, feeling the urgency to be with him again. This wasn't like on the beach. I need more than that.

I wanted everything he had to give.

His eyes were filled with desire, and the more I watched him, the more rapid my heart beat. I could see my chest moving up and down as he just stood there taking me in. His hands made it to his shorts and he slowly unbuttoned them and let them fall. With one tug his boxers followed suit.

Chance leaned into me again, this time climbing on top of me. I scooted myself back on the bed until my head reached his pillows, the whole time never taking my eyes off of him. He laid his body beside mine and propped himself up with his elbow, while his other hand traced circles around one of my breasts, but never touched my nipple. I let out a soft moan as his hands mimicked that same pattern on the opposite side.

He bit his bottom lip when he rolled his flat palm between them. I honestly did not know how much more I could take. I felt that at any moment, I was going to explode. Chance continued to savor every inch of my body, just like I'd asked him to.

I made a second attempt to reach out and touch him, but he gently seized my hand and brushed it against his lips. He closed his eyes for a moment, and I could only assume it was to regain some composure considering how involved he'd become. His rock-hard cock pressed into my leg, allowing me just a hint of how turned on he was becoming. Chance shifted his weight and leaned over to brush his closed lips against my hardened nipple. I arched my body toward his mouth, because the sensation was becoming blissfully unbearable. Finally he opened his mouth and slid his fabulous tongue over where his lips had just been. The air from his breath hit the wetness and sent more tingling sensations down into the very core of my sexual desire. When he took my nipple into his mouth I began to shudder.

His mouth kissed my belly button, but continued to travel down to my thighs. I felt like a ticking bomb and I knew that he was fully aware of what he was doing to me. He pushed one of my knees up and buried his mouth into one of them. I could first feel his tongue and then small nibbles as his teeth brushed against my tender skin.

I was sure I knew what was about to happen, but instead he kissed my shaved skin right above that sensitive spot between my legs. Then he used his tongue to lick up my abdomen until he reached the skin in between my breasts.

Chance's lips finally made their way back to my lips. I kissed him eagerly; stroking my tongue against his in a ravishing manner. I ran one of my legs over his ass, and finally wrapped them around his back, causing him to be positioned over top of me.

Chance pulled away from our kiss and looked me in the eyes. I noticed immediately that they were filled with tears. I reached up for his face wondering what could be wrong, but he just froze.

In all of my efforts to make Hope's request a reality, I'd lost myself. Each touch, every kiss led to my heart breaking more and more. I couldn't do this to her. She needed to know.

"Chance, what's wrong?" She asked.

"Hope, I don't think I can do this anymore," I confessed.

Her eyes filled with worry. "Why? What did I do? Please tell me. Don't stop being with me tonight. I can't -."

I put my finger over her lip. "Shh. I can't just be with you tonight, Hope. I don't want to stop being with you at all. You're worth the risk. I don't care if we have to sneak around for months. I'll do whatever it takes. Tell me you feel the same. Tell me I'm not imagining this thing between us is so much more than either of us has ever experienced."

Hope began to sob. I pulled her into my arms and rolled us over so that she was now on top of me. "Are you okay?"

"You aren't imagining it. I feel it too," she announced as the tears fell down her cheeks.

I took her face into my hands and used my thumbs to wipe away the wetness. "We'll figure this out. I promise." I looked her directly in the eyes when I said it. I wanted her to know I meant it with all of my heart.

That promise was something that I was going to hold onto. I had no idea how we were going to hide our feelings around her father, and my sister, but I knew I couldn't push her away again. Hope pressed her lips against mine, and started to run her hands down my stomach. I slid mine down between her legs and knew instantly that I needed to take my time. She was too special not to savor, and she needed to know it.

Her legs pretzeled mine while our bodies thrust in sync.

"Does it feel good?" I asked with my lips against hers.

"Yes. Don't stop," she answered.

We climaxed together, holding each other tight until we could both finally relax.

I pressed my lips against her forehead and then buried my face into her neck.

We eventually switched positions so that her weight was on me. As she drifted to sleep, I tickled her back with my fingers.

Hope's breathing slowed and when I was sure she was asleep, I finally let my eyes close. I wished that we could have stayed awake all night, but we were both exhausted. I found myself wondering if my lovemaking was good enough for her. I'd never been asked to do that, and everything I'd done just now was out of raw emotion.

Before I finally let myself fall to sleep, I kissed her one more time. "I love you," I whispered, knowing she couldn't hear me.

It was the first time I'd ever said those words and really meant them. I thought I had felt that way in the past, but after feeling what Hope did to me, I knew it had been something else altogether.

I didn't know how we were going to make it work. Hell, I didn't even know if it was possible. I just knew that I couldn't be away from her. Even if we had to meet away from the house once a week, I'd do it.

It was time to tell her the truth about everything. If she still accepted me and wanted me after she knew my past, then I would confess my true feelings.

I was so nervous, even afraid that she would be sickened by me or leave me like everyone else did. I didn't want that to happen. God, I didn't know what I would do if she looked at me the way all of my ex-friends had. She had to be told though. She had to understand why her father didn't want us together. She needed to hear the truth from me, not my sister, and especially not from her dad.

I felt a tear falling down my cheek as I prayed this wasn't going to be the last time I got to hold her in my arms. Losing her would be the final nail in my coffin. I just knew it.

I squeezed her tighter, and finally let myself fall asleep, knowing for right now she was right where she wanted to be.

20
Hope

Chance woke me up with gentle kisses all over my face. I opened my eyes to his smile, but immediately started to panic about my father coming home and catching us. Then I remembered that we still had another day to be together.

"It's still early, baby. Go back to sleep."

I smiled and wrapped my arms around him. "So, this isn't just a dream?"

"What do you mean?"

"You still want to be with me even though we have to sneak around?"

He moved a piece of hair away from my face. "Hope, I would do anything to be with you. It would kill me inside if I didn't at least try to make this work. I can't live this close to you, seeing you every day and not want more."

I couldn't help but let out a faint laugh. I was so overly excited to hear him say those words to me. It was all I'd wanted. We could make this work. It wasn't like my dad paid that much attention. "We can wait until they go to bed at night and I'll sneak over to your place, or we could just go out somewhere when we know they're staying home."

He chuckled and pulled me close. "We'll make it work. For now, let's just lay here together."

"Sounds great to me."

It wasn't long after us deciding to relax that Chance jumped up, seeming over-excited about something. "I have an idea. There's a dinghy out in the old shed that we could take to the State Park and put it in the lake. It's got a little motor that goes with it, and I'm sure we could make a day out of it. I don't know if you've ever been fishing, but I hear it's a good spot."

Honestly, I didn't care where we spent the day as long as we were together. "That sounds perfect." I didn't have to tell him that I'd spent last summer out on that lake with my ex-boyfriend. His father had a boat with a cabin that we'd spend the night in. I'd tell my mom that I was staying with Rylee, and I'd sneak out with him. He's the one who taught me how to fish, among other things that Chance probably didn't want to hear about.

Besides, we were too limited on our time together to drudge up the past. I wanted to live in the present, spending every available moment in his company.

"I'll pack up the dinghy while you make us snacks to put in the cooler."

"Cool deal. I'll meet you in the house." I didn't waste time on goodbyes, instead I hurried inside to change and make sandwiches. While getting everything out of the refrigerator I thought about whatever Chance wasn't telling me. He kept making it a point to throw the past into every discussion about us being together, as if it was going to change my mind.

Ideally it would have been nice to say that I didn't wonder what he was hiding from me. The fact that he continued bringing it up only concerned me more. In the back of my mind I figured it was probably something as tragic as his mother's death. She obviously died suddenly, and Chance felt somehow responsible. In all honesty I knew it was most likely his guilt over her death that was causing him so much grief. No matter what, it didn't matter. I'd spent day after day since I'd moved in thinking about ways to be around Chance. Now that I had a real opportunity to make it happen, I wasn't about to dwell on something that may or may not have happened.

Chance drove my car to the state park, the whole time talking about how he'd come to this place to clear his head. I didn't want to spoil the fun by letting him know I'd visited it plenty of times, including the swinging rope at the quarry.

I hadn't been back since a girl jumped and ended up drowning. It took divers two days to recover her body.

Once we pulled up in a parking spot, Chance and I got out of the vehicle and began grabbing our things.

I carried the cooler and bag, while he used the cigarette lighter plug in my car to operate the air pump. The dinghy quickly filled with air, tripling in size. I watched him affix the small motor to the back and drag it into the water's edge. While he held it, I carried everything over and sat it within, before putting one foot inside. Just as I went to bring my other leg over the boat moved. I ended up in a split, soaking wet on the sand outside of it instead.

Chance was hunched over in hysterics as I stood up and gained enough composure to jump inside of the small watercraft. He hopped in with ease, still laughing at my clumsiness. Soaked, and annoyed, I decided to remove the shorts and tank top. I felt his eyes on me immediately, and knew for a fact that it had caused him to stop laughing. He licked his lips, making me giggle. "Ah, I see how you are."

I tossed the wet clothes towards him as we pulled further away from the water's edge. "How am I?"

"One track mind. That's all I'm going to say."

He shook his head and let out an air-filled chuckle. "You got me. I'm not even going to argue."

He didn't have to. It made me happy to be able to get his attention at the drop of a hat. Our day was about being together, so no matter what we were wearing, or not, I was going to have a good time.

Chance

It was amazing how in such little time I'd been able to feel alive again. For a while I'd been settling for what I figured I deserved. I wasn't just punishing myself, I literally wondered if the world would be a better place without me in it.

Hope had changed that.

From the moment she walked through my door, and into my life, everything had changed. Instead of dwelling on what I'd never have again, I was looking forward to what I could.

There was only one problem with letting myself live again. I knew more than ever that I had to come clean about my past to her. I owed it to her to hear it from me. I couldn't allow myself to feel this good with that lingering over my head. Hope was about to find out my deepest, darkest secret, and I knew that it could change all of what we were finding in each other.

Once we'd gotten out to a good spot, I turned off the little motor and stared over at Hope. With her wearing another bikini, it was difficult to look at anything else. She crossed her legs in the small area and smiled. "What?"

"You're just so beautiful, that's all." She was. I'd dated my share of hot girls, but Hope made them all look plain. She didn't have to cake makeup on her face either. She was a natural work of art. It made me think back to my time playing baseball. The girls would come out to the games decked out, obviously to hook up with the players. I'd always had a girlfriend, but it didn't stop them from trying. They practically threw themselves on us time and time again. It was flattering at first, especially when I was so nervous to do well. The distraction helped even if only for a few minutes. After the first couple of college games I'd had enough. They were a nuisance.

I couldn't see Hope acting that way. She wasn't shy by any means, it was the opposite. She was able to carry herself in a way that was dignifying, instead of needy. I knew that when she kissed my lips it was because she wanted to be with me, the person who was inside, not the ballplayer that had an opportunity to get them out of the town they lived in.

Believe it or not, that kind of petty drama was a given when it came to being a sports player. It was one thing that I'd never miss. Perhaps it was the only thing. Considering that my chances of ever playing in the majors were far gone, Hope had given me that glimmer of optimism that I might be able to finally move on. The risks of being with her outweighed whatever was stopping me. I was going to do what was needed, and when she turned eighteen we'd find a way to tell her dad, or move out together on our own. We'd make it work.

"You got me out here on this lake. What's next, Chance?"

She waited patiently for me to reply, bringing me

179

back to reality. "We take these two rods and we catch us some dinner."

"Eww, I'm not gutting fish later. I'm just going to put that out there right now."

I snickered. "Damn, you spoiled all my fun." I waited a second for her to catch on that I was teasing her. She let out a laugh and held her hand out for the rod. "Do you need help baiting? I caught these worms in the front yard." I pulled two large worms out of the zipper pocket of my swimming trunks.

Her face curled up immediately. "Oh my God. Please don't tell me that you had them in your pocket this whole time?"

"They were against my leg. It's not a big deal. They're just worms." I ripped one in three parts and put the rest back in my pocket. "Here, allow me." After baiting her hook she cast her line in the water. I copied her, casting mine a little further out. "Not bad for a girl," I teased.

"If we weren't in the middle of the lake I'd walk away from your snarky attitude today. What's gotten into you?"

"I seem to think I've gotten into you, Hope. I mean, I *am* the one with the magic penis." I knew I was testing her nerves, but I liked it when she got annoyed. Her face tightened and she'd do her best to keep poised. Besides, when we fought about little things it reminded me how precious she was becoming to me; it reminded me that I had someone in my life again.

"You're hopeless."

"You love me, shut up." I realized what I'd said too late. Hope's face turned beet red and she quickly looked away when our eyes met. I didn't know whether to take it as an offense, or a compliment that she was in shock. I decided to do the first thing that came to mind, which was to change the subject. "After this we can go over to that rope you want to show me."

The tense moment was over as she replied, "Yeah, definitely."

We caught two fish that were on the small side; therefore we threw them both back. I could tell she was getting bored, so we pulled in the lines and took the boat back to the shore. Once we'd packed it back up in the car, we brought out a blanket and cooler, and found a quiet spot.

Hope and I laid facing each other as we ate. We talked about life in general, and the past two days we'd spent together. Her smile was so contagious, and I couldn't remember the last time I'd felt so content. With the truth lingering over my head, I knew I had to prepare myself in case this was going to be our last day as a couple. There was a big chance that when Hope heard about my past she would want nothing to do with me. I was determined to make the best of what I had in front of me. Need be, I'd beg her for forgiveness.

I thought about saying those three words to Hope, but if I did that and then told her the truth later, she'd think it was all some ploy to keep her. I couldn't do that. Hope needed to want to be with me for her own reasons, not mine. I couldn't let her see me weak, but I knew it was going to be a challenge.

We stayed at the state park until after the sun set, which we watched while cuddled up in the blanket together. The stars came out and we pointed at the ones we recognized. Each minute that passed was only bringing me closer to my confession, making it impossible to think about being happy.

If this was our last night together I wanted to

memorize everything about her. I took in the scent of her shampoo in her hair, and the way her smooth skin felt when I caressed it. I kissed her more times than I could count, and made sure to make her smile as much as humanly possible. These were the moments that I wanted to treasure, no matter what the outcome.

If she walked away from me, I'd be able to look at her knowing that if only for a short time, we were happy together.

It would have to be enough.

21
Hope

    For the second night in a row we made love until we both fell asleep entangled together. Chance was such a beautiful person, inside and out. I was emotionally in awe of him, and the things he did to me. Physically, he was so appreciative. He was always making sure I was happy. I'd never been with someone who wasn't selfish, so of course it was amazing to experience.

    When I realized what day it was I shot up in the bed. Chance seemed to do the same, noticing my wide eyes staring back at him. "Shit. I need to get out of here."

    "Why don't you grab some clothes and get dressed? When you're done we can walk over together," he suggested.

    I jumped up and started running around the room looking for my clothes. Chance pulled a clean shirt out of a basket and tossed it my way. It was just a plain white t-shirt so nobody would even know the difference where I'd gotten it. Now if I would have tottered in the house wearing a Penn State shirt, well that would have been harder to explain.

My dad wasn't due back yet. With the time it took them to drive from the secluded cabin, it would at least be around eleven before they walked in the door.

Chance was waiting by the pool when I got outside. He glanced over and gave me one of his famous smiles before I reached for his hand. We entered into the back of the house, and just as we'd thought, there wasn't anyone home. While Chance made his way toward the living room, I ran my bag of stuff upstairs and changed my clothes. When I came back downstairs he had a serious look on his face.

I froze in place and started to panic. The color had left his cheeks, and his morning smile had disappeared. "Sit down, Hope. Before we can move any further with whatever this is, you need to know the truth about my past. I can't keep you in limbo any longer. If you're willing to sneak around with me, you need to know why your dad is so adamant about me keeping my distance. After I explain everything, I'll let you decide if we have a future." He paused for a second before grabbing my hand and pulling me down to sit beside him. "I just need you to promise me that you'll listen to everything before judging me."

I shook my head up and down. "Of course. Whatever it is, I'll listen." I just knew it was going to be about his mother. He was too good of a man for it to be anything else.

Chance looked down to his hands. He was rubbing them on his knees like he was having trouble with this. I leaned into him. "You can tell me, Chance. Don't be afraid to talk to me."

He looked over in my direction and gave me a quick smile before his face went back to being serious. "I don't know if you're aware of it, but I actually went to Penn State on a scholarship. I got in with both academics and baseball.

I'd played ball my whole life, on as many teams as my mom could get me on. It's all I ever wanted to do. I'd always attended public school and couldn't believe when the recruiters started contacting me in my sophomore year of high school. To have that happen is major. You can imagine how it made me work even harder."

I clutched his hand and played with it as he continued.

"I'd never been away from home before, and the first semester was really an adjustment for me. In the beginning I threw myself into my classes and stayed in my room, but as the weeks went on I started making friends. My first friend I made was a girl named Chrissy. She was quiet like me and our professor thought we would make good study partners."

He looked up at me, displaying a very confused grimace.

"We started spending a bunch of extra time together, even when we weren't studying. I promise you that it was completely plutonic. We were just friends that enjoyed hanging out. That's all it was, especially for me."

He obtained a bottle of water off the table and took a sip. "When I met my now ex, Veronica, our friendship started to taper off. My ex was jealous of me being friends with another girl, and I was tired of having to make excuses to Chrissy, instead of telling her it wasn't my idea to stop hanging out."

"Sophomore year started and my relationship became more serious, but the whole time Chrissy reached out and tried to remain friends. Every time I'd say no, she'd come back with another invite."

Chance sat back against the couch and stared at the television as he kept explaining.

"My ex was a selfish bitch. Looking back I realize that we were never in a real relationship. She just wanted someone to dress, order around, and be at her beck and call. So winter break was fast approaching and I buckled down to study for my exams, while she went to her family's place in the Hamptons to drink and party it up with her richy friends."

He put his hands through his hair, and then rubbed his knees again. "We got into this huge fight because I wouldn't go with her, and she actually told me that if I didn't go we were over, but I knew I couldn't. I had to maintain a certain grade point average to keep my scholarship, which required me to stay back and study. In a group of text messages she brutally dumped me, as if I was just an object she could toss out."

"I took the news hard and ended up leaving the library to go to a party. Chrissy spotted me immediately, and we began heavily binge drinking. This creep kept following her around, so she begged me to pretend we were a couple. I was comfortable around her, and the alcohol made us seem like we were more than friends anyway. Soon the room started to spin and we headed outside for some air."

"Chrissy proceeded to throw herself at me on the porch of the frat house. I wasn't expecting it and she caught my arm with her nose, causing it to start bleeding everywhere. I felt so horrible about the whole thing that I insisted she come up to my room and get cleaned up. I swear to you, Hope, I meant nothing else by it, but we'd had a lot to drink and my body and mind weren't in the same place. We marched up to my room holding hands and laughing. She was pinching her nose as the blood continued to pour out."

Chance stood up and began pacing around the room. "I got her into the bathroom and helped her with the bleeding. She went through a whole towel and it still dripped into the sink for at least ten minutes more before subsiding. Anyway, once she was cleaned up she sat on my bed next to me and confessed how she'd had feelings for me for over a year. She already knew that Veronica broke up with me, and I guess she figured this was her chance. She leaned in and kissed me, and I let her. I was emotional and drunk, and you have no idea how I wished it never happened, but we ended up having sex."

"After it was over, I told her how I still had feelings for Veronica, and that nobody could find out what we had done in case we got back together."

Chance kneeled down in front of me. He clutched my hands and looked into my eyes. "That was the last time I saw Chrissy; that anyone saw her. Her parents reported her missing when she didn't arrive home, and after the police asked around I became the prime suspect in her disappearance. Two days later they found her body in a nearby culvert. She had been brutally beaten and left to freeze to death in the nude."

Chance buried his face into my legs. He began to sob and I ran my fingers through his hair telling him it would all be alright. I had to admit that I was a little frightened, not that he was going to hurt me, but because of the whole situation.

"People from the party had told police we were together so they got a search warrant and came into my room, where they found a ton of her blood, and a used condom with both of our DNA on it. They arrested me a few days later when they got all of the evidence back from the labs. With all they had and the eye witness accounts it wasn't hard for them to lay the book on me."

"Veronica and her father returned from their trip, and

he agreed to be my lawyer if I swore I would never go near his daughter again. At first she believed I was innocent, but as more evidence piled up, I was left with only Buffy and my mother at my side."

He started to break down again, and I held him tight in my arms. While he continued to cry he started talking again. "My mother had a massive heart attack a week later. She died right in front of me. There wasn't anything I could do to save her. She was healthy, Hope. She was fucking healthy, and I killed her; I broke her heart and killed my own mother."

I was flabbergasted. How was I supposed to react to everything that he'd told me. "Oh my God, Chance, you can't blame yourself for that." I was trying to get him to calm down. "I can't imagine what that was like for you." I could tell from the way he was looking at me that he was desperate. He'd kept it bottled up for so long that he couldn't handle it anymore. I had a huge choice to make, but I wasn't sure I was in the right state of mind to do it. We sat there in silence for a few minutes, neither of us wanting to strike up a single sentence.

Finally, after some time, he managed to calm down enough to speak to me again. "When it was time for court, Veronica's dad was getting ready to make a plea bargain, but one of his partners found a loophole in my case and got me acquitted. The evidence had been tainted somehow during the collection. Anyway, after burying my mother and paying for the attorney's, and then finally being kicked out of school, I had to move in with Buffy. My mom's retirement, and life insurance were all gone and we had nothing left for me to go back to school. The whole fucking town knew my face from the news, and of course nobody believed that I was innocent. We received letters from Chrissy's family asking me to confess so they could have closure. Buffy had to take on more shifts to pay off the rest of my mom's bills, find us a bigger apartment, and also because she couldn't stand being around me. I got that it was hard, but for a while I honestly believe that she thought I was guilty. I could see it in her eyes, Hope. My own sister thought I'd raped and killed my friend. She actually thought I'd be capable of something so heinous. Do you have any idea how something like that felt?"

I couldn't imagine it. The idea of going through that alone was horrible. On top of it all they'd lost their mother. "No. I can't." I was trembling while holding him firmly against me. I could see how the evidence said one thing, while the real truth was buried. If it had been my family I would have wanted that closure. With all fingers pointed at Chance it was difficult to even look elsewhere.

Buffy met your dad a little after everything went down. It took him a while to come around me, and even longer to act like I wasn't a murderer. I could tell he was skeptical. As they got closer I seemed to get pushed off to the side. I think in some ways it helped her get over her suspicions. Your father never said anything about it to me. He moved us here and the rest is history, aside from him forbidding me to be with you. You can probably understand now why he did it, and it has nothing to do with my age."

He sat up, pulling me into my arms, and peering in my eyes. "Hope, I swear to you, I'd never hurt another female like that. She was my friend and I would've never allowed her to leave if I had any idea that was the last time I'd see her alive. I swear to God!"

I pulled him into my arms. I don't know how I knew, or maybe I was just too naïve and caught up in the moment to consider that he may be lying. Something in my gut told me he was telling me the truth; it was telling me that I could trust him with my life. After all, he'd saved me before. If he was the guy that everyone suspected him of being, he could have raped and killed me the afternoon on the side of the road, or when he left the bar with me in tow. "I believe you, Chance. I believe you."

I could see appreciation in the way he held his grin. He was thankful that for the first time since that terrifying ordeal he had someone on his side one-hundred percent. I wasn't going to be that person who questioned the possibility. I knew without a doubt that this man in front of me was innocent. "You don't know how much this means to me."

"Yes, I think I do. You're not alone, Chance, not anymore. I believe you."

He hugged me so tightly, sniffling against my shoulder. This was a side of Chance that I never knew existed. His emotional side didn't mean he was a sissy. Instead it showed me that he was capable of feeling pain. It showed me that what I was feeling inside of my gut was the real deal, and not some kind of infatuation.

He pulled away holding my shoulders. "There's something else you need to know, Hope. Remember that night that we were at the bar? Our first night together?"

I nodded my head.

"Someone disappeared from the bar that night. The police got a hit on the video surveillance from the nationwide mug shots. They came asking me questions about it. The video shows me leaving with a female and people gave my description. When they saw my criminal history they hunted me down and told me not to leave town."

"You left with me, Chance." I confirmed. I already

knew about the disappearance, courtesy of my best friend.

"You don't understand, Hope. You're underage, and your father didn't even know we'd met. I couldn't say that I was with you even if I wanted to."

"I don't care about what happens to me. You have to tell them we were together. I'm your alibi, Chance." This guy had the worse luck on the planet. He was now being pegged for a second crime.

He shook his head. "No way! I won't get you involved."

We both turned our heads toward the window when we heard a car pulling up out front.

"They're home." I said in a panic.

Chance kissed me. "I'm going in the kitchen. Run upstairs and don't come down until you hear us talking," he urged.

Without even thinking about everything he'd told me, I rushed up the stairs toward my room.

22

Chance

Telling Hope the truth was easier than I'd originally thought. Once I started the whole story came pouring out. She believed me and it meant everything. I hated to send her upstairs after confessing so much about myself, but we couldn't risk being found out, especially now. I made my way to the kitchen and started to make coffee. By the time the front door opened it was already brewing and I was leaning against the counter.

I heard Buffy first as she called out. "Hello, we're home!"

I headed out of the kitchen and into the foyer. Buffy was beaming ear to ear. She dropped her suit case and held out her arms for me to hug her. I gave her a big squeeze and finally let her go as Mark walked into the house. I reached my hand out and shook his, the whole time wondering if he suspected that I'd slept with his only daughter.

"Where's Hope?" Was the first thing out of his mouth.

"I have no idea. I came in to make coffee, and then heard you guys coming in the door," I lied.

"HOPE," Buffy called up the stairs.

Perfection came walking down the stairs in a pair of pajama pants and hoodie. She had pulled her hair up, but it looked like she'd just gotten out of bed. "Hey, I didn't hear you come in."

She never looked in my direction and it was a good thing, because if my eyes found hers they would know the truth immediately. This was a dangerous game that we were playing.

"We have some news and it involves the both of you. How about we leave everything here. I want to make a big family breakfast and tell you all what's going on." Buffy was all smiles, making me wonder what she had up her sleeve. All I could think about was going on some kind of family vacation together, and sneaking around trying to catch alone moments with my girlfriend.

"Can I get a shower while you cook?" Hope asked.

"I can help you cook, sis," I offered.

Buffy snatched my arm and pulled me into the kitchen, while Mark started carrying the luggage into the laundry room.

"So, how was your weekend, little brother?" She asked as she started pulling out things from cabinets and the refrigerator.

"It was fine. I just hung around here and worked on the roof for a while. What about you? How was your trip?"

She smiled cheek to cheek again. "It was fabulous, but we can talk about it when we're all together."

"Okay, should I be nervous?" I leaned across the counter. "Are you kicking me out, or hiring a new carpenter? Am I working too slow?" I asked.

"Chance, get a grip!" She laughed. "It has nothing to do with you, it just affects you indirectly. Stop assuming."

I shrugged and made a cup of coffee while she began cooking. I noticed she was making French toast. It was something that my mother showed her how to do when we were kids. They made this vanilla cinnamon butter to go with it that made it taste even better. The smell filled my nostrils, but it wasn't breakfast that filled my mind. It was Hope.

I found myself watching the kitchen doorway, just waiting for her to come into the room. I heard the phone ring and Mark getting into a conversation with one of his clients about a new property. I started juggling, or attempting to juggle some oranges while I waited.

My sister rolled her eyes and motioned to a stack of plates and silverware. I dropped the fruit back in the basket. Once I took the plates, she told me to set the outside table, so I headed onto the patio.

When I started to set the table I got a whiff of Hope's shampoo, and it took everything I had in me not to turn around and pull her into my arms. She smelled delightful and I found myself missing her already even though we were standing just feet apart.

I twisted my head to glance at her, but when I noticed she was doing the same, I turned away. "Get yourself together," I mumbled to myself.

Hope and I needed to be careful. We couldn't act like we were involved, but it was obviously impossible to avoid each other. We had to be cordial without revealing our desire to be together. It was harder than we thought. When I looked at her, I wanted to melt into her eyes. She was breathtaking, and her running shorts with that tight shirt did more for me than it should have been doing.

"Good morning, Chance." Hope said loud enough that Buffy could hear.

"Hey, Hope. What's new? What'd you do last night?" I asked, praying she went along with the ruse.

"Nothing much, downloaded some new music to go running to today," she announced, but as she approached the table she added, "I spent the weekend with my boyfriend and last night he made passionate love to me until I collapsed in his arms. It was amazing."

I had to turn away from the house. Her face was red and I could tell she thought she was funny. "So, what's he like?" I asked as we sat at the table across from each other. We could hear Mark talking from in his office and Buffy was busy inside attending to the stove.

Hope played with her napkin, folding it in different directions. "He's kind, and considerate. He puts everyone else's needs before his own. He has the biggest heart, but tries to hide it away. And...I think about sleeping with him every CHANCE I get." She over-enunciated my name.

"Hope! Calm down, please. You're making it difficult for me to focus," I confessed while pointing between my legs.

She giggled. "You're the one that asked. I can't help it. In fact, after last night and this morning, I wish we could just rip everything off of this table and bang like wild animals."

I looked up at her in shock, but saw her winking at me. She immediately started giggling. We were caught off guard by Buffy bringing out two large trays of French toast and sausage, while Mark followed behind her with orange juice and coffee.

"What's so funny out here?" Mark asked.

I froze, but Hope took over. "I was laughing at something that happened yesterday. Chance was climbing on a ladder while I was going running. He must have thought it was locked into place, but when he started climbing up it was collapsing. His face was priceless."

They all began laughing, but I was in shock that my little princess had told a complete white-lie without breaking a sweat.

"Hope, do you mind scooting next to Chance so that I can sit with your dad? We had such a fun weekend, I don't think I am ready for it to end yet," Buffy announced.

Hope stood up and headed in my direction. When she sat on the bench beside me her leg brushed against mine. Knowing her mood, she had probably done it intentionally. This was going to be a lot more difficult than I'd imagined it in my head.

My sister broke my train of thought. "So we have something important to tell you. Mark why don't you tell them."

"As you both know I'm crazy about this woman, and after much consideration I've asked her to be my wife." Mark seemed like he was on cloud nine.

Hope was taking a drink of orange juice and immediately spit it out in front of her. It went over her plate and on her face. I handed her some napkins. "Sorry, it went down the wrong hole, I guess," she said while cleaning up the mess.

"Well, I suppose congratulations are in order." I reached over and shook Mark's hand then

got up and gave my sister a big hug. I knew she was beside herself with excitement. We finally started eating as

Buffy and Mark talked about their romantic weekend. Hope and I kept touching our legs together, knowing it was the closest to hand holding we could get.

Finally after a moment of silence, Buffy got all giddy. "This means that you two will be each other's niece and uncle. Isn't that totally cool? We'll all be a real family."

This time I was the one spitting out my coffee. "I don't think we should label it, sis. You are making me feel old. Hope is only like sixteen or something. She isn't young enough to call me her uncle. Maybe if she were a little girl or something, it would be different. I don't expect her to call me uncle Chance."

"I'm almost eighteen," Hope corrected.

Her father gave a curious look. "Not until the end of the year, sweetie."

"Whatever! I hate that my birthday is the last day of the year. All of my friends are legal adults and I can't do anything I want, ever!" It was very obvious that she was not taking the proposal well. I wanted to hug her, but I couldn't.

"Hope, please don't ruin breakfast," Mark pleaded.

"Sorry. Buffy, I'm happy for you and my dad. I can't wait to help plan the wedding, if you will let me. Breakfast was fantastic. Now if you'll excuse me I'm going for a run. I'm obviously on edge for some reason this morning. Maybe I just need to go clear my head."

Hope stood up and took her plate into the house. She never looked at me or back toward her father.

"Wonder what's gotten into her," he said with a laugh.

"Probably, just girl problems. Us women get our period and it messes us all up. I'm sure she's fine." Buffy stated.

I stood up from the table. "I need to grab a new paintbrush at the hardware store. Hope borrowed mine and forgot to clean it out. The thing was hard as a rock when I found it still stuck in the roller tray. I should have those posts done by dinner time. Thanks for breakfast and congratulations you two. I'm real glad you have each other." I said before I headed into the kitchen.

I hurried into the pool house, located my keys then ran right into the garage where I found a brand new paintbrush and stuck it in my pocket. I jumped on my bike and began looking for Hope, knowing damn well she didn't want to be alone.

Hope

I had to get out of that house. I don't even remember if I cleared my plate off the table. The combination of being around Chance and hearing my dad's announcement was too much for me to take. How could he ask her to marry him without seeing if I was okay with it? I knew it wasn't my decision, but he could have at least talked to me about it. I liked Buffy a lot, and albeit she was more like a big sister than a step-mother, but factor in the relationship with me and Chance, and it was a complete cluster fuck.

I wanted to scream, but instead kept running as fast as my legs would let me. The summer sun was beating down on me and I'd forgotten to grab anything to drink. Between the tears and the sweat, I was having a hard time seeing through my wet eyes.

A familiar sound came roaring around the corner behind me, and I slowed down my pace even before he was in view. Chance pulled up beside me and handed me a helmet. I jumped right on the bike, and he took off out of the neighborhood.

I wrapped my arms tightly around him. With one of his hands he squeezed mine, and I felt a rush of relief to know that we were together.

When we finally made it to a nearby park he pulled in and turned off the bike. I hopped off the motorcycle and waited for Chance to pull me into his arms, and kiss me tenderly. "Are you okay?" He asked as he placed his forehead against mine.

"Not really."

He let out a short laugh. "That was certainly a surprise."

"You're telling me. I didn't even know how to react. I feel like such an idiot for running out. Your sister must hate me for ruining her excitement."

Chance led me to a bench and we sat down next to each other. He captured my hand and played with it as he spoke. "Buffy will be fine. She should have known this would all be hard for you, Hope. You just moved into the house after not speaking to your father for a long period of time. There is no way that this would be easy for you."

"Well it doesn't help that the guy I want to be with is going to be my uncle," I blurted out.

"That is not even funny."

"No kidding. I thought I was going to choke on my breakfast when she said that."

"Well, one good thing can come out of this," he suggested.

"Yeah, care to share?"

"They will be so caught up in planning that they won't notice how crazy we are for each other." He had a point.

I brought my head up and kissed him lightly on the cheek. "You're crazy about me?"

"Hope, I never would have told you about my past if I wasn't. You don't know how many times I wanted you to know the truth." He put his head against mine.

I place one of his hands in between both of mine. "None of that was your fault. You have to know that."

He nodded and shot me a smirk. "Sometimes I do, but there are some days I can't help but blame myself. The worst part is that they never even looked for another killer. The newspapers always talked about how the real killer got away with it, referring to me. It really tears me up inside knowing that."

"Chance, please don't take this the wrong way, but if it weren't for your past we would've never met. I have to think that something good comes out of something horrible." I smiled and stared at his hand that I still held.

He turned to face me more, suddenly pulling me on his lap. "I can't imagine never knowing you. You've made me remember what it's like to have a friend, and how it feels to love someone."

His words shocked me, and it wasn't because I thought he was lying or that it wasn't the appropriate time to tell me. I just couldn't believe he'd said it. "Did you just say what I think you said?"

He looked directly into my eyes and smiled. "Maybe."

I smiled back at him. "Well maybe I feel the same."

He pulled me tight against his chest. "You better."

"I wish we could stay here all day." I looked around and saw nothing but nature. It was secluded and peaceful.

"Yeah, well I can't stay much longer. I told your dad I was going out to get a paintbrush at the hardware store." Chance explained

I sat up and looked at him. "You better get going

then."

He laughed and reached for something in his back pocket. "I'm surprised you didn't feel it when you were on the bike behind me." A paintbrush in a wrapper sat in his hand.

I busted out laughing, unable to control my shock in reaction to his quick thinking. "Wow, you thought of that fast."

"It was nothing compared to your story about the ladder," he added.

I leaned over and kissed him lightly, but when he began to kiss me back it turned into much more. I ran my hands over his face, and held them as his mouth found mine once again. When he pulled away we were both breathless. "I don't know how long I can last without touching you," I confessed. "I need to be close to you." I kissed him again, so slowly that it implied everything I expected it to.

"You won't have to wait long," he promised.

We held each other for a few more minutes before climbing back onto his bike and heading in the direction of our neighborhood. I assured him that I would be open-minded about my father and Buffy's upcoming nuptials. To be honest all I wanted to do was think about him. It wouldn't be hard to put my father's wedding out of my mind.

I really did want them to be happy, except I just feared being the one to break the news to my mother. She'd been through so much lately. First my grandfather died and now my grandmother had to be put into a home. Plus she had lost her job and had to sell the house. This would crush her.

I couldn't begin to figure out how I was going to look in her eyes and hurt her. Knowing Buffy like I did, she was bound to call every newspaper and have it listed. Hell, she probably had called to have engagement photos taken already.

I could just picture it now she and my father in a fashioned embrace while Chance and I stood behind them with googly eyes for each other. That would go over fantastic.

I squeezed my arms around Chance even tighter. Our alone time was almost over and I wasn't ready to let him go.

When he finally pulled over he gave me a quick kiss and finally sped away. We couldn't be caught like that, so I understood completely. As he drove into the distance I felt like a part of me was gone. My heart ached and I ran as fast as I could to get back to my house and be able to see him.

When I rounded the block that my house was on I decided to slow down. I didn't want to arrive just minutes after Chance, so I walked the rest of the way. I finally made it down the long driveway and was met by my father having a word with Chance. When he sauntered away from him he quickly patted him on the shoulder. I had no idea what the discussion was about, but I couldn't help having a guilty conscience.

Chance had already begun painting the wooden posts on the front of the house. Seeing him with a brush reminded me of being in my room. I wished we were alone again with that bucket of paint, a couple rollers, and my bed.

He looked back at me and gave me a wave before turning back around and getting to work. My father came back out of the house with his briefcase this time. He walked over to where I was standing and pulled me in for a hug. "I'm sorry if we caught you off guard this morning, sweetie. We didn't mean to upset you."

"It's fine, Dad. I'd just woke up and wasn't prepared for hearing big news like that yet. I feel better after my run though. It's all good."

He smiled. "Well I'm glad to hear it. Listen, I gotta run out and show some commercial property to an investor. I don't know how long I'll be so Buffy was hoping that you and Chance would want to watch movies later. Please try and be nice to her. She really cares about you, Hope."

"I'd love to hang out with them, and I promise to be nice. Good luck with the investors," I said as I happily ran into the house.

I didn't see Buffy when I got inside, so I hurried up and headed into my room. After gathering some clean clothes I went into the bathroom. As I reached in to turn the water on I heard someone knocking. I walked to the door first but no one was there. Then I turned around and saw Chance standing at the window.

I pulled it open quickly. "What are you doing?"

He smiled, displaying his perfect teeth. "I'm trying to work, but then I saw what you were doing. I didn't want you to freak out if you saw me staring."

"That's illegal you know. You're a peeping Tom," I joked.

"You can handcuff me right now, Hope. I wouldn't even put up a fight." He laughed, while still looking at me with intent.

I leaned out and grazed his lips. "Don't tempt me."

"So are you giving me permission to watch?" He asked.

"What do you think?" I started pulling off my shirt and backed away from the window while sliding my shorts off slowly. When I stood up he was smiling but moving out of my sight.

"That is so mean," he said in the distance.

I took my time in the shower, and not because I

204

wanted to tease Chance. I was half tempted to pull him inside. I just wanted to let the water run down my face and relax. When I got out I didn't see him anywhere around. He may have had to go get one of his famous cold showers he'd told me about.

I wrapped myself up in a towel and started to get dressed. When I was done applying lotion to my legs I headed into my bedroom. After about five minutes someone knocked on my door. "Come in." I was hoping to see my boyfriend.

Buffy tottered in and sat down beside me on my bed. "Hey, can we talk?" She asked.

"Sure."

"I feel like an idiot for how I dealt with things this morning. I was so excited that I didn't take into consideration that it would be hard for you. I am so sorry, Hope. I really love you like a sister and I don't want to lose that if I marry your dad. I know that sounded convoluted, but it's the truth."

"Buffy, I feel the same way. I am sorry too. I should have been more understanding. You love my dad and he loves you. You guys should be able to do whatever you want."

She leaned her head on my shoulder. "So, are we cool?"

"Absolutely," I said.

She threw her arms around me and squealed like she was describing a high school crush.

"I was thinking that you might want to watch movies with me and Chance. Your dad is going to be getting home late. You know how those investor meetings go. They almost always end up at some golf course and country club."

I smiled, only thinking of being in the same room with Chance. "That would be great."

24

Chance

Mark had pulled me aside and asked if anyone had come over to the house while he and Buffy were gone. I assured him that nobody did. That wasn't a lie.

We were burying ourselves into an endless mess, but there was no other place I wanted to be. Hope was fully aware of my feelings now, and she would never let me stop even if I wanted to.

My sister had this brilliant idea to have a movie night, and I would have declined if it weren't for the fact that Hope was going to be there. Buffy had this problem of getting the worst girly movies ever made. I usually fell asleep after the first twenty minutes, and her shortly after. We'd end up taking days to finish, well she would at least.

I finished painting the posts on the front and back of the house, and headed to my place to shower. I imagined that my sister would order pizza and we would just veg out all night. Hope had no idea what she was in for.

When I was all cleaned up I headed over to the main house. I called out for my sister, but she wasn't anywhere to be found. I then snuck up to Hope's room. She was sitting at her computer with headphones in. I strode up behind her and kissed the back of her neck.

She jumped before turning around and pulling me into a hug.

"Where's my sister?"

"She just left to go grocery shopping and grab the movies," Hope explained with an ornery grin.

"So, we're alone?" I needed to verify.

She placed her soft lips against mine. "I was just getting ready to come visit you. I had to wait until she at least pulled out of the driveway."

"What were you going to do when you found me?" I asked, even though I already knew the answer.

"What do you want me to do?" She bit down on her lip, while awaiting my answer.

"I can think of a million things I'd like to do with you, but for starters I think we need to do this." I leaned down and pressed my lips against hers again. She gripped the collar of my shirt, and pulled me even closer to her face. Her lips rubbed down my neck and she bit me before she ran her tongue over the bite mark.

"You smell so good." She whispered.

We started taking off our clothes as fast as we possibly could. "What if someone comes home?" I asked in between kisses.

"We should just hurry." Hope pushed me down on her bed.

Hope moved her hands up my thighs and kissed me

on my belly button, and then with her tongue she worked her way up to one of my nipples. She obtained it with her teeth and slowly pulled it. "Oh God!"

Then she climbed on top of me, straddling my legs. Her tongue found mine and she played with it, teasing me with her own. We didn't have time for slow passion; we needed to hurry so that we didn't get caught.

Hope reached down and grabbed me. She lifted her body and then we were one. At first she was rocking slow, but soon picked up the pace. She used my chest to balance her weight while she guided her hips back and forth. It didn't take us long to become overwhelmed with each other. This girl had all of my attention, and there was nothing I wasn't willing to risk to be with her.

When her body began to lose control it was difficult for me to be able to hold out. A few seconds after she slowed her rhythm, I was sent into a frenzy.

Hot.
Sweaty.
Passionate.
Love.

Hope leaned her face toward me and kissed me slowly. I couldn't help from wrapping my arms around her keeping her close to me. After a few minutes we both agreed that we needed to get dressed before Buffy returned home. The grocery store was just ten minutes away, and the movie rental was out of this big video box right inside of that same location. Depending on what Buffy needed, she may already be on her way back.

Hope and I attained our clothes and began dressing. I

noticed her birth control pill package lying on her dresser and I couldn't help but grab it. "Please make sure to take one of these every day. We already have a lot of explaining to do."

"I never forget, Chance; you don't have to worry about that." She kissed me one more time.

After doing a quick check out the window, Hope and I held hands as we sauntered down to the living room. She turned on the television while I went into the kitchen and made us both some tea, and then headed back and sat on the couch to cuddle next to her. When we heard Buffy pull up we scooted apart and acted like we were surprised to see her back so soon.

"Oh goodie, you're both already here. I'm so excited." Buffy said as she came into the room. "I got us two movies to watch and extra butter popcorn."

I picked up the movies and rolled my eyes as I looked at the first one. Who wrote these cheesy stories anyway? Hope looked over at me and I held up what would be a nightmare for me to sit through.

Buffy left for a second then came running back into the room. "I forgot to give you your movie." She handed me a movie out of her purse, and I immediately smiled. She'd gotten me a horror flick even though she hated them.

"I know I loathe them, but I figured that we could all sit on the same couch and you could protect Hope and I from whatever's on that DVD. You do have two shoulders we can hide behind, ya know." She disappeared into the kitchen to make the popcorn.

I got the biggest smile on my face as I headed over and put my movie in, ignoring the other two. I sat down next to Hope and leaned into her. "Do you like scary movies?"

"Actually, I do," she whispered.

"Damn, I was hoping you could hide your eyes in my shoulder."

She smiled back at me. "Oh, that can be arranged."

Buffy walked back in the room with a giant bowl of popcorn. We turned off the lights and all three of us sat on the couch ready to watch. About halfway into the movie Hope located a blanket and wrapped it around herself. I slid my hand down to my side and slipped it under the blanket without making it obvious to my sister. It was there that I found her fingers waiting to be held.

Buffy fell asleep while Hope and I continued to watch the movie. Her hand never left mine and I found comfort being able to do such mundane things with her. She was so special to me and I couldn't help but love the fact that she enjoyed these kinds of movies.

When it was over I leaned over to Hope. "I better call it a night," I whispered.

She brought her chin up and brushed her lips over mine. "Okay."

"Walk me into the kitchen?" I asked in a quiet tone.

She nodded and followed me in there with our cups in her hands. I leaned down and kissed her lips. My thumb came up and rubbed her bottom one. "See you in the morning, baby."

I headed out toward my place. It killed me to do that.

I made it in the door, grabbing my pack of smokes. If I couldn't be with Hope tonight then I was going to have my first cigarette of the day. I stripped down in my living room to only my boxers and headed out to the picnic table, where I'd watched Hope seduce me just days ago. The smoke filled my lungs and I realized how lonely I was without her close to me. It was unbelievable how in just a short amount of time I'd come to love someone so much that I didn't want to be away from them.

She had no idea how grateful I was for her.

There was the giant issue of her father warning me to stay away from his daughter, and the fact that the local cops were breathing down my neck for an alibi that I couldn't give them.

I know Hope said she wanted the truth to come out, but I couldn't let her do that. If she told the cops we were together, I would be out of trouble with them, but have to then deal with Mark. It was a lose-lose situation.

I finished my cigarette and put it out in one of my sister's new flower pots. I would have to remember to remove it in the morning so she never saw that I'd done it. She hated that shit.

I went in the pool house and tried to find something to watch on television, but my mind was elsewhere. I couldn't stop thinking of Hope, and wondered what she was doing, and if she was thinking about me too.

Finally I headed into my room and lay on my bed. I was getting ready to play around on the internet on my cell phone when I got a message.

It was from an unknown number, but there was only one person it could have been.

Hope

I couldn't stand being in my room, so I snuck downstairs and got Chance's number from my father's office. I got so excited that I started texting before I had even made it back to my room.

I miss you already ~ Hope

I stared at my phone and when I didn't get a reply I wondered if Chance was awake, or even if this was still his phone number. I located my stuffed frog he'd won me on the boardwalk and hugged it.

Finally my phone vibrated.

Me too! ~ C

I got a big smile on my face.

So what are you wearing? ~Hope

A pair of long plaid pants. A Hawaiian shirt that is button up. And some argyle socks. ~C

Lol. I bet that looks so hot on you. ~ Hope

I can't sleep. There is something wrong with my bed. ~C

What? Did you break it? ~Hope

You're not in it. ~C

I held the phone to my chest and started laughing.

What would you do if I was? ~ Hope

I would hold you all night long. ~ C

:)~Hope
<3 Goodnight ~C
<3 Goodnight ~Hope
I wished we could talk all night long, but I needed some rest. It had been a long emotional day for me. I hugged my stuffed frog tight and finally fell asleep.

25

Hope

When I woke up Buffy was sitting on the edge of my bed. I didn't even have to open my eyes all the way to know it was her. Her bright pink tank top was burning my eyes.

"Oh hey, Buff. What's up?" I asked.

"Sorry to come in your room so early. I actually had something I wanted to talk to you about."

I tried to focus and listen, but I was not a morning person. "Okay, is it about the wedding?"

"No, actually it's about my brother," she stated.

Her eyes were fixed on mine and I didn't know what to do. If I changed my expression she would know I was hiding something. I remained as calm as I could. "What about him?"

"Well I was wondering if you have seen him with anyone, especially when we were away?"

"Oh, um...no, I didn't see him with anyone." That wasn't a lie. He'd been with only me the whole time.

"Hope, I won't be mad if he asked you not to tell me. I know he's been seeing someone. He's acting different, and last month I found him naked in his bed, after he left a bar we were all at together. Now I know my brother and he doesn't sleep without clothes." She sounded certain. I knew otherwise.

"I swear to you that I didn't see anyone over the weekend or ever."

She gave me a quick smile. "Damn. Did he ever leave and stay somewhere else over night?"

I shook my head. "No! I saw him everyday at least a couple times. If he went anywhere I didn't notice. I wasn't his keeper though. If you wanted me to keep tabs on him you should have said something."

Buffy stood up and headed toward my door. "It was worth a try I guess. He won't talk to me about it. Maybe it's my imagination." She started walking out of the room. "Sorry I woke you up. I just didn't want to ask in front of your father or Chance."

"It's fine. I'll see you downstairs," I announced.

Well that sucked. I obtained my cell phone and texted Chance.

Buffy just asked me if I saw you with anyone while they were gone. She mentioned the morning she found you naked when I was hiding in the shower. I didn't tell her anything. Just wanted you to know. ~Hope

Wow, she won't give up will she? Thanks! C-ya soon. ~C

Definitely! ~ Hope

I climbed out of my bed and got dressed. Today I was going to visit my mother. I hadn't seen her in weeks and I wanted her to be informed about my father's plans. Maybe it wasn't my place to tell her, but she would kill me if she found out from someone else. I threw on some sweat shorts and the white t-shirt that smelled like Chance. Then I headed into the bathroom to wash up, and finally make my way downstairs.

215

Buffy was outside doing what looked like Yoga. My father was in his office talking on the phone.

Finally, Chance came walking into the kitchen as I opened the refrigerator.

I felt a hand brush over my butt. "Good morning, beautiful."

"Hey, yourself."

He was eating a banana and I couldn't help but watch his lips as he did it. "What are you doing today?"

"I am going to see my mother. It's been a while, and I really need to get out of this house."

Chance knew not to take it personal; well I hoped that he didn't.

"I guess you're going to spill the beans to her?" Chance asked.

"That is the plan."

I heard my dad coming into the room. "What's the plan?" He asked.

"I um, I'm going to have lunch with Mom today," I confessed.

"Hope, it's okay. It's fine. She needs to know." He squeezed my shoulder. "Don't worry about it, sweetie. I know you're going to tell her sooner or later."

"Thanks, Dad. I just don't want her hearing about it from anyone else." I ambled outside toward my car, not really wanting to be in the same room with my dad yet.

I couldn't stay inside with either of them. Being around Chance and not being able to touch him made me want him more. My father was keeping us apart; well he thought he was at least. The last thing I wanted was for Chance to have to move out. If I couldn't see him I'd go insane.

Once I started driving, I realized I wasn't prepared to face my mother with the information I had on my dad and Buffy.

She was going to freak out. It wasn't because she was still in love with him, in fact she hated him. I think she would be hurt and possibly feel jealous. She had lost everything while he was living it up, becoming wealthier than when they were together.

I pulled into the driveway behind my mother's car and took a deep breath. It was going to be a long day. Suddenly, I wished I was back at the pool house in Chance's arms.

My sister was fishing around trying to figure out who I was involved with. I couldn't be pissed at her, because I knew she was just looking out for me. The problem was I wasn't sure how deep she was going to be looking. I had to start being more careful about being around Hope. If Buffy suspected it was her she would freak out.

As much as I cared for Hope I had to keep thinking

about the big picture. In just a few months she would be eighteen, and could make her own decisions about who she wanted to be with. I was fully aware that she wanted to be with me, but I found myself wondering if we wouldn't just be better waiting it out. If we did then nobody would get in any trouble.

I lit up a cigarette and watched my sister doing some ridiculous stretches. "You look so stupid. Is that supposed to make you lose weight?"

Buffy shot me a dirty look. "What's your problem today?" She asked.

"I was just kidding. Get a grip. What are you doing today?"

"I'm going to finish watching the movies I got and then return them. I think that Mark had invited some people over to discuss business. Do you think you can find somewhere else to eat tonight? Maybe like at your new love interest's place or something?"

"You're fishing for something that doesn't exist, Buff." I tried to get her to drop it.

"Chance, you're my brother and I love you, but I know you're seeing someone. You've had this spark in your eyes ever since that morning I found you sleeping naked."

I rolled my eyes. "You're crazy. It gets hot in the pool house. I drank myself into a stupor, showered, and passed out in my bed. No harm no foul, sis. Get over it."

She stopped her stretching and marched over to face me. Her hands were on her hips and she squint her eyes like she was trying to read my mind. "No, I'm not, but you are if you think you can hide her from me for much longer. What's the big deal? Is she ugly or something?"

I turned and started walking away from her. "I don't

have time for this shit."

"Being that I am kind of your boss, I would say you have all the time in the world. Now tell me the truth. When have you ever kept a relationship from me? Is she married or something?" She just kept pushing.

"Jesus Christ, Buffy, please stop it already." I looked directly into her eyes. "It was a one-time thing, okay?"

I was an idiot.

"Why couldn't you just tell me then?" She asked.

"Because there was nothing to tell. I picked someone up at a bar and took her home with me. We had a great time and then she left. That's it." I explained.

"Was it the woman who went missing?" Buffy asked.

"Hell no! I never even saw that woman. From her picture in the paper she looked like she was over forty. Why would I take someone that old home with me, Buffy? I may be a lot of things, but I've never been desperate. If I wanted to pick up a chick that didn't know about my past, and fuck her brains out, I guarantee it wouldn't be hard. I've never had a problem in that department, and you know it. Please say you believe me."

She clutched my arm and pulled me to sit down next to her. "I always believe you, Chance, but I also know that you've been acting different. All of a sudden you seem...I don't know, like happier. I just don't understand how a one-night-stand could result in that."

I sighed. "I'll find someplace to eat tonight, and when I get home I'll stay in the pool house. It really isn't a big deal."

I got up and walked away from Buffy, but my nerves were now shot. I went inside and changed my clothes. Then I jumped on my bike and headed to the nearest bar that was open at eleven am on a Tuesday.

The bar was empty and it was just how I wanted it to be. I pulled out my license and slid it across the bar before ordering my first beer.

"Bad day, kid?" The male bartender asked.

"Bad life." I handed him cash for the beer.

A female voice said something right before slipping beside me. "Did you hear me?" She asked.

"No. Sorry."

"I said my name is Chelsea."

"Chance, my name is Chance," I blurted out.

The woman twisted a straw around in her mixed drink while she looked at me from top to bottom. "I'd love to take a CHANCE with you," she confessed.

I swallowed hard. "No, you really wouldn't."

"I beg to differ. In fact I'm sure that you and I could find something better to do than sit here at a bar all day drowning our sorrows. What do you think?"

I gave her a half-smile. She was built nice and had long blonde hair. She was wearing low-cut jean shorts and a shirt that tied at the bottom, exposing her navel. She pulled a piece of ice out of her glass and ran it over her lips before putting it in her mouth. I knew she was taunting me.

"Thanks for the offer, but I can't," I admitted.

"You don't want to, or you can't? Because in my book they are two different things." She placed her palm on my thigh, I guess expecting that it would do the trick.

I gripped her hand and removed it from my leg. "I'm gay," I announced.

"Well, that is just a cryin' shame," she retorted.

"Guess we have to just hang out here." I said, even though I wanted to burst out laughing. I couldn't believe I'd said it. I also couldn't believe I was passing up on a no-strings-attached-sex-fest with this chick, but I was. She may have been very attractive, but she couldn't even compare to Hope. There was no use even trying to make my feelings for her go away. It wasn't going to happen, and I refused to be THAT GUY, who sleeps with one person to get rid of another.

For the rest of the afternoon I planned on sitting at this bar, alone.

26

Hope

After noticing the large 'For Sale' sign in the yard I approached the front entrance to my grandparent's house and took a deep breath. It wasn't going to be easy to face my mother and break her heart. It may have been the hardest thing that I ever had to do. I stood my ground and pushed open the door, knowing that when I came back out the damage would be done.

"In here, honey," my mother called out from the kitchen.

I walked toward the back of the house to find her doing the dishes. When I noticed how many were in the drainer I had to ask. "Was someone else here?"

"What do you mean?"

When I thought about having my own agenda I decided that it would be best to save my concerns for a later time. "Nothing, never mind." I sauntered over and gave her a big hug, stalling the inevitable.

"You look so beautiful, Hope. Have you done something different with yourself? You're just glowing." Since

I knew for a fact that I certainly wasn't with child, I took her compliment to mean that I appeared happy for a change. I knew why I was glowing. Hell, I was probably radiating with happiness. "Nothing is new. Just trying to get settled in at Dad's house," I lied.

"Well you look fantastic. What have you been up to?" She asked.

"Nothing really. I like to run in the morning. The neighborhood is really quiet. I painted my room. I've even been doing some reading, and a lot of swimming." I didn't tell her about the golf lessons, or our family dinners every night.

My mom turned her attention back to the dirty dishes. "Have you seen Rylee lately?"

Oh crap! I didn't know if she had talked to Rylee's parents. This was horrible. "Yeah I saw her the other day. We went to the beach." I winged it.

"Her mother said she's been spending all of her free time with you at the new house. She said she's practically living there. Doesn't your dad and his, whatever she is, have a problem with that?" My mother asked while she dried her hands off with a dish towel.

"Um, no, Dad works a lot and Buffy doesn't mind," I lied again.

"I still can't believe your father is involved with someone named Buffy." My mother shook her head, but through her stiff glare I could tell it hurt her.

"Actually, her name is really Matilda. Her mother named her after her dying grandmother." It was something Chance had told me one night during one of our pillow talks.

My mother calmed her tone. "Well I guess Buffy is better than that. So...what is she like?"

I shrugged my shoulders. "She's actually nice. She

223

keeps Dad in line. Her cooking is really good. Her brother said that she went to culinary school after she graduated, but never pursued a career."

I realized what I'd said too late. "Her brother?"

"His name is Chance. He lives out back in the guest pool house." Here comes the third degree.

"I wasn't aware. Is he older than his sister?" She asked.

Shit!

"No, he is twenty something, I guess. I never really asked. He's working on the house for them. I only see him in passing and at meals." Wow, another big fat lie.

"Is he handsome? Does my little girl have a crush on an older man?" She teased.

If she only knew...

"No, Mom. Geesh," I said defensively.

"Well I just hope that your father had the sense to tell him how young you are. I wouldn't want him staring in your window like some common creep."

I rolled my eyes feeling defensive of Chance, even though I knew he looked in my windows. "So, how have you been?" I tried to change the subject.

My mom led me into the living room. I noticed a bunch of boxes lying around the room.

"It's been hectic. With work and packing I haven't had time to do much else. There is something that I wanted to talk to you about though."

"I think I already know." How could she have found out already?

She seemed shocked. "Oh, honey I didn't want you to find out this way. I wanted to be the one to tell you, but I just haven't had the time. So are you okay with it?"

"Yeah I was upset at first, but I guess it will be okay as long as he is happy I shouldn't care right?"

My mother looked utterly confused. "Honey, who is HE?"

"Dad. Isn't that who you're talking about?" I asked.

"No! Does he have news that you know about?"

Darn darn darn!

"Well, I didn't want it to come out like this, but he and Buffy are engaged." I watched her face turn bone white.

She folded her hands before looking up at me. Her lips were tight and her brows creased. "For the love of...That. God. Damn. Son. Of. A. Bitch! How could he just up and marry the first floozy to come along? Well I hope she takes him for everything he has. It will serve him right."

I shook my head and put my hands up to my face. "Mom, please!" She had to calm down.

"Sorry, Hope. That was uncalled for." My mother apologized. "He's just taken so much from me, and now he gets to live a new life, as if he didn't destroy mine."

"It's fine. Not meaning to change the subject, but what was your news?" I asked.

"It isn't important."

"Mom, come on. What is it?"

"I met someone. He's a nurse that works at the nursing home. We only had one date, but he brings me coffee when we share the same shifts. He is so nice, Hope. You would really like him. He was married for ten years to a woman that never wanted children. I told him all about you. I can't wait for you to meet him," she admitted.

I gave her a big smile and leaned in to hug her. "That's great, Mom. You needed to get back out there. Dad's loss is your gain. Don't worry about him and Buffy. Seriously, just worry about you from now on. I'm just glad that you're happy."

"I got an offer on the house yesterday too. They want to settle before the month ends."

My heart broke, but I realized it was something that had to happen. "Wow, that was fast. Do you need help moving? Oh my gosh, did you even find a new place yet?"

"As a matter of fact, yes. Sam has a couple rental properties and one of them is available. You are going to love it sweetie. It has new carpet and appliances."

"Who is Sam?" I asked.

"Oh, sorry. He's the new guy I'm seeing," she explained. "Why don't you come back in the kitchen and I'll make us some lunch and tell you all about him."

For the next three hours my mother wouldn't shut up about the new man in her life. Part of me wondered if she'd even remembered the news about my father and Buffy.

When she finally had to start getting ready for her shift I headed out. After the shock of everything I figured it had gone over better than I expected it to. Although she freaked out about my Dad, it was soon forgotten.

It seemed like my mother was turning a new leaf with her luck. I just really hoped she didn't look any further into Buffy's brother. If she asked me to move back in with her I would freak out.

I would miss Chance so much and it would be impossible for us to have any alone time unless we met in public, which was not my idea of alone. I was going to have to keep my fingers crossed that my mother was too caught up in her new life to worry about mine.

27

Hope

Before I left my old community, I pulled over and texted Chance. Part of me just wanted him to know I was thinking about him.

Hey ~Hope

Immediately I got a response.

Hey, Baby. Where are you? ~C

I got ready to text back and my phone started to ring. "Hello?"

"Hey. What are you wearing?"

Loud music filled the receiver. I couldn't imagine him having anything like that playing at home.

"Where are you?"

"At the bar. Trying to fight off this sexy lady next to me. She wants a piece of me."

My cheeks burned, while I became annoyed with jealousy. It was rather disturbing that he'd speak to me that way. Thinking he was testing me, I kept quiet, patiently waiting for him to admit it was a joke.

"Hey, are you still there?"

I felt like hanging up...

"Yeah."

"She asked me to hook up with her, but I told her I was gay." He began laughing at himself. "She doesn't hold a candle to you, baby."

"Are you drunk? Why would you say you were gay?"

He cackled to himself before answering. "Because nobody can know we're together right now."

"She doesn't know who I am though."

"Hope, don't fight with me. I miss you."

He was drunk, and the sheer knowledge of his intoxication left a bad taste in my mouth...

"Chance, where are you?"

"I don't fucking know. I drove out toward the park, and then I saw a bar. I've been here since Buffy asked me who I was sleeping with."

"She what?" My emotions began to go awry. This was not something that I could take lightly. His answer would determine if I could go home or not.

"Yep. I told her you were a one-nighter. Well I didn't say it was you. She doesn't know ANYTHING!" His words were slurred and drug out.

"I'm on my way to get you. Can you come outside?"

"Why don't you come inside and have a drink with me? I want everyone to see the guy I'm banging. You're the best gay boyfriend. I like how you bend over and take it." He hooted at his statement, as if it was entertainingly humorous.

Chance may have thought his actions were comical, but I wasn't amused. He sounded horrible, probably having derived from his bad day.

"I am *not* coming inside. I'll call you when I arrive, and you will get your butt out to my car."

"You're so beautiful, Hope. You're the most beautiful person in the whole world, no, the whole universe. I just want to box you up and keep you in my pocket like a little toy."

"Thank you, I think. You're pretty great as well, when you're not intoxicated. Maybe you should just come outside now. I will be there in five minutes."

"Are you coming to see me, baby?" Of course it was in one ear and out the other. This was like babysitting a child.

"Oh my God. Please go outside and wait for me. Don't you dare get on that bike!"

"Okay, baby. I will see you outside on Friday."

Before I was able to say anything the line went dead. I attempted to call it back, but he never answered, so I pressed the gas pedal to the floor, driving as fast as my car would take me. When I arrived at the bar, his motorcycle was the first thing I spotted. A rush of relief hit me when I knew he was still there. I jumped out of my vehicle and headed in the direction of the entrance, except at the last second I heard someone throwing up.

My feet moved swiftly, making it around the corner to spot Chance on his knees. He reeked of alcohol and vomit as I leaned down and handled his shoulder. "Chance." The odor was so pungent I was forced to cover my nose to refrain from becoming sick myself.

He brought his arms up and hugged me. "Hey, baby. What are you doing here? I didn't cheat on you with that woman. Aren't you proud of me? I could have hit that shit. She wanted some of this cock right here." He pointed to his crotch, as if I wasn't aware of its location.

I had to ignore the jealous fears that overwhelmed me, despite the fact that I wanted to make sure he hadn't messed around. In his condition it was impossible to begin to rationalize. "Chance, you have to get up." I urged him to stand. He'd used his arm to wipe the access bile from his face, while his balance was non-existent.

"I can't. Did you know I just threw up? Yep that's what happens when I drink too much."

He was slurring his words, spatting out ridiculous declarations, while making no sense. I wanted to laugh, but I was more concerned about how I was going to get him into my car without a fight.

"Can you please stand up?" I asked.

"I would do anything for you, Hope," he said as he strained to get himself in a vertical position. He began to sway backwards, but luckily I got a hold on his arms and was able to steady him better. We strolled over to my vehicle, and I exasperated myself more when I fought to get him inside of it.

Chance started opening my glove compartment and rummaging around inside. "What are you doing now?" My agitation was apparent, not that he was in any condition to even notice.

"I'm looking for my pants. Hope, have you seen my pants?"

I started laughing. "Yes. They're on your ass."

"You're so smart and pretty," he said as he stroked my face. "You have nice breasts too. I noticed them first."

"Maybe you should stop talking," I proposed

He put his hand on the steering wheel, causing me to stop backing up. "Wait. We can't go home. Mark is having some meeting there. Buffy told me to fend for myself tonight."

"Where are we supposed to go then?" I asked.

"We could still go home. If they aren't out back we

can sneak in the pool house. Maybe then you can show me your boobies. I really like them, you know."

I rolled my eyes again and started backing up. "So you keep telling me."

"No, I really love them, Hope. I want to marry your breasts. Both of them. I need to be a tit bigamist."

I continued to hoot at his drunken comments the whole ride home. Luckily it was only about a ten minute drive. When we pulled up at the house, I noticed strange vehicles parked outside. My car was smaller, easier to hide alongside of the garage, giving us a straight walk to the pool house.

"Stay here while I go check out back," I suggested, as I stepped out and paced around to make sure we were in the clear.

Once I'd searched out back to make certain we were alone, I headed in the direction of my car to grab Chance. I could hear commotion in the house, but it was coming from the well-lit dining room. I knew I needed to sneak Chance in on the side where he had his secret smoke breaks. There was lots of high greenery everywhere, and in the dark we would be undetected.

When I reached the car Chance was all but passed out. I had to literally drag him. He tried to speak, but I placed my hand over his mouth as we passed the window where the dinner party was taking place. Once we managed to make it to the pool house, I searched inside of his pockets and located his keys. After unlocking the door, he immediately went tumbling inside. I closed it behind us keeping the lights off.

Chance was rolling around the floor in hysterics. I didn't know whether to be annoyed or feel sorry for him. "Get up. I need to get you into the shower, so you can sober up."

"Will you get in with me?" He asked. He stuck out his bottom lip like a small child would. As cute as I found it, I knew I had to be the mature person and get him straight.

"I can't. My father is right across the yard," I clarified.

"Please. Don't you want to? Don't you want to get naked and ride me all night, baby?"

"Chance, don't beg. You know it's not going to happen." He reached to grab me, but I pulled away enough to where I could point him in the direction the bathroom.

He smelled like vodka and vomit with a hint of cologne. It was retched.

When he finally made it inside the tiny bathroom, he whipped his dick out and began peeing in the toilet with no regard for me even being in the room. I started the shower and helped him out of his clothes. Though difficult, I managed to get him to participate. When I tried to get him under the water, he wouldn't budge.

"Chance, please. You're covered in puke. Just get in and get cleaned up. You smell horrible."

"Please come with me," he attempted to pull me in. He was much stronger than me. I tried to stay out, but ended up tumbling down on top of him. The shower curtain and rod fell on us. When we were finally able to get up, I fixed the curtain the best I could. He fought to pull me in again. "Please. I need you. I just want to feel your skin against mine. Please, Hope."

"I can't. I want to, but I can't." Instead I leaned in and started to get him cleaned up. After having him spin around a few times, I decided he was clean enough to get dressed.

I held out a towel and waited for him to step out of the tub before wrapping it around him. He decided to brush his teeth, for a taxing ten minutes, in which I told him they were clean several times, but he continued doing it. Finally, he followed me into the bedroom and pulled me down on the bed with him.

His body hovered over mine as his fingertips played with my cheek. "You're so perfect to me, Hope. You make me want to live. You're all that I want, all that I need. You're everything. God, I love you so much."

It was impossible not to feel overcome. Those words were such a big deal in any relationship. Ours, yet brewing for a long period of time, had been a struggle. For him to have deep feelings for me left me speechless.

He wiped my cheeks. "Why are you crying?"

"Nobody's ever said something like that to me," I embarrassingly admitted.

"It's the truth. I'm so in love with you. I know you think I'm just drunk, but I swear it's true. You make me smile again."

"Chance," I managed to whisper as his lips hit mine.

He pulled away. "Yeah."

"I love you, too." I didn't wait for him to respond. Our next kiss was intense leaving us too caught up in each other to discuss anything more.

28

Chance

    I woke up in bed with only a pair of boxers on. When I sat up I realized that my head was pounding. While still holding the back of it, I stood up and headed to find the Tylenol. To my disappointment I was all out. I pulled on a pair of shorts, and after relieving myself in the bathroom, I headed to the main house.

    When I got to the kitchen door I realized I had no idea what time it was. I didn't want to wake up the whole house so I peeked in and saw it was after ten in the morning. I crept inside, but didn't hear any movement.

    Thankfully, my sister had made coffee. I made myself a cup and counted four Tylenol, tossing them back with the hot brew. There still wasn't any sound coming from around the house. I walked to the foyer and looked outside. Only Hope's car was sitting out front.

    I climbed up the stairs heading to her side of the house. Her door was shut, but I opened it slowly. She was sound asleep, and I couldn't help but take in her beauty. I strode in and leaned over to give her a kiss, but as I stood to walk away she snatched my arm. Still groggy from her sleep, she attempted to focus. "What are you doing in here?"

"What happened to me last night?" I whispered. "Where's my bike?"

She sat up and I couldn't help but notice the small tank top she had on. "Stop staring at my chest," she accused as she adjusted it, hiding some of her cleavage. "You got drunk off your ass at the bar, so on my way back from my mother's I picked you up and brought you home. I got you cleaned up and stayed with you until you fell asleep. Your motorcycle is still at the bar."

"You took care of me? Did my sister and Mark see us?" I asked.

"No. Once you fell asleep I went inside through the front. They still had company and thought I'd just got home," she explained.

"I don't remember anything," I admitted.

Hope looked upset. I couldn't understand why. "I knew it was too good to be true." While grabbing her, I tried to remember what would make her so upset. It was coming back to me in small pieces.

"What are you talking about? What did I do?"

"It wasn't what you did. It was what you said."

"Did I say something wrong?"

"No, it was perfect," she said quietly.

"Well whatever it was, I meant it," I assumingly announce.

Hope turned around and put her head in her pillow. "Forget it, Chance, it doesn't matter."

"Please don't be mad at me." I tried to reach for her, but she pulled away.

I was hurt, but had no right to be. I'd acted like an ass. *What had I been thinking?* I should've never gone out to a bar.

I was such a loser.

I left Hope in her room and went back downstairs. On the counter I found something that might make her smile. I got out a pen and a piece of painters tape and hiked back upstairs. I sat the object on her dresser and walked out without saying a word.

I hid in her bathroom across the hall waiting. The anticipation was killing me, and for a moment I figured she didn't hear me come back the second time.

I couldn't believe he didn't remember last night. I was a fool to think someone sober would say that to me anyway. I heard Chance come in my room, but I didn't want to talk to him. I wasn't really mad, just disappointed. As I stood up to head into my bathroom something caught my eye.

A red apple sat on my dresser. Taped to it was a note.

I don't remember what I said last night, but when I woke up this morning I knew I missed you.

I love you so much. Please don't be mad. I can't be without your smile for long.

I had to choke back the emotions. I quickly ran into the bathroom to brush my teeth, so that I could find him and kiss him right away. As I ambled in I saw him leaning against the sink. My arms wrapped around him.

"Does this mean you forgive me?" He asked with his hands cupped around my face.

I nodded my head yes, before he leaned down and kissed me.

"So much, Hope." He whispered in my ear, before leaving me alone to get myself cleaned up.

When I looked in the mirror I couldn't believe he hadn't changed his mind. After washing my face, I managed to get a brush through my hair. I ran back into my room and put on some clothes I wore to run in then headed downstairs.

Chance was outside, skimming leaves out of the pool. I jumped when Buffy marched into the room. "Hey, Hope, what are you doing?"

I held my heart. "Buff, you scared me. I was just..."

"Looking at my brother. Yeah I noticed."

"Please don't say anything," I said in a panic.

She smiled and sat down. "Hope, I may be his sister, but I'm not blind. I know girls think he is attractive."

"Where is my dad?" I asked trying to change the subject.

She was looking straight at me with her hands across her chest. "He had to meet with investors on the new building today. He won't be home till late. So let's get back to my brother. How long have you been seeing him?"

I choked on the glass of milk I was drinking. "What? I don't know what you're talking about."

"Oh really. Then do me a favor. Walk out there and hug him."

"What? Buffy, you're crazy. I couldn't do that."

"Sure you can. If it's nothing I'll see it for myself, but I'm pretty sure I have things all figured out now. Come on, Hope, let's go." She grabbed my arm and pulled me out the door.

She pushed me ahead of her and watched as I sauntered over to Chance. He looked up and saw the tears in my eyes, before I couldn't say a word. She would hear me anyway. As ordered, I wrapped my arms around him. At first he didn't react, but as I pulled away I felt his arms going around me. I knew that she was watching, but I still pulled myself out of his hold and looked into his eyes. His concern was all I could see. "I'm so sorry," I whispered.

"I think that both of you need to get your asses over here and explain some things to me right now," she demanded.

Immediately Chance knew. He looked so hurt as we walked over to the picnic table.

She stood up and began pacing back and forth. "So how long has this been going on?" She asked.

"What are you talking about, Buffy? What's going on?" Chance acted like she way off base.

"Don't you dare do that, little brother. I've known for weeks that you were different. I sat up at night wondering what could have changed in your life. You never go out and you don't have any friends anymore. Then when I got back from my vacation, I went into the pool house and found your dirty laundry. I discovered a bra under your bed that was white lace and a bag of sandy bathing suits, one of them belonging to me."

"So what. I took Hope to the beach. That doesn't mean anything," Chance argued.

"Did you hear me say I found the bra?"

I sat there shaking with my hands up to my face.

"Yeah, so what? I brought some chick home from the bar. I told you that."

"That isn't how I figured things out, Chance. The other night I pretended to be asleep when we were watching movies. I saw you two so close and I know you were holding hands under the covers. Then last night I was in the kitchen and saw Hope getting you inside the house. I checked and your bike was nowhere to be found. You obviously came home together."

"So what. We're friends, Buffy. That is it." I'd never heard Chance act so defensive.

"Hope, look at me," Buffy ordered. "Are you and Chance just friends?" I hated to be put on the spot, because I was a terrible liar.

I looked from Buffy to Chance. He appeared to be furious. "I said leave her alone, Buffy."

"Just one more question. Hope, how many times have you slept with my brother?"

Chance put his body in between mine and Buffy's so that I couldn't see her. "Leave her the fuck alone!"

"Calm down. I just wanted you to admit it." She sat back down across from me. When she looked in my direction she could see that I was crying. "Did you guys really think you could hide this forever? If Mark discovers this he's going to flip."

"Are you going to tell my father? Please don't, Buffy," I begged.

"Of course not. He would kick Chance's ass and make him move out."

"Thank you," I whispered quietly.

"How serious is this thing between the two of you? Is this just something fun for you, Chance, because I can't let this continue if you're just using her?"

Chance looked over at me. He sat down beside me and took my hand. "She's never been a game to me, and for the record we fought this. We tried so hard to avoid each other when she first moved in, but we'd already been together and..."

Buffy cut him off. "What do you mean? How did you know her?"

I lay my head down on the table, while coming to grips that this was actually happening. "Remember when we first met, and you and Dad said I could look around? Well, I kind of walked into the pool house when Chance was getting dressed," I explained but Chance cut me off.

"Then when she left I went out for some smokes. She had pulled over to the side of the road and this guy was harassing her. He was trying to coax her into his truck. I got him to leave and stayed with her until she could calm down." Chance said as he looked over to me. "Then, you and Mark took me out to that bar."

"Okay, you're losing me. You told me you hooked up with some random chick." Buffy stated.

Chance looked toward me and winked. "That wasn't exactly the truth. You see, Hope's stupid friend scored them some fake I.D.s. I spotted her in the bar and let her know that you and Mark were there too. She'd been drinking and her friend wouldn't leave, because she met some guy. I brought her back to the pool house so that she could sober up, but one thing led to another and the rest is history," Chance explained.

"Oh my God. You two hooked up before Mark

introduced you? So this had nothing to do with you living here together?" She asked.

"No, in fact up until last weekend we barely even talked, but finally we couldn't stand it anymore. At least that's how it was for me," I could feel my cheeks burning as I confessed.

"I love her, Buff. This whole time I've been trying to protect her from this." It warmed my heart hearing him say that.

"So, my brother is in love with my soon to be step-daughter. Should we call the Maury show now or wait until your father finds out?" Buffy asked.

I was freaking out. "He can't find out. He won't understand. Please Buffy, if you care about me at all you won't tell him," I begged.

She shook her head and ran her hands through her hair. "You guys are really putting me in a bad situation." She got quiet for a second. Chance held my hand and rubbed his thumb against mine. "This is what's going to happen. I don't want to see it. Do not do anything that would make him think there is something between you. And that goes for you, Hope, I saw how you looked at him and that's how I tied it all together. He can't know. When you turn eighteen you two can decide what to do. I am not going to let this ruin my wedding. Do you both hear me?"

Chance and I both nodded our heads.

"For the record, I think you are made for each other, but if anyone else asks I will lie." She then left us outside alone.

Chance turned to face me. "Are you okay?"

"Maybe, I'm just dreaming. Did that really happen?" I asked.

He kissed the top of my head. "It happened, but she won't tell. I considered telling her a while back, but then you moved in and it just wasn't that easy."

"Do you want to break up with me now?" I asked.

"Are you kidding? I just told you I loved you and I'm sure I said it last night. When you're drunk you say the truth, and that's also how I knew you really wanted to be with me that first night."

"Actually, I think I wanted you ever since I first saw you. I couldn't get that picture out of my head until that night we were together, and then I just had a better image to keep in my mind."

I leaned my head against his chest. "Loving you makes me happy. This mess with my parents and having to move in with my dad, who ignored me for so long, it wouldn't have been nearly as easy if you weren't here."

"I'm not going anywhere," Chance said as he kissed me in broad daylight right on the lips.

We both jumped when Buffy yelled out the door. "I can see you two!"

We both laughed. Chance stood up and held out his hand. He looked back at his sister, laughing as she shook her head at us. "See you later, Buffy."

"Where are we going?" I asked.

"Hopefully to get my motorcycle, if it's still there," he teased.

29

Chance

It was obvious Hope was worried about my sister, but one thing that I knew for sure was that she always had my back. The fact that I loved Hope made me more sure that she would keep our secret. It was honestly easier for me now that she knew. I think that it was harder for Hope though. She hadn't said much since Buffy's confrontation.

She sat on my couch with her hands on her knees. "Hope, is everything okay, beautiful?" I asked.

"I don't know. I think I'm just a little freaked out right now. I mean, don't get me wrong. In a way I'm glad she knows, but what are we going to do if she tells my dad? I can't let you get kicked out of here. I would rather stop what we're doing and have you here than have to lose you all together," she explained.

"Baby, there's no way in hell that I'm going to let you walk away."

She looked up at me with those shining eyes.

"Hope, this isn't some fling for me. If it was then I never would have told you about my past. You have to know how important you are to me," I explained.

"I do know. Sometimes it's just so hard hiding it. Why can't everyone just understand that we care about each other?"

I knelt down in front of her and covered her hands with mine. "It's just six months, Hope. We get to see each other every day and now we don't even have to hide it from Buffy. This is a good thing. Besides, it was only a matter of time before she figured it out. Everything will be fine." I leaned in and waited halfway for her to kiss me. She met me and pressed her lips against mine. "Don't you want this? Do you still want me?"

"I get that you think I'm too young, but I know what I want. Yes, of course I want this. I want you." She smiled and traced her fingernails over the skin of my arms. "I love you."

Hearing her say it would never get old. Unfortunately, it only showed me that she was going to take risks to be with me. That could be so dangerous for our relationship. "Maybe we should slow down some. Things have gotten really intense between us. I don't want you to get freaked out, but we've got to be more careful," I explained.

Hope stood up and staggered past me. She held out her hand and led me into my bedroom. Once inside, I cupped my hands around her face and pulled her lips into mine. She backed away and lifted off her shirt. I did the same. She gave me a quick smile and removed her shorts, and I followed her lead.

"We need to talk about this, Hope. This isn't going to solve anything." I wanted her, but knew this didn't resolve any of our problems. If anything, it made them worse.

Then Hope unhooked her bra.

I watched her breasts fall out from within the lacey fabric. She leaned down and removed her panties, before climbing on top of my bed. I removed my boxers and got under the covers after her. When I found that warm body, I nestled myself against it. I loved how she smelled like honey, and I couldn't get enough of her smooth skin.

"We're supposed to be getting my motorcycle," I said in between kisses.

"I just need to be close to you for a little while. I feel weird, like something bad is going to happen."

"Please don't even talk like that. Everything is going to be fine."

She made sure she was touching me. "Please just hold me. I need to be close to you. Pretend you never have to let go."

I did as she requested, but after only a few minutes I realized being naked next to her made me want more. It was impossible to rationalize with myself when we were in this current predicament. "Hope, I don't know how much longer I can lay naked next to you, and not get some. I'm so turned on right now it isn't even funny," I explained.

I felt Hope's hand feeling around between my legs. Her head disappeared from on top of the covers, and then I felt her lips, right there, so warm and pleasant. Her hands began to explore around down there and just when things started getting good, I heard my front door opening. Hope froze in place and I actually had to grab her arms and pull her up to the top of the bed.

"Chance, it's me. Mark just called. He's on his way home. I'm not kidding about you and Hope. You two can't be in here when he gets home."

"OKAY!" I yelled.

Hope looked over at me. "Do you want me to finish?" She reached down under the covers with her hand.

I stopped her before she made it any worse. "Let's just go and get my bike. We can finish this later." It was a promise.

"All right," she said as she leaned over and kissed me.

Hope and I got dressed and headed out to get my motorcycle. I met her in her car while she ran inside to get her purse and keys. When she climbed into the driver's seat, she had a weird look her face.

"What's wrong?" I asked.

"Nothing. I just feel like Buffy is the one acting funny now. She kept staring at me, like I was hiding a million dollars or something."

"I think you're just panicking. Everything will be okay. Please trust me." I had to believe that we were going to be okay, because any other outcome would be terrible.

Hope started her car and we headed out of our long driveway. "I do trust you. You've never given me a reason not to," she explained.

"I appreciate that."

We made it out of the neighborhood before either of us said anything else. Hope was on edge and I felt like if I spoke I would say the wrong thing. Finally I decided to change the subject. "So have you decided what you want to do once the summer is over?"

She glanced over at me before looking back to the road. "What do you mean? With us?" She asked.

"No, with your future. Have you thought about going to college?"

Hope shrugged her shoulders. "I don't know. I hate school work, so I never really wanted to attend college. I guess with everything that's happened, I haven't been thinking too much about it."

I put my arm over her head rest. "College is important. You should give it a try. It can be hard at times, but it's very different than high school."

"You sound like my father, Chance."

"Sorry." I rubbed the back of her neck. "I just think since you graduated early, with honors, that you would want to look into all of your options. Virginia has great colleges. I also got offered a spot at Virginia Tech before staying home in Pennsylvania to attend school. Now that I look back, I wonder if I should have just left the state back then."

"If I tell you I'll look into school will you leave me alone about it?" She asked.

"You hate it that much?"

"Yes, I do," she confirmed.

We pulled up to the bar, and my motorcycle was the only thing in the parking lot. "Well, at least it didn't get stolen."

I started to get out of the car, but Hope pulled me by my arm back inside. "Chance, wait. My dad will probably be home when we get back. In case I can't talk to you, I want you to think about this." She leaned forward and kissed me, starting out slow, but soon her whole tongue was sliding over mine. I could feel the growth between my legs, and backed away before I had the urge to take her right in the car.

I kissed her on the forehead. "See you later, baby." I said before I headed toward my bike.

Hope waited for me to get on and get it started before she drove off. If Mark decided to stay home this afternoon I would have to go back to taking a cold shower.

30

Hope

When I arrived home the first thing I noticed is that my father wasn't there yet. I ran into the house so that it would seem like I had been there for a while. Then Buffy came walking into the living room to greet me.

"Hey, did you guys get his bike?" She asked.

"Yes, listen I'm sorry about everything. I wanted to tell you, but I was so scared that you'd tell dad. I don't know what I'd do if Chance had to move away." I don't think I was telling her something she didn't already know, but it was more to the point of having her on my side in case something bad happened.

"Chance is my brother, he's my blood, and there is no way I would betray his trust. Hope, I know him better than he knows himself. It wasn't hard to figure out that you were the reason he was being so secretive," she explained.

"I feel bad about it."

"Your father is almost twenty years older than me. I'm in no position to judge either one of you."

We heard the door open, and at first I wanted to rush into Chance's arms, but that wasn't who walked in the door. It was actually my father and he wasn't alone.

"Buffy, honey, can you set three extra plates on the patio tonight?" He asked as he strode in.

I was speechless. Behind him was someone from my past; someone I hoped I never saw again. "Hope, I think you already know Greg Thomas and his sons Trevor and Michael."

"Yeah, I know them Dad. Why are they in our house?" I wanted to know why my ex boyfriend was standing in front of me in my house.

"Hope! Have some manners. Mr. Greg and I are working on a project together in town. I invited him and his boys here to discuss business over an early dinner." My father explained.

Trevor had made several attempts to get back with me ever since I dumped his ass. He was standing behind his father looking me up and down. He was the last person that I wanted to be around, and I certainly didn't appreciate the way he was staring at me. I rolled my eyes. "Excuse me, I need to go change."

I started walking up the stairs when I heard my father again. "Hope, we'll be out at the pool. Why don't you get your bathing suit on, and come out to join us. I'm sure your friends would like to catch up."

I wanted to scream, but I knew I had to remain calm. I didn't want to piss off my dad. "Buffy, can you come here a second?"

Buffy met me in my room. I felt like I was already starting to hyperventilate. "What's wrong, Hope? How do you know those guys?"

Tears fell down my cheeks as I gently sobbed in my

hands. "Trevor is my ex-boyfriend. He's an asshole and I hate him. How could my father think that it would be okay? Did you know about this?" I asked.

"Of course not! I would have warned you." She gave me a hug. "What do you need me to do?"

"I need you to tell Chance what's going on. I don't want him getting the wrong idea. Please, Buffy." I was being irrational. Just because they were here didn't mean I had to get back together with him. I just wanted to be able to ignore him until they left.

Buffy agreed to let Chance know what was bothering me, so that he didn't worry. In the meantime, my father had his own agenda. I changed into the ugliest bathing suit I had, and finished the ensemble off with a giant cover up. He met me when I was coming down the steps.

"Hope, honey I need you to be extra nice to Trevor tonight. His father is a potential investor in one of my largest projects. I can't have him walking away because my daughter pissed off one of his kids," he explained.

"Dad, please. I broke up with Trevor a long time ago, and I really don't like him anymore. Can't I go somewhere for the night?" I begged. "Can I just say I had something else to do?"

"No, Hope! I need you to do this for me. Just entertain them." My father started to raise his voice and I knew there was no getting him to change his mind.

I headed downstairs and stayed close to Buffy while she started preparing the food for the grill. My father had already made his way out to the patio, and I saw all three of the guys had beer bottles in their hands.

When I spotted Chance, I got butterflies in my stomach. He was so gorgeous. That man could be making millions modeling underwear. His body was so perfectly chiseled that it was almost a sin to look at.

Buffy caught me glaring. "Hope!" She said as she smacked me on my butt.

"Sorry, I can't help it," I confessed.

Buffy laughed. "My girlfriends used to love spending the night so that they could stare at him. We were seniors and he was just a measly freshman, but that didn't stop them all from inviting him to their prom."

I looked over at him again, before he disappeared into the pool house. "I believe it." I said biting my lip.

"Seriously, Hope, could you stop undressing him with your eyes?"

"Yes, sorry. Here let me take that out for you," I offered.

I picked up the tray of steaks and carried them out to the grilling station. My father was standing there waiting for me. "Thanks, sweetie."

"Can I have a beer, Dad?" I asked obnoxiously.

"No you can't, young lady!" He replied.

I rolled my eyes. The two assholes were drinking and one of them was the same age as me.

I caught Trevor looking at me, before calling me to come over where he and his brother sat. "What have you been up to, Hope?" He asked.

"Nothing much. Just hanging out here for the most part."

I saw Chance come out of the pool house again. Our eyes met for just a second, and it was so hard not to smile. He gave me a quick wink before anyone noticed he was there.

Trevor wasn't paying any attention to our new company. "Have you been to the beach lately? I could take you sometime if you wanted."

"Actually, I just went last week. It was the best day of my life." I said loud enough that Chance could hear.

He gave a half smile before I heard my father calling us all over from across the patio.

"Greg, I'd like you to meet Buffy's little brother Chance."

Chance extended his hand out to the old man. "Nice to meet you, sir."

Trevor's older brother jumped in. "Hey, is your last name Avery?" He asked.

I could see Chance tense up. "Yes, it is. Why?"

"I saw you play ball once. Man you're an awesome short stop. Where do you play now?" Michael asked.

Chance's jaw clenched. "My mother died not too long ago, and I decided to take some time off from ball."

"Man, you played like Ripken himself. I bet you could get picked up by a triple A team easy."

"Thanks. I haven't played in a while though," I could see how much that hurt Chance. I wished I could help him get his old life back.

"My name is Michael, by the way, but you can call me Mike." He held out his hand and shook with Chance. "So are you going to school around here this fall?"

He glanced over at me for a second. "Actually, I was considering it."

That's why he asked me. He wanted us to go together. I should have figured.

"You should check out Virginia Tech man, it's great there. I have some friends on the team and none of them can play like you."

"Maybe I will," Chance replied.

253

I sat down in a chaise lounge about six feet away from the guys. They seemed consumed in their baseball talks, and I started to relax knowing that Chance was being sociable.

I closed my eyes for a second and felt someone sit down beside me. When they opened I was met with Trevor's stare. His hair was lighter from being at the beach, but those lying blue eyes were exactly how I remembered them. "Hey, sexy. So what were we talking about before?" He asked.

"I don't remember!"

"Oh yeah, the beach. So who gave you the best time of your life?" He asked.

"None of your business, Trevor. Did you overlook the fact that we weren't together? Did you forget me telling you that you would never have any part of *this* again?" I waved my hands around my body.

"Oh, I remember. It turned me on."

I had to look away on account of wanting to literally slap that cocky grin off his face. "Trevor, please just leave me alone. We're not friends. We never really were."

"I never asked you to be my friend, Hope. You were my girlfriend. We fucked. That's all I wanted out of you." He laughed before standing up and heading in the direction of the guys. I hated him so much, and wondered if he was going to go over there and gloat about sleeping with me to Chance. Of course he wouldn't know that we were together, but that wouldn't stop him from putting it out there. I think all I ever was to him was someone that he could brag about. It made me sick to my stomach. More than anything I wanted this family gone from my house.

Buffy finally came outside with two margarita glasses in her hand. She handed me one and winked. My father noticed right away. "What are you doing giving her alcohol?"

"There isn't alcohol in hers, Mark," she said.

I took a sip and knew right away that she was lying. The tequila burned going down my throat. Buffy seized my arm and led me to the pool. "Come on, Hope, let's get in and relax."

I gave her a smile before realizing I was wearing the ugliest bathing suit. "Hey, Buff, where is that suit that I borrowed for the beach?"

"It's still in the laundry room. Why?"

"I'll be right back," I announced.

Trevor was an ignorant bastard, and he was never going to touch me again. He didn't deserve me, or anyone for that matter, and I felt like rubbing it right in his face.

31

Chance

I didn't feel like talking to these rich guys about how easy they had it, but Buffy asked me to be nice. She also told me that Trevor was Hope's ex. I could read between the lines. I saw what Mark was trying to do, and I didn't appreciate it. That was his daughter and he thought he could get in good with the father if the kids got along.

I was surprised Buffy hadn't caught on to that. She was usually really good about reading people.

I didn't know what Trevor had said to Hope, but after he walked away I noticed she was gone. Buffy was climbing into the pool, so I headed over to ask her. "Hey, where did Hope go?" I whispered.

"She um, you'll see I guess, but Chance, please remember to keep your cool tonight. I can't have you losing your shit and costing Mark this deal."

"You're scaring me, Buff. What's she up to?"

"She's putting on a bathing suit."

"What suit? Not the? Tell me it isn't that one." I asked, but my worst fears were confirmed when Hope came back out of the house. She immediately started removing the cover-up to reveal the skimpy bikini she wore for me at the beach. Every single one of her perfect curves was accentuated. I wanted to run over and hide her, and I certainly didn't want to have to watch them eying her up. This was pure torture.

Sure enough I saw Trevor and Mike standing there with their eyes all over her.

"This is just fucking great!" I said to my sister before walking back toward the guys.

Hope smiled at me in passing, but I was pretty pissed about her wearing that in front of them, well in front of anyone for that matter. I thought that suit had been for me, for our special day at the beach. I assumed that she wore that as a gift to me. Instead she was flaunting that body of hers all over the place. I wanted to punch something.

Once I got over to the guys I noticed that even Mr. Thomas was admiring Hope. I kept clenching my fists, avoiding making a big deal out of it in fear of Mark seeing me. Finally she got into the pool with my sister. Between the two of them, I wanted to bury myself. Was I the only one here that felt like they were being violated?

Trevor nudged my shoulder. "Dude, you are so lucky to live in this house."

"Why is that?" I asked, despite the fact that I knew what he was going to say. I just needed him to make one asshole comment and I'd bury him in the ground.

"Shit, if you ever saw Hope naked you'd know," Trevor announced then snickered.

It took every bit of my being not to take my beer bottle and hit him over the head with it. I could feel my hands trembling.

"I fucked up letting that one go. She was a great piece of ass," he added.

I downed my beer like I was in a race at a frat party. I had to remain calm. They couldn't know how I felt about Hope. "I guess I don't really look at her that way. I mean she's going to be Buffy's step-daughter."

"Dude, you are kidding right? Look at her and tell me you wouldn't hit that," Trevor taunted.

I reached in my pockets pretending I lost something. "Oh shit! Be right back, man." I said as I ran into the pool house. I checked every cabinet until I found a small bottle of Jaeger. I took two shots and grabbed my cigarettes. I happen to look down at my phone and saw I had a text.

When you see me in this suit just remember I belong to you. I love you, Chance. ~ H

I knew Hope was in the pool so I didn't write her back. I shoved the phone back in my pocket and took another shot. It was going to be a fucked up night.

When I got back outside Buffy had turned on music. Mike and Trevor were closer to the pool and when they saw me they waved me over. I held up my cigarette letting them know I would be a few minutes. Mark's view of me was restricted by bushes so I could look at Hope without being in trouble.

She was sitting next to Buffy sneering with her frozen drink in her hand. She spotted me and smiled. I mouthed the words "I love you".

Buffy saw me smoking. "When you're done get your butt in here with us, little brother."

258

I finished my cigarette and headed over to the pool. Mike ran behind me like he was my golf caddy and handed me a beer. "Thanks man."

"No problem. Hey you got anymore smokes? My dad doesn't know, but I really need one."

"Sure." I handed him one and my lighter and he disappeared behind the pool house.

Trevor sat next to me at the other end of the pool. "So who's Hope seeing?" He asked.

I took another drink and was thankful that I was already starting to feel the effects of the shots. "I have no idea. Why?"

"I just wanted to know what kind of douche bag she is putting out to now. I had to tell her I was a fucking virgin to get her to sleep with me. Her body is amazing, but she has no idea how to work it. It is a shame."

Calm down!

"Didn't you just say you wanted to sleep with her again?" I asked calmly.

"Well yeah, I'd fuck her every day if I could, but it ain't the best I ever had. She never even liked taking off all of her clothes. Hell, sometimes she was wearing more than she has on right now."

I wanted to smile so badly. Hope was nothing like he was describing. She loved being naked around me and our sex was amazing. As much as I wanted to kill this dude, I also wanted to laugh at him. He had no idea who she was, he never did.

"So how long were you together?" I asked.

"About a year. She said I just wasn't her type anymore. Whatever that shit means. If you ask me I think she may be batting on the wrong team, if ya know what I mean," he laughed.

"Yeah, I get it."

"Now her friend Rylee is a great piece of ass. She isn't as pretty, but damn that girl knows how to work it. We hooked up a couple times. I'd definitely hit that again," he noted.

"Man, did Hope find out?" I asked wondering if that broke up their relationship.

"Hell no! She would never talk to Rylee. Nah, we hooked up on nights where Hope had to study. A few times I drove her home and she gave me head. That was just mediocre though," he said all nonchalantly.

I really hated this dick. He needed to have the shit beat out of him. I didn't know what Hope even saw in him. He was such an asshole.

I tried to avoid looking in Hope's direction, but as the night progressed, and the girls got out of the pool to eat, I found myself glancing her way more often. It was friendly and nobody seemed to even notice it was happening. She would be caught up in a conversation and glance at me for just a second. When our eyes met we would turn away, but it let us know we were thinking about being together.

After dinner Buffy made herself and Hope more drinks. I could tell she was starting to relax more, because she was looking my way quite often. I knew it was time for me to get out of sight before her father discovered the real person she desired at this party.

I waved goodbye while walking to the pool house and closed the door behind me. It was hard being inside when I knew Hope was out there with that creep. I tried to watch television, but couldn't stop muting it to hear what was happening outside. When I noticed it had gotten quiet, I looked out the door. Everything had been turned off and I could see people standing in the kitchen. As I looked further I noticed that I couldn't spot Hope.

Just being curious, I tottered outside and lit up another cigarette. I kept hearing this sound, but I had no idea what it was. I sat on the picnic table and leaned back just relaxing. I figured Hope had gone up to bed and would text me when she was ready.

I put out my smoke and went to hide it in the flowerpot. As I turned around I heard the noise again. It was coming from the main house, but outside of it. It almost sounded like an injured cat crying. I turned the corner and tried to focus into the darkness and spotted three figures.

They also spotted me. I don't know what made me do it, but I started running toward them. All of a sudden two of them ran away and left one to fall to the ground. Once I got about five feet away I knew who the figure was.

It was Hope. She lay there on the ground with a ripped shirt and a busted lip, with her underwear down to her knees. I ran to her side.

"Hope, Jesus, are you okay?" I don't know why I said that because it was clear that she was anything but okay.

She was shaking profusely and seemed almost incoherent. I picked her up and started carrying her toward the kitchen door. I heard the voices out front and the sounds of car doors, but I ignored it and kept walking toward the house. Hope was my first priority. Once I knew she was okay, someone would have hell to pay.

Buffy was in the kitchen cleaning up and ran to get the door for me.

"Oh my God, Chance, what happened?"

"I went outside for a smoke and heard this noise

coming from the side of the house. When I ran over there they had her pushed up against the house. They left her there and ran away. I am going to fucking kill those little bastards."

"Chance, calm down. Get her sitting down and get me the first aid kit. Where is Mark? You need to go find Mark." Buffy frantically cried out.

Like a mad man I ran around from bathroom to bathroom until I found the kit, then I opened the front door to look for Mark. He was waving as a car pulled out of the driveway.

"Mark, you need to come in here. There is something wrong with Hope."

He followed me into the kitchen and couldn't believe his own eyes. His daughter who had just been fine was now beaten, shaking and bleeding.

"What the hell happened?" He ordered an explanation.

"I found them doing stuff to her beside the house. They ran away when I approached them." I explained quickly.

Mark looked confused. "You found who?"

"Seriously? It was Mike and Trevor. Who else would it be?" I asked.

I was getting more pissed by the minute. *Take care of your daughter.*

"I just saw them. They were acting fine. There is no way they would do something to Hope. They have known her since they were children. Now tell me what really happened, Chance, or I will be forced to call the police."

Buffy interrupted. "Mark, he wouldn't lie."

"Really, Buffy, I'm getting really tired of you taking up for him. You know what he is capable of. He probably heard all of the good things happening to those boys and got jealous." He turned to Hope. "Hope, honey did Chance do this to you?"

"No!" She said.

"Who did this to you, sweetie?" He asked.

"Chance saved me, daddy. He always does. He wouldn't do this." She said before breaking down and sobbing in Buffy's arms.

I had to look away for my own good, but I honestly couldn't take my eyes off of her. She was in pain, and I wanted to be the one holding her.

"This is impossible. Hope, tell me what happened," Mark demanded.

In between cries she held her bruised face up and started telling us how she was hanging up the wet towels when Mike came up and grabbed her from behind, pulling her to the side of the house. She said he held his hand over her mouth so that nobody would hear. Then she said that Trevor was there. He pulled down her shirt, ripping it, so that he could grope his dirty hands over her breasts, and then he reached between her legs and started fondling her. She said that when they heard me coming they ran away.

Mark was frozen, and I was waiting for an apology. "I wouldn't lie to you, Mark. It was those two little assholes. You need to call the police." I said while handing him a phone.

"I don't want to get the police involved. There's too much at stake here," he admitted.

Buffy kept shaking her head, her eyes filled with tears.

"You were going to call the police on me, but you won't call on them?" I asked, feeling so pissed. I looked over at Hope who was still in Buffy's arms. "I'll check on you later. I need to get the hell out of here, before I say something I might not regret," I announced, as I looked to Mark then headed out the door.

I wanted him to feel like shit. That was his daughter and he was choosing money over her. He was as low as they were.

32

Buffy stayed the night in my room with me. She held me tight just like my mother would have. I never had a sister, but she was just as close. I didn't care what she was to my father, I would always just think of her as my big sister.

My father came in the room several times to try and talk to Buffy, but she refused to speak to him. After time he stopped bothering us and we were able to go to sleep.

I heard my phone vibrating and Buffy got up and handed it to me. I already knew it was from Chance.

Are you okay, baby?~ C

Still shaken up. I can't believe that happened. Buffy is sleeping with me tonight. ~ H

Tell her not to leave your side. ~ C

She won't. ~ H

I wanted to hurt them, Hope. I still want to hurt them. ~ C

I do too. I love you, Chance. Thank you for saving me again. ~ H

I love you too, and I WILL ALWAYS SAVE YOU. See

you in the morning. ~ C

I put my phone down and nestled myself back under the covers.

"Did you tell him you were okay?" Buffy whispered.

"Yeah, he knows you're with me."

"I'm not going anywhere, Hope. I've been attacked by guys before. I know how scary it is," she admitted.

The next morning Buffy waited for me to get myself cleaned up before she even went to brush her own teeth. My lip was still swollen, but I wasn't as bruised as I'd first assumed. My face had a red mark over my eye, but that was it. I had one small bruise on my abdomen, and two giant marks resembling fingers on each of my arms.

Buffy insisted on taking pictures of each mark so that if my father came around we could give the documentation to the police. When I finally dressed into something comfortable, I waited downstairs for Buffy to get changed. Once she found me in the kitchen, she started making me something to eat. I sat up at the breakfast bar, my elbows on the countertop, leaning my chin on my fist.

"So have you seen Dad?" I asked her while she was buttering my toast.

"Nope, it looks like he left for work already."

I played with some sugar that had spilled onto the countertop, making funny shapes with my finger. "Thank you again, Buff."

"Hope, I love you. I want what's best for you, and I'll always be here no matter what happens with me and your father," she explained.

"I love you like a sister," I blurted out. "Our relationship is important to me.

Buffy turned around with a big smile on her face. I noticed her glancing toward the door so I turned to see what she was looking at. Chance was walking into the kitchen with a bunch of flowers in his hand. They were carnations and obviously weren't picked from someone's garden.

"Good morning, ladies. Hope, these are for you," he said as he leaned over and kissed my forehead.

Before he could stop me, I pulled him in for a hug. His arms wrapped around my back, and I felt completely safe. Having him comforting me only made my emotions go into overdrive. I began to sob against his chest, and when he didn't let go, it only reminded me what could have happened if he hadn't found me.

He rubbed my back, while I continued to cry. "It's okay, baby. I won't let them near you again. I promise."

I appreciated what Buffy had been doing, but Chance always saved me, even from myself sometimes. I couldn't get what Trevor did out of my head, but suddenly, with Chance's arms tight around me, I felt protected again.

"I love you." I whispered in his ear.

He leaned down and kissed my nose. "Me too."

Chance got himself some coffee and sat next to me to eat his breakfast. Buffy said she wasn't hungry, and I knew it was because she and my father were having problems over what happened to me. I appreciated that she took my side, but I felt bad for her being in the middle.

I wondered if she would've been on my side had Chance and I not been involved. Would she have just thought I was some spoiled brat kid, trying to get my daddy's attention?

Just as we finished eating we heard the door shutting. My father marched into the kitchen. He never even acknowledged me, but instead asked Buffy to come into his office. I felt hurt, but as they left the room Chance put his hand on my leg. "You okay?" He whispered.

"As long as you're here I'm fine."

We sat there leering at each other, until we heard loud hollering coming from the office. Chance and I both got up and crept closer to the hallway so that we could hear what they were saying.

"I won't let you do that, Mark. Do you have any idea what he has been through? You owe him an apology. I can't believe it was so easy for you to jump to conclusions about him. Was it that much easier for you to accuse my brother than those little assholes?" Buffy slammed.

"This business deal could determine our future. I can't let some misunderstanding affect that. Hope is going to be fine. She's a strong girl and she never has to see those boys again. I don't see why we can't just let it go," my father snapped back.

"Let it go? Are you fucking kidding me? Your daughter was sexually assaulted last night, and you want to let it go?" Buffy yelled.

"I would hardly say she was sexually assaulted, Buff..."

Buffy interrupted him. "If it weren't for my brother she could have been raped. They exposed her and fondled her. What is your fucking idea of sexual assault, because obviously we have different views?"

"I refuse to argue about this shit with you, Buffy. I've got too much riding on this deal to have teenage drama get in the way. Go find your brother. I need to speak with him." My father ordered.

We ran back into the kitchen until we saw Buffy

emerging. She had tears in her eyes, and I could tell she was not a happy camper. "Chance, Mark wants to see you."

I led her to sit down while I sat next to her.

The men's meeting wasn't loud like he and Buffy's. After about twenty minutes Chance came walking into the kitchen. He didn't say a word as he sauntered past us and headed outside.

Buffy got up and immediately went running after him. It killed me that I couldn't be outside with them, but I didn't want to get into trouble.

My father came into the kitchen and I turned to face him. "Hope, I'm very sorry about what happened. I wasn't aware of what Chance did for you. I didn't realize he would do something so noble. As far as what happened last night, I can only ask for you to try to let it go. I have too much at stake to ruin this deal, and I realize that's hard for you to understand. It's what has to be done."

My eyes filled with tears. I hated him.

I got up and ran outside toward the pool house. He wasn't going to keep me from checking on Chance. I didn't care if I lived out of my car.

As I got closer to the pool house, I could hear them yelling.

"I don't have a choice, Buffy." Chance was losing his calm demeanor, more by the second.

"You could have said no. Do you have any idea what this is going to do to her?" Buffy asked.

"Of course I do, don't you think this is killing me? I don't know what else to do. I'm kind of stuck, and Mark knows that. Can you blame him? He knows if I stick around I'm going to the authorities. If it was up to me they'd be in jail instead of with their daddy at some club. This is bullshit, and he knows it. It's not like it's forever. It's just until the deal is over. I'll be back. I've got no other options," he exclaimed.

My heart started beating faster. I knew something was wrong, so I rushed into the pool house and stood there waiting for an explanation.

"Maybe I should leave you two alone," Buffy suggested.

I shook my head. "No, please stay."

Chance pulled me over and sat me down on the chair. "Hope," he said before getting choked up. "I have to leave."

This couldn't be happening.

That son of a bitch didn't believe me last night, and then when he saw me protecting his daughter he couldn't take it.

He sat me down and asked how I felt about the whole ordeal, as if he gave a damn. I assume my answer set his plan into motion, because I told him there was no way that I was keeping my mouth shut about what Trevor and his brother had done to Hope. He must have made some calls last night or early this morning, because I was on the next flight to South Carolina to work on the construction of a hotel. He didn't give me an option. He said it was an opportunity I needed to take and that he had done a lot to get me the position.

I did not thank him. In fact, I wanted to hurt him. He was such a fucking coward. Now I'd have to abandon Hope when she needed me the most. It broke my heart, and it killed me more that I had to be the one to tell her. She was never going to understand.

"What do you mean you have to leave? Where are you going? When will you be home?" She asked.

My eyes filled with grief, and I didn't want to feel like a pussy, but this was torture. "Your father got me a job working on a construction site in South Carolina. It will last for a few months, and then he said I can come back."

"No! No way! This can't be happening. Why would you agree to it? Please, Chance, you can't just leave me here." Hope was clinging to my arms, her words becoming hard to make out, because she was crying so badly. "You can't leave. You can't leave me here all alone."

"Hope, I don't have a choice. I haven't had much time to think about this, but I assume he wants me to be out of the picture until this deal is finalized," I explained.

"Do either of you see how convoluted this is? I don't care about his freaking deal. He takes everything from me. First he broke up my family, and now he's ripping us apart," Hope screamed.

I tried to grab her, but she pulled away. "He doesn't even know about us, Hope. Would you please just listen to me?" She refused. Instead she buried her face into her hands. "Nothing between us has to change, baby. We can talk every

271

day, and I will find a way to come home on the weekends or something."

Buffy put her hands on Hope's shoulders and started rubbing her back. "In the meantime I can keep talking to your dad. We'll get Chance home as fast as we can," she assured us.

"No! This can't be happening. He saved me. He saved me last night and this is what happens? I don't understand." Hope sobbed harder, and it was excruciating for me to hear it. I watched her petite body shaking, not knowing what I could do to take the pain away.

I knelt down in front of her. "Hope, look at me."

She finally looked up past her tear filled eyes. "There isn't anything you can say to make this better. My father has done nothing but hurt me, and now he's taking the person that I love the most away from me."

"I know. Please just calm down. I know that things seem horrible right now, but we're still going to see each other. I'll call you every day. The months will fly by and then I'll be home," I explained. "I promise that I'll come back for you."

My heart was breaking even more seeing her reaction to all of this. I wanted to walk in that house and punch that bastard in his face. His daughter needed support, but instead he was torturing her, and he didn't even realize how much.

"I'm going to head into the house. Hope, don't be too long okay?"

The shades were down in the pool house, so that Hope's father couldn't see in if he were outside. "Hope, I love you. I promise you that we're going to get through this. I swear it."

She fell into my arms and I let her cry. I could feel

272

pain washing over me, so I held her tighter, trying to think positive, even though I knew we'd just hit yet another huge hurdle. "Why can't we just leave? We could run away, and they wouldn't be able to stop us," she suggested.

I wished it were that easy. "Hope, you're not eighteen. I could be charged with kidnapping."

"I would assure them that it wasn't true."

As much as she pleaded with me to understand, I knew how the law worked. "Baby, it's not that simple. I know it feels like it's a good idea, but I promise you that it isn't. If I take this job then I can come home to you. If we run away, we'll never be able to be a family. I don't want to lose my sister, and I know you don't want to be away from your mom. Please try to understand."

While I held her tight in my arms, we both went through the motions of saying goodbye. This wasn't easy, and I wasn't sure how I was going to be able to walk out that door when I knew she was so distraught. After all, Hope had changed me, giving me a reason to want to live. The idea of losing that was tough on me. What if she found someone else? She was young and beautiful, with a friend who liked to flaunt herself around town. Hope didn't know what Rylee had done with Trevor, but I did. She wasn't someone I trusted with my girlfriend.

To prevent any further repercussions, Hope retreated back to the main house, leaving me to pack alone. I can't say that I didn't lose it a couple of times, imagining how my life was fucked up yet again. It didn't matter where I turned, because somehow I was always in the line of fire. This time I was losing more than my self-worth.

I was facing the fear of losing Hope.

33

Hope

When Chance told me he had to leave, I felt like my whole world was crashing down on me. Buffy and I drove him to the airport and we both cried as he left to board his plane. I spent the entire ride home pleading with her to help me get him back. I begged her, but knew there was little she could do. My dad had his mind made up, and according to Buffy, this deal was the biggest he'd ever been involved in. It was so large that it would allow him to retire early.

I understood my father's reasoning for wanting to keep the peace temporarily, but I couldn't accept that he'd sent Chance away, and neglected the fact that I was assaulted. A crime had been committed, yet he'd done nothing.

I wished that there was a way to prove to my dad that he was destroying me. More than anything I wanted to tell him that we were in love, and that he was breaking my heart.

Chance called us once he'd made it there safely, and later that night before he went to sleep. He met his new boss, and had checked into the motel where he'd be staying at.

That first evening he called me to tell me he was going to bed, I immediately broke down, just hearing his voice. I closed my eyes before saying anything, imagining that he was only ringing me from his cell phone in the pool house. "I miss you so much, already."

"I miss you too, baby. The time is going to pass by quickly. Before you know it I'll be home. I promise."

"You shouldn't have even left, Chance. I can't believe this is happening." My sobs kept me from being able to continue. I had to take a few breaths to control my emotions. "I wish you were holding me."

"Close your eyes. Don't say you are and you really aren't. Seriously, just do it."

I followed his directions, feeling like it was a stupid idea. "Okay. They're closed."

"Can you feel my arms around you now?"

"No." I refused to play this juvenile game. This wouldn't solve the emptiness in my heart.

"Hope, please just appease me. Close your eyes and imagine us being back on that beach, the sounds of the waves are crashing as we look out at the setting sun on the horizon." He paused a second. "Are you with me?"

I nodded with my eyes shut, even though he couldn't see me. "Yes," I whispered.

"Good. Can you feel my arms wrapped around the front of your body? You're leaning against my chest, and your body is so warm, baby. The wind keeps whipping your hair around, and the mist of the incoming waves are causing it to dampen."

"I remember," I said as I imagined being there in his arms, so tightly held, safe, and happy.

"When I miss you I think about that moment. I picture

us together, where no one can hurt us. It's just me and you and that big ocean. We may be miles away at the moment, but you're with me when I close my eyes. Your dad may have sent me away, but it's not going to change what we have."

"How am I supposed to put on a straight face when I'm going to be missing you so much?"

"Tell him it's stress from what happened to you. Make his ass sweat bullets for not nailing those two little pricks to the wall."

"Believe me, I plan to. If he thinks for one minute I'm going to let that go, he's got another thing coming." I had so much pent up anger when it came to my father, and it wasn't just because of his latest acts. It was derived from years of not being around.

"Are you gritting your teeth? I can hear it in the way you change your voice. It's so cute. I can picture the way you tighten up your lips, and squint your eyes."

"Stop. I don't do that." I sat up and looked at my reflection in the mirror, making that same face, and holding in my hysterics because he was spot on.

"You do so." Chance snickered. "You're so cute when you're defensive."

"Well you're so cute when you're shirtless."

"Is that so?" He was taunting me to continue. "What if I told you that I was shirtless right now? Are you picturing that?"

"I am now," I giggled.

"Maybe you should take off your shirt. I mean, it's only fair if I have something sexy to picture."

I plopped down on my bed, letting my head hit the pillow. I wasn't removing my shirt if I didn't have to. "I'm already in my bra."

"You're full of shit, Hope. Come on. Go lock your door and get naked for me. I'm going to give you a bedtime story, and it requires your undivided cooperation."

As humiliating as it felt. I put the phone on the mattress and began taking off my clothes. While I knew he could still hear me, I spoke. "This better be worth it, Chance. If you tell anyone I did this, you'll be sorry."

He laughed. "Don't worry, baby. I won't tell if you don't."

"I can't believe I'm doing this." My bedroom door was already locked, so I climbed under my covers, feeling modest even with being all alone in the room.

"Are you naked?"

"Obviously. Do you want me to tell you that I'm touching myself," I asked sarcastically.

Chance hooted. "This would be a lot easier if you went along with it."

"This is incredibly weird. I'm all alone in my room. Do people actually do this?"

"Close your eyes and run your fingers over one of your nipples."

"No."

"Just shut up and do it. Please, baby. I need this."

When he put it that way I knew I had to go through with it. I closed my eyes, reluctantly grazing my nipple with my nails. Immediately my body reacted to the touch. "Mmm, I'm doing it."

"Good girl. Now slide that hand down further and touch your pussy. I bet it's so warm."

I continued down until I reached that spot. My smooth skin was in fact warm, just liked he'd said.

"Now slip your fingers inside and start rubbing

yourself. Do it the way my tongue feels. Pretend it's me getting you off."

I moaned. "It's nice."

"Hope, I'm so hard."

I wanted to laugh, but knew I'd ruin the moment. The idea of us both being alone on a bed made me snicker to myself anyway. "So what are you going to do about it?"

"Oh, I'm going to let you suck it. That's what."

Hearing him boast about what he wanted me to do sent chills throughout my already sensitive body. I knew we weren't physically able to be together, and while Chance was making the best of the situation, I finally subdued myself into accepting that this was the only way. "You want me to lick it first?"

He groaned, causing me to react with a huge grin. He was totally getting aroused from this. I too was feeling new sensations. "Suck it hard, Hope. Keep rubbing yourself. I'm close, baby."

I rubbed myself harder, keeping my eyes closed as I envisioned his tongue doing all the work. Even before I heard his deep breathing on the phone, or the sound he made when his body tensed up, I was already beginning to convulse. My ass lifted off the bed as I continued massaging my throbbing clit. In a matter of minutes I'd brought myself to climax, and although it was hot, I felt a bit ashamed, as if it was naughty. I waited for Chance to reply, since I felt a tad bit embarrassed.

"I made a mess," He laughed to himself. "I better let you go so I can clean myself up. Thanks for playing along, Hope."

"You're welcome. It was ... interesting."

"You liked it. I know you did."

"I wish you were here. It's not the same."

"I'll be home before you know it. Listen, I'll call you when I get done with work. I'll be thinking about you until then."

I pulled the covers up to my neck, refusing to redress when my body was still sensitive. "Me too. Goodnight, Chance."

After we'd hung up I stared at my ceiling, trying to come up with a simple solution to being able to act normal when my heart was breaking to pieces. This wasn't a choice that either of us would have made. There was one person to blame for my utter loneliness, and unfortunately I shared a blood connection to him.

I refused to speak to my father, even at meals when he sat at the same table with us. Buffy finally gave in and started talking to him after holding out for a week. He seemed remorseful, but the damage was done.

Chance called me at least twice a day. He called to wake me up in the mornings and then to tell me goodnight; although, sometimes our nighttime talks would last for hours. One good thing about him being away was that we got to communicate a lot more than we did around the house. We didn't really have to hide. Since I spent most of my time in my room, my father never even knew, not that I even cared.

Buffy called Chance every few days, always making it a habit to bring it up at dinner time when my father was around. She talked about how much he hated it, and wished he could be here where his only family was.

Obviously, the news of Chance being homesick did not faze him in the least. He played golf with Mr. Greg at least once a week. They shot the shit over the phone, and I even heard him mentioning Trevor and Michael in a positive conversation.

Since my mother had finally moved into her new home I wondered if I could get away from my father, but once I saw the size, I knew why she hadn't asked me in the first place. It was tiny and only had one bedroom.

Her boyfriend Sam was a great guy. He had an outstanding sense of humor and seemed to be madly in love with her. I could tell immediately why she was so crazy about him. He made me promise that once a week I would come over to his place and have dinner with him and my mother. She was thrilled that he'd asked and I knew I'd keep that promise.

Day after day I looked for things to do to get me out of the house. I called Rylee so many times that I'd started wondering if she was angry at me. I kept getting this vibe that maybe Chance didn't care for her, even though they'd never officially met, except for that night in the bar.

Finally, one night while on the phone, Chance told me why. He explained how Trevor said he and Rylee had slept together behind my back. I'd been going on and on about her being such a trustworthy friend and he said he couldn't take it anymore. Words could not even describe how betrayed I felt. We'd been best friends for so long, and it was difficult to fathom her doing something that would destroy that trust I'd had for her. I got so angry about it that I finally called her, ready to ream her out for being a shitty person.

At first she denied it, making me feel guilty about accepting it as the truth. I was content to believing that Trevor had made the whole thing up to get to me, but soon after she called me crying saying that it happened a couple times when they were drinking.

I said a few choice words to her and simply hung up, shocked by her actions, and disgusted that she'd done them.

She called me repeatedly until I finally answered after letting the news sink in for over twenty-four hours. "Hope, please hear me out. I need to tell you -."

I cut her off. "Save it, Rylee. Trevor is a loser, and if you want to waste your time with someone like him, that's your business. As far as our friendship goes, well it's going to take me a while to trust you again. The thing is, I've moved on. I broke up with Trevor a long time ago, because he was an asshole. Now I have a boyfriend that loves me, and treats me with respect. If hooking up with my sloppy seconds is what you prefer, go ahead. Karma is a bitch."

"Hope, wait. Don't hang up. I'm sorry. I swear I am."

"Rylee, I don't care. You screwed my boyfriend behind my back, and I don't even care. I'm that happy with Chance. He's a man, which is something Trevor will never be."

"Please don't hate me. I love you, Hope. You're my best friend." She was sobbing on the other end of the call. I don't know why, but I felt sorry for her pathetic ass.

"I need time to get over what you've done to me."

"Okay. I understand." She paused and I heard her sniffling. "I'll always be there for you, Hope."

I hung up before I could say something that I would in turn regret. Unlike my untrustworthy friend, I clung to the hope that one day we could mend whatever had been broken. By the end of that day I was content with not talking to her until I could get over the shock of it all.

Since I was so overjoyed with mine and Chance's relationship, I knew I should just let it go. I had enough to worry about, like figuring out how I was going to sneak off to see my boyfriend.

Some days, I would spend all of my time in the pool house. I told my father I went in there to study, but I never really did. What I actually went there for was to catch a hint of Chance, whether it was on his sheets, or even on his clothes in the closet. I'd made his bed, and then climbed in it so many times that I'd lost count. It never happened without tears. I felt lost, lonely, and destroyed.

Chance convinced me to enroll in community college to get me out of the house, so when September came around I gladly found reprieve. I was enrolled in three classes that kept me occupied enough to where I wasn't utterly miserable with depression.

Then, just when I thought nothing else could bring me down, I got news that would utterly take my breath away. It was an early morning that my father caught me in the kitchen. Buffy wasn't anywhere in the room, and just as I turned to head out to get away from him, I noticed him covering his face with his hands. "Hope, we need to talk."

My heart began to race as I faced him, seeing the hurt in his eyes. Right away I panicked, assuming he knew about my relationship with Chance. Perhaps he was coming clean that he'd known all along and sent him away for that very reason. Nothing could have prepared me for what came out of his mouth. I sat down in front of him, waiting for the blow that could end everything.

"I'm listening."

"Honey, I didn't want to be the one to tell you this, but your mom is in the hospital."

"Did she get into an accident? Oh my God is she going to be okay?" Right away I was worried.

He looked down as he responded. "The thing is, she's been sick for a long time now."

"Sick? Does she have pneumonia or something?" I was confused. I'd talked to my mother and she hadn't mentioned a cold. In fact, she seemed happy with her new boyfriend, and her little apartment.

"Look, your mom didn't want to worry you. She thought she could beat this without you having to find out."

"Find out what?" There was no point of him beating around the bush. I needed answers. "Dad, please tell me."

"She's got Myocarditis."

Before he could explain more I blurted out, "What's that?"

He motioned for me to give him a moment. "It's a heart condition. She's had it for years, always knowing this day might come."

He was scaring me. "What are you saying? Is she going to die?" Saying those words made me immediately begin to tremble. My teeth shattered as tears dripped down my cheeks. "Just tell me the truth."

"She's being treated for it. It can be very serious."

"So she could die?"

"Hope, we can't even think like that right now." It actually shocked me that he seemed to care.

I shook my head. People said that when things were bad. "No, this can't be. I've lived with her my whole life. She's taken care of me, and worked a normal job. The only time I've ever seen her cry was when you left. She can't have what you're saying. You have to be wrong."

"I wish I was. Listen, I know you're upset, but this is the real reason you moved in with me. She knew her health was failing. That apartment she moved into is closer to her doctor. She's been aware all along that there would come a time when she'd need more progressive treatments."

I was in denial. There was no way my mother would have lied about something so serious. She'd always taught me to be honest. "Where is she? I need to see her, so she can tell me this is all a mistake. You're just trying to hurt me." I stood up and ran out of the house, desperate to find my mother, and put my fears to ease. I didn't even make it to my car before hunching over with disbelief. I couldn't fathom that this was actually happening. More importantly, how could she have hid something this severe?

My father came rushing out of the house toward me. He lifted me up and held me in his arms. Though still angry with everything we were going through personally, I clung to him for comfort. He kissed the top of my head as I lost all control of myself. To be honest, I don't even know how long we stood there in the middle of the driveway. Once I'd finally settled down enough, my father pulled away. "Hope, your mother asked me to bring you to the hospital to see her. She wants to talk to you about what's going on. It's going to be okay."

As much as I wanted to see her, I didn't know how to look at her lying in that hospital bed. My mother had always been my rock. She'd protected me, seeming like the strongest person on the planet. Now, all of a sudden, I was being told she was weak. Her fragile state left her vulnerable. It almost felt like she was a stranger to me.

As reluctant as I was, I loved my mother, and knew she needed me. After all, she'd given me the best life she could. She taught me how to be the woman I'd become. I owed her everything. Convinced that I was going to be strong, I agreed to allow my father to take me to the hospital.

During the ride I didn't hold back from breaking down. More than anything I wanted to call Chance, because I knew he'd somehow be able to soothe me. Instead I was sitting next to my father, who'd time and time again let me down.

Once inside of the hospital it became obvious early on that my father had visited before. He knew where to lead me, and once we reached her room, he motioned for me to enter alone. I looked back at him before making my way inside.

No words could begin to describe how I felt when I saw my mother in that bed. Hooked up to monitors, she turned to see me approaching. I watched her reaching a hand out for me to grab. Once I'd taken it, she smiled while displaying weak eyes. "Hi, mom."

"Hi," she said in a whisper.

It was impossible to try to remain calm. There was no way that I could see her in this kind of condition and not feel overwhelmed. This woman meant everything to me. "I'm sorry."

"Please don't cry."

I wiped my face off and faked a smile. "Sorry. This is a lot to take in."

"I'm glad you're here." I could tell she was struggling to communicate. "It's going to be okay."

"I don't understand."

"It's never been this bad before. The medicine makes me loopy. We thought it was time you knew the truth, just in case."

"Are you going to die?" I had to know the truth. I was still in denial that this was really happening. This woman, so fragile, wasn't the person who'd raised me. This wasn't the same woman that cursed under her breath at my father. I barely recognized her, which was odd because we'd been together recently.

She attempted to squeeze my hand, but failed. "I'm

trying not to."

I turned when I heard someone coming in the room. A nurse, wearing cat scrubs came inside and began checking vitals. She smiled when our eyes met. "I'll just be quick."

"I need to know more. Is there a doctor I can talk to?" It was too hard for my mother to speak in full sentences. I needed someone to give it to me straight.

"Let me page the doctor for you." She jotted down the information and headed back outside.

While I waited, I smoothed out my mother's hair, helped her sip on some ice water, and sat on the edge of the bed to be closer to her. Finally an older man entered. He held out his hand. "My name is Dr. Hodgins. I'm your mother's physician."

"I need to know what's going on. Please, can you tell me what's happening to my mom?"

He nodded. "Sure. Your mom suffers from something called Myocarditis. It's a condition with the heart where an infection causes inflammation."

"Is she going to die?" Maybe he would give me a straight answer.

"I'm treating your mom with systemic corticosteroids. Even though this bout is the worst she's suffered, I'm optimistic she'll be back to herself in a week or so. Of course, because we're dealing with the heart, we need to keep her in the hospital until she improves."

"And then what? Won't it come back again?"

"Your mother can live a normal life as long as we remain one step ahead of this. Because her heart doesn't work normally, she's required to stay on medication, which also prevents these flare ups. In rare cases a transplant is an option, though we're not near that degree as of yet."

I was trying to process everything he said, yet the transplant scared the shit out of me. The idea of my mom being on some waiting list to receive a heart, that she'd probably never get, was horrifying.

I sank down in the chair next to the bed, covering my face to hide my tears. This was not how I saw my day going, and the image of my mother next to me in this bed was something I couldn't soon forget. I hated how weak she looked, and that there was nothing I could do for her.

My father came into the room after speaking to the exiting doctor. He had a soda in his hand and offered it to me. "Here. Drink some ginger ale."

By this point my mom had fallen asleep. She finally looked peaceful, which made it easier to look in that direction. "I don't want to leave her."

"They won't allow you to stay the night, Hope."

"I'm staying here, dad. I don't care about the rules. I'll hide in the closet if I have to."

My father wasn't amused by my announcement. "Don't be ridiculous. We're going home. You can come back tomorrow. By then she'll have improved. The doctor said she's doing great."

I kept staring at my sleeping mother as I spoke. "Can I get what she has?"

He reached over and touched my shoulder, causing me to look up at his standing body. "No. It's not genetic, Hope. Most of the time it's contracted virally."

"I can't lose her, dad." There was this constant burning in my throat as I swallowed back my tears. "I'll never be able to live with myself if something happens to her and I wasn't here. Please, let me stay. If I get in trouble I'll call you. After everything you've put me through, I think you could at least have some compassion."

"Hope, about that," he started.

"Save it, dad. I've got enough on my plate, don't you think?"

I don't know if it was the way I peered into his soul, or the fact he knew I wasn't going to budge from my seat. My father sighed and leaned over to kiss me on the head, before heading out.

I honestly don't know how long I sat there after that listening to monitors. When my mother didn't wake up again, I must have fallen asleep. Before I knew what was happening, a nurse came in with a pillow and blanket. At first I was startled until she began to cover me up. I looked right at her, shocked that she was allowing me to stay. With only a smile on her face, she checked my mother's vitals and exited the room, closing the door all the way behind her.

Settled that they were allowing me to stay, I stood up and sauntered over to the edge of the bed. My sleeping mother still looked so comfortable, and I didn't want to wake her, so I spoke in a whisper. "I still can't believe you were sick. Why didn't you tell me, mom? I spent the last year so caught up in school that I didn't even notice something could be wrong with your health. I feel like it's my fault that you're in here. You've been under so much stress, with the sale of the house, and everything else." I reached my hand up to touch her cheek. "Please don't die on me. You've got to recover so I can tell you about the man I'm in love with. Dad wouldn't understand. He sent him away, and now I feel so lost. The two people I care about the most are hurting, and I don't know what I can do to make it better. I feel so worthless." When I began to cry again, I knew it was time to back away from the bed before I woke her. She didn't need the extra stress of

worrying about me. For now I was content with her waking up and seeing me beside her.

34

Hope

Watching my mother recover was sometimes agonizing. It took me a whole day to conjure up the courage to talk about it with Chance. By then he'd called me numerous times without getting an answer. I was too distraught to turn my phone on and begin to comprehend how to explain everything that was happening.

I wasn't just broken from his absence, but also torn to pieces as I watched my mother fighting to heal. I think once I'd told him everything it calmed his nerves. He seemed genuinely worried about my well-being. I assured him that I would get through it, but knew it caused another strain on our already struggling relationship with him being so far away.

I think that I'd originally given his leaving so much attention that when I made my mom first priority it seemed as if I was pushing him away. It wasn't on purpose, but it didn't make it easier for Chance, who was seemingly all alone.

My mother was able to return home after eight days in the hospital. Her boyfriend drove us over to her apartment, and helped me get her comfortable. She still wasn't cleared to work, but at least could be home. I slept on her couch for an entire week, preparing her food, and helping her get cleaned up. She assured me that she was well enough to do it herself, but my fear of losing her had kicked in, not allowing me to let her out of my sight.

I think by the thirteenth day she was sick of me. She sat me down and begged me to go home. Perhaps she wanted alone time with her new boyfriend, or maybe I was a little annoying. At any rate, I reluctantly left.

I think it took me a while to understand that she was better. The flare up had gone away, and she got back to her normal lifestyle, with the help of medication as a preventative. Without having to focus on her twenty-four-seven, I was faced with the agony of the fact that I'd ignored my boyfriend. We'd still talked, but it certainly wasn't as much. Two times a day had turned to one short goodnight call. Chance seemed distant, and I wondered if our time apart was changing how he felt about me. He was an attractive man. For sure he could go out and find someone that would give him attention.

Day after day I dwelled on what he could be doing behind my back. Sure, each night he'd say those three words before hanging up, but the connection felt broken. I think the more time that passed made it even harder for me. I played out scenarios in my head of driving down to South Carolina to catch him cheating. Finally, I couldn't take it any longer. I went to Buffy for answers.

"Can we talk?" I asked as I sat down on the couch next to her.

"Sure, what's up?" She didn't take her eyes away from the television.

"Do you think Chance has another girlfriend?"

She seemed shocked as she turned to face me. "Why would you think that?"

"I don't know." I shrugged. "I guess he seems distant."

"Hope, he's two states away. From what he tells me, he's super homesick. Had it not been for your mom getting sick I'm sure he would have asked me to sneak you down to see him. As far as finding someone else, my brother can be difficult, but he's honest. If there was someone else, he'd tell you."

I appreciated that she was giving it to me straight, but it still didn't settle my roaming mind. The only way I was going to be at peace was if I confronted the actual source.

I waited until he called that night to address my concerns.

"Hey, baby. How's it going?"

"It's good. I miss you, Chance."

"That's good to hear. I miss you too." I could hear giggling in the background. My stomach literally dropped.

"Is someone there with you?" I'd considered how I was going to ask him if he was cheating on me, but this changed everything.

"What? No. It's just me. I'm in my room." More giggling, and it was definitely a female.

"Chance, you can tell me the truth. I'm a big girl. I can handle it. What I can't handle is a liar."

"Hope, it's not what you think."

That's all I need to hear to end the call. That was a classic line to try to get out of trouble. I wasn't having it.

Chance had someone else in his room while he was calling me. I hung up the phone, and ignored the slew of callbacks from his number. When I refused his calls, he rang his sister's phone. She walked in my room, sat her phone down on my dresser and headed back out. I could hear him yelling my name, but put my ear buds in to ignore him. I'd been cheated on before, but somehow this was way worse. Maybe it was because I was absolutely in love with this man. It wasn't a puppy love either. It was deep, and he obviously didn't feel the same. All I could think is that it was all my fault. Had I not ignored him to take care of my mother maybe I could have held onto him while he was away.

I cried myself to sleep with visions of him sleeping with other women. The more I pictured them, the worse they were. I felt sick to my stomach imagining someone else touching him the way I had. I wondered if he kissed them with passion, and if they offered something extra that I didn't know how to do. I became upset with myself, so much that I knew I wasn't going to sleep until we had it out. If he thought he could screw whoever he wanted, he needed to hear how hurt I was.

It was four in the morning when I picked up my phone and dialed his number. After three rings he answered with a groggy voice. "Hope?"

"How could you?"

I could hear him adjusting. "You're freaking out about nothing."

"Nothing? Do you have a zip code rule or something?"

"What the fuck are you talking about? It's four in the morning, and after spending hours trying to get you on the phone, I'm exhausted. Whatever you think I did, you're way off base."

"I heard female voices. I heard her laughing when I asked you questions."

This made Chance laugh, which pissed me off. "Baby, you're being irrational."

"Are you laughing at me?"

"It's shocking how jealous you are, that's all. I think it's time I come home for a visit to reassure you that you're my girl."

I hated that he was being almost comical about it. "Don't bother. When you come home I won't be here. I can't stand cheaters."

"You think I'm cheating on you? I should be the one who's mad here. Obviously my girlfriend has no faith in what we share together."

"I heard the voices. Stop lying to me. Please, Chance, be decent and tell me the truth."

He sighed loudly against the receiver. "Fine, you want the truth?"

"Yes, that's why I called. I want you to have the balls to break my heart, asshole."

He laughed again. "This is bullshit."

"It is," I agreed.

"Get your computer, Hope."

"What? Screw you. Just tell me the truth."

"I'm trying to. Get your damn computer so I can get this over with and go to bed."

I located my laptop and opened it. A video chat was coming through from Chance so I accepted it. "I'm sending you a file, but it's too big to text. Don't you dare hang up."

I waited as it loaded and came through. As the video played I couldn't believe what I was seeing. The giggling I recognized right away, I just couldn't understand how I'd been so mistaken.

When I was silent he took it upon himself to address me. "I think you owe me a fucking apology, Hope. How the hell does someone cheat on their girlfriend, with their girlfriend?"

I kept watching the video of me in the pool, swimming around and laughing at something Buffy was saying. I hadn't known he'd recorded me, but there it was plain as day. There was no mistaking the voice I heard. Chance had been telling the truth, and I felt like shit.

"Oh, God. Chance I'm so-."

"Forgive me for being blunt, but I'm going back to bed. The next time you want to accuse me of some kind of bullshit, make sure you ask first."

"Chance, wait!"

He hung up the phone before I could get another word in edgewise. I felt so horrible that I didn't sleep for the rest of the night. By morning I was so exhausted that it was impossible to move from my bed. My depression only escalated when Buffy came in the room to get her phone and I had to explain what happened. I could see the disapproving stare she gave me before walking out.

Crying wasn't going to solve anything, though. I knew better than to think that sobbing all alone in my room was going to make me feel better. Since I wanted to be alone, I decided to spend the day in the pool house, in Chance's bed. I wasn't sure how long I'd been sleeping, but woke to my phone ringing. I picked it up without even checking to see who the caller was, on account of my ears being oversensitive. "Yeah?"

"Yeah? Is that how you apologize?"

I sat up in his bed, realizing Chance was waiting for me to answer. "Sorry. I didn't expect it to be you."

"Who else would it be?"

"I said I was sorry."

"I can't believe that you thought I had some random chick in my room, Hope. It's hard enough being here without you, but now I've got to worry about my girlfriend losing her shit."

"Why didn't you just tell me that you had a video of me?"

"I tried to last night, before you went all ballistic."

I felt so ashamed of my actions. "I'm so stupid."

"Hope, I love you. Before all that shit happened last night I was going to tell you that I got a weekend off. I'm coming home to see you."

My mouth dropped. "Seriously? You're coming home?"

"Not for good. The job's still not done. I've got a weekend, and I plan on spending every moment with you."

"So you're not mad at me for being an idiot?"

"Yeah, I'm mad. You didn't trust me. It sucks." I could hear how much it affected him. Trust was a serious issue for Chance, and I'd overlooked that when I accused him of being with someone else.

"I'll make it up to you."

"You better. I expect lots of kissing, and having my way the whole time I'm there."

I giggled, reminding me of the one I'd heard over the phone. "That can be arranged." Immediately I felt warm all over my body.

"Good. I'll call with the details of my flight."

I was giddy. Chance was coming home to visit, and I

couldn't wait to wrap my arms around him. "I love you."

"I know you do. I'll call you later, baby." When he hung up everything had changed. I had something to smile about, and I don't think I could have frowned even if I tried my hardest.

After two long months of agony Chance got three days off to come and visit. Buffy never mentioned it to my father, but he was rarely home anyway. The new strip mall was taking up all of his time. Buffy said she would tell my dad I was staying at a friend's house, so that Chance and I could have the night together.

I drove to the airport myself to pick him up. I was so excited that I missed my exit twice, and when I finally pulled up to get him, I locked my keys in the car with it running. While a nice officer got my car opened, I spotted Chance walking towards me. I ran as fast as I could and jumped into his arms. He swung me around as I squeezed him tight.

This was the moment that I'd waited so long for. I felt complete, like nothing else in the world mattered.

Chance

Hope had no idea how much I missed her. I couldn't believe she was finally here in my arms. I tried to get home to see her every week, but my boss was a real prick. Apparently the hotel we were building had a deadline, and if we finished it ahead of schedule they got a bonus. The crew had to work on weekends and one guy got one weekend off at a time. Since I was the newest on the crew, I was the last person to get that benefit.

Being away from Hope had been so hard on me, but I tried to keep myself busy. I impressed the bosses by working overtime almost every night. Little did they know it was because I didn't want to sit in my motel room and miss Hope anymore than I already did. I would work late enough to where I could go back to my room and call her, and then crash for the night. I felt like a robot, falling into the same daily routine for two months.

Having her back in my arms felt like heaven. "God, Hope, I missed you so much."

She pulled away only to press her lips against mine. "I missed you too."

I looked around and noticed she was alone. "Where's Buffy?"

"She said she wanted to give us the night together. We have a room about a mile from here," Hope explained.

I couldn't help but smile. "Really? A whole night alone? No interruptions?"

Hope nodded and bit down on her lip. It was a little reaction, yet so sexy to me.

"What are we waiting for then?" I said as I picked her up and carried her to the car.

I was surprised when an officer gave Hope her keys. "Have a good day, ma'am."

"I locked them in the car." She explained while getting into the passenger side.

I climbed in the driver's side, snatched the keys out of her hand and started up the vehicle. We made it to the hotel in less than five minutes. Apparently, Buffy had paid cash for a room and reserved it under my name. Hope waited patiently as I checked in and got the room keys. When we reached the inside of the elevator I couldn't control myself. I pulled Hope into my arms and kissed her bottom lip. My tongue slid over it and then made its way into her mouth. When hers brushed against mine for the first time, I became instantly aroused. It had been too long.

The sound of the elevator opening made us break out of our lip-lock. An old woman with a walker waited for us to exit. She was shaking her head and giving us dirty looks. We laughed as we passed her.

Hope and I made it into the hallway and finally located our room. Once the card slid into the key slot the green light lit, and I flung the door open. Our bags dropped at our feet and we made it to the bed without even noticing what the room looked like. I didn't want to waste a single second with her, because we'd both been deprived for months.

Hope's hands gripped my shirt and guided it over my head. Her lips were pressed against mine again, until I pulled away. "Don't you want to slow down?" I asked between kisses.

"No!" She stated while starting to kiss me on my chest. I'd been standing, but she tugged me down on the bed next to her, immediately beginning to unbutton my jeans. "Please don't slow down, Chance. I want you inside me. I need to feel what it's like again."

Her shirt had buttons, but it didn't once I was finished tearing it open, revealing her see-through white bra. It hooked in the front, and I didn't waste time freeing her beautiful breasts. While she finished removing it off of her arms, I cupped both of her mounds and pinched them with my fingers. "I missed these."

Hope bit down on her lip while slipping off her pants. They were made from some stretch kind of fabric that took no time to disappear from her legs. Fortunate for me, her panties came down with them.

Hope lay naked on the bed beneath me and I couldn't help but take in her beauty. She was still as beautiful as I remembered. I stood up to finish removing my pants, but I never took my eyes off of hers. When I climbed back down on top of her, I immediately found her lips. If I could kiss her all night I would have been happy. Her soft skin played against mine as her tongue slid into my mouth. Our kisses deepened and our teeth kept clanking as they intensified. My hand cupped one of her breasts and I used my fingers to pull her little nipple toward my lips. Hope's body flexed and she let out a moan as I sucked it in hard, making a sound myself when I finally let go.

Her legs intertwined with mine. She used her strength to flip herself on top of me, sitting straight up. I couldn't help but admire her body, while she took her fingers and ran them over my face, slowly moving it across my lips, so that I could kiss them as they continued moving down. They made their way down my neck and then to my abdomen. When she reached my navel she slid her hands back up against my chest. "I think your muscles are bigger." She said as she leaned down and kissed my bare skin. Her hips were moving back and forth against me and I knew she could feel how ready I was.

"Did you miss me, Chance?" She asked, while trying to catch her breath.

"Obviously," I said, as I seized her by the waist and started rocking her harder against me.

Her hands reached up and cupped both of her own breasts. "I can't believe you're here with me. I want you. Make love to me."

"Oh, you want me, do ya? Show me how much. Give me a reason to savor every single inch of this body until we're both satiated. Please," I requested.

Hope smiled as she sat up enough for me to slide right inside of her. We both shuttered with the first thrust, but then I slowed our pace down as our hips worked together. I held Hope's ass and used my arms to push myself inside of her deeper. She moaned, but it wasn't because she was in any pain. Her fingernails dug into my chest as she cried out, seemingly being carried away with ecstasy. It stung, but also felt good. "Oh yes!" I called, as she began moving faster. I

301

tried to follow with her rhythm, but lost myself in the moment of my own release. I pulled Hope down onto my chest and clung to her until I finally lost all control of myself. My body began to spasm while I closed my eyes and felt that ecstasy I'd been deprived of. Hope stayed close and tickled my stomach as she lay on one side of me. I kissed her forehead. "I love you."

"I know." She said. I could tell she smiled from the way her voice sounded.

35
Hope

Waking up with Chance next to me was the happiest I'd been in two months. His strong arms were wrapped around me and even though I was wide awake, I refused to move. Last night had been amazing and after three separate encounters we finally fell asleep. I wasn't sure what time it was, but it didn't even matter. As long as I was here with him, nothing could be better.

When he finally stirred, gently kissing my forehead, I slid my mouth up to his. I missed his lips, more than I wanted to admit. It made me seem pathetic.

"Good morning, baby," Chance whispered.

"It is good," I replied.

"What time do we need to check out?" Chance asked. I shrugged. "Ten."

"Want to get a shower before we go?"

"I really don't want to go. I don't want to have to pretend that you mean nothing to me. I waited too long for you to come home." I was sick of all of it. Once and for all my dad needed to be told the truth. He couldn't keep us apart.

Chance sat up and cupped my face into his hands. "You think I want that? Hope, I have counted down every single day until I could see your beautiful face in person. All the pictures and video chatting was great, but this is what kept me going; knowing that one day I could come home to you. I promise you that if I have to climb into your bedroom window tonight, I will. Nothing is going to keep me away from you today, baby. Do you understand?"

I nodded my head and let the tears fall on Chance's hands that were still holding my face. He pressed his lips into mine again. "How about that shower?"

The hot water felt so nice and being this close to my fabulously handsome boyfriend was even more satisfying. Chance took his time washing my hair while feeding my neck and back with soft kisses. He grasped the bar of soap and began washing my neck, then slowly made his way across my entire back. His slippery hands wrapped around me, gently massaging the soap onto each of my breasts. He wasn't being sexual, per se. He just wanted to be with me.

When he finished washing me, I did the same for him, concentrating on his sculpted chest first. His arms seemed bigger since he left for the new job, and I admired how strong they felt when they wrapped around me. I couldn't help but smile when my soap-covered hands made their way to his backside and maneuvered around. Chance was perfect and he was everything that I could want. I must have cried a million times when he had to leave, but now that he was here, I felt the need to celebrate.

Just like old times, Chance climbed out of the shower and wrapped a towel around me before getting one for himself. He kissed the top of my forehead as we both began brushing our teeth. It was normal everyday things like this that made me enjoy being around him.

When we checked out of the hotel room Chance took me to breakfast. We both got pancakes and coffee. We sat there for a while after finishing up, talking. It was funny that we still had things to discuss. Our late night phone calls lasted so long that we knew everything about one another. My father may have distanced Chance and I, but he'd only helped us get to know each other better. If I thought that I loved him before he left, albeit it had only intensified now.

I tried to pay for breakfast, but Chance insisted. When we got back into the car he had a big smile on his face.

"What?" I asked.

"I have something for you," he said.

"Is it a kiss?" I asked, as I leaned in for one.

He moved forward and brushed his lips over mine. "Nope, it is something else."

I was getting more excited by the second. "Tell me what it is."

Chance reached in his bag and pulled out a small pouch. It wasn't anything fancy, but it did have a pretty blue ribbon. "I stole the ribbon from your bedroom one day. You were wearing it the day we first met. I kept it with me the whole time I was gone, in my wallet."

I pulled the ribbon that I now recognized, feeling a hint of redness rush through my cheeks knowing he had something with him that was mine. When I removed the ribbon he took it and put it in his pocket. "This is special to me, so don't mind me taking it back." He winked.

Chance's face got bigger as I dug inside of the velvet sack. I pulled out the chain and gasped at what I saw hanging from it. There were two hearts that were separate pieces, one said Hope and the other said Chance. They were small hearts made of plain white gold that hung over top of one another to appear like it was just one charm. When I didn't understand it, Chance explained.

"I wanted you to have something special so I had these made. You can wear them every day and your father will never see my name, because it will be hiding under yours." He took the necklace and showed me.

"I love it. Thank you so much. I'll never take it off," I exclaimed. I'd personally gotten jewelry as a gift before, but nothing so sentimental.

"That's what I was going for when I got it." He laughed.

Putting that necklace around Hope's neck made me feel content. I'd bought that for her with my first paycheck, and couldn't wait to give it to her. I pulled it out every night as we talked on the phone and traced her name with my thumb. It was probably so ridiculous, but I clung to whatever I could; being alone sucked so badly. While my co-workers were hitting the town going to strip clubs, I resorted to staying a hermit in my motel room, knowing my girl was at home waiting for me to return. I wasn't taking this second chance at life for granted.

While she drove she played with the necklace. I could tell it meant so much to her, which in turn meant a lot to me. As soon as I spotted that charm that hid a secret one behind it, I knew it was perfect. Unless she shook it, nobody would ever see my name.

Hope drove the slowest I'd ever seen her drive on our way back to the house. I wondered if she was going to hang a left and drive us out of state, so that we didn't have to pretend anymore. I missed my sister, but being without Hope was unbearable. After the night we'd just shared, I couldn't imagine looking in the opposite direction when she entered the room. I was in awe of her, and desperately needed to make up for lost time.

When we pulled into the long driveway I heard Hope sigh. She dreaded this part of my visit and I could feel her pain. I squeezed her hand. "Baby, I promise we'll be together tonight."

"I know. I just don't want to wait, and I don't like sharing you," she pouted.

"Trust me, Hope, I plan on going to bed early tonight. Don't you?" I winked so she'd catch on.

"Hell yeah. I feel tired already," She said sarcastically.

I brought her hand to my lips. "I fucking love you, and I'm home now. Nothing is going to keep me from holding you in my arms tonight."

"Then let's get this show on the road."

Hope left her bag in the car and walked with me toward the house. Buffy came running out and hugged me immediately. "If he asks, I called Hope this morning to grab you from the airport," she whispered.

"I missed you too, sis." I said as I watched Mark approaching us.

"Hey, Chance. I didn't even know you were visiting this weekend. How've you been doing?" Mark asked.

I tried to remain calm, but I was still pissed about what he had done to his daughter. There was no way I would ever treat her that way. "I wanted to surprise everyone, and I pretty much hate the job. The money is good, but when it's over, I plan on coming home and going back to school. This isn't what I see doing forever."

Mark raised an eyebrow. "Sorry to hear it isn't going that great. Well, come on inside and get comfortable. I think the pool house is the way you left it. Sometimes Hope goes out there to study, but I doubt if she made a mess."

Hope had indeed spent time in the pool house. She'd called me many times from inside. Although Mark was still talking, I was picturing her rolling around in my sheets taking in my manly scent. When I started to smile, I realized they were all standing around me.

"It is really good to be home," I announced.

Buffy talked Mark into going out to dinner, and with Hope still not speaking to him much, he said yes immediately. He hadn't even made a big deal out of her picking me up from the airport. Maybe me being away had given him time to realize I would risk my life for her safety, not cause her harm. Maybe he felt bad for sending me away, or perhaps he felt sorry for everything Hope went through. It was obvious she was in a good mood, which was probably rare. Aside from him being there at first with her mother's illness, he'd gone back to business as if nothing happened. It irked me.

After being home for only about half an hour, Mark got a phone call and had to run to the strip mall to meet with a potential new lease. Buffy had hugged me a million times and finally allowed me to breathe. As soon as Mark's car pulled out of sight Hope was back in my arms. We strolled hand in hand to the pool house and closed the door behind us. Buffy said she would text us when he was back so Hope could just walk outside and act casual.

The funny thing was that Hope didn't seem fazed by her father. I think she would have been okay with him seeing us together. Her animosity towards him was a little disturbing, and I realized that she had just reached her breaking point. There may have been no way for them to fix their relationship. The man had let his daughter get sexually assaulted while he sat back and did nothing to the kids involved. That was a crime in itself.

When we got inside the pool house, I noticed how clean it was.

"I came in here a lot more than both of them know about. In fact, I snuck out at night and slept in your bed a few nights. It might sound creepy, but I just wanted to be near you, well as close to you as I could be," she admitted.

"Hope, I carry around a damn ribbon in my wallet. I have no room to talk," I said confidently.

"The house is clean except for the sheets. I refused to change them. They still smell like you." She smiled and marched toward the bedroom.

I followed her, while still picturing her rolling around in the sheets. "You know we don't have much time right?" I said, as I watched her shirt come flying off and land on my head.

"We have enough time."

I smiled and met her on my mattress, minus my clothes.

36

Hope

I'd wanted to spend the afternoon alone with Chance, but my father arrived home only an hour after he'd left. He and Buffy decided that we should all go to the Country Club to have an early dinner. Chance headed to the pool house to get cleaned up, while I stayed inside the main house to do the same.

My plan was that at the last minute I was going to tell my father I preferred to drive myself, in case they wanted to stay later. I knew Chance would volunteer to ride with me, which would give us some more alone time.

The fall weather was causing it to be cool outside, especially in the afternoons, so I made it a point to wear something that I could put a sweater over. I chose a strapless black dress with blue and white designs in it. It came up above my knees, but looked cute with a cardigan on top.

My hair had really grown since the summer, which now covered my entire back. I curled each of the ends and pulled the sides up so it looked fuller. After putting on a bit of makeup, I stood back and looked at my appearance. My most

311

favorite part of the whole outfit was my necklace from Chance. It hung perfectly in the center of my chest.

Satisfied that Chance would be impressed, I headed downstairs. Buffy decided to wear something other than pink. She wore a navy blue suit that made her look older than she normally dressed; a strand of pearls were wrapped around her neck, while her hair was curled to perfection.

"You look beautiful," I said as she came downstairs.

"So do you. Wow!" She replied.

My father followed behind and put his arms around Buffy's waist. "You will be the two best looking women in the club tonight."

"We better be," Buffy said as she gave him a once over. "Hope, why don't you go see if Chance is ready yet."

"Okay." I said calmly, but really I wanted to simultaneously scream and jump up and down.

I was wearing heels, which made it impossible to run toward the pool house. I adjusted my dress at least three times before making it to the entrance. When I opened the door, I could smell Chance's cologne. I followed the scent toward the bathroom and lost my breath at how handsome he looked.

Chance was wearing a pair of black pants. His blue polo shirt displayed every muscle on his arms and chest. While he had been away, I washed all of the clothes he still had in boxes and then hung them up. He obviously appreciated my hard work by wearing one of the outfits.

"Well, don't you clean up nice."

Chance took one look at me and flew out of the bathroom. "Hope. Damn, you look fantastic." He kissed me gently on the lips. "And thanks for the work you did in my closet."

"You're welcome." I said, as I wiped my lip-gloss off his lips. "They're waiting for us."

"Let me just get my wallet and I'll be there."

I decided not to push my luck with my father and headed out to the driveway. As I approached the car, I heard Chance running to catch up behind me. "Sorry you guys had to wait," he said.

"It's fine, Chance. Are we ready to go?" My dad asked.

I interrupted. "Um dad, I was thinking I should drive my own car. If you guys want to stay late, I can head home early. I just want to have the option, you know?"

My dad creased his brow and looked over to Buffy. She gave him a nod and his face calmed. "Probably a good idea, sweetie. You know how I get when I run into my golf buddies."

I started to walk alone to my car and heard Chance calling. "Hope, wait! I'll ride with you, so you don't have to drive alone." He turned to face my dad. "Is that cool with you guys?"

"Of course it is," Buffy announced.

Chance got into the passenger side before I'd even opened my door. "Good plan."

"Thanks!" I said, as I started the car.

We got out of the driveway and followed my dad out of the community. Chance suggested that I not follow too close so he could kiss my hand and play with my hair. Luckily, when we came into town my father ran a yellow light and we stayed when it turned red. At the same exact time, we leaned into one another for a kiss. "You're so beautiful," Chance said, as he looked into my eyes.

We were interrupted from our sweet moment when

the person behind me started honking, because the light had turned back to green.

That old woman had ruined our make-out session. If I hadn't missed my girlfriend so much, I wouldn't have minded. Hope welcoming me home was even better than I'd thought it would be. She seemed different, but yet, still the same. Her hair was longer and something about her face made her seem more mature, but whatever it was, I loved it.

Working that construction job had been pure hell. There'd been so many times where I wanted to buy a cheap car and come home. I played out in my mind how I'd pick up Hope and we would drive as far away as we could. Hope and I would sit awake at night talking about everything.

Mark had only made us stronger and now that I was back, I knew I needed to pull him aside and tell him I didn't want to return to South Carolina. I would have appreciated the job if I hadn't met Hope, but I had something to live for now, and being away from her was killing me.

As if she was reading my mind, Hope brought up the

topic. "I'm not going to let you get back on that plane, Chance."

I grabbed her hand and kissed it. "Are you going to wrestle me to the ground?" I asked sarcastically. "Because, I think I would really like that."

"Don't act like you want to go back. Based on your performance last night, I'd say you were glad to be home."

I chuckled. "Are you kidding me? Don't ever ask that. Of course I want to be home." I looked over at Hope, and ran my hand across her cheek. "I don't want to ever go back, Hope. I just want to be here with you."

We came to another red light and Hope looked over at me. "I know, I know! I guess I'm just on edge. I finally have you back and all I keep thinking about is the fact that you have to leave," she confessed.

"I'll find a way to stay. I've saved up some money, at least enough to get a place and be able to pay for a few months until I can find a job here. I'll do whatever it takes."

Knowing that Hope was worried, and the fact that we were on our way to have dinner with the person who put us in this situation, was ridiculous. I hated seeing her hurting.

"Maybe we should just tell him we're together?"

I ran my hands through my hair. "Hope, it's not that easy. He could refuse to let me see you. He could get your mother involved. We only have a short time before your birthday. Just let me handle it. I'll figure something out."

"What if you don't?" She asked.

"I will. Just relax. I'll handle this."

She looked worried. "Well I can't handle you being gone again. I know I sound like a selfish little girl, but it's true. It hurt so much. I needed you. My mom got sick and I felt like I was alone. I needed you to hold me and reassure me that she would be okay, even if at the time it wasn't true. None of this has been easy for me," she admitted.

We were getting close to the club, and I knew I needed to calm her down before Mark started poking around with questions.

"Hope, I adore you, and I assure you I'll do whatever it takes."

"Thanks. I know you will. I'm sorry for being so annoying about it. I just can't imagine ever losing you."

I leaned over and kissed her cheek. My lips touched the base of her ear. "You will never lose me, and I don't find you annoying. I actually feel amazed every time I hear you say how much you want to be with me."

Hope smiled. "It's good to have you back, Chance."

"I know," I said, as I rubbed the back of her neck.

We finally turned into the club, and prepared for a long night with her father. Who knew what kind of conversations we would have, or what we'd eat. My concerns were more about keeping my distance from Hope, when all I wanted to do was tell the world she was mine.

37
Hope

I hated the Country Club. Trevor had brought me every weekend when we'd dated. His father was a fixture, who probably kept the place in business. Before me, Trevor had found this establishment to be a great place for banging chicks. In fact, this was where he'd taken my innocence.

One night a bunch of us kids snuck on the grounds and took some of the golf carts out. Rylee had hooked up with some football player and they went rolling out onto the greens somewhere, leaving me alone with Trevor.

He'd made many advances toward me having sex with him. At first they were sweet and innocent, but the longer I held out, the more physical he became. The truth was that Trevor always scared me and I found myself doing things so that he wouldn't yell at me, or call me awful names. On nights like that night, he threatened to tell the whole school I had an STD, or that I was a lesbian which was why we weren't sleeping together. He threatened to say that I'd let his friends have their way with me all at the same time. You name it, he'd said it to scare me. That night he used the excuse that

317

everyone was doing it except for me. He said my pussy was going to dry up if I didn't start putting out. Finally, after crying for a long period of time, fearing that I'd be the laughing stock of the school, I laid down on a patch of green grass and let him have his way with me.

I wasn't ready. I didn't even want it to happen.

I wasn't in love with him.

Of course, being inexperienced left me without the knowledge of foreplay. I was completely dry when he entered me, which made it hurt even worse. I suppose I could have told someone, but felt too ashamed for doing it. After that night I didn't care anymore. It was just sex, and it meant nothing to me. It's another reason why I knew I couldn't be with someone like him. I was tired of being controlled for acceptance.

Just thinking about that night made me so angry.

"What's wrong, Hope? I thought you were okay?"

I shook my head while I continued looking for a parking spot. "This is where I lost my virginity. I hate this place."

I suddenly thought back to when I knew I was truly ready to have sex; the moment when I knew that I wanted a guy without any doubt. I was confident with my body, and knew exactly how I wanted to feel. It had been my first night with Chance. After that night nothing with Trevor seemed to matter anymore. It was that night that made me see the difference. It showed me that I never loved Trevor, even when I tried to in order to make myself feel better about my choices.

Chance had showed me love and what it was like to actually make love. He would never force me, or hurt me and I appreciated him so much.

"Why didn't you just tell your father that you wanted to go somewhere else?" He asked.

"Because ever since he got this stupid membership he's been hell bent on spending every second here," I explained. "Besides, it was a long time ago. I don't care anymore."

We started to get out of the car. "Was it with the dick head?" He asked.

"Yes!" I held my head down, trying to not think about him. "It was horrible, Chance. I wish I had just waited for you. You have no idea how much I wish that."

Chance stroked my cheek and smiled. "He can't hurt you now, Hope. I will never let him touch you again. I may not have been your first, but I damn sure want to be your last." Chance smiled when he said it, sending a wave of butterflies throughout my body. He could do that to me, where no one else ever had before.

My father and Buffy approached us and we all toddled inside together. We appeared as a family. I guess a really messed up one at that. Apparently, my father had reserved us a table ahead of time, so we didn't have to sit in a more common area of the restaurant. Our table was circular, and since Buffy slid in right next to my dad, Chance and I were able to sit together. He and I were able to touch legs the whole time. It may not have been much, in fact, it was seemingly innocent, but it was enough for me to feel connected to him.

Once we ordered our food, my father started talking to Chance about the town he worked in. He even had the nerve to ask him if he'd met anyone special. I felt Chance's leg start rubbing against mine as he answered. "There is nothing there that I want. I go to work and then head back to the motel. It's lonely, and I feel like it just drains the life out of me."

"I'm sorry that it isn't working out for you, Chance. I know Buffy hates that you're so unhappy. Perhaps it is time for you to come home." Before Chance could reply or I could scream, my dad started talking again. "I would have one condition if you came back though, Chance."

Whatever it is, just take it...

"I don't know what you said, or how you managed to do it, but you convinced my daughter to enroll in college." He looked over at me. "Buffy told me all about it." Then he looked back to Chance. "Thank you for that. I want so much for her and I could not be prouder. Therefore, my condition would be that you mentor her and help her get through any hard classes. I know how smart you are. College is tough. She can use the guidance."

I could tell that Chance felt ecstatic. He still didn't care for my father's actions, but he could finally come home and I was so happy. We could be together, and still have animosity toward my dad. After all, he was a complete douche.

Was this really happening? Was I being asked to come home and spend time with Hope? I didn't waste any time accepting his offer. "Of course I'll help Hope. I plan on enrolling there myself next semester anyway."

Mark held up his drink. "Well since we're celebrating, Buffy and I have another announcement."

He turned to my sister, and I half expected her to yell out that she was pregnant, but instead she just gave him a smile. "We decided to get married on New Year's Day," Buffy announced.

A rush of relief went through me and I know it was the same for Hope. It wasn't that neither of us wanted Buffy to have children, we just needed to be able to reveal our relationship first. "That's great news," I replied.

"Mark and I are going to have the wedding here with just a few close friends, and we want you both to stand up for us," she said in an excited voice. Buffy started clapping and had a huge smile on her face.

"Sounds great, guys." I said as I took another swig of my beer. I focused my attention to my girlfriend's leg. Being this close to her was becoming difficult to remain calm. I wanted nothing more than to take her home and celebrate the fact that I wasn't going anywhere.

When our food finally came everyone got quiet and started eating. Halfway through, Hope asked me to scoot out so that she could use the ladies room. I hadn't noticed a change in her demeanor, but I couldn't help get this feeling that something was wrong. The last thing I needed was to draw attention to how concerned I was about her in front of her father. All of my plans on coming home would be ruined, and I'd be back to living hundreds of miles away from her again.

After about two minutes I noticed Mr. Thomas heading to our table. I cleared my throat as he approached and fought with myself to put on a smile.

"Hey there. I didn't know you'd be here tonight," he said.

"Ah, Greg, we're celebrating Chance coming home, and setting a date for the wedding," Mark explained.

"Well congrats on both. Why don't you all join us at our table for drinks?" Greg suggested.

Once he'd received a few reluctant glares, he saw we were going to say no. "Aw, come on. Are you really going to pass up on free booze, Mark?" He pressured.

As Mark and Buffy signaled the waiter as to what we were doing, I still hadn't noticed Hope. When we stood up to move to the table in the other room with Mr. Thomas, I noticed why Hope had gotten upset. Sitting there at the table was Trevor and he wasn't alone. I remembered the slender darkly tanned girl from the bar, and pictures in Hope's room. He was with Rylee and they were all over each other.

Not wasting any time on a missed opportunity, I

turned to Mark. "I am going to go find Hope and tell her where we're going."

Mark gave me a nod, right before realizing how bad of an idea this really was. His face turned pale even as I toddled past him. He's lucky I didn't jack his ass up for being so selfish. Obviously his daughter wouldn't want to be near Trevor. He belonged in jail.

Buffy looked like she was ready to cry. I kept walking, determined to find Hope before she had to face them.

The ladies room was just off the main dining area. As I ambled toward the door listed "ladies", an older woman was stepping out. Without any regard for who might see me, I rushed inside.

I could hear Hope's sniffles even before I approached the stall. Lucky for me there were no other women inside. "Baby, it's me. Are you okay?"

I heard the door unlock and crack open. "No," she said as I entered and closed the door behind us. "Did you see who he's with? I don't get it. She knows what he put me through. She saw the bruises he gave me before, before I sent her the pictures. She knows he used to make me have sex with him, Chance. I told her how I hated it."

"He what?" I started to rush out of the stall with all intentions of killing the fucker, but Hope seized my arm.

"Please, Chance, don't! He can't hurt me now, not ever. Don't risk being sent away again. I just got you back," she pleaded.

"Fine, but we should have called the police before. In addition, Hope, as far as your friend goes, she deserves him. She obviously only cares about herself. Let the money-hungry bitch get what's coming to her," I suggested.

"It's not like I wish for her to get hurt. Even after all

the lies; I wouldn't want that to happen."

Hope and I stopped talking when we heard the door opening. I climbed behind her and stood on the toilet in case they looked under the stalls. When I heard the voices, I knew everything was going to play out differently.

The female was giggling, while the male voice was mumbling between kissing sounds. "Trevor, wait! You shouldn't be in here. We're going to get caught."

"Fuck them. My father will raise Hell and they won't do a thing about it," he said.

Slow moaning sounds came from outside of the stall. "Oh, that feels so good. Don't stop, Trevor. Oh yeah, you know what I like," she purred.

I pulled Hope into my chest. This was unreal.

Suddenly, we heard the door to the next stall open and their bodies began slamming against it. More nasty sounds were being made and I was sure Hope was about to lose her dinner. I leaned down and pressed my lips against hers while I covered her ears with my hands. I knew it didn't help much, but I was trying my best to keep her sane.

Their next words made me cringe. "I should have picked you from the beginning, Rylee. That little bitch friend of yours was a waste of my fucking time. I'm not even going to count how many times she denied me," Trevor said.

"Mmm, I tried to tell you that, baby," Rylee replied.

"Stop running your mouth and start sucking my dick. I need to cum."

This little punk was going down, just as soon as I got my girl out of this bathroom.

I could see the shock and pain on Hope's face as I climbed down from the toilet and slowly opened the door to the stall. At the very last second, it creaked.

Hope and I turned around to see Trevor and Rylee looking back at us wide-eyed. "You've got to be kidding me." Trevor said while trying to re-button his shirt. "Now you decide to put out in bathrooms, Hope?"

Hope couldn't restrain me. My fist went right into Trevor's jaw. He managed to keep his balance and smile before coming at me. "Don't you ever fucking touch me you cock-blocking prick. You can have your little bitch and her church-going attitude. I don't fucking want her," he said as he took a swing at me.

Despite the fact that I was directly in front of him, I was able to duck making it so he only clipped me on the edge of my shoulder.

I hadn't even noticed the girls trying to separate us, but when my sister spoke, everyone froze. "What the hell is going on in here?"

"Nothing to worry your pretty little head about, blondie, not unless you want in on this." He motioned to his body.

I raised my arm to hit him again, but Buffy jumped in front of us. "Let me tell you something you little fucking prick. You're lucky that I didn't cut off your little dick and feed it to the birds for what you did to Hope. You're scum, and you deserve nothing in life. Now you've involved my brother, and I've reached my breaking point. If you so much as look at either of them again, I will call my friends, who will call their friends, who happen to have ties to the mob, and they will never find your body parts when they're done with you. Do you fucking understand that?"

Trevor's eyes were huge, and he started to say something back, but Buffy hauled off and smacked him clear across the cheek. "Come on, you two, we need to get away from all this trash." Her last words made her look at Rylee. My sister obviously knew exactly who she was.

Once outside of the bathroom, Buffy turned around and made sure our clothes looked okay. She faced Hope. "Your father wanted me to give you your purse and tell you that your food is boxed up and waiting by the exit. He said he had no idea that they were here. As soon as we sat down he told the waiter to pack your things, and to go and to tell Chance to take you home. He said he is so sorry, Hope, and I believe him," she explained.

Hope nodded her head while I reached my arm around her and marched us out of the building. For the record, at this point, I didn't give a shit who was watching. Hope was safe with me, and I wanted everyone to know it.

38

Hope

Seeing and hearing Trevor and Rylee was horrible. How did I end up in that bathroom at the same time they decided to get it on in a public place? I had the worst luck ever.

Thankfully, Chance was with me and managed to get a good punch in before Buffy tore Trevor a new ass. The situation had been intense, but I'd never wanted to laugh so bad in my life. Rylee looked like she wanted to die. Just when I didn't think I could love Buffy more, she gave me another reason.

Once Chance and I got to my car, he insisted on driving us home. I didn't argue with him over it, because it was pointless. I kept replaying Chance punching Trevor in the face, and every time I felt exhilarated. Maybe it was wrong of me to want that bastard to pay for what he'd done to me and probably many other girls. It really hurt me that Rylee would want to be with someone like him after she had known firsthand what he'd done to me.

"You okay, baby?" Chance asked.

He took my hand as he continued down the lane of

the Country Club. I noticed him making quick glances at me when I didn't answer him right away.

"I'm fine. I should have never assumed they wouldn't be there. It's a weekend for God sakes."

Chance let go of my hand so that he could move it around while he was talking. "Hope, I wanted to kill him, for today and everyday he put you through hell."

"He's not even worth it. He never was."

"So what are you doing tonight?" He immediately changed the subject.

I gave him a sly smile. "I was planning on spending it with this hot guy. He has strong arms and rock hard abs, and the nicest ass I've ever seen."

"Damn, he must be a lucky guy."

"He is!" I boasted.

We both started laughing, which was something that we really needed considering the shitty evening we were having.

"For what it's worth, I wish I was your first. I would have taken my time and waited until you were ready. I'd never take you for granted."

I touched his hand and smiled. "I know. Trust me, I know that. So, not to change the subject, but how long do you think we have before they come home?" I asked.

Chance shrugged. "Probably no more than a half hour. The way Buffy talked they weren't really that happy about being around Trevor. Are you sure you're okay?"

I ran my hand across the top of Chance's neck. "I've waited forever to have you back home with me. All I want is to spend time with you. I actually think that Trevor helped us out, in some kind of messed up way. Did you see how my father wanted you to take me home? He trusts you with me.

That's got to be a good sign."

Chance chuckled. "Trusts me. That's not a good thing, Hope. Not while I've been hiding a relationship with you from him for months. When he finds out that will be the last thing he does."

We pulled into the driveway then got out to head into the main house. Chance pulled me into his arms. "I'm so happy that I never have to spend another night away from you again. God, I missed you."

I wrapped my arms around his neck, letting him pick me up to carry me into the house. He sat me down on the couch, but only so that he could get comfortable beside me. When my Dad and Buffy came home, we would see their car pull up and be able to separate quickly. "I can't wait for you to tutor me," I laughed out loud admitting it.

"Oh really? What subject do you need help in first?" He asked as he pushed his body on top of mine. He stared down into my eyes waiting for a response. I could already feel his growing bulge pressing on his pants. My body reacted by becoming increasingly hot. I felt like I needed to rip off my clothes and give myself to him, with no regard for when my dad would return home.

"I think I need mouth to mouth and then maybe some physics, or chemistry," I said, as his lips slowly brushed mine.

"I don't think you have any problems in chemistry. We already have that subject taken care of." He kissed on my ear lobe and then my neck. "Your skin tastes so good."

Things started to progress quickly. Chance's hand began roaming as he kissed me, and soon found my breasts under my dress. He pulled the front completely down for easy access. For a moment he sat there silently looking at me, then he slowly moved forward and nibbled on each of them before coming up to my lips for another kiss. Just as I grabbed his shirt to remove it, we saw headlights pulling into the driveway. Chance hopped off of me, and I made a mad dash for the stairs.

I immediately threw on some different clothes, and was already heading back down when they came in the door. I could tell from the look on their faces that something was wrong.

"Hope, where's Chance?" My dad asked.

Before I could answer, I heard his voice coming toward us. "I'm right here. What's wrong?"

"The police are on their way," Buffy interrupted. "We tried to get him to reconsider, but he refused."

I started to panic. "What are you talking about?"

My father approached me. "Trevor is pressing assault charges on Chance, sweetie. Buffy explained what happened to Greg and me. He's not involved in his son's actions."

"Well, how do you know they're coming?" I asked in a frantic.

"It's okay, Hope. I can handle it." Chance interrupted.

Buffy chimed in. "No, it isn't okay, Chance. You already have a record. You'll be found guilty for that fact. This is bad," she explained.

"Let me tell you both something before I get hauled away tonight. A couple months ago, I caught that son of a bitch sexually assaulting Hope. Then today, he had the nerve to bring her friend into the bathroom and talk shit about Hope while they were banging each other. When I confronted him, he talked more shit about her. There is no way I will ever regret hitting him. I would do it again in a heartbeat. Hope doesn't deserve to be treated like that." Chance did his best to explain, but as my father raised his eyebrow, I could see

330

that he read between the lines.

"I appreciate that you took up for my daughter, Chance. It seems like you have been there for her more than once." My father said as he gave Chance a pat on the back.

We watched the headlights pulling into the driveway, followed by two officers marching toward the front door.

My dad let them in, while Chance stood between Buffy and I. Even before the officers spoke, I had tears forming in my eyes.

"Sorry to bother you tonight folks. Are you Mr. Chance Avery?" The officer asked.

"Yes, sir, I am."

"Please turn around." While pulling out the handcuffs he started giving him his Miranda rights. "You have the right to remain silent. Anything you say can and will be used against you in a court of law. You have the right to an attorney. If you cannot afford an attorney, one will be provided for you. Do you understand the rights I have just read to you? With these rights in mind, do you wish to speak to me?"

Chance looked down at the floor. "Yes, I understand those rights."

I didn't know what came over me, but I threw myself in front of the officer, preventing them from taking Chance out of the house. "No! Please you have to wait! He was protecting me. I was being assaulted."

Part of it was a lie, well kind of. Trevor might not have assaulted me today, but he did two months ago. They didn't need to know that.

"Are you saying that you want to come in and make a formal charge against Mr. Thomas?" One officer asked.

"Hope, sweetie calm down," My father blurted out.

"No, Dad! I won't calm down. I won't let Chance get in trouble like this for protecting me. Trevor should be the one in trouble." I looked at the officers. "Yes, I will come and tell you the real truth."

"Officers, my daughter is not eighteen. Don't I have the right to prevent her from perjuring herself?" My father asked.

"Stop it. You can't take him away. He was protecting me," I reiterated.

They all seemed to be arguing with me, but as if time froze and left me and Chance alone in the room I caught his stare and everything stopped. I didn't hear the arguing. I didn't hear anything. All I saw was the man I loved.

"Miss, if you would like to follow us down to the station to file charges against Mr. Thomas, feel free to do so." They said as they started taking Chance out of the house.

Buffy stopped me before I could run after them, but the tears became worse.

Before the car pulled away, my father had a lawyer on the phone. We all packed into the SUV and headed to the station.

At first, my father was quiet, but after a few minutes he shocked us both. "Hope, I need to know if you've ever been intimate with Trevor. He has a reputation at the club and I want to know the truth."

I was afraid, but I wanted my dad to hate Trevor. "Yes. He was my first. He practically forced me then too. He'd said I didn't love him if I didn't go through with it. He cheated on me and lied to me, and if Chance hadn't been there over the summer, he would have raped me, while his brother stood there watching," I confessed.

It was difficult to admit it out loud. In some ways I

knew I was breaking his heart, more than any other thing in life possibly could. Through our struggling relationship I finally saw my father; the one that helped raise me when I was little.

He got all choked up and then began hitting the steering wheel. "How could I have been so stupid? Damn it! I brought him into our home. I did this," he yelled.

Buffy reached over to grab his shoulder, and I leaned forward doing the same. "You didn't know, dad. Nobody knew. Chance was the only one."

"I sent him away; away from the only family he has, for a fucking business deal, and now he gets arrested for keeping you safe?" His remorseful words touched my heart. He was finally opening his eyes. "Honey, I'm so sorry." He looked to Buffy. "And I'm sorry the most to you, Hope. God, I can't believe I put a business deal before my own daughter's safety."

"Dad, let's just worry about Chance. He's the important one tonight. We can deal with everything else once he's home safe."

For the rest of the ride to the jail we all remained quiet. Once we got inside we were told that Chance was in intake. My father left Buffy and I to find out what bail would be set for. After we waited another forty minutes he came back out and said that Chance couldn't face the judge for a bail hearing until morning and there was nothing that we could do.

I thought about going straight to an officer and filing a report about Trevor, but I had thought of another plan while I waited.

During the drive home my father and Buffy talked about going to court in the morning, and how they were going to deal with things. I pulled my cell phone out of my pocket and searched for a number I never thought I would be using again.

39

Hope

This was my last resort. I buried my pride and built up the strength to do it; and then I texted the number.

Rylee we need to talk. ~ Hope

We were almost home before she responded.

We really don't have anything to say. ~ R

No, there is A LOT to talk about. U owe me. ~ Hope

Look, I'm sorry. ~ R

I'm pressing charges against Trevor for sexual assault. ~ Hope

Please don't!!! ~ R

This is what is going to happen. You are going to bring Trevor to talk to me right now. If you don't show, I'm going straight to the police. ~ Hope

What if he doesn't want to come? ~ R

Then I guess he can call a lawyer. You may want to tell him I have pictures of everything he did to me and witnesses. ~ Hope

Where? ~ R

The park in one hour. ~ Hope

Rylee didn't write back, but I knew she was going to

do her damndest to get Trevor there. The last thing she wanted was for her meal ticket out of this town to be incarcerated or have a criminal record.

Once Buffy and my dad went inside I ran up to my room and changed my clothes. I decided on black capris and a black shirt. I wanted to be invisible when they showed up, in case they weren't alone. Before heading out I ran to the pool house and found a bat that Chance kept in his closet. There was no way I was going there without something to defend myself.

On the way, my heart was pounding through my chest. I heard my phone ringing over and over, but knew it was my dad. If I told them what I had planned they never would have let me go through with it.

When I pulled up I realized I was alone. The park was empty and dark with only the sounds of insects harping in the distance. I exited my vehicle and sat down on a bench located directly in front of where I parked my car. The headlights illuminated where I sat, causing it to be difficult for me to see the approaching vehicle. I could hear the tires on the gravel road and decided to stand up to see how close the car was getting. When it pulled up beside mine, I tried to remain calm by holding my head up high and focusing on what I had come there for.

Trevor stepped out of the car first. He looked angry but I refused to fear him anymore. If he wanted to hurt me, it wasn't going to happen. After what he did to Chance today, and the things that he'd said to me, I wouldn't care if I killed him myself. When he got about five feet away from me I yelled at him. "Stop! Don't come any further," I warned.

"What do you want, Hope? Why have you drug me out here in the middle of nowhere? What do you think you're going to accomplish?" Trevor questioned.

"I have a proposition for you," I replied.

Even though I knew I was in quite a predicament, it felt good to be calling the shots.

"Okay, let's hear it."

"I want you to drop the charges against Chance."

"Hell no! Why would you think I would do such a thing? Do you think I owe you some kind of favor? Everything I did to you was because you wanted it, Hope. Stop acting like you didn't like it. Everyone likes what I have to offer." Trevor was an egotistical bastard. He was the scum of the earth.

I snickered. "It's so funny that you ask that." I held the bat tightly in one hand, but began circling around Trevor. For some reason I felt like I had someone standing behind me, ready to attack Trevor if he made any moves. "I never enjoyed it, Trevor. In fact, being with you was like giving myself thousands of paper cuts. You disgust me."

"You expect me to do you a favor after you claim I disgust you? Are you fucking insane?" Trevor asked.

I pointed the bat at his head. "No, I'm not crazy, but I can be if I need to. Now, here's my deal. You are going to drop the charges against Chance, or I will notify the police of how many times you sexually assaulted me. Included in that confession would be the documented photographs to prove what happened."

"Anyone could have given you those bruises, you little bitch. Are you really trying to blackmail me right now? Nobody is going to believe that story coming from you, Hope. Everyone knows how poor your mother is. They will just assume it is some ploy to get money from my family."

I hadn't considered that Trevor would be smart enough to turn things around on me. The truth was that everyone in town knew my mother; it was a small town. The fact that he brought her into this made me angrier. "We have video surveillance at the house, Trevor. How do you plan on getting your way out of that one? Not to mention that your brother was involved. If I go after you, he goes down too," I lied.

One minute Trevor was standing five feet away, but in a matter of only a second he had jumped on top of me, causing the bat to fly out of my hand, choking me. "You stupid little cunt! I'm going to kill you." He roared, as his hand squeezed harder, constricting my airflow.

I tried to claw at him, kicking with my legs, and even punching him, but I couldn't free his adrenaline-fueled hold. Just as I was about to lose consciousness, I felt his hands release me.

Rylee stood over me with the bat in her hand. Next to me, rolling around in pain, was Trevor. He was holding his side, screaming in agony. Rylee extended a hand to me as she kept a close eye on Trevor. "Are you okay, Hope?"

My throat was in immediate pain, but I managed to get out a "yeah".

Rylee hiked over to where Trevor was still curled up. "Get up, you son of a bitch!" She ordered with tear-filled eyes.

I had gotten myself up and leaned against the car. My throat felt like it was scratched from the inside, and just out of natural reaction I held the outside of my neck.

Rylee pushed Trevor with the tip of the bat. "Sit down on your ass, Trevor. I can't believe you were going to actually hurt her, maybe even kill her. I thought that you had changed. I thought you finally wanted a life with me, but your anger ruins everything."

Trevor scrunched up his face and spit at her feet. "You were never anything but a common whore, Rylee. You knew damn well that all I wanted from you was some easy ass. My father would never let me get serious with someone like you."

I couldn't see Rylee's face because her back was to me, but I knew what Trevor said was like a kick in the stomach for her. The park was silent for at least a whole minute. Rylee never backed away.

Finally, she moved closer to him, poking him with the bat. "This is how things are going to go." She pushed the bat into his side, causing him to squeal in pain. "You're going to get up and get into my car in the backseat. I'll climb in beside you, to prevent you from moving an inch. Then we're going to drive to the police station, where you will be dropping all of the charges against Chance Avery. If Hope's evidence isn't enough to convict you, I am sure that an eyewitness testimony will," she threatened.

Trevor didn't say a word. Instead, he held his head down and finally got up and started walking toward the car. Rylee had the bat pushed into his back the entire time. When I got into the driver's side, I handed her my keys with my pepper spray attached. I didn't have to tell her the reason; she nodded and pointed the bottle at his face.

While I began our drive back to the station I heard Rylee saying, "I'm so sorry, Hope," from the backseat.

Maybe I could forgive her someday, but for right now all I wanted to do was to see Chance, nothing else mattered to me.

Trevor reluctantly made his way into the station and immediately began pleading his case. He told the officers that Chance had reacted in self-defense and that he didn't wish to press charges after all. A detective came and did a thorough interview with him, in which I have no idea what was said. Once I saw his father come into the station I knew the shit had just gotten serious. As they walked back toward Rylee and me, she held my hand. I think she was afraid of what they'd say to her.

"If I never see either of you again, it will be too soon." He said as he sauntered out of the police station doors beside his father.

I started to get up and go after him to give him and his father another piece of my mind, but Rylee pulled me back when she saw Chance emerging from a closed door. Our eyes met and I couldn't help but run toward him. We embraced and I immediately started to cry. "I'm so sorry."

"How did you get me out, Hope? What did you do?" He asked.

No part of me wanted to be mad at him for assuming I had to do something shady, but wasn't that what I had done? "It doesn't matter. Trevor will never bother us again," I promised.

Rylee gave Trevor the finger and we all staggered out to her car. On the way back to get my vehicle she drove while Chance and I stayed locked in each other's arms in the backseat. When we finally reached the park I leaned inside the window and thanked Rylee, before getting into my own car and driving us home.

It was no surprise that Buffy and my father were frantically waiting for my return.

40

Chance

Seeing Hope at the police station felt like a dream. I still didn't know how she changed Trevor's mind, and part of me was afraid to ask, but I trusted her. When she came into my arms for the first time I knew I wasn't dreaming. She felt so warm, just like being home.

I didn't say anything to her in either of the cars on the ride home; instead, I just held her hand and gazed at her beautiful face. She seemed happy, almost satisfied, in a way that I hadn't seen in a long time. Of course, when we pulled up at the house we were faced with two very distraught family members.

Before they approached us, I had to know what had happened. "Hope, care to fill me in?"

She looked over at me and then back to her father and Buffy. "I told you already that Trevor will never be a problem for us again."

"Should I be worried about you?" I asked.

"Nope. I'll be fine. I just finally stood my ground and threatened to turn him in for everything he ever did to me, and I also kind of said that we had video surveillance of the outside of the house."

I laughed. "Wow! Well here come the parental units. Maybe we shouldn't be so close together?"

Hope squeezed my hand. "I'm tired of lying, Chance. I think we should just tell him."

"I just got back, Hope. Do you really think that is a good idea?" I asked, but as I did, I heard the car door opening on my side.

"Chance? How did you…? What the…?" Buffy said.

We both climbed out of the car at the same time. "I can explain, but I think we all need to go inside," Hope said.

When her father looked at Buffy, he had a concerned look on his face. He put his arm around her as they headed inside, but never said a single word to either of us, which I found weird.

We all headed into the kitchen. I leaned against the counter after Buffy had handed me a beer while she and Mark sat at the breakfast bar waiting for an explanation.

I looked over to Hope and then back to them. "Hope is going to have to tell you how I got out. She did it all herself."

Hope looked at her dad. "Well first I need to go back to last year. I guess you already know about mine and Trevor's relationship, but it was worse than I ever led on. Dad, on several occasions he forced me to do things with him." Hope put her head down. She couldn't look him in the eye.

"I will kill that bastard!" Mark yelled.

Hope looked up at him as the tears ran down her

cheeks. "When I got the nerve to break up with him, I severed all ties, and then eventually moved here with you. He still tried to call, but I never spoke with him, not even once."

I looked up at Mark who still seemed like he was fuming. "How did you get Chance out, Hope? Did he make you do something? Did he make you be with him again?" Mark asked.

I cringed at the thought.

"No! No way, dad! I texted him and Rylee to meet me in the park. I took Chance's baseball bat to protect myself. I only went there to threaten him, not to do anything physical." Hope seemed to be thinking about her next words. "When I gave him an ultimatum, he came at me. Eventually Rylee stepped in and saved me. With her on my side I was able to convince him that I had proof of what he'd done to me and I would use it against him if he didn't drop the charges against Chance."

I couldn't help but smile at her as she talked about her brave move, and there was the fact that she knew where I kept my favorite bat, and also that she'd used that bat to harm Trevor.

I wanted Hope to stop with the story and leave it at that, but Mark wasn't finished with his interrogation.

"Hope, it's really nice of you to do so much for Chance, but I have to wonder why you would risk your life in a dark park for him? You were very foolish and could have gotten yourself killed," Mark said.

"It doesn't matter. The charges are dropped and we're all here together, right?" Buffy chimed in.

Fear stabbed me in the gut when Mark looked from me to Hope. "No, that isn't it. For the past two months, I have regretted sending Chance away. I honestly feared that he was

343

a bad influence on you, Hope, but now I see that you two are great friends. I'm sorry. I'm sorry I wasn't there for you; for both of you."

Marks confession made me feel guilty and I worried what Hope was thinking, and what she would say next. I just got home and I couldn't leave her again. It will kill me, especially after this.

"I think Chance has proven that he would do anything for this family. It wasn't fair for him to get into trouble because he was helping me." I wanted to scream out loud how much I loved Chance, how I loved him for always saving me, how he would never hurt me or leave my side. I wanted everyone to be able to see us holding hands; to know that I was his and he was mine.

However, it was just impossible...

My father was finally seeing Chance in the positive and not the negative that he'd always assumed. It was important for me to keep things that way. If my dad knew that Chance and I were intimate then everything would be ruined. I couldn't take the chance, literally.

Before I could make any more excuses for myself, my dad and Buffy looked at each other and nodded. "Well it's been a really long day. Maybe we should all just call it a night," he suggested.

"Yeah, I am pretty tired," Buffy admitted.

Chance leaned against the counter. He snatched the last apple in the wooden bowl and took a big bite out of it. I watched as his lips covered a part of the fruit. I realized half way through that I had begun licking my lips. Just as fast as I'd started, I turned around and stopped. "Yeah, I'll be right behind you guys. Goodnight!" I said as they headed toward the stairs.

"Goodnight, sweetie! Goodnight, Chance!" My dad announced.

I leaned on the other side of the counter and watched Chance taking another bite of his apple. With his mouth full of fruit, he smiled. "So are you really heading up to bed?" He asked with one eyebrow cocked.

I reached across the counter and grabbed the apple from him. Before he could argue, I took a big bite out of the same side of it. "Mmm. Do you have another option for me?" I whispered.

"Maybe," he said with a half smile.

"So what do you have in mind?" I asked curiously while biting down on my lip.

"Did you ever sneak out of your house when you were a kid?" He asked.

I put my head down, feeling like I had missed out on something. "Not really. My mother would have known, and I was too good when I was really little to even consider doing something like that."

He leaned over and gently ran his fingers across my mouth. All I could do was watch him biting down on his own lip as he did it. As his finger trailed over my bottom lip I licked

345

the tip slowly. When he didn't remove his finger, I sucked it into my mouth and drug my tongue against it.

I could see the eagerness in his eyes. "If you continue to do that, I'll be taking you right on this counter top with no regard as to who may see us."

I climbed on top of the counter top until I was directly in front of him. I was risking it all, but nothing else was on my mind. My lips reached his and I immediately felt his hands in my hair, pulling me deeper into our kiss. I gripped the collar of his shirt and did the same thing. Our tongues mingled together, and I could feel my body tingling everywhere with eagerness.

Chance backed away. Our foreheads pressed together as we both gasped for air. "Your bedroom or mine, Hope?" It was all he could get out.

"Give me ten minutes?"

He pulled my legs down in front of me and kissed me slowly once more. When he moved away, he opened his eyes and looked right into mine. "Please don't make me wait too long."

41

Hope

It only took me about ten seconds to make it up the stairs to my bedroom. I obtained all of my pillows and put them under my covers making it appear like a person was in there. My father had never come in my room to wake me up so I figured I was safe from that. If for some reason he sent Buffy upstairs and I wasn't there, she would know where to find me.

Once I had the bed looking as good as I could get it, I headed over to the mirror and let my hair down. My natural waves looked disheveled, but that was how Chance liked it. I stared at my plain clothes and decided to change into a small cami top with matching shorts. The material was so thin that I could almost see my nipples through it. I looked at myself in the mirror knowing Chance would go nuts when he saw me, in a good way of course.

Climbing out of my window was easy, but with my dad in bed already, I decided to just go downstairs and saunter out the back door. I still had to maneuver my way around the bushes so they couldn't see me walking if they were in their bathroom, but realistically they would have to be standing in their Jacuzzi tub, as their bathroom was the mirror image of mine.

When I got to Chance's door I went right inside. He was standing there without a shirt waiting for me. After pulling me up against his chest and kissing me right away, I realized he hadn't seen my choice of pajamas. What I was wearing was nothing erotic. My own mother had bought them for me as summer pajamas, but I hated how thin they were and never wore them. I pushed Chance into his chair, the first place I'd ever seduced him, the place where it all began for us.

He tried to pull me back toward him. I smiled but continued walking backwards. He noticed immediately why I was doing it, and I found his eyes focusing on everything but my face. I watched his lips parting and his tongue slipping out for just a second before he bit down.

"What's your favorite part about me, Chance?"

"Definitely your knees," he said calmly, while never taking his eyes off of my body. I watched him lick his lips, causing me to react by licking mine.

I tried not to laugh, but let out a small chuckle before continuing. I gripped the bottom of my cami and pulled it up revealing my navel. "I want you to kiss me here first," I said as I pointed to my abdomen.

Chance started to get up. "No stay!" I ordered.

I let go of my cami and reached both hands around the back of my neck. It made my chest stick out more, and I watched as he started readjusting the way he was sitting. My hands slid slowly down the front of my neck until finally reaching my breasts. As I slid my fingers across the fabric where my nipples were, I stared right at him. "Then you can kiss me here."

Chance looked like he was uncomfortable, but not like he was in pain. He put his hand between his legs, as if to hold something down. I smiled before sliding my hands down my waist and over my backside.

"Where do you want to touch me first, Chance?" I asked, as I slowly ambled toward him, taking very small steps.

When his hands immediately slid under the outside of my shorts, I let out a gasp. "Everywhere," was all he said before his lips found mine.

Chance's hands traveled to the back of my butt while he pulled me to sit on his lap. I leaned my body back thinking he was going to take off my shirt, but he gently ran his fingers up the fabric of my cami top. "Hope, you have no idea what you do to me."

His palms cupped my breasts. I wanted him to be touching my bare skin, but he continued teasing me over the fabric. I began rocking my body back and forth while sitting on top of him. He reached around and gripped both of my butt cheeks, as he began pulling me into him harder.

"I want this," I whispered.

We kissed slowly, savoring the fact that we had all night. "I know, baby."

I felt Chance's hand slide up the inside of my shorts. He could immediately feel my readiness when his fingers reached my pussy. I was so turned on that I was panting for him to touch me there. "Please don't stop," I begged.

I felt his finger enter me. I rocked my body up and down as he guided it in and out. The friction sent thrills deep into my core. I wanted to scream when my body started to uncontrollably convulse. When I leaned my head on his shoulder to catch my breath, he put his mouth against my ear. "I'm just beginning."

349

Chance guided me to stand up, and he quickly climbed out of the chair. He leaned me over and stood behind me, running his hands up to my hips. He tugged me back until my ass was pressing against his erection.

Within seconds, he had grabbed the elastic of my shorts and pulled them down off of my backside, revealing my naked ass. He rubbed one of the cheeks before I heard the zipper of his pants sliding down. I stood there bent over just waiting for him to be inside of me. It was as if I needed him to be closer to me than he already was. I couldn't explain why I needed him; I just knew that I did.

Chance was gentle as he slid inside of me. He picked up the pace almost instantly. I could tell he liked this position, because he was in total control. His hands were tight around my waist and with each thrust, it felt like he entered a little more. When we finally both climaxed, he collapsed his spent body over my back. I could feel the sweat from his chest against my hot skin. His breathing was heavy, but he continued kissing my back.

"I fucking love you."

Chance stepped right out of his pants, leaving them on the floor in the living room. I followed him into the bedroom where he pulled down the covers for me before climbing in himself. He held one of his arms up, allowing me to cuddle my body against his. "This is where you belong."

I looked up into his brown eyes. "I'd do anything for you."

"I know, Hope. That means so much."

I closed my eyes and easily fell asleep knowing that he wasn't going anywhere, because he already was home.

I held Hope in my arms and couldn't fall asleep as easily as she had. My mind was a crazy mess of what had transposed in the last two days. Just a few hours ago, I was in a jail cell, but now I was home in my bed with my beautiful girlfriend in my arms. Technically, I hadn't been charged when Trevor must have showed up at the station. I was still in a holding room waiting to be processed. One minute I was preparing to be fingerprinted, and the next I was being released.

It was all surreal considering all that had happened. Even though the charges were bullshit, they still would have stuck, had it not been for my witty girlfriend.

Mark had done a one-eighty and was now okay with me never going back to South Carolina again. He seemed genuinely okay with me being friends with Hope. It wasn't exactly what I wanted, but it would do for now. At least he knew that I'd never hurt her.

For so many nights I had to lie awake missing her. Talking to her just wasn't the same as being near her. I missed her touch and the way that her skin smelled and tasted. I longed for her beautiful smile and those sweet kisses she gave only me. She brightened my days, and without her it seemed like I was living in a storm.

There were some nights that I broke down. Part of it may have been the alcohol I was consuming, but I truly missed her. It felt like a part of me was missing. I didn't understand how my feelings for her had intensified, until I saw her at that airport. She was everything to me; my reason for living.

Her little seduction tonight was unnecessary. She already knew I wanted her. She didn't have to wear certain clothes or act sexy. I didn't care how she looked, because she would always be perfect in my eyes.

I couldn't explain it and I didn't want to. I squeezed my arms tighter around her and kissed the top of her head. This wasn't a dream. I was really here in the pool house.

I assumed that being back would warrant me to make some major decisions about my future. Since I had talked Hope into registering for college, I knew it was time for me to do the same. It was already too late for this semester, but by next semester, I would be sitting in classrooms again.

It had been such a long time since I wanted a future, but now that I had Hope I could see myself having a real shot at life. I wanted to be someone that she could be proud of, not someone who lives in a pool house, because he has given up the will to do anything with his future. I had to change.

I finally closed my eyes and imagined my future with Hope. I could see us graduating college and buying our first place. I pictured us being engaged and the look on her face when I actually popped the question. I thought about us starting a family and the birth of our first child.

I wanted all of these things now.

But...what if she wasn't sure about me? What if I was just a *now* relationship? What if Hope did not want me forever? Those possibilities consumed my thoughts. She was younger, and could change her mind at any time.

I slid myself away from Hope's sleeping body and sat up in my bed. My fingers brushed away the hair that was blocking her face. It was frustrating just imagining a life without her. There was a possibility that she didn't know what she wanted her future to be yet. She surely didn't know when we first met. The only thing Hope had been sure of was how much she hated school.

Realizing that I was frantically pushing myself to a breaking point, I cuddled my body against Hope's and managed to close my eyes until I finally fell asleep.

42

Hope

The next two months flew by. With all of the wedding plans moving in full-force, Buffy didn't leave me much time to study for my classes or spend time with Chance. He had returned back to his normal routine with ease, and after the first week he was back to repairing things on my dad's house.

I kept up with my courses the best I could, using my boyfriend as my study partner. I truly believed that he studied for my classes more than I did. During his free time he began looking into courses he could take the following semester. In the two months that he worked in South Carolina, he'd managed to save nearly ten thousand dollars. He worked a lot of overtime and on weekends, and since he had nothing to spend his money on it just kept accumulating. The community college expenses were not anything like Penn State, so Chance had plenty to get a good start on courses. He was already two full years ahead of me with credits, and I knew that if he had gotten a scholarship to Penn State then he would excel right past me in academics.

It didn't matter though, because all I wanted to do

was be with him. There were times after running around with Buffy that I would be in the same room as Chance and still miss him. It was something about him that just drew me in. There had been quite a few guys in my classes to ask me out, but none of them compared to my boyfriend. Sure, some of them were good looking, but none held a candle to Chance.

Day after day we would sneak passionate kisses in the yard behind bushes, or wherever we could. When my father would leave the house for meetings we would spend the afternoon in the pool house. At least three nights a week I would either sneak out to sleep next to Chance, or he would come in to be with me. There were many times that we weren't even intimate with each other; we just wanted the closeness. No matter what time of day it was, I was thinking of Chance Avery.

When I turned eighteen in a month, everyone would finally know our true feelings for one another. Most of them would assume I was too young to know what I wanted, and probably even feel the same way about Chance's intentions, but they would be wrong. I wasn't naïve enough to believe that our future held butterflies and rainbows, but I did know that Chance was in love with me as I was him. We had never really had a sit down discussion about marriage, but both of us mentioned how much we wanted to always be together.

Today was no different from the rest. I had a math class in the morning and afterwards Buffy and I were going for our dress fittings. I was all too thrilled when she picked out a pink colored dress for me to wear during the ceremony. Even my father and Chance had to wear matching bow ties and vests. Chance thought it was hysterical, saying it was exactly how he envisioned Buffy's big day. One day he teased me about wearing pink so much that I nudged him in the gut.

After he finally stood back up from being hunched over he promised to leave me alone about it.

I don't even know why I hated the color so much, but all I knew is that if I ever had a child, who happened to be a girl, she would not be wearing that color.

When class was over Buffy and I headed out to the next town over to the dress shop. She hadn't picked anything expensive, and I was starting to understand that she was always modest with her spending. Chance told me that she was an excellent money manager and never overspent for anything. He said that Buffy had actually found our house without my dad's knowledge. He'd been looking at newer homes in normal communities, but for what they were asking, my father was able to get double the space and have an extra pool house attached.

When I met her I assumed she was this stereotypical blonde, hungry for my father's money, and someone to take care of her. After knowing her for a while, I had found that it was the exact opposite. Buffy took care of my father. She cooked him gourmet meals and managed his finances, and always made sure his clothes were in pristine condition. She entertained him, and filled him with laughter every time they were close to each other. Most of all, she was kind and loyal to him and to me. I appreciated her so much and I knew for a fact that she was the best friend I had ever had in my life.

Buffy tried to stay out of mine and Chance's relationship. It wasn't because she wanted to, but because she didn't want to be involved if my father ever found out.

He and Chance started doing more together. At night, they would have a few beers and watch sports highlights on television. Some days when it was nice, my father would pull Chance from working on the house and take him golfing. I think Chance would have enjoyed it more if he didn't always have to look over his shoulder for the idiot Trevor, every time he was at the Country Club.

As he and my father continued to bond, we struggled with the certainty that my dad finding out about our relationship was not going to go over well. We'd even had several arguments about that such topic.

I hated fighting with him, but I knew that the closer it came to me being eighteen, the closer I was to possibly losing my boyfriend. Since I'd been working hard to rebuild a relationship with my dad, and keep a close eye on my mother I couldn't imagine losing Chance. We had to find a way to convince my dad that we were better together.

Things had really changed in the last two months for me. Mark had been a completely different person. He not only included me in some of his outings with his friends, but he wanted us all to be a family more around the house. Hope and I both took advantage of the situation, knowing we could be together all of the time. The hardest things were not being able to touch each other. Some nights after dinner we would sit around for hours shooting the shit. It was never that our conversations were boring, but it was hard to know that we could be somewhere else alone.

Hope was my girlfriend, no matter if we had to hide it or not. She knew how important she was to me and that was as good as things could be for the time being.

The wedding was fast approaching and Buffy seemed to be freaking out more on a daily basis. Her newest conquest was to have Hope involved with everything possible. Part of me was happy that they were so close, but I felt like she was keeping me away from having alone time with Hope.

Buffy made it her life mission to save money, so traveling to several towns away for something cheaper was always what she ended up doing. She would take Hope around with her for the company, and they wouldn't get back until late in the evening.

Mark didn't seem to mind. Some days we would both take off early and go to the golf course, or sit around watching football and drinking beer. The subject of Hope and I never came up and I wasn't even sure what I would say if it did.

I still had no idea how we were going to confess about our relationship. Since we have been together for many months now, it would be harder than at first. Sometimes I regretted prolonging the inevitable.

Hope seemed to be content with our situation. Sure, we both wanted to be able to be out in public without wondering who would see us, but we also appreciated the time we did get to spend together and it made it even better.

She had adjusted well to her first semester of school and I made it a point to help her study whenever we got the opportunity. Mark encouraged it, so it was necessary that we did what he asked.

We had about one more month of walking on eggshells and then we could come clean about our relationship. I had already registered for the next semester and made sure to take as many courses with Hope as I could. I already had taken most of her normal classes, but we chose several that we could take together.

I figured that Hope would complain about school, but she never seemed to struggle. My plan was once she turned eighteen, and college started back up after the New Year we could stop hiding our relationship and live together. I hadn't really mentioned it to her yet, but I planned on doing it the next time we were alone.

Again, everything depended on how her father took the news. At this point in our relationship I knew that if he went off the deep end, and kicked me out of the pool house Hope would come with me wherever I went. I hated the idea of that, but the truth was Mark had told me to stay away from his daughter, after we had already been together.

I hadn't heard from Hope all morning since she went out for her fitting with my sister. I'd been out at the hardware store with Mark picking up some new windows for the front of the house. He and Buffy decided to replace them all at the same time.

We rented a trailer and piled them all on it to get them back to the house.

I'd been busy this morning and it kept my mind off the little amount of time I'd seen her this week; but there was something that I needed to talk to her about before she heard it from my sister. I didn't think it would be a big deal as long as Hope knew ahead of time.

My sister had decided to invite all of her friends from

back home to the wedding. There was only one problem that I had with that; it was Susan.

Susan had been a friend of my sister's since they were in kindergarten. She used to spend the night with us every weekend and she even went on family trips. When I became a teenager and started noticing girls, she was the first crush I ever had. I used to try and sit close to her just to get a whiff of her hair. At first she thought of me as the creepy kid brother of her best friend, but as my body started to change, so did her opinion of me.

One night after a football game I tagged along with my sister to a party a senior was throwing. I didn't know anyone except Buffy and Susan, and my sister was already up some guy's ass as soon as we got there. Susan stayed back with me and fed me beer after beer. Finally, after a few hours she asked if I wanted to go upstairs and lay down. I agreed and headed up there thinking she was just being nice.

I was wrong.

Susan threw herself on me, and I wanted it even more than she did. After that first time, we continued to sleep together until I left for college. We never were a couple, but when my sister finally found out she flipped. She didn't talk to Susan for months, saying she deflowered her brother. It wasn't like that, but Buffy never got over it. During the time when I'd gotten into all the trouble, Susan came back into our lives saying she knew I could never do anything so horrible.

Buffy begged me not to get involved with her, and honestly, I never wanted to, but Susan never stopped trying.

I needed to tell Hope about Susan before she came to stay. Hope's birthday was one day before the wedding and I couldn't let something from my past ruin it. If Hope heard it from anyone else, she would think I was hiding something.

Finding the time alone with Hope was becoming scarce and every minute she was with Buffy, I feared she would find out.

43

Hope

For the past two weeks I'd been alone with Chance only three times. We saw each other daily, but private time was just not happening. Our quick kisses and sneaky embraces continued, even though our late night cuddling seemed non-existent.

It wasn't that either of us didn't want to. Chance begged me most nights to come to bed with him, but school had me so overwhelmed. Chance was such a smart person and he loved school. I was determined not to disappoint him. The problem was that it took all of my extra time, even after my study sessions with him to understand anything I was supposed to know already.

This morning seemed like all the other mornings, except Chance was already in the kitchen. His ornery smile was flashing across his face, making me want to burst out in laughter. "Good morning, sunshine," he said while still grinning.

"What's with you, and where is everyone else?" I asked.

Chance leaned into me and gently rubbed his nose

against mine, before pressing his lips over mine. "They had to go Christmas shopping. We're all alone."

I wrapped my arms around his neck and kissed him again. "Well I wonder what we could do all day."

Chance picked me up and sat me on top of the counter. He moved toward the fridge and started gathering items. "I am going to make you breakfast first. Then I plan on spending the rest of our day helping you study, in bed of course."

"I don't know how much I can learn if we're in bed, Chance. To be perfectly honest with you I don't think I can concentrate on anything other than you."

He continued to gather ingredients for our breakfast. "Oh, we will study. I promise you'll be fully prepared for those finals. I have a plan." He seemed sure of himself.

"A study plan? You've really thought about this haven't you?" I asked.

"Buffy sent me a text this morning saying that she and Mark decided to go out shopping last minute. I knew you had to study, but I miss you, so I implemented a plan so we could be together and study at the same time. Aren't you curious about the plan?" He asked.

I started swinging my feet while sitting on the counter. Chance didn't have his face to me, but I knew he was smiling. He was dancing around as something fried in the pan in front of him.

"Okay fine! What is the plan, since I can tell that you're busting to tell me?"

Chance spun around, caging me in with his hands on either side. "So this is how it works. You will be thoroughly quizzed on all courses. When you pass all of the questions on each subject, I will remove one article of clothing. If you fail a topic, the clothes go back on. So, in order for you to have some of me today, you have to be prepared for all of your finals." Chance had a huge grin on his face. He bit down on his lip while he waited for my response, still only inches from my face.

"What if I cheat?" I taunted.

"Not possible! This study proposition is fool proof. When you get your answers right you can have me, otherwise you get none of this." He laughed as he pointed from his head to his feet.

I rolled my eyes. It sounded like a good plan and it was possible it would motivate me to try hard. I was in. "Alright. We can study your way."

"Perfect." Chance turned around and put two pieces of toast and some eggs on a plate. "Here, you need to eat before we get started."

I took a fork and put my eggs inside of the toast to make a sandwich. I loved watching the yolk run out of the sides then later dipping it. Chance curled his lip up as he held his toast up and gently dipped it into his egg.

"You do realize that mine tastes exactly the same as yours does?" I asked.

"Whatever. It's just weird. I prefer to dip. It seems more classy."

I laughed. "Oh yeah, because eating an egg with toast is so classy. You're ridiculous."

"You love my quirks, Hope." He stuck out his tongue at me then put his plate in the dishwasher. "When you're ready to be schooled by all of my wisdom, head on over, baby."

"Maybe I will, or maybe I won't." I teased.

"Oh, I know you will. You can't resist this." He lifted

his shirt revealing his rock hard abdomen. I felt like licking my lips, but would have only let him know he was right about me not resisting. "See you soon." I watched him walk toward the pool house.

I grabbed my plate and cleaned it before heading up to my room to change my clothes. Chance had acted so cocky about me not being able to resist that I decided to get a shower. The longer I took, the more impatient he would become. I knew that he was ultimately helping me, but I wanted to be the one who was irresistible.

When I got out of the shower I looked out the window toward the pool house. I could see Chance standing at the door. Just as I went to turn away, he waved to me.

"Son of a bitch! How did he know?" I said to myself.

Obviously, he knew me too well. I took the towel off my head to brush my hair before heading in my room and putting on a cotton sweat suit. By the time I finally made it to the pool house Chance was sprawled out on the couch. The textbooks were in front of him with paper surrounding them.

"There she is....Mrs. I always know what Chance is thinking and there is no way he has the upper hand on me," he cackled out.

"Shut up!" I said as I ran over and jumped on top of him. "You still want me, so who cares?"

"True. How about you hop off of me so we can get serious up in here." He put on a game face, avoiding eye contact with me.

I rolled my eyes again. "Fine." I removed myself from Chance's magnificent body and sat down next to him. He pointed to the chair across from where he was; the chair where it all started.

"Get over there and do not get up until we're

finished. Got it?"

I shook my head and laughed as I headed over to the chair, as if he were punishing me.

A friend of mine at Penn State used to use this study plan with his girlfriend, except she was the one testing him. He said she never let him tease his way out of studying. Hope hated to study, and she would be the first person to admit it.

Once she sat down and stopped trying to argue her way out of it, I grabbed the first book and began with the questions.

For her math class she did all right, but didn't answer enough questions correctly on the first time around. She got frustrated a few times, so I grabbed the notes that she'd taken and taught her little things to remember the answers easier. When she appeared like she understood it better, I quizzed her again. This time she only missed one question, which in turn required me to remove one article of clothing. It was a wise choice for me to layer up too. When I removed the t-shirt to show that I had an undershirt underneath, she wasn't pleased.

"Seriously? When have you ever worn one of those? Did you steal that from my father's laundry basket?" She asked, frustrated.

When we got to her next course, which happened to be chemistry, she tried to distract me. She unzipped her sweat jacket revealing only a bra underneath. "It is really hot in here today." She said as she fanned herself. "I feel like I can't breathe. Maybe it's best if I strip down to my underwear."

I stared into the book and refused to look at her. Finally, after a few minutes she focused her attention on me only being one shirt away from a naked chest.

Hope must have enjoyed Chemistry class because she did well on my quiz the first time around. I stood up and acted like a sexy male stripper, as I removed my undershirt.

Before I could turn around, I heard catcalls coming from Hope's chair. I sat down on the couch, like it never happened. The key to this study session was keeping my ground. If I gave her an inch, she'd take a mile and we'd end up in my bed.

"There should be a rule that states you can't act all sexy when removing your clothes. That is so not fair!" She wasn't angry. I knew that look she was giving me. It had nothing to do with emotions. Hope was hungry for attention, and I refused to give it to her until we completed every course.

I held the next textbook high enough that Hope could not see me smiling from behind it. I love when she got frustrated. Her face became red and she gritted her teeth when she spoke.

Her next course was psychology. She did horrible on the first quiz, so I decided to take a break for lunch. I headed into the kitchen to make us something to eat. When I felt Hope's arms wrapping around me, I welcomed them in, but realized immediately what was happening. I grabbed her hands and removed them. "Hold up. Just because we're breaking for a bit doesn't mean you can sample the merchandise."

"But, Chance, I want you," she said with a pouty face. "We're all alone."

"Get back in there and go over your notes. We still have two subjects to pass before you can have some of this goodness," I teased.

"You suck," she said as she strolled back into the living room.

"That's you later!" I yelled back.

I made us both a sandwich and took them into the living room. Hope grabbed the plate and started eating, while she gave me dirty looks. I knew this was all her game to try and sway me from letting her off the hook from studying.

When we finished eating I dove right back in. Eventually I taught her a jingle to enable her to remember her questions easier. After the third attempt, she passed. I didn't hesitate when I removed my jeans and let them fall to the floor.

Hope sat back and watched me. She bit down on her lip and it took everything in me not to march over to her, pick her up, and carry her to my bedroom.

The last subject was a business management class she was taking. She managed to enroll in the class late to gain an extra credit for the semester. Hope seemed focused and within thirty minutes had answered almost every question correctly. She did a silent clap with her hands and pointed to my boxers. I gave her a big smile as I grabbed the elastic band on them and played with it. I pulled them down just enough so that she still couldn't see anything that was hiding inside of them.

"I don't know. Maybe I should have made that last test harder," I teased.

Her body language was effortlessly letting me know that we were done with this game I'd been playing. Hope wanted to get down to business, and I wasn't about to stop her.

44

Hope

I was determined to ace that last test, not only because I couldn't wait any longer to see Chance without clothes, but also because I'd never studied that much in my entire life. It was already three in the afternoon and it felt like Chance and I hadn't had alone time, even though we'd been together all day. Chance gave me a big smile before leading me into the bedroom. He was never forceful with me, and I appreciated it since my history with Trevor had been so violent.

His gentle touch gave me butterflies, each and every time. I enjoyed being with him and feeling him so close. His arms wrapped around me even before he took off his boxers.

"I think I just need one hug before you seduce me." He tantalized me with his sense of humor.

"Let's stop beating around the bush, Chance. Drop em!" I demanded.

"I plan on beating around your bush for the next couple of hours." His cackle was deep.

"Seriously, I don't even have a bush."

"You know what I meant." Chance sat me down on the bed and he knelt between my legs. "Actually, I need to talk to you about something important, Hope," he said in a serious tone.

I studied his face and all of the humor was gone from it. He put his hands on both of my knees and looked directly into my eyes.

"Whatever it is, you can say it." I trusted this man. There was nothing he could say that would make me think otherwise.

"Has Buffy talked to you about any of her friends?" He asked.

I had no idea what he was getting at. "No. Well not really. She said some of their names and talked about fun things that she did when she was my age, but nothing in particular. Why? What's wrong with her friends?" I asked.

Chance's face was indescribable. I couldn't read him like I normally could. "There's something that you need to know before they start getting here for the wedding; something that I need to fill you in about."

"Why does it seem like this is really serious all of the sudden? You're scaring me." Chance stood up and started pacing around the room. "You're making me nervous, Chance. Just spill. I can't take this weirdness with you. We just had a fun day, and all of a sudden you look like you just saw a ghost." It bothered me.

"Buffy has this friend named Susan. They did everything together when they were younger, but things changed and they grew apart, I guess."

"You aren't making any sense. Susan is in Buffy's wedding. Why are you telling me they grew apart?" I asked.

He put his hands up to his face. "Ugh! This is harder than I thought it would be," he admitted.

"What is? Dammit, Chance, just tell me."

"Susan and I had a thing," he confessed.

I froze. Not because it shocked me that he was with another woman. That was obviously something I knew about, but I was shocked that, number one, I didn't know, and number two it was Buffy's so-called best friend. Before I could say anything, Chance interrupted me.

"Hope, Susan and I had a weird kind of relationship. We were never exclusive. It was more of a mutual agreement. We would hook up every once in a while, but that's all it was, just a hook up for me."

I could hear the words coming out of his mouth, but I just couldn't believe he was telling me. I never imagined him being that type of person; the kind that had a fuck buddy, per se. Then again, I could see why he'd go along with it. He was strappingly handsome, and she was obviously older. My question was why he'd be so weird about explaining. Something was going on, and I was afraid to ask what it was.

"Chance, do you have feelings for her?"

"No! Of course not, but when things went wrong in Pennsylvania, she was there for me. It only stopped when we moved here. I hadn't spoken to her in over a month before I met you and I haven't talked to her since. I swear. It never meant anything to me except a good time."

"I still don't understand. Are you telling me this because you think she might still want you?" I'd already accused him of cheating on me in the past. I couldn't feel this jealous without him getting upset. I had to trust that he was being honest with me, because I knew in my heart that we were on the same page.

He sat down beside me and took my hand into his. His eyes turned to me. Right away I could see the worry in his eyes. "I'm telling you this because we're hiding our relationship. When Susan gets here, she'll just assume I'm single. Hope, I can't tell her about us, unless you want your father to know. I'm not saying that I know for sure she would tell, but I know that she would be jealous that I'm in love with you. I never felt that way about her. I'm just concerned that things could get awkward while she is here. I don't want you to ever doubt how devoted I am to us. You need to keep that in mind."

"I'll be eighteen on the thirty-first of December. As much as I'd like to make an official announcement about us, I know I can't ruin the wedding. If you tell me that I have nothing to worry about, I believe you." I couldn't imagine seeing him with another woman. It would tear me apart inside, even if he was rejecting her. It was the fact that she could touch him in front of everyone when I still couldn't.

I squeezed his hand. "You're right about not telling her. I don't want to risk our family going into turmoil, because of something we have been doing behind all of their backs."

"Hope, I promise you that I have no interest in being with her ever again."

"You had to like her a little to want to sleep with her. What does she look like?"

He shook his head. "No. We're not even going to talk about this. It's irrelevant, and we're wasting time on each other talking about it."

"Fine." I smiled, realizing that we were in fact alone with nothing but time to spend naked. "Are you going to take off your drawers or do I have to beg?" I was certain that we could get back to where we'd left off quite quickly.

As Chance began to remove his boxers, I thought about how much I hated someone I hadn't even met yet. He may think that everything was okay, but I was definitely worried. Somewhere in the back of my mind I wondered what this woman could be thinking about seeing him again. Perhaps she had hope they'd hook up again. I didn't know how I'd be able to sit there watching her flirt with him. It was definitely going to be difficult.

I'd finally told her about Susan. She didn't need me to go into any specific details; it would have just made her more upset. I knew that I had to tell her. Susan was going to come here and assume I was free to hook up with, and I had no way of telling her anything different.

She was a free spirited girl who didn't like taking no for an answer. That mixed with the simple fact that we already had history together was a bad thing. She was going to try to get me alone, and Hope would probably flip out about it.

I dropped my boxers and climbed into bed with my sexy girlfriend, who was already removing the rest of her clothes. I loved the way that her sweat suit fit her body, but when she took it off, I liked her new appearance better.

As much as I wanted to be intimate, I knew it was just as fun to sit there admiring just how perfect she was to me. Her smooth skin had a glow as the light came in through the mini-blinds. She lowered her chin and looked over at me watching her. When her lips separated I immediately licked mine. She was feet away from me, but I could recall exactly what it tasted like to have her tongue in my mouth. Her long eyelashes batted as she blinked, and a half-smile formed as she intently gazed at my naked physique. "See something you want, baby?"

"Oh, I think you know I want it all." She seemed confident with her reply, and I knew it was because she knew exactly what was about to happen. The anticipation alone was making my dick hard. I pulled Hope on top of me and all of my current worries vanished. She had that effect on me. The way her hands touched me, or the way her body connected with mine, made every other sexual partner weak in comparison. We were in sync with one another, and though she lacked the experience that other's carried with them, Hope knew me. She understood me in a way that none of them had before. For that reason alone I knew she was the one.

I'd never kissed anyone and felt the passion that I did with her. She had this electrifying demeanor with everything she set out to do. Hope left me in awe, and I craved the attention she gave me. She'd given me a second chance, and I would never take her for granted.

I lay next to her and stroked her hair. "Do you have

any idea what you mean to me; what it's like to finally feel like I matter?"

Hope traced my lips as she replied. "Why do you think I'm here with you, naked in your bed?"

I let her suck on my finger while I closed my eyes and focused on speaking. It was becoming a task with the current actions. "I don't want you to ever forget how important you are. Without you, my life would be meaningless. You make me want to be a better person."

"Chance, you were already a good person. Don't you see that? Don't you know that you got dealt a shitty hand? It wasn't because you deserved it." She smiled and leaned closer to my face. "Now, would you please make love to me, before I burst?"

"Burst? Hell yeah! I wouldn't want you combusting." I teased her for the choice of words she'd used.

For the next half hour, I kissed every inch of Hope's body. I started slowly below her knees and then worked my way up to her neck. When I got to her most tender spots, I took my time and used my tongue to savor her sweetness.

Hope's body jerked in ecstasy as I slid my head between her legs and pleasured her until she screamed my name. Just as I had finished, she pulled my face up to hers and kissed me deeply. She always knew how crazy it made me when she did that. My rock hard cock beckoned for attention immediately.

Hope positioned herself on top of me, and when our bodies became one, she took control of the movements. I intertwined our hands, while she rocked back and forth on top of me. I wanted to grab at her hips, but I couldn't make myself let go of her hands. Things were perfect, and our bodies seemed in sync with one another.

For the second time, Hope began to pick up the pace. Her loud cries let me know that she'd reached euphoria once more. Seeing and hearing her in that condition got to me. I felt a burst of release, and succumbed to my own reward.

Afterwards, I rubbed her back and played with her hair while she remained on top of my sweaty body. "How do you do that?" I asked.

"Do what?" She asked as she rested her head on my chest.

"You make every time just as good as the first time, maybe even better," I admitted.

I felt Hope shrug her shoulders. "You're just being nice because I gave you some." She didn't get it.

"Nope, it's the truth. You're so damn irresistible. All I want to do is be with you."

Hope began rubbing the top of my chest with her fingers. "Can I ask you something?"

"Of course you can. Ask me anything, baby."

"Did she love you?"

Except that. Damn! "I don't know, Hope. I don't want to know."

"How long did it go on? I mean, how many times?"

I didn't count how many times. Hope was fishing for answers and she really didn't need to know details like that. Hell, I didn't even want to think about them. Doing that with Susan made me feel sneaky. When my sister found out she flipped. It definitely contributed to their severed friendship. Obviously they kept in touch, but they were never as close as they were. I think Buffy refused to trust her, even though she wouldn't admit it.

"Can we please not talk about it? I'm not trying to be

mean or hurt your feelings, and I surely didn't tell you that to make you feel insecure. I just wanted you to know the truth, so that if she said anything you would not get the wrong idea about us. Please, can we just lie here together without the third degree?" I begged.

"I'm sorry. You're right." She wrapped her arms around me.

"I want you to sleep here tonight. Do you think you can sneak out later?" I asked.

I could feel Hope beaming as she lay against my chest. Her head began to nod up and down. "I'll find a way."

"Hope?"

"Yes?"

"What do you want for Christmas? I mean, you haven't told me anything." I needed ideas, because I had that and a birthday to shop for.

"Surprise me. I'll love whatever you choose. My necklace is my most prized possession. It'll be hard to beat that," She taunted.

"I smiled, knowing exactly what I wanted to get her. She would love it, I was certain.

45

Hope

I woke up in Chance's arms early the next morning. Sneaking out hadn't been a problem the night before. My dad and Buffy came in from shopping around nine and went right to bed as a result of exhaustion.

When I looked at the clock I knew I had plenty of time to cuddle with Chance before anyone noticed that I wasn't in my room. I couldn't wait for this charade to finally be finished. Maybe other people wouldn't be able to understand how Chance had fallen in love with someone that hadn't turned eighteen yet, but it wasn't like he was dating a child. I was a woman who was old enough to make my own choices. I'd come on to him at first, and though he tried to push me away, our chemistry was undeniable.

I'd been with other people, well one other person, and that relationship lasted a year. I was familiar with commitment. I'd graduated high school and was now attending college. What more could they expect out of an adult? I was on the right track, and I had one person to thank.

The three-year difference in our age meant nothing

to us when we looked at the big picture.

There had been so many times when I wanted to tell my mother about him, but each time I had chickened out. If my mother was in the wrong kind of mood or not feeling well, it could have sent her over to my father's house on the warpath. She couldn't afford to stress about things. I had to play my cards right so that nobody got hurt.

When I finally felt Chance's strong arms squeezing me tight, I knew he was awake. "Good morning, baby," he said with his eyes still closed.

"How did you know it was me?" I joked. "I could have placed an imposter here to fool you."

"Your morning breath gave it away," he kidded.

"Ha ha." I said as I leaned up and purposely kissed him.

"I knew because I never once let you out of my arms last night, and because your skin always smells like heaven."

"I like your answer. I'll let you live to see another day now." I stood up and headed into the bathroom, where I found my spare toothbrush that Chance always kept for me.

"Mind if I use your toothbrush?" I joked. He gagged at the idea of sharing toothbrushes, even though I'd done it before. I found it funny that he had little quirks. I stood there waiting for him to reply, but I didn't hear him. Then he suddenly appeared in the doorway, standing there naked in front of me.

"You have your own, smart ass. Watch out for a minute. I have to piss." He said as he walked toward the toilet and began going, while I stood there brushing my teeth.

"Seriously? I hate when you do this."

"Do what? I am going to the bathroom. You go to the bathroom at least ten times a day. What is the big deal?"

"You never want privacy though." I was a woman who sometimes needed my privacy. There were things that a female needs to do without a man in the room.

"No. I do want privacy, except from you. I have nothing to hide from you. I want to be able to share everything. We all poop, Hope. It's natural human disposal."

I cringed as he'd said it.

"Don't give me that look. I know that's what you're getting at. Trust me I eat the same food as you. I'm fully aware that you sometimes have to shit. Everyone does it."

"Oh my God, please stop. This is so embarrassing."

He stepped behind me and wrapped his arms around the front of my waist. "Everything about you is sexy to me. Don't be embarrassed. If you need privacy, I understand. I just get a kick out of giving you a hard time about it." He kissed my shoulder and stepped back.

"Why do you always know what to say? You suck!" I wanted to act mad, but I knew I couldn't. He was utterly amazing.

"I suck because I say the right thing? You do realize that is a contradiction right?"

I laughed out loud. "Yeah, I know."

Chance sauntered out into the bedroom. I knew he was getting dressed. He may be comfortable around me naked, but he didn't generally traipse around like that. He always had on a pair of boxers. I enjoyed him either way, but I always feared my father would walk in on us being together in this house, naked, and it scared the shit out of me.

I headed back into his room behind him. I didn't want to seem like a stalker but I loved to look at him. Chance was bent over, like that first day we met. He was slipping his boxers on around his ankles and started pulling them up. I noticed all of the muscles in his back moving, and for a second it was so perfect that I had to close my eyes; looking at Chance this way, made me want him. He was so tan and so perfectly sculpted. I pictured being in his arms and how he could carry me around like I was a bag of feathers. His strength was so appealing to me.

"Like something you see, cause you're literally staring a hole in my chest."

I cleared my throat. A slight part of me seemed embarrassed, but that was only because I'd been caught. "Actually, I like everything I see." I bit my bottom lip. "The things I want to do to you right now are sinful". I managed to say with a straight face.

Chance shook his head and slid a pair of shorts over his boxers. "If you continue to watch me and talk like that, I am going to snatch your ass up and fuck you all over again," he threatened.

My nipples tingled as I licked my lips. "Mmm, what's stopping you?"

A shirtless Chance came walking towards me. He didn't waste any time grabbing my waist and pulling me against his lips. He kissed me so hard that I thought I was going to lose consciousness.

I put my hands over his chest and pushed him down on the bed. He watched as I removed my top and then my bottoms, before climbing over top of him. I licked his navel and placed small kisses all over those beautiful abs of his. He played with my hair as I drug my lips over his tanned skin.

I sat up and ran my hands over his stomach again playing with his belly button, then finally making it to where the elastic on his shorts sat. As I worked, I could feel his readiness pressing against my hand and I focused on pulling the shorts down.

It was ironic how I used to hate being intimate, and I loathed the idea of having other partners, but Chance made that all go away. I loved him, maybe even from the first time our eyes met, as corny as that seems. Maybe his body pulled me in, but his demeanor and kind soul showed me what it is was really like to love someone. Chance had been saving me since before he really knew me. That meant more to me than anything. He was truly my best friend.

46
Chance

Hope wasn't very cautious with her father being in the house across the yard. She had successfully gotten me back into bed. I have trouble saying no to her, especially since I'd been back home. Being away from her was painstaking and I never wanted to experience that again.

As she removed my shorts I wondered if I should stop her. Hope massaged my thighs with her hands, and placed kisses on my stomach which made me crazy. It was the little things she did to me that made me want her like there was no tomorrow.

When I couldn't take it anymore, I grabbed her and pulled her body up to meet mine. Without any effort I slid into her and she let out a small moan as it happened. I watched as my beautiful girlfriend sat straight up, and placed her hands on my thighs behind her for support. It caused her chest to stick out further, and as she moved, so did her breasts. I couldn't help but reach up and run my fingers over her nipples. They were so hard, beckoning me for attention.

"Does it feel good, baby? That's it, ride me. Fuck, you're so sexy. Touch yourself. You know what I like."

Hope smiled as I ran my hands down to her small waist and began guiding her yet harder. I watched as the grinding became rapid. She threw her head back and let out a beautiful cry as she reached up and squeezed both of her own nipples. "Chance..."

When I heard that, I couldn't help but finish myself. Hearing her say my name turned me on, but seeing her touching herself made me erupt. It was like a direct order sent straight to my penis. This time Hope collapsed on top of me. We were both breathing heavy, when we heard my door open.

I grabbed Hope, who was still attached to me by her legs, and carried her into the bathroom. I lifted her up, sticking her in the shower, then turned on the water and jumped in myself. I hoped that whoever was here did not notice the water turning on after they'd already marched in.

As Hope stood there in the shower behind me, I heard two sets of voices. We were caught, I just knew it. All I could think of was that my life was officially over. I was about to die at the hands of her father.

I heard my sister's voice first. "Chance? How long are you going to be in there?"

I stuck my head out from behind the curtain, even though she clearly was not standing in the bathroom. Then I realized Hope's clothes were thrown all over my bedroom. This couldn't get worse.

"I just got in. What's up?" I tried to sound calm.

"Mark and I need to talk to you. We will just wait in

the living room until you finish," she yelled.

I looked down at Hope who appeared as if she was going to be sick. "I love you." I whispered in her ear. "No matter what happens, we'll find a way."

I pulled back and watched as she mouthed the same words to me. Figuring this might be our last time together, at least for a while until I either recovered from Mark beating the shit out of me or somehow being arrested for sleeping with a minor, I started washing Hope's hair. She closed her eyes and didn't fight me. When I started to do my own and then wash my body I saw the tears in her eyes. She knew why I was taking my time, and her fear matched mine. Before turning off the water, I gave her one last kiss over her lips.

"It will be okay. I promise," I whispered.

I turned off the water and reached a towel for Hope first. I helped her out and grabbed a towel for myself. When I made it to the hallway I peeked out realizing Mark was sitting in a chair with his back facing us. Buffy was sitting across from him, not even noticing me standing in a towel. I grabbed Hope and led her into my bedroom so that she could get dressed at least.

Before I could even find shorts she was already fully dressed, sitting on the edge of my bed. I threw on my clothes and kissed her one more time, trying not to get choked up over it.

When I headed out to the living room, I knew it had only been about ten minutes in total from the time they had come into the apartment. I threw on a t-shirt as I made my way into the room where Buffy and Mark sat waiting.

"Morning, you two. What's up?" Even though I knew what was up. I tried not to look Mark in the eyes as I sat down next to my sister, reliving all of the ways his daughter had satisfied me only a short time ago.

Mark had both hands on the ends of the chair's arms. To me, it appeared he was trying to control his temper. I could feel the beads of sweat already starting to form across my forehead, even though I had just gotten out of the shower. I didn't care if he hauled off and hit me. I'd gone against his word time and time again. There was no way he would understand how I felt about her. This could only end badly.

47
Chance

I was prepared for anything. If he wanted to call me out about being with his daughter, I was going to tell him the truth. I was in love with her and probably had been since we started this affair. She made me want to live again and I couldn't imagine spending one day without her. That had to count for something.

When his mouth opened, I hung my head high and waited.

"So, as you know the wedding is just a month away. Your sister and I drove a few towns over to shop for Christmas. I realize that this may be too forward of me to ask, but I wanted to know if Hope had talked to you about school? I know that you help her study all the time, and I think it has been a big influence on her. Did you know she hates school?" Mark asked.

So far, I wasn't getting the crap beat out of me.

"Yeah, she mentioned it a few times. And to answer

your question, no, she never really talks about it. Why? What's up?"

Mark looked over at Buffy and then back to me. "Chance, I have some connections here in Virginia. I have made several calls on your behalf, and I personally went to college with the baseball recruiter over at Virginia Tech. I know I should have talked to you first, but I felt so bad for sending you away to South Carolina. I want you to know that I trust you and that I'm sorry."

"I'm not sure I'm following you?"

"My friend, who is the recruiter, he knew of you, Chance. He watched you play in high school, but you'd already picked Penn State. Anyway, his short stop broke his leg last week and they say he won't be able to play for at least a year. I told him how you lived with us and were planning on enrolling at the community college next semester. After explaining everything that happened, he pulled your transcripts and saw your college grade point average. They want you to play for them, Chance, at least for one year. What do you say about that? Would you like to go back to school at a university instead of a community college?"

I was stunned; this had nothing to do with Hope, but actually it had everything to do with her. "I'm kind of in shock right now. Do I need to give you an answer this minute? I've already enrolled at the community college," I stated.

"He needs to know before they look into other options. They'll need to know by week end."

I was surprised, excited, and even overwhelmed. Who was this guy? How did he know all of these important people? My mother always said 'Don't look a gift horse in the mouth' and I finally got it! "Wow, I want to say yes, but I think I need a couple days to think about it. I feel like I'm dreaming." I scratched my head, looking to my sister for some kind of sign. "Why did you ask about Hope? What does she have to do with this?"

"We figured if Hope saw you going there, she would want to follow. She looks up to you, almost like you're her brother," Mark replied.

Holy shit! Her brother? He was so wrong...

"Okay. Just give me a little time to think about it. I'll let you know what I decide by lunch time." I watched as he and Buffy got up and began walking away. "Mark thanks for this. I really thought I'd never get an opportunity this big again."

"We just want you to be happy, Chance. What happened in Pennsylvania was unfortunate, but it's over. It's time to move on with your life. You deserve more than living in a pool house forever," Buffy said before they headed out.

I watched them enter into the main house, and then locked my door. I needed to start doing that.

"You can come out now, baby. They're gone."

My girlfriend came creeping out of the bedroom. Her face was expressionless.

I grabbed her into my arms and kissed her on the forehead. "That was close. I've got to lock that door when you spend the night."

Hope sat down on the couch and I sat across from her on the chair. "What are you going to do, Chance?" She asked.

"It all depends."

"On what?"

"On you, silly. I don't want to do this without you. I promised that I wouldn't leave you again," I stated.

"I can't ask you to do that, Chance. You have to make your decisions about what is best for you. I want you to be happy, and I know how much it hurt you when you had to stop playing ball. This is your second chance. You have to take it," she explained.

"Hope, things are different now. My life has changed. I don't want to do this without you." I admitted. "Besides, I might have to live with roommates at a dorm for the first year. You're the only roommate that I want, Hope. Don't you get it? You are my future. I want to be with you for the rest of my life." I knew that was a major confession, so I let it sink in before saying anything else.

Hope stood up and faced me. "Chance, I can't talk about this right now. I'm so sorry. I have to get out of here."

I grabbed her hand and tried to keep her from leaving. Tears ran down her face. I didn't understand what was happening. I thought she would be excited. Why was she running away?

"Hope please wait. Tell me what's going on. Is it because we'll be living apart? Please talk to me," I begged.

"Chance, I can't do this. I can't take away your future when I don't know what I want for mine. I'm so sorry, but that also includes us. I love you, but I don't know if I want this forever. I just don't know. I'm so sorry. I have to leave." She darted out the door, without another word.

I stood there in shock. What was happening? Did she just leave me? I was crushed.

I'd just gone from citizen high to citizen low.

Hope

I couldn't let him blow an opportunity like this. I did what I had to do. I lied.

Chance was everything to me, and he was the only future that I wanted, but to see him struggle with a decision like that because of me made me so angry. He should have said yes, even before speaking to me. The fact that he waited for my decision was wrong. I couldn't be with him when I knew he would regret that decision forever.

Once he was enrolled and doing well I would tell him the truth. If he still wanted me then, we'd figure it out.

Suddenly, I realized what I may be giving up. I wanted to run back to him and tell him I was lying, but I couldn't. I just kept running down the street; running from my reality of what I'd just pushed away. I was forcing Chance away so that he could have a real second opportunity at a life that should have been his in the first place. Just because he met me didn't mean he had to pass on it.

I'd gotten about three blocks from my house when I heard a familiar sound. Chance's motorcycle pulled up beside me. "Hope, what are you doing?" He demanded an answer.

"Chance please, I can't get into this with you right now," I said while trying to avoid his face.

"I know what you're doing. I won't let you do this to

us, because you think it's the right thing for me. You're wrong. I know you love me. I know you want this. I know you want our future." I felt burning in my throat as I focused on denying his claims. I wanted to tell him he was right. Running into his arms would have been so much easier. I just couldn't live with myself knowing that I kept him from something he thought was out of his reach. I had to let him want to try.

"You need to do this. Just accept the offer and see this through. Please," I begged.

He grabbed me by the arm and forced me to look at him. His hands cupped my face. "There is no fucking way I'm going to let you do this, Hope."

"I don't want what you want anymore," I lied in a low tone. It took everything I had to keep a straight face. I felt like I'd just stabbed myself directly in the heart.

"Stop lying!" Chance grabbed both of my arms. "Please don't do this to me." His eyes filled with agonizing pain as I watched the first set of tears drop down his cheeks. "You make me want to live again. I don't want this if you aren't a part of it."

Just seeing my handsome boyfriend shedding tears because he feared he was losing me made me start sobbing. I put my hands over my face to try and hide my emotions from him. "I just want you to be happy."

He tugged my hands down. My vision was blurred by the amount of liquid in each of my eyes, but I could see that he was looking directly at me. "Don't you get it? Don't you understand? You *are* what I want. I may not have known it then, but from the first moment I met you, I knew you were important. I know we're young, but there was never a doubt for me. I love you and I want to marry you, and someday have our own family."

I shook my head. "School is important, Chance. You can play ball again."

A couple cars passed, reminding us that all of this was transpiring in public for anyone to see. I was at the point where I didn't care. I ached from the inside out, knowing that this decision was going to destroy me while still going along with it.

"Dammit, Hope! Are you even listening to me? Yes, I was excited about the offer, but none of that is as important as us. I want you to do something. I want you to look me in the eyes and tell me that you don't feel the same way. If you can say that to me then I will believe you. I will accept Mark's offer and throw myself into Virginia Tech. I need to hear you say it though."

I took a deep breath and looked up at him. His eyes were red and it was apparent that he was frustrated. I didn't know what to do. On one hand, I wanted to throw caution to the wind and give in to my own desires.

"I can't, Chance." I looked down at the ground.

He put his hands around my face again. "Stop fighting me. I'll always choose you." He said as he put his lips on top of mine. "I'm already enrolled in the community college and have my schedule picked out. I am not throwing away anything that I need in my life. I promise you."

Realizing that my father could come driving down the road at any moment I backed away from Chance. "Maybe we should talk about this somewhere else," I suggested.

"Do you trust me?"

"With my life."

"Stop trying to make my decisions. You aren't some summer fling, or some young love. Besides, I haven't played ball in such a long time. I don't know if I could even get back into it the way I was before."

I looked away, feeling defeated. "Fine."

He ran his hands through his hair as if he wasn't satisfied. "Do you want a ride back to the house?"

"No! I'm just going to pretend I was out for a run. I'll meet you back there." I watched as he climbed back on his motorcycle. "Wear a helmet next time."

"Sorry, I saw my future running away and I didn't have time for safety." He gave me a wink and took off toward the house.

I ended up walking the whole way back giving me time to reflect on what had just happened. I guess I was an idiot to think Chance would just give up on our relationship. The cards were all on the table now. Chance was very clear about his intentions with where our relationship was going. He was right about one thing. I wanted the same.

There was a part of me that wished he would have just said yes. The separation would be something that we dealt with already; surely, we could do it again. Maybe he was right about not being in the same place he was when he played ball last. I didn't want his decision to be based on just me. I hated that he would do that.

Perhaps he would have said no after thinking about it. It bothered me, but not as much as the look in his eyes when I lied to him. I couldn't do that again.

48
Chance

It really ticked me off that Hope assumed she could just walk away without a fight. Had she not been in the bed with me earlier confessing our feelings? She was insane to think I'd let her go just because a scout looked my way.

Sure, for my entire life baseball had come before anything. The murder of my friend, and my absence from the world had shown me what else was important. I no longer dwelled on what could have been, and now looked to what I might be able to have. What I knew for sure was that I needed to wake up to Hope's smile every day for the rest of my life. Her name said it all; she gave me hope.

Once I got back to the pool house I sat there waiting for Hope to show up. She took her time getting back, and I knew part of it was because she had to show her face in the main house before paying me a "friendly visit".

She ambled in the door and stopped immediately when she saw me sitting there. "Before you say anything I want to apologize."

"I'd prefer it if we just forget it ever happened. Hope, I'm going to college, and I plan on getting a degree. Even if I went to a school a couple hours away, it wouldn't change anything between us. Besides, I'd want you there with me."

She smiled and swayed her body as she stood there. "I don't want to lose you. If you say you want me with you, I'll be there."

After much consideration we decided to go spend a day at Virginia Tech to check out the campus and the baseball organization. Since mine and Hope's falling out she'd been more positive about me at least seeing it through. I wanted her to come with me, and Mark had pushed the idea just as much in an optimistic way, thinking Hope would fall in love with the campus and would want to go too.

Our day had been planned out so we took Hope's car knowing that Mark wouldn't allow her on my bike. It was starting to get entirely too cold to be riding a motorcycle around anyway.

We left early in the morning, and by the time we'd made it to campus we'd stopped three times. Once was to get gas in Hope's car. The next was because Hope drank a large coffee and couldn't hold her bladder. The third was because she said she was starving to death. I didn't mind though, because anytime with her was nice. I still liked teasing her about it though.

When we walked onto the campus I noticed that it was a bit overwhelming for Hope. The community college was nothing compared in size to this, and she seemed genuinely afraid. While the sports coordinator showed me around she tagged along behind us, taking more of a sister approach as opposed to my girlfriend. It was easier that way for both of us since we never knew who the friends with her father were.

After we'd toured what appeared to be the entire sports facility we took a break for lunch. Hope and I purchased some sandwiches from the cafeteria and found a shaded spot in the grass. The sun was shining, and thankfully the temperature was over sixty degrees. I pulled Hope between my legs after we were done eating. While the breeze blew her hair around her face, we watched as the students congregated all around us.

"So what do you think?" I asked.

She shrugged. "So far it seems pretty cool. It's bigger than I imagined it to be. How about you? Are you ready to move out here?"

"The facility is nice and it seems like they have a good program going here, but you know I'm nervous about starting back up again. It's really been a long time. I don't know if I'll be ready enough to play this coming spring," I admitted.

I kissed the top of her forehead. She pulled my arms across her chest tighter. "So, how far do you think the dorms are away from each other?"

I wondered if Hope was actually considering going to school here. I'd explained to her about the strict curfews that I would have to abide by if I was on the team. Between practice and classes, our time together would be limited. I knew it was hard for her to take, because it was also difficult for me. I didn't like the little time we had now, and then it would be cut into half. Sure, we could be together more freely, but by then she would be eighteen and it really wouldn't matter too much. We planned on telling Mark about our relationship once the wedding was over.

"We need to go meet that guy about it now actually." I lifted Hope up easily to a standing position then stood up behind her. Since the sports director was not around I could hold her hand without her worrying who would see. When I grabbed it, she looked up at me and smiled.

The next hour or so was spent exploring around the large property. The dorms were situated in different areas on campus, and honestly there was no way to tell where one would be placed. Hope seemed uneasy as we toured each room. They were small, and although she was used to a small room at her mother's, she now had a huge one that she didn't have to share with anyone else.

When the guy giving us the tour talked about roommates I thought Hope was going to pass out. I squeezed her hand to let her know I hated it too.

Once we were finally done toddling around with the guide he offered that we could explore anywhere we wanted to. Hope and I thanked him for his time and began walking around the different buildings. Of course, this university offered so much more than the community college. It was a good school.

As we were strolling through, we heard someone calling my name. I continued holding Hope's hand, not really caring anymore who would see. The baseball director that knew Hope's dad was approaching us. I still never let go of her hand. She looked up at me and I winked at her, letting her know that I just didn't care. No matter what, we were going to be together.

"Mr. Avery, I forgot to give you this information booklet. It has all kinds of questions and answers, and if you can't find anything feel free to give me a call. Also, we need to set up a time for you to come in and practice with the team. We need to get a feel for your playing skills. I've seen you play, but others are curious if you still have what it takes," he said.

I grabbed the brochure and shook the guy's hand. "Thanks! I'll be glad to come in whenever you suggest."

As he strode away I looked at Hope and shrugged. We'd finally toured every inch of the campus and climbed in Hope's car with sore feet. The college was listed as twenty six hundred acres, but it seemed like we walked forty miles.

Hope decided to drive home while I looked through the information that we'd gotten from the tours and the sports director. I was already familiar with most of the information. Most universities have the same type of guidelines. One thing that caught my attention was that freshman needed to live on campus, but after that they could live off campus. There was even a coed dorm available. I knew Hope and I couldn't room together, but if we were in the same building it would be easier to spend time together. Besides, neither of us would be there on scholarship. That meant we could live off campus together if we wanted.

Maybe I was getting overly excited. Just imagining being in college with Hope at my side was overwhelming. She may have overreacted before, but now she seemed just as interested as I did.

"Did you like it?" I asked.

"Kind of a lot to take in. How about you? Are you ready to sign on the dotted line?"

I grabbed her hand and kissed the back of it. "I won't go anywhere without you. But yeah, I can see myself walking around campus with the hottest woman on the planet."

Hope giggled. "I'm not that hot, Chance."

"Um, then you must be looking through a dirty mirror. Yes you are, baby." I looked over at her driving. She had her hair up in one of those messy buns. She was wearing a small amount of eye makeup, but not too much. Hope was so tan that she never needed to wear makeup. "In fact, just looking at you makes me horny." I taunted.

"Chance! I. Am. Trying. To. Drive."

"What? It's the truth. I mean, if you need to pull over so that I can show you, I won't be opposed," I said convincingly.

She shocked me. "Okay. Where shall we pull over, smartass?"

"Seriously? That would be awesome."

Hope took her eyes off the road and looked over at me. "I was kidding!"

"Damn." I wasn't convinced. I took my hand and slid it down the inside of her thigh. "Are you sure?"

I watched her bite down on her lip. "I don't want to get caught."

"Chicken," I teased.

I ran my hand up and down her thigh again, this time putting a bit more pressure. I leaned over and kissed her on the neck, and then the bottom of her chin. "Let's just find an old abandoned road for a little while," I suggested.

"We are in the middle of nowhere. Are you kidding me right now? Have you not watched horror movies where inbred cousins slaughter people in broken down vehicles?"

"No, I'm not kidding and what the hell? That's fiction. Come on, baby, I want you so bad. It's difficult to be around you and not want you. I think you fed me a love potion, because I never used to be this sappy."

"Oh my gosh, you're being so stupid!" She laughed.

"I want you to kiss me until my lips hurt." I kissed her neck again and nibbled on her ear. "If you aren't going to pull over, you should at least let me drive, that way you can straddle me."

I saw her famous half-smile forming. "Stop talking about it. I can't concentrate on the road."

"Sorry, I can't help it. Your body is sending me subliminal messages. It's saying...Chance...I want you so bad...take me, Chance...oh yeah...I want it." I started laughing after I said it.

"I don't say that," she corrected.

"Yes you do." I said as I ran my hand through her hair that was coming out of the bun.

She started giggling again. "Whatever."

I was smiling from ear to ear. I could tell she was having a good time with my humor, or else I wouldn't have taken things too far.

"So are we going to park or what?" I pushed.

We were on a country road and had passed several old dirt driveways that were clearly abandoned or possibly hunting property. "Turn into the next opening."

She shook her head as she started driving onto a little hidden driveway. "I can't believe you're making me do this."

I kissed her on her cheek slowly then reached my lips to her ear. "I'm not making you do anything, baby, well nothing you don't want to do," I teased.

Hope threw the car in park and within seconds she was sitting on top of me. Her hands were all over me, and mine all over hers. We were in the middle of nowhere and didn't have to hide our actions from anyone, so I planned on taking full advantage of the situation.

49

Hope

I can't believe that Chance talked me into parking in the middle of nowhere for some afternoon delight, but he had, and I loved every second of it. Once I put my car into park I climbed right over and began groping my boyfriend. I wasn't sure how serious he was really being when he was telling me to do it, but after a while I was just as interested in the possibilities.

Chance had the strongest hands and he knew just how to use them. We were trying to make do with the little space we had in the car, but it was not working out as good as we had anticipated. Even my backseat was small in comparison to Chance's body. He stood nearly six foot tall, and maneuvering both of our bodies was quite complicated.

"Let's get out," he suggested.

Chance opened the door without taking his hands off of me. He'd reached behind and opened it then guided me out only to press me back against it. I stopped kissing him to look around at the property. We were on a long driveway surrounded by huge trees. It was cloudy out, but it seemed shaded also. Chance didn't waste any time when he picked me up and sat me on the flat part of my trunk. I wrapped my legs around his waist and pulled him toward me. My hands slid up his hard chest. It was enjoyable to feel every muscle as I brushed over them with my palms.

I felt my bra loosen and with one swift tug. He'd removed my top with little effort.

Chance bit down on his lip as I watched his hands pulling away my straps, exposing me to whatever was out there in the woods with us. In heat of the moment, I didn't even care. I was too turned on to contemplate anyone being out there beyond the trees.

"Is there a blanket or something in the trunk?" Chance asked.

I ran my tongue against his neck and slid it up to his ear. "Yes," I whispered.

He pulled away from me and began his embark toward the driver's side of the car; as I grabbed a shirt to cover my naked chest. It was hard not to notice the protruding bulge in his pants. "Hurry up," I ordered.

"I am," he shouted, as he got to the driver's door. "Shit!"

"What is it?" I jumped down from the car, heading in his direction.

"It's locked. Go around the other side and hit the unlock button," he suggested.

I ran to the other side of the car and tried the passenger side door. "Oh, crap." Then I quickly tried the back door that we came out of. "Oh no, no, no! It's locked, too."

"Fuck! I must have leaned you against it as we were getting out. Shit!" Chanced leaned his head over the roof of the car.

"What are we going to do?" I asked.

"See if any of the windows are cracked." He suggested.

We both looked on our sides. "Nothing!"

"Same here." I rubbed my face with my hands. "What are we going to do?"

Chance came over to my side of the car. He took me in his arms. "Right now we are going to pretend we aren't locked out of the car." He pressed his lips against mine and removed the shirt from my hands.

"Chance we shouldn't," I said, as our lips pressed together.

His lips worked their way down my neck, and then gently across one of my exposed breasts. My head fell back, and I knew I was losing the battle. "We can't," I repeated.

He reached for my waist, pressing me gently against the car. "We can." He wasted no time unbuttoning my pants.

"We shouldn't." It was my last attempt, except the sensations were too strong. I couldn't fight the desire I had for Chance when he was touching me. I wanted him to continue, and I didn't care if we were doing it outside, while being locked out of the vehicle.

The next time he pressed his lips on mine I wiggled myself out of my pants. Just as fast as I'd done that, I proceeded to unbutton his pants. Chance picked me up and I wrapped my legs around his waist. My arms went around his shoulders, and within seconds he entered me.

Being with him like this was so erotic. We were exposed in the woods. It was private, but not really. I pulled Chance's shirt over his head, while hearing a car go by on the road we'd came in on.

We felt the raindrops hitting us, but did nothing until

they became heavier. We should have stopped, but the more the rain hit Chance's body, the more I wanted him. His chest was so slick when my palms glided over it. I leaned forward, lapping up the drops of water off of his skin. The sounds of our bodies slapping together echoed off the trees, along with our matched bout of moans. I reached up, taking a handful of his wet hair and pulled his lips into mine. Our slippery mouths played together, each kiss intensifying with our steady pace. Chance pushed me back, allowing my body to lie flat on the car. He ran his hand over my slick breast, circling my nipple with the wetness from the downpour. Thunder rumbled in the distance, sending chills all over me. This wasn't just crazy, it was dangerous, making it the hottest sex I'd ever experienced.

I savored Chance's lips again, sucking the water off of them, and then licking them dry. He teased me with his tongue, pulling away when I leaned in, and with no warning Chance picked up his rhythm. He pumped into me so hard that I cried out each time our skin smacked together. My toes curled as I felt myself losing control of my muscles. As I clung to him overwhelmed with passion, he tightened up, closing his eyes, drawing his ending out. He held me tight against him, and let the rain continue to fall down on us.

We were two people, naked, in the middle of the woods, too caught up in each other to care about anything else.

Finally we came to the realization that we were going to run out of daylight. Chance paced around, I assumed to think of ways to resolve our problem.

"Now what do we do? We're soaking wet and it's getting cold," I said as we began looking around for our clothes. Putting them on was pointless considering they were all in puddles beneath our feet, but we did it anyway. The rain continued to fall and even though we were up shit's creek, I couldn't help but admire how beautiful Chance looked soaking wet. He was so irresistible that I had sex with him while stranded in the rain. He was making me lose my mind, and I felt invigorated.

Chance looked around the woods. I had no idea what he was doing, but he seemed like he knew.

The rain was really coming down now. I hugged myself trying to keep warm. Chance came back to the car with a giant rock in his hand. "I promise I will pay to have this repaired, Hope."

All I could do was nod. I just wanted to be warm.

I hated having to break Hope's window to get inside the car, but neither of us had our phones. We were stuck in the woods in the middle of nowhere. It wasn't like I could easily flag someone down to help us. It was starting to get dark and pretty cold, not to mention that the rain wasn't letting up.

When Hope saw me with the rock she didn't overreact. I chose the passenger rear window, because it was the smallest. When the rock hit it the tiny tempered glass pieces crumpled in and outside the car. I took my hand and reached in to unlock the door. Once it was open I got Hope inside and ran to the driver's side to get the car started. When the heat came on, Hope looked relieved. She rubbed her hands together in front of the vents when her teeth chattered. I knew exactly how she felt as I began the same process.

"I thought we were going to freeze to death," she admitted.

I watched as she continued to hold her hands up to where the hot air was blowing. We were both soaking wet. Before I pulled out of the wet dirt road I remembered she said she had a blanket in the trunk. I ran to the rear of the car and grabbed it, and after I got back in wrapped it around Hope to get her warm faster.

"Is that better?" I asked, while my teeth were still chattering.

"Much." She gave me a quick smile as I climbed to the back and made a makeshift cover for the broken window out of an old bumper sticker I found on her backseat. I bit the sticker into small pieces so it acted as tape, and used a piece of cardboard from an old taco box I found on the floor. It was a good thing Hope had a messy car.

"Okay, now let's get you home." I climbed back into the driver's seat and put the car into drive.

"Chance?"

"Yeah, baby?"

"I love you."

I looked toward her. "I love you too. I'd do anything

for you. You know that."

After about a half hour of driving, Hope fell asleep. We only had another half hour to go, so I didn't bother waking her.

Driving home in the silence gave me a bunch of time to think about everything that happened. I enjoyed visiting the school and seeing what all of our possibilities could be, but I just didn't feel as excited as I would have anticipated.

I wanted more than just to play a sport forever. Finishing my education was important as well, but I was looking at a bigger picture now. I could do all of those things and have Hope by my side. I didn't need to separate the two. We needed to make the decision to move together. I wouldn't do it without her, because I knew that once school was over, she was my future. I couldn't risk giving that up for any reason.

It wasn't that Hope would deliberately make me give something like that up. She wasn't like that at all; in fact, she would have pushed me toward it, forsaking her own happiness for mine. It pissed me off when she put her needs last. I wanted her to be happy too. In all honesty, Hope was the kind of girl that didn't need much to make her happy. She made do with what she had and was generally satisfied with it. Whatever we were to decide, we needed to do it soon. With Christmas and the wedding, things were about to get hectic.

When I pulled into the driveway I noticed that the living room light was on. Without waking Hope I managed to reach into the passenger side and lift her into my hold. She wrapped her arms around me, but it was obvious she was still half-asleep. Mark met me at the door and held it open while I carried Hope upstairs to her room. I received some curious looks when they saw her disheveled hair and blanket. I knew as soon as I sauntered down the stairs I would be drilled by the sergeant himself.

Sure enough, I hit that last step and he was there waiting. "What happened to you two?"

"Hope thought she hit something so she pulled over. We both jumped out of the car, but one of us must have somehow hit the damn lock button. When we went to get back in, we were locked out. Our phones and everything were in the car. I had to break the window to get us inside." I confessed, although only half was the truth.

"I assume it was already raining?" He asked.

"Yep, it had just started. Anyway, Hope said she had a blanket in the trunk, so once I got her safely into the heat I grabbed it, and made sure she was warm enough."

"Thank you, Chance. You are always keeping her safe. I really appreciate it." He gave me a pat on my shoulder. "So come in here and tell me how it went today. Did you see anything you liked?"

"Do you mind if I grab some dry clothes?"

"Not at all," he replied.

I ran out to get changed and came back in feeling much better.

We met in the kitchen, and I started pouring myself some tea immediately. "It was really nice. The fields are great there. Seems like they have a lot to offer."

"What about Hope? Did she seem interested?" He asked.

I shrugged my shoulders. "Some things she really liked, but you know Hope. She hates school. I don't know what she wants honestly. Maybe giving her a goodnight's sleep will help."

"So, have you made up your mind?"

"I don't know yet, Mark. I mean, I haven't played in a while. I don't even know if I'll still be good enough," I admitted.

"I don't mean to keep pushing you about it. I just want Hope to get a degree in something. She has no clue what she wants to do with her life. I feel like if she has you there, she won't feel so reluctant about it. You're friends, and you could be a mentor to her like you are here at home."

If he only knew how I mentored his daughter.

"I will talk to her tomorrow about it," I announced.

"Thanks for taking her today. She never would have gone with me," he admitted.

I laughed. "Probably not."

I took my drink and headed out to the pool house. Hope was already waiting for me in my bed.

"Hey, how did you get in here?" I asked as I crawled in beside her.

"I went out the garage door while you and dad were talking. I locked my bedroom door and he already thinks I'm sleeping. I just wanted to be close to you. I'm still sort of cold," she confessed.

I cuddled my body up to hers. With one final kiss to the top of her head, I easily fell fast asleep knowing she was right where she belonged.

50

Hope

Waking up in Chance's arms was something that I wanted to do every day for the rest of my life. It didn't matter where we were as long as it happened. His strong hold wrapped tightly around me and I'd never felt safer.

Knowing I needed to get back inside of the main house before I was detected missing was getting easier. When I snuck out I would wear my running clothes. Exiting Chance's pool house from the rear was simple, and I would return to the house without my father knowing any different. Most of the time, he didn't even notice me coming in anyway.

I kissed Chance on his perfect nose. "Good morning."

He kept his eyes closed but gave me a welcomed smile. "Morning."

Chance nestled his face into my hair. I actually think he enjoyed smelling it, since he did it often. I let him hold me close, because I was not ready to get out of his warm bed.

"What are your plans today?" I asked.

"Well I would love to stay right here in this bed and hold you tight all day, but I guess that isn't very feasible." He sighed. "I need to run out and get this Christmas shopping done so that I'm not out there with all the crazies."

"Can I come with you? I have to get something for my mom, and I also wanted to pick out Dad and Buff's wedding gift."

I felt little kisses on top of my head. "Of course we can go together, after I get your window fixed. I almost forgot about it happening." He was quiet for a second. "Do you want to get them something from the both of us?"

Chance knew I didn't have much money. I had saved some when I was in school and even worked a small job as cashier at Rylee's mom's consignment shop, but it was dwindling away. My father was always leaving me twenties and since Chance and I are a couple he never let me use them, so I had a stash from that.

"Yeah, what do you have in mind? I don't have a whole lot to spend," I confessed.

Chance started running his hand over my arms. It felt good but gave me goose bumps immediately. "I was offering to pay for all of it, Hope. We're a couple. Plus, I don't think you realize how much money I made when I went away. You know I was working almost eighty hours a week and forty of that was double time? I saved almost every cent I made. I will buy the present from both of us."

"I don't want you to have to do that." I felt like I was worthless, and I certainly didn't want him to feel like I'd ever use him.

Chance turned me around and looked directly into my eyes. We were so over the morning breath issues, in fact we never even discussed it. "Hope, I want to spend the rest of my life with you. I'm completely okay taking care of you and our children. If you decided that you don't want to finish school, I

will be fine with that too. I'm in this for the long haul and I
want to take care of you."

His words were perfect, but one thing stuck out. They
were actually shocking to me. "Children, as in more than one?
How many do you want exactly?"

"We can start with nine boys. After that you can have
your girls," he teased.

I picked up a pillow and hit him with it. "Do you know
what my body would look like if I had more than nine
children?"

"It doesn't matter, because I will still love you.
Besides, your body would only have changed because we
created so much perfection. Every stretch mark will remind
me of that." Chance's words made me want to cry. They were
beautiful.

"I don't know what to say." I pushed the pillow out of
the way and leaned in to kiss him. Then I whispered in his ear.
"You know the probability of me having nine children that are
all boys is highly unlikely."

"How about we start with one and go from there? I
only wanted nine to have my own ball team, so I guess I'll just
have to be the coach of our child's team, whether it's a girl or
boy." He kissed me again.

"When will we be having this child?" I was afraid to
ask. It was understandable that Chance wanted to discuss our
future. I remember wondering what I'd name my kids when I
was still one myself. I think it just represented long-term. As
much as I wanted that, it was scary going into uncharted
territory.

He shrugged. "Whenever you decide to go off the pill.
I don't think Mark would have the heart to kill his grandchild's
father. I'm not saying I want to do it now, but if it did happen,

I wouldn't be pissed about it."

"You seemed to have put a great deal of thought into this. Do you have names already?" I asked curiously, knowing darn well that getting pregnant at eighteen was not on my to-do list.

"Of course I do." I watched dimples forming on his cheeks, and knew this was going to be good. "The girl will be named Faith, and our son will be Lucky."

I burst out in laughter.

"What? Don't you think that's good? We can have one of those country signs made over our door. Instead of it saying Faith-Hope-Love, it will say Faith-Hope-Chance-Lucky."

I continued laughing until I was sure I was going to pee myself. I got up and ran for the bathroom. It was becoming a habit for me to just go with the bathroom door wide open, so I decided to continue the conversation. "What would the dog's name be?"

"Oh that's easy, Rumplestiltskin," he yelled.

As I was trying to get up to finally brush my teeth, I cocked my head into the bedroom door. "What the hell? Why?" I asked while still in hysterics.

"Have you ever known a dog with that name? I mean, if I take him to the park I want him to know I'm talking to him. I think it is quite genius actually." Chance was still in bed with both his arms folded behind his head.

I rolled my eyes and let out another chuckle. "You know that is ridiculous right?"

"Probably."

Looking at the mess on the top of my head, and brushing my teeth with the brush stuck in my mouth, I continued to speak. "So when do you want to head out to the stores?" I asked.

"Well since the mall is about an hour from here, I would say soon," he replied.

I ran back into the bedroom and jumped on top of him. I had fresh breath, and had managed to get my hair looking halfway decent. "Get up then. I'll meet you in the house in a half hour. I'm going to go run around the block, and then hop in the shower." I leaned in to kiss him.

He pulled me back down on top of him. "I just need one more hug from the future mother of my children and caretaker of Rumplestilskin." He continued with his early morning bantering. As much as I wanted to stick around I knew I had to get myself motivated. I got up and headed out of the pool house, just like I did almost every morning, leaving my cute, half-naked man in bed.

After finally managing to get myself out from under my warm blankets I jumped in the shower, and then dressed. I had to call two different places before I managed to get someone that could repair Hope's window while we shopped.

When I headed into the main house I found the three of them glued to the television in the kitchen. They barely took their eyes off of the screen. "Good morning, people. What's so interesting?" I asked.

Buffy didn't say anything; instead, she grabbed the remote and turned up the volume.

Investigators found the woman living in Ohio. It appeared that the incident had been staged so that the woman could run away from her life here in Virginia. Since there were never any formal charges in her disappearance, the case has been closed.

After adjusting the volume back down on the television, they all turned to look at me.

I took a sip of my coffee. "What? I told you all I had nothing to do with it."

"We're just glad everyone else knows that now, Chance," Buffy admitted.

"Buffy's right, you have to feel some kind of relief knowing you don't have that lingering over your head," Mark added.

"I do, but I knew all along that I'd never met the woman." I took another sip of my coffee. "So I managed to find a shop near the mall that can fix Hope's window today. She and I have some wedding and Christmas shopping to do, so we're going to drop it off," I explained. It was great that we were actually allowed to hang out together. It sure made being together easier.

"Thanks for taking care of that so quickly, Chance. I was going to make some calls about that this afternoon," Mark replied.

I finished my cup of coffee and rinsed it in the sink. "It wasn't a problem. Besides, I'm the one that had to break it."

"Yeah, but you did it so that Hope wouldn't freeze to death," Buffy got her two-cents in.

When I finally looked up to meet Hope's eyes, I noticed that her hair was down and the natural waves were showing off her highlights. She was wearing tight jeans that tucked into a pair of black riding boots, and a sweater that showed off a lot more cleavage than it probably should in the shape of a V. I tried not to stare, but I couldn't take my eyes off of her. She caught my gaze. "Are you ready to go, Chance?"

I was wearing one of my Penn State hoodies and a pair of jeans that were meant to have small rips around the pockets. In comparison, we really didn't match up well. "I'm just going to change my shirt. I think this might be too hot once we get into the crowded mall. I'll be right back."

I ran straight toward my closet and found a short sleeve V-neck that I usually wore when I went out. I kept the jeans on, but grabbed my leather jacket, which happened to match Hope's boots. With one last spray of cologne, I headed to the front yard where I found my beauty waiting for me.

Hope bit down on her lip when she took a look at what I'd changed in to. "My boyfriend is yummy," she confessed in a low enough voice that no one else could hear.

"He doesn't compare to my girlfriend," I joked. "Seriously, Hope, you look fucking amazing."

She smiled and started her car. "Thank you."

I couldn't take my eyes off of her for the entire car

ride. At one point she held her hand up to shade herself from me, because I kept taking pictures on my phone. When we finally got to the glass shop I jumped out and opened her door for her. I wanted everyone there to know she was taken.

The mall was right across the main highway from the shop, so it was easy for us to walk over there and get our shopping done while we waited.

I held Hope's hand as we crossed the busy road, and even as we strolled from store to store. I noticed people looking at us, and I couldn't help but smile. We were both dressed pretty nice; compared to a few people that were actually shopping in raggedy old pajama pants.

When we got into a major department store I headed directly toward the household section. "Where are we going?" Hope asked.

"We are getting your dad and Buff one of those new coffee machines that makes one cup at a time."

Hope giggled as we approached the said machine. "You're getting them something we can use too? How awesome is that?"

"My ideas are always kick-ass, baby." I threw her a smile before turning my attention to the selection.

We ended up picking out the biggest machine, and after buying a specific coffee and the accessories I wasn't worried about them thinking we bought it for ourselves too.

Hope decided she wanted to get her mother a charm bracelet. I thought it was a great idea, because they could always add to it. We found a jewelry kiosk in the center of the mall and started working with an associate to gather the charms Hope was looking for. Before Hope caught on, I saw the chick checking me out. I tried to be polite and smile, but she immediately got all googly eyed.

Just as I saw Hope had noticed, I grabbed her hand and kissed it. I looked directly up at the girl. "Do you have any large diamond rings here?" I asked.

Her eyes got really big. "No, we only sell accessory jewelry. There is a fancier store right down there though if that is what you are looking for," she explained in a shitty manner. I wanted to laugh in her face. Why did chicks do that when the guys were obviously taken already?

Hope was looking up at me as I gave her a wink. "We're going there next, baby. I can't wait to get that thing on your finger." I announced loud enough that the girl would hear playing off how she'd reacted.

We paid for our things and headed on our way. Hope stopped me after we were out of the girls view. "I can't believe you did that."

"Did what? I told her that I wanted to get you a ring? It was the truth," I confessed.

She didn't know how much I wanted her to have it. I know we were young, but it was a promise that when we were ready, we would do it.

"You know I can't wear something like that around the house, Chance. At least not for the next few weeks." She corrected.

"Fine, I'll wait!" I gave in. "So who're we shopping for next?"

"Actually, I need to get you something. Do you want to pick it out yourself?" She asked.

"Hell no! I like surprises. In fact, you being in a giant box would be awesome. Do you think you could put yourself under the tree?" I joked.

Hope looped her arm into mine as we walked. "I don't think that would be a feasible option."

We both laughed. What she didn't realize was that I was truly picturing her coming out of that box, naked of course. "Well how about you go shopping for me and I go shopping for you, then we can meet back here in thirty minutes," I suggested.

"Okay, it's a deal. No peeking at the bags though."

"You too!" I threatened and pointed my finger at her. "And no talking to hot dudes." I added.

Hope started stepping away from me backwards. "The only hot dude in this mall is already mine. See you later, baby."

Hearing her call me baby was hot! She needed to do it more.

51

Hope

After finishing shopping with Chance, I couldn't wait for Christmas to get here. I'd made plans to spend time with my mother, and was eager to give her the bracelet that Chance had helped me purchase for her. I was also contemplating introducing them. It was exciting for me to finally be able to show him off as my boyfriend.

Buffy and my dad had gone out for a Christmas Eve party and left he and I alone for the night. I'm sure Buffy knew what was going to happen, but my dad sure didn't. They'd been so caught up with wedding plans, that Chance and I were able to spend all of our time together.

Since the temperature outside had dropped, he was working on projects inside the house, so I usually just hung out or helped him.

Chance and I had made plans for an all night marathon of A Christmas Story and National Lampoon's Christmas. There was no other two favorite movies of mine that I could watch over and over during the holidays.

Chance made us hot chocolate and we cuddled on

the couch together.

"Do you want to open your present?" I asked anxiously.

"What about tomorrow?"

"I have something normal to give you then. This present is just for us," I confessed.

Chance got a huge grin on his face, and I could see those shallow dimples showing. "Sure. Can I give you one of yours then?"

"Okay."

I ran up to my room to get Chance's present ready, while he ran out to his place to get mine. I was so nervous and wondered if this was some mistake. It certainly wasn't something I was comfortable with.

When I had put the finishing touches on it, I heard Chance coming in the kitchen door. I ran downstairs and hid until he was parked comfortably on the couch. I snuck up behind him, tied the bandana around his eyes, and then turned on the song 'Santa Baby'.

I was so nervous that my body was shaking profusely. I started rubbing Chance's legs and made sure he didn't try to touch me. By the time I'd sat back on his lap, he knew what was happening. His hands slid from my neck to my very tiny Santa's helper bra and panties. They were both red velvet with fur trim, but the fabric was non-existent at that.

When Chance felt the fabric, he quickly pulled off the blindfold. "Holy shit!" Was all he could say.

I stood up right in front of him and swayed my hips slowly from side to side. I squatted down and came back up running my fingers over my exposed abdomen. The black heels I had borrowed from Buffy's closet were actually easier than I thought to dance in, and I felt extremely sexy with them on.

I picked up my foot and drug my heel between his legs, making sure it brushed against his hardness. His eyes never left my body. He kept biting his lip and contorting his face, like I was torturing him. I ran my hands through my hair, letting my hands linger behind my head. I turned and readily shook my ass right in front of his face. Then I kneeled on the floor, crawling my way up to his lap, so I could lick him across his lips.

Chance's hands were on my chest as he cupped my breasts in his hands. He tugged at the tiny bra and allowed them to fall out of the top. His tongue brushed against one of my nipples and I felt it trigger a reaction instantly between my legs.

All of my nervousness had subsided as Chance ran his hand down my abdomen, and reached into my decorative panties. When his finger found out how hot and ready I was, he began sliding it in and out of me. My legs straddled his body on the couch as he continued to move his finger deeper into my folds.

I thrust my head back and felt the sensation growing between my legs. Finally, I erupted and felt it running through my entire body. "Oh, yeah," I cried out!

I didn't waste any time unbuttoning his jeans and pulling it out with my hand. Chance ripped off my Santa panties right before I jumped back on top of him. His mouth found my nipple again, the exact moment his hard cock entered me. I moved up and down in a steady groove. The room had once been chilly, but it was now scorching hot. I gripped Chance's shirt and pulled it up over his head. I just wanted to see that chest, the one that I thought about so often. I used his shoulders to push my weight up and down, while he tugged at my waist to assist. My breasts were bouncing in his face, so he stuck out his tongue to catch my nipple. He pushed them together licking them both at the same time.

"Please don't stop, Hope. Fuck me, baby," he murmured as he licked both nipples again.

This time we both screamed out in a simultaneous bout of extreme bliss. I collapsed on top of him, allowing his strong arms to keep me close. "That was awesome," he whispered in my hair while still out of breath. "Can you wear that every year for me?"

"Mmm, of course."

Hope's present to me was AMAZING! I was glad she finally let me touch her, because I was about to explode in my pants just having to watch. She had no idea what her body did to me, and with only a week until her eighteenth birthday,

I was becoming anxious. We decided we were going to wait until after the New Year to tell the whole world about our relationship. We were both concerned that her parents wouldn't approve, at least at first. We'd been sneaking around for so long now that it was going to hurt more than help.

"Would you be mad if I gave you both of your presents tomorrow?" I asked.

"No. Did I do something wrong?"

I shook my head "Baby, you did everything right."

"I guess I can wait," she replied.

Since I knew that Buffy and Mark were going to be home really late, it was just another reason for Hope to sleep in my bed tonight. I wanted to wake up and be the first person to wish her a Merry Christmas.

"How about we head over and climb into bed? We can continue watching the movies from my room."

We both stood up and gathered our clothes. Hope ran upstairs and grabbed something to wear in the morning when she went for her run. We then headed to the pool house. My mind was all over the place as we climbed in next to one another. It wasn't just Christmas that excited me. It was Hope turning eighteen.

When I woke up it was brighter than normal. I climbed out of bed to go to the bathroom, and stopped to look out the window. It had begun to snow and the grass was already covered. Realizing it was Christmas morning I hurried to go to the bathroom, brush my teeth and grab Hope's secret present.

When I got back into the room she was already sitting up leaning on her elbows. "Come back to bed," she purred.

I climbed onto the mattress and handed her a shoebox that I had tried to wrap myself. The ribbon was in disarray, but it served its purpose enough.

She looked at me having no idea what the gift was, and began to unwrap it. To her surprise, the box was empty, so it seemed. She shook it and heard something small hitting the sides. She grabbed the ball of tissue paper and started ripping it apart.

Hope froze when the tiny ring fell onto her lap. She held it in her hand and looked up to me.

"Chance?"

"Hope, I know we're young. I don't want you to feel like this is something we have to set in stone. Our love story has been complicated from the very beginning. It seems like we always have some hurdle standing in our way. I bought you this ring as a promise. I promise to always love you and want to share my life and my future with you. You don't have to wear it, but just keep it until you're ready."

Hope looked at the ring. It wasn't gigantic, but it wasn't too small either. The heart diamond in the center was only a half carat, but the band was covered in tiny diamonds all the way around. "If you don't like it we can return it. I picked out white gold because it goes so well with your skin." When I realized I was starting to ramble, I shut up, desperately waiting for a response.

When she remained silent I felt as if this purchase had been a huge mistake. How could I have thrown myself out there without considering it could backfire?

Hope looked up at me, and I noticed her eyes were filled with tears. In that instant I felt like she was going to tell me she couldn't accept it.

I was panicking.

"Chance, this is so beautiful. I don't know what to say. I certainly didn't expect anything like this from you. It must have cost a lot of money."

"Well, I paid off my motorcycle that I'd bought on my credit card, and it was just begging me to buy something else with it. It doesn't even matter what it cost, Hope. You mean everything to me."

Hope put the ring on her finger, and I got butterflies watching her admire it. "What if I don't want to ever take it off?" She asked.

"Well as happy as that makes me, I think you might want to at least wait one more week," I suggested. "So does this mean you like it?"

"I love it! I want to wear it forever."

I couldn't contain the size of my smile. "I love you. It represents that promise. Merry Christmas."

"I love you too, Chance, Merry Christmas."

Once Hope and I were ready to let go of each other, we both finally made our way into the main house. Like always, my sister had made a huge spread of food. She greeted me with a big kiss while I snatched her up for a hug.

Hope and I had already sat out the gifts under the tree; we'd even shook the ones with our names. Once we had breakfast and coffee we headed into the living room to exchange presents.

Hope and I handed Buffy her first box. Buffy smiled and began opening it. When she pulled out a custom made apron she stood up and put it on. Her name was embroidered at the top and all kinds of pastries were in different patterns all over it, but the best part was that it was almost all pink. "Oh my gosh, I love it! Thank you guys so much."

I looked over to Hope and smiled. "Hope picked it out. She wanted you to have something for your new shop. You're going to need something like that with all the cakes you're going to be making." Part of Mark's big deal was that he got to lease one of the properties for his and Buffy's new bakery. She was more than thrilled about it. I think it helped Hope see that even when her dad was being selfish, he had more than money riding on the deal. He was doing it as a surprise for his wife-to-be.

"You're right, little brother. Here." She handed me a package. "This is from Mark and me."

The small box looked like it could only fit jewelry, but when I opened it I found a set of keys. "What's this?" I asked.

"We got you an old clunker. Don't get too excited it barely passed inspection, and could use some TLC, but Mark knew this old man who died, and his son just wanted to get rid of it. You need something that has four wheel drive and a roof on it," Buffy announced.

"Thanks, guys. This is awesome."

After walking out to check out the old red Chevy truck, we went back inside and continued to exchange gifts. Hope and I had gotten Mark some new towels that attached to his golf clubs with his initials sewn on them. We also gave him two packs of his favorite golf balls and matching covers for each of his clubs. He seemed thrilled.

Hope gave my sister her last package from us, which turned out to be her favorite gift. She had taken a picture of Buffy and I with our mother, and had it enlarged and put on a canvas. We both had tears in our eyes when she saw us standing there with Mom. "This is amazing you guys. Thank you so much."

Mark got right up and started hanging it at the top of

the stairs for her. She just kept looking at it. She and Mark had given Hope something to hold her IPod to her arm while she ran, and some new running shoes. They gave Hope a gas card that contained two hundred dollars. She was elated with that gift. Gas was expensive after all.

"Here, Hope. I got you a little something," I said as I handed her the package. She opened it up and saw that it was two concert tickets to one of her favorite bands.

"Wow. Are you going to go with me?" She asked.

"If you want me to. I bought the second for whoever you wanted to take," I said, knowing darn well I'd be her date.

Hope handed me a large box. "This is for you, Chance."

I looked up at her, wondering what could be in this box. When I opened it, I gasped. Inside were three separate canvases, kind of like Buffy's. All three were of me playing baseball and she had them done in black and white. They were all three about ten inches square and I traced my own image, as I looked at them. "These are awesome. Where did you get these pictures?" I asked.

"Actually, I gave them to her when she told me she wanted to get them done. Your living room needs some help brother," Buffy admitted.

"Thank you so much. I reached out and hugged her with one arm, and it took everything I had not to pull her in for more.

Finally, when all of the other small gifts had been exchanged, Hope and I handed Mark and Buffy one last gift each. They both looked to one another and reached into the matching gift bags. When they pulled out a sweatshirt from each bag, they seemed confused, until they unfolded them and saw what they said.

Large letters saying VT were written across the front. They looked to each other and then to us.

"Hope? Does this mean you'll transfer and go to Virginia Tech too?" Mark asked.

"Yeah, it does," she replied.

He took her into his arms. "Thank you, sweetie. I'm so proud of your decision."

Hope hugged him back. "You should probably thank Chance. He practically begged me," she fibbed.

Mark extended his hand out anyway. "You're a good guy, Chance. I'm happy to have you as part of this family."

I shook his hand back and wondered how long he would think that.

For the rest of the afternoon Buffy fed us until we couldn't move any longer. The snow continued to fall, but Hope still needed to visit with her mother. I didn't want to worry about her out on the roads, so I asked Mark if I could just drive her over in the new truck. I'd never met her mother, but now was as good time as ever to do so.

Mark didn't hesitate to say yes, considering it was for his daughter's safety. I think he and my sister wanted some alone time anyway.

I helped Hope get her gifts together and we climbed into the truck. I hoped that meeting her mother wouldn't ruin the perfect day we were having, but prepared for whatever might come.

52

Hope

I managed to wear the ring backwards on my right hand so that no one would notice, but I refused to take it off. Chance kept looking at me admiring it as we drove to my mother's house.

"I'm going to tell her about us."

"You don't want to wait?" I could sense he was nervous. We'd waited too long already though. I was sick of keeping it a secret. Chance was my future and there would soon be nothing standing in our way.

I shook my head. "No, she'll be able to tell. It's best that I just tell her."

Visibility was becoming difficult, but he still took one hand off the wheel and grabbed mine. "Whatever you want to do, Hope. Your parents knowing won't change the way I feel about you."

"I know."

We pulled up at my mother's house and she opened

the door to greet us. When she took one look at Chance, I could already see the curiosity in her eyes.

"Merry Christmas, honey. Come on inside and get warm. This weather is beautiful, but so cold and dreadful as well."

"It's great to see you. You look well."

"I am. I'm doing so much better. My new medication is keeping me going, that's for sure."

It was good to hear. I worried with my decision to go off to college if she'd have another flare up. That would be difficult to handle being a couple hours away. Still, it wasn't far enough to where I couldn't drive to reach her.

Once we were in the house and had removed our coats we sat down in front of my mom. "Mom, this is Chance," I announced.

My mother leaned over and shook his hand. "Nice to meet you. So you're the guy who lives out back?" She asked.

"Yes, ma'am. I'm Buffy's younger brother," he explained.

My mother looked from me to Chance. "May I ask how much younger?"

"I am twenty-one." I watched his Adam's apple move as he swallowed. I could tell from the way he was carrying himself that he was nervous.

After she just sat there staring back at him, I couldn't take it anymore. "Mom, Chance is my boyfriend," I blurted out.

She smiled briefly then got her motherly look going. "It's not surprising. Living under the same roof had to help that along."

From her sarcasm I could tell she wasn't thrilled. "Chance lives out back in the pool house. We aren't under the same roof." I gave him a smile before continuing. "I'm practically eighteen already, but if it makes you feel better, I can break up with him for the next seven days, and then get back together." My flip comment caused her to calm down.

"That's not necessary. I want you to be happy."

"Speaking of that...Chance talked me into attending Virginia Tech. We're both starting there next semester. He's playing baseball for them," I explained.

"Where did you attend school before?" She asked.

Chance cleared his throat. "Penn State. I had a full ride there, but after my mother died, I took some time off."

He didn't have to tell her about what else happened. The past was in the past, and I wanted him to not have to think about that part of his life anymore.

"Wow, Penn State. That's amazing. You must be extremely smart," my mother noted.

I looked over to Chance and noticed he was blushing. "I think school is important. That's why I kept pushing for Hope to go. I think she needs to get a degree in something that she loves."

He reached over and grabbed my hand. My first reaction was to pull away, and my mother caught on immediately. "Exactly how long have the two of you been hiding this relationship, because I know your father and he would never allow this to go on in his house?"

I squeezed Chance's hand. "Since June. We met before we knew about Buffy and Dad. When I moved there we'd already...ugh-gone out. We tried to stay away from each other, but it became difficult. You're right, Mom, he doesn't know. We've only told you."

Chance squeezed my hand tight. "I love your daughter, Miss Ryan. I'd never hurt her. I realize you might think I am too old for her, or that us living so close is a bad idea, but I can assure you that Hope is in good hands."

"I appreciate your honesty, Chance. Actually, I think you're wrong - at least about my approving. Honestly, I couldn't have picked a better person myself. I didn't care for her last boyfriend very much. Excuse my French, but he was a bit of an ass. She needs someone that appreciates her. You seem like you have that taken care of, so you have my blessing. With my recent health problems, it makes me happy knowing she's not alone."

"Mom? Really?" I couldn't hold my excitement in. I ran over and hugged her. "Thank you so much. This is the best present ever."

"What are the living arrangements going to be?" She asked. "When you do tell your father, granted he doesn't want to cut off this guy's genitals, what are you going to do?"

There were some things that my mother did not need to know. "Chance and I will be living in separate buildings at school."

"I would be a bad mother if I didn't ask," she admitted. "Though, it doesn't really matter. Once she turns eighteen, I have no say."

"Are you going to tell Dad?" I asked.

"As much as I would like to hurt your father, I think I'll keep my mouth shut about this." She ran her hands across her legs. "How about we open some presents?"

I liked that my mother changed the subject. All in all, she seemed to genuinely like Chance. I wasn't sorry for waiting to tell her. Who knows how she would have reacted before, but today was Christmas and I was almost legally an adult.

"Chance helped me pick out your gift, Mom. I hope

you like it," I said as I handed her the box.

My mother opened the neatly wrapped package and her eyes lit up. While she took her time looking at all of the separate charms, I started explaining what each one represented.

"The baby boot is to remind you of me. The house is to remind you that you always gave me a wonderful home. The heart signifies how much I love you. The book is to show that you have a daughter who is attending a university."

She had tears in her eyes. "Oh, honey, I love it so much. Thank you."

Once my mother calmed down she handed me a small package. "I wanted you to have this. Your grandmother gave it to me before she lost all of her memories. Since I didn't have a lot of spending money, I decided it would be something perfect that you could always keep."

I opened the box to find a diamond tennis bracelet. "Holy Crap, mom. I can't take this."

"Yes you can. I never get dressed up anymore anyway. Here, let me put it on you." She reached over and wrapped it around my wrist. As she was doing so, she noticed my ring that I had turned backwards. "Oh my goodness what a beautiful band. It's so small and dainty."

She looked at the ring, but never noticed that the other side had a rock on it. "Chance gave it to me for Christmas."

She looked up to Chance. "You did great picking it out."

We spent the afternoon with my mother. She made us lunch and we talked about how her boyfriend was taking her to see his whole family. When I asked where he was, she stated he had to work at the nursing home until four.

The weather was getting worse and we knew we couldn't afford to stay much longer. My mother seemed to be getting concerned about it herself. I was surprised when we went to leave. She reached up, hugged Chance, and said something in his ear. He smiled and nodded his head before following me to the truck.

The day was going great. I had my girl around my arm, and we'd just told her mother about us. She took the news better than I could have imagined and Hope seemed thrilled about it.

The roads were really getting slick and I had to drive slowly in order to keep us from sliding off into a ditch. The entire ride home we'd been the only vehicle on the road. It made me nervous when we reached the country roads that a snowplow hadn't even visited yet. I wasn't used to driving such a big vehicle, and I worried if I took a turn too fast we would be in big trouble.

"I'm just going to take my time, Hope. I want us to get home in one piece," I announced.

"That's a good idea," she said as she scooted in the seat right next to me and buckled back up. "I hope you don't mind me changing seats. I felt so far away from you."

"Have I told you how awesome you are?" I asked.

She put her head against my side. "Not in the last ten minutes."

"I love you." I never hesitated when I said it, because it was the one thing I never doubted.

"I know you do, Chance. This really is a beautiful day."

After a long ride, we made it home in one piece. I almost choked when we pulled up behind a Jeep with Pennsylvania tags. "Oh, shit!"

"What? Who is it?" Hope asked.

I should have known that our perfect Christmas would have come to an end sooner than later. I shook my head and placed it on the steering wheel once we came to a stop. "It's Susan's."

Hope grabbed my arm. It was snowing too hard for anyone to see us in the truck. "Who cares. She can't hurt us right?"

I shook my head again. "Here's the problem. She likes to drink and run her mouth. Knowing Buffy, she won't tell her about us in fear that she will blab after a bottle of wine. If she doesn't know we're together, she's going to try to hook up. I swear to you that I have no interest in being with her, but not being able to give a reason could become a big problem."

"I appreciate your honesty. It'll be fine. It's just a few days anyway. After that we can tell everyone."

I looked into her eyes. "You're right."

"Then let's go in and say hello to this Susan."

I was reluctant, but we couldn't sit outside and contemplate our plan. It was going to be a long couple of days, even if Hope thought it wasn't going to be a big deal.

53

Hope

I wanted to picture Susan as some older woman who was overweight and maybe missing a few teeth. She was the opposite of that. In fact, she was the opposite of me. She had very long straight hair that was obviously professionally styled. Her face was beautiful and the makeup she was wearing made her look like she was a movie star. Unlike Buffy, she was dressed classy in some kind of tunic sweater and her long legs were exposed with only a pair of leggings that accented her narrow hips. She had a glass of wine already in her hand, and as we strolled in the door, I watched as her eyes lit up. It was like she immediately had locked Chance in as a target. It was that moment when I knew she was exactly the threat Chance had warned me about.

The beautiful woman walked right past me and took Chance into a long embrace. "Oh my God, Chance, it's been so long. I've really missed you. I hope you don't mind me coming in a couple days early. I just wanted to be able to catch up with you. You look amazing." Before he could get a word in edge wise, she leaned in and kissed him straight on the lips.

I swallowed hard and tried to keep from screaming. Buffy came up behind me and sensed my anxiety. She grabbed me gently by the arm. "Susan, don't be rude. This is Hope, Mark's daughter I was telling you about."

She slowly let go of my boyfriend and turned to face me. I watched as she looked from my hair to my feet, and then finally extended her hand. "Nice to meet you. I guess I didn't realize he had a kid in high school."

"Actually, Hope's in college." Chance corrected her and gave me a wink before anyone could notice.

"Well you're very cute. I bet she has lots of hot young men coming over to swim in that pool with her."

"Not if I have anything to say about it," my father interrupted.

I watched him walk into the room. They were all holding drinks, and when Susan, the now bitch-I-wanted-to-choke noticed Chance was empty handed, she took it upon herself to drag him into the kitchen by his hand and attend to his thirst, or whatever else she had in mind.

When I couldn't see them any longer it made me feel jealous, vulnerable, and mostly angry. Chance was mine, and beyond the fact that we were together in secret, I wasn't going to let ANYONE, especially this chick ruin my life.

"How was your visit with your mom today?" My dad asked.

"It was nice. She was impressed with Chance for some reason," I tried to say nonchalantly.

"Well he's an impressive kid. It looks like he may be preoccupied for the next few days though. The way Susan talked, they go way back," he replied. I couldn't help but notice how my dad seemed excited for Chance. More than anything I wanted to run to my room and cry.

He may as well have kicked me in the gut, or stuck his hand into my chest and ripped out my heart.

"So, where is she sleeping? Do I need to get the guest room ready?" I asked.

Please don't say the pool house. Please don't say it...

"Actually, she put her things out in the pool house already. She said Chance wouldn't mind. Besides, he needs to be around a good woman this time of year. I don't want him being alone and depressed." My dad explained.

I caught Buffy looking at me. The worry in her eyes was obvious. She knew I was about to lose it.

I could hear a woman laughing in the kitchen, and felt the tears accruing. Before it was obvious to my dad, I excused myself.

"I am just going to go upstairs for a bit. It isn't like I can drink wine with you all," I said sarcastically.

"I think Hope should be allowed to have a glass of wine with us, Mark. It isn't like she'll be driving," Buffy stated.

"She can have a glass at dinner," he said.

I rolled my eyes and marched upstairs to my room, hearing Susan laughing even when I'd gotten to my room made me want to get in my car and drive away.

I flopped down on my bed and began crying my eyes out. I don't know why I couldn't handle things. I knew he wasn't doing anything with her, but it hurt so much anyway. She put her things in the pool house. God only knows what she packed to wear to bed. I was so beside myself with jealousy that I refused to go back downstairs. I couldn't see her hanging all over him. I couldn't watch her seducing him. It was agony, like I was being tortured from the inside out.

In all honesty it was bullshit. Chance was mine.

I had to keep telling myself that.

I hadn't realized that I had fallen asleep until a knock at my door woke me up. Chance came sauntering toward me. "Hope, baby, are you okay?"

"No! I can't stand it. I hate her for touching you. This isn't fair. I feel like a kid being punished. How can I be in the same room with little miss hands? How can I smile when I want to stick my fingernails in her eyes?"

He laughed at my response. "I like it when you're protective."

"Well I like it when she packs her shit and leaves. If you think I'm okay with her sleeping in that pool house you've got another thing coming, Chance. I will cut you off. No, I'll give you back this ring."

"Jesus, woman. There's no need for drastic measures. I don't plan on sleeping in the same place as she does. Once she has enough to drink, she'll pass out. It's not going to even be an issue."

"If you say so. It's still going to be a while, and she obviously can't keep her grabby hands off of you. She acts like you're a piece of freaking meat."

"I happen to like being referred to as a piece of meat, when you're hungry."

I shoved him away from me. "Jerk."

He shook his head, leaned in, and kissed me on the lips. "They asked me to come get you for dinner. Hope, I am so sorry she's here. There's only one woman in this house that I belong to, and it's always going to be you. Try to calm down enough to have Christmas dinner with me."

I finally looked up at him. He knew I'd been crying; it was obvious. "She's not sleeping in the same house as you!" I reiterated.

"The hell she is. No fucking way, Hope. I won't let that happen, I told you. Please calm down."

I started to feel better just hearing him say he wouldn't allow it.

He leaned down and played with the ring on my finger. He brought it to his lips and kissed it. "Nothing will come between us. Please know that."

"Okay, I'll try." It was all I could say.

"Twenty minutes," he said. Chance leaned down further and pressed his lips against mine. "The only person who'll be in my arms tonight is you."

I watched Chance walk out of my room, and I finally got myself out of bed. I ran over to the mirror and started doing my makeup to hide the redness. I decided to change my clothes, for some revengeful attention at the dinner table. I wouldn't be treated like a child in my own house.

The tight black dress was low cut and accented every curve of my body, especially my large breasts. Susan could kiss my ass. I had one feature that she did not and I was fully prepared to have Chance staring at them during the whole meal. Two could play the seductive game, and I already knew who the winner would be.

I let my hair fall down my back and the natural curls fell right into place.

The voices were coming from the dining room, so I ran into the kitchen. I took two shots of some clear liquor that my father drank with coke. Both went down smooth, and since I hadn't heard anyone calling me, I took one more.

My hands ran down my dress and I made sure it was sitting perfectly as I sauntered into the room. Everyone stopped talking. Chance was in the middle of taking a drink when he literally started to choke.

"Hope, you look amazing." Buffy announced. She pointed her hand to sit across the table from Chance. "Sit down. I poured you a glass of red. I hope you like it."

"Thank you." I tried not to look at Chance, but I could feel his eyes burning into my body.

When I caught a glimpse of Susan she seemed to also be staring me down.

Most of the dinner discussion was Buffy and Susan reliving their youth through stories. They included Chance in a few, but after the first bottle of wine I noticed Susan getting a bit too open about her and Chance sneaking around when they were younger. At one point he actually got up from the table and got himself a beer.

The liquor was really showing its ugly face by the time dessert was served. Buffy had made some fancy shit that she probably spent hours on. I could barely feel my fingers, so poking at the pretty designed cake was fun. I found myself laughing out for no reason at random times.

"Hope, are you okay?" My father asked.

I was sick of hearing that bitch talk about all the places she had fucked my boyfriend. I looked up and smiled. "Just dandy, daddy."

Chance's stare burned into me, and I couldn't help but laugh at him. In fact, I couldn't stop laughing at EVERYTHING.

"What is wrong with you?" My father demanded. "You couldn't be drunk from one glass of wine."

"Plus some shots!" I said while still giggling.

Chance looked upset with me. I couldn't have him mad at me. He tried to mouth me the word sit down, but I stood there staring at him.

With no regard for us or our future, my drunk self did

something horrible. I pointed across the table at Chance and Susan.

"Do you want to hear about my first time?" My body started swaying and in the corner of my eye I saw my father coming at me. "My boyfriend forced me to sleep with him, and after several attempts he took me while other kids at the Country Club sat there watching us. Then he fucked my best friend the same week."

My father had come up behind me and grabbed me. He was pulling me out of the room apologizing to everyone for my actions.

"Let go of me," I screamed.

"You're embarrassing yourself, Hope. What's the matter with you? Why would you drink so much? Did Trevor try to call you? This isn't like you. Did something else happen?" He asked.

I stood on the first step and looked my dad in the eye, by this time Chance and Buffy were standing in the doorway. I looked over at Chance. "I miss my boyfriend. I wish we were together but we aren't. He is with someone else now." I cried like a little baby. My dad didn't know I was talking about Chance, and my drunk self couldn't even begin to think about what I was saying. He obviously wasn't really with her.

I ran upstairs to my room and locked my door. Finally, after a few hours, I saw Buffy standing over my bed. "Take these." She handed me two pills. "Hope, I'm so sorry. I can't believe she was throwing herself on him like that. I should have known better."

I didn't want to talk about it. I wanted to know if Chance hated me. "Where's Chance?"

"Downstairs with your dad and Susan," she explained.

"I can't watch them, Buff. It hurts too much." I started

to cry again.

She shook her head and hugged me. "I never should have kept this from your father." As she continued to comfort me she spotted my ring, which in my drunkenness had turned diamond up. "Oh my god, is that?"

"Chance gave it to me. It was his promise to me," I confessed as tears ran down my face.

"Why are you crying? I should be the one crying." she admitted.

I let her hug me. "He'll never forgive me for tonight. I was such an ass."

"That man is in love with you, Hope. Nothing will change that. Please calm down. I'll make sure he comes upstairs. Just give me a few minutes."

I watched Buffy leave the room. The laughing had finally stopped downstairs and I wondered if everyone had just gone to bed. Not knowing where Susan was, I snuck down the steps. They were in the kitchen except for Chance. Before I could turn around to walk into the living room, I felt his arms around me.

"I am so sorry, baby," he said as he cupped his hands over my face.

"I can't do this anymore, Chance. They *all* need to know the truth."

He wiped a tear from my cheek. "Come to the pool house tonight. Spend the night in my arms and we'll talk about telling him."

"Okay."

He kissed me one more time before going back into the kitchen. I sat down on the step and listened for a moment.

Chance didn't waste any time. "I am going to call it an

early night. I have a headache, and just want to lay down."

I heard some commotion, but when I ran upstairs I noticed him going into the pool house alone. He looked up and blew me a kiss before turning off his light, so that I could sneak in undetected.

When I started getting my clothes together I heard a knock on my door. I hid the evidence and opened it to find my dad.

"How are you doing, Hope?" He asked kindly.

I shrugged and held my head down embarrassed. "I'm fine, just really sorry."

"I've been drunk many times, sweetie. I am not really mad at you, just concerned about things you said. Do you miss Trevor?"

"No way! I hate him, dad, I swear."

He put his arm around me. "I want you to be with a good guy, Hope; someone that will love you and treat you with respect."

"I want that too."

"We can start over in the morning, okay?" He asked.

I nodded. "Sure."

When I heard he and Buffy talking to Susan down the hall I locked my bedroom door, and ran down the stairs. Once outside, I made my way to the pool house in no time at all. Chance was sitting there waiting for me.

I flew into his arms squeezing him so tight. "I'm so sorry. I couldn't handle it. She wouldn't shut up."

"I should have left the table. She was just trying to get a rouse out of me. You have to know I hated it too," he said.

Chance picked me up and carried me from the living room to his bedroom without releasing my lips from his.

We lay on the bed on our sides just staring at each

other for a long period of time.

"You looked beautiful tonight."

"Thank you," I whispered.

"I like it when you're jealous. You're scary, and unpredictable."

"Don't mess with me. You never know when I'll snap," I teased.

"Just as long as you take it out on me, you little tiger."

We both laughed before getting comfortable again. My Christmas may have suffered a bump in the road, but it was ending just as perfect as it started.

54

Chance

It was a mistake to even think Hope would be okay with Susan's grabby paws all over me. The woman wouldn't get the hint. All I wanted was for Hope to be with me, out in the open. So many times tonight I just wanted to tell Mark. We'd made it this long, but I didn't know if I could go until New Years.

Hope and I were deep into a kiss when someone knocked on my door. She sat up, shirtless, and looked at me. "Who do you think it is?" She whispered.

It was late, and I was sure that Mark and Buffy had called it a night. "I don't know. Just stay there. I promise I'll get rid of them." I said as I headed out of the bedroom. The snow made it bright outside, even in the middle of the night and I could see that it was Susan.

I opened the door and she came pushing in. "I can't believe you had Buffy make up the guest room," she said.

I turned to face her. She was wearing a long winter coat and stood with her hands on her hips. "Sorry. I'm not in the mood for company, Susan."

She started to approach me. "Don't you remember how good we were? How good I made you feel?"

"It was a long time ago," I admitted.

"Let me remind you then." She opened the coat to reveal some skimpy lingerie.

I turned away from her. "Please put the coat back on."

She didn't listen. Instead, she came toward me and pressed her lips against mine. I pushed her off of me. "Dammit, Susan, I said no. Get a fucking hint."

"What the fuck, Chance? Are you gay?" She asked.

"No, of course not. I have a girlfriend now, and I love her," I confessed.

She started buttoning her jacket finally. "Buffy didn't tell me," she said embarrassed.

"I didn't want anyone to know. Please don't say anything to them. I don't want them knowing my business, " I said as I pretty much pushed her back out of the door.

"If you change your mind, you know where to find me," she said.

I made my way back into the bedroom. Hope was sitting up hugging her naked chest. "I can't believe you didn't get dressed."

"I think I want to get caught. I can't hide this anymore, Chance. Look at everything we've had to go through. I can't stand it."

"Me either," I admitted as I pulled her back into my arms.

Hope finally fell asleep, but I stayed awake wondering

how all of this was going to play out. I needed for her to be cool for a few more days. Once she was eighteen, they couldn't stop us.

Three days later, things were still weird being around Susan. She'd gone from throwing herself on me, to eerily watching my every move. Mark had pulled me aside twice and asked what was wrong with her. It was hard to tell him that she wasn't Hope.

Buffy made Hope a beautiful birthday cake and dinner. Her father had gone out and got her a new laptop for deciding to go to school, and she was so surprised. I slipped her a gift in private. I had printed out a photo we took at the beach that time we went together. I made a paper frame for it and wrote a note on the back about how much she meant to me.

Hope's birthday dinner was also the rehearsal dinner for the wedding. We had a house full, and there was a bunch of people stopping by. After the minister who was performing the ceremony had gone over all of the details, everyone began to leave. Of course, that left the five of us in the house again to ring in the New Year.

Susan had drank a bit too much, and was attempting to grope all over me again. This time she cornered me in a hallway and wouldn't take no for an answer. I shook my head, pushed her away, and called it a night.

Hope joined me after an hour of waiting, and I gave her the other half of her present. We rang in the New Year and afterwards, I spent at least thirty minutes kissing her, with my lips, my tongue, on every inch of her body. When my head reached her tender skin between her legs, she cried out in ecstasy. I love satisfying her and for the first time I didn't have to hide it.

We fell asleep naked in my bed, and when Buffy came in to wake us up, Hope never even moved. "Seriously? You guys want to get caught on my wedding day?"

"She's an adult, Buff, let her enjoy it." I stated while still holding her close to me.

"Okay, well before you spill the beans to everyone, could you at least give me one day to get married?" She pleaded.

Hope and I sat up, realizing how much it was upsetting her. "Sorry, Buff. We're being selfish. You're right. We can tell my father about us another day. What is a few more days, right?" Hope said.

"Well, I came in here to let you both know that your dad and Susan are already up. We have a bunch to do, and I just knew Hope was in here. I would appreciate it if you could get yourselves up and arrive in the house at separate times," she said frustrated.

"We'll get there when we get there. Calm down. You're just being bitchy because you're nervous."

Buffy held her hands up in the air. "Whatever, Chance! It is my day, you know?"

When she stormed out I pulled Hope down for another kiss.

"Maybe we should head to the main house," she suggested.

"Yeah, probably." I kissed her once more. "But, I hate pretending that I don't want you." He looked up at me and licked his lips. "Because, I always want you."

A few minutes later Hope and I got up and made our separate entrances into the main house, like my sister wanted. Buffy finally calmed down, and we were able to start getting everything ready. Since they decided to have the service at the Country Club, we all had to pile into cars and make our way there.

The service started at two and only about twenty people had been invited. The wedding party was just one of Mark's friends and myself, and then Hope and Susan.

Buffy had spent hours upon hours making centerpieces with mason jars. She and Hope had taken at least ten jars out back and spray painted the insides silver. She found these pink and white flowers that matched her colors and filled the jars. I thought it was stupid until I was standing there looking at the finished product.

I should have never doubted my sister's creativity. She was amazing.

Hope came down the aisle first, and I felt like I was going to lose it because she was so beautiful. Her hair had been curled to perfection and she looked like a china doll. She caught my eyes while she marched and never even paid attention to her father noticing. I was shocked when he turned and nodded at me, as if knowing she was looking at me.

My sister looked beautiful marching down the aisle and she seemed so happy. I wanted to walk her, but she insisted on doing it herself.

That was my sister.

Her dress wasn't old-fashioned. As a secret surprise to me, and a promise to our mom, she had taken our mother's wedding dress that she kept, and had a professional dressmaker alter it to her tastes. Tiny fabric roses lined the top of the strapless dress. They also surrounded the circumference of the entire base. I'd only seen pictures of my mother's dress, but Mark filled me in about it right before she came down the aisle. I got choked up about it, even before I saw her. My mom would have been so proud of my sister and the life she'd made. She had a man that adored her, and had stuck by me, even when I was at my worst.

During the ceremony, I couldn't take my eyes off of Hope. When the minister asked them to repeat the vows, I mouthed "I do" to Hope. She did the same to me. I noticed Susan staring at me the entire time and realized she must have thought I was saying the words to her. I'd ignored her for days, but she still wouldn't let it go. It made me feel sorry for her, but not enough to care about her being upset.

After the ceremony, as we were stepping out, I was supposed to walk with Hope, but Susan threw herself in front of her and took my arm. I watched Hope's eyes get big, and at that very moment, I realized she'd reached her breaking point. I tried to get her attention, but her hateful eyes bore into Susan.

"What do you think you're doing?" I heard Hope ask.

"Taking what's mine. It's time to celebrate," Susan spat out.

Before I even knew what was going on, I saw Hope pulling Susan away from me. "He'll never be yours, you bitch," she screamed.

The music finally stopped while Mark and Buffy stood watching in disbelief.

"Little girl, I don't know what kind of crush you have on him, but I can assure you he is way out of your league." Susan gritted her teeth and shoved Hope. I knew in that instant that things were about to get ugly. In a matter of seconds I watched as our secret unraveled in front of us.

I grabbed Hope, assumingly praying that she'd stay silent until I got her into another room. Mark and Buffy were busy at the far end of the room, but quickly saw the commotion. As the congregation surrounded them with congratulations, I pulled my girlfriend along, ducking into the room beside the one we were in.

She forced her arm out of my grasp. "What the hell?"

"Think about what you're doing."

Susan rounded the corner. Her eyes filled with confusion as she approached. "Look, kid, I don't know what you're trying to pull here. It's obvious you have some crush on Chance. If your daddy found out he'd blow a gasket. Go on and be a good girl. Chance and I need to get some things straight."

I swallowed the lump in my throat, preparing to watch Hope react. While wedging myself conveniently between them, Hope lunged alongside me. "I'm not a little girl." She shoved Susan, forcing her to fall down on her ass. She arose quickly, staggering toward Hope full-force. Hope managed to yank a chunk of Susan's hair, causing her to retreat backwards. While standing her ground, I saw a fire in Hope's eyes. She'd held in her jealousy for days, letting it brew until she was steaming.

As the women taunted each other with words, I watched Mark hauling ass into the room and Buffy was right behind him.

Hope pushed Susan again. I could hear Buffy gasping.

"You whore! You have no idea what I can do," Hope yelled. I tried to restrain her, but she was steady going at Susan. "You've been here for days throwing yourself at him like he's a piece of meat. How pathetic are you?"

Susan turned toward me. "How do you stand living

with this shit? Mark, come get a handle on your kid. I don't have time for this."

"Hope! Stop this now!" Mark ordered. Once he separated them, he looked at his daughter. I knew what he was seeing. The truth was written across her angry face. "What's the meaning of this? Dammit, ever since Susan came here you've been acting crazy. I want the truth, Hope. What's gotten into you?"

My stomach started to knot up, like everything was going in slow motion. Hope wouldn't look at me and there was only one reason that would happen. She was going to tell him, and she knew I'd try to stop her. Before I could yell, scream, or grab her by the hand and run out of there, she just started talking. "I love him, Dad."

He clearly had blinders on. "What do you mean you love him? Honey, this is all about some crush? I get that you've been spending a lot of time together, and you see him as someone you can trust, but -."

"I've loved him since before you even introduced us. We'd already met when I came to live here."

I caught Buffy's stare, and knew she was scared to death that he'd learn she was in on the secret.

"I don't understand. How is that possible?"

Here it came. With my heart beating out of my chest, I turned to look at Hope, listening as she finally came clean about us.

"I can't keep lying about it anymore. We've been a couple since the summer."

"A couple? What...Wait a minute. You're telling me that this isn't a crush you have for Chance? You're saying he's been involved with you for months?" From the tone of his voice I knew I was in deep shit. I clench my fists together, preparing for him to come at me. After all, I'd been screwing his daughter. What father wouldn't want to kill me?

He turned and looked at me with so much animosity. Hope wouldn't back down though. "We tried to stop, but it only made us stronger." Tears filled her eyes. "Dad, this isn't Chance's fault. It was me from the beginning."

He pointed in my direction. "I want you out of my pool house. Do you hear me?"

I nodded, knowing that there was nothing I could do. He'd warned to stay away. "Yeah. I hear you."

"Dad, no. Please, you can't do this. Chance didn't do anything wrong." Hope was pleading, while my sister remained silent.

I felt Susan tucking her arm inside of mine. I turned to look at her, shocked she'd not gotten the hint. "You can come home with me. I've got a spare room, not that you'll need it."

I tugged out of her hold, giving her a dirty look as I backed up. "I'm not interested. Don't you get it, Susan?"

"Dad, you can't kick him out. If he goes, then so do I." Hope placed her hands on her hips and waited for him to reply. He looked from me then back to his daughter.

"This is going to be dealt with before the night is over. This is not happening under my roof." That threat was geared to me, not his daughter. He thought he could control the situation. It was obvious that he didn't have a clue about the seriousness of our relationship.

When her dad grabbed her arm to pull her back into the next room, she retracted it, stepping away from him. "No. I'm not leaving Chance in here with her. I refuse to watch this slut try to put her claws into my boyfriend anymore."

"Who are you calling a slut, you little tramp?" Susan added.

Buffy put her body in front of Susan's and Mark held Hope back. "This has to stop, Susan. Leave her alone. Just let them be."

I wanted to say something, but I was in shock. My sister had tears running down her eyes. We'd ruined her ceremony, and now she was going to start her marriage in a battle with her new husband.

Mark turned to Buffy. "Did you know?" He seemed hurt, like she'd defied his trust in the worst way possible.

Before she could answer, I interrupted. "She didn't know. We didn't tell anyone."

He turned to face me. "Oh, now you speak? You promised me, Chance. You promised that you wouldn't touch her." The pain in his eyes ripped right through me. "I told you when she first came to live with us that she was off limits."

"You're right. I did promise you, but I'd already fallen in love with her." I took a deep breath, preparing myself to be hit with a fist. "I fell in love with her the first night we were together, and it was weeks before she moved in with us."

He seemed so confused. I couldn't even begin to look in Hope's direction, after confessing that I'd loved her for so long.

He ran his hands through his hair, never taking his eyes off of his daughter. Had it not been for my being afraid he'd come after me, I would have laced my hand with Hope's.

"I don't understand. You couldn't have met her," he reiterated.

Hope interrupted, "I met Chance when I first came to see you here. Then we crossed paths again later on that day." She shook her head. "It's a long story. Then after that, he saved me when Rylee snuck us into a bar you all happened to be at. I didn't want you to catch me, and when my friend

458

refused to leave, Chance got me out of there."

Mark's eyes lit up. He knew exactly when it happened. He turned to me. "When the police came, they asked you questions you wouldn't answer? Is that because you were with my daughter?"

I nodded my head. "I found out how old Hope was after the fact. I swear I didn't know. She was in the bar, for Christ sakes. Anyway, I knew I couldn't let the police know that she was a minor, so I lied to keep her safe, and me out of jail. I didn't want you to find out about that night for several reasons; one being the fact that she was your daughter." *This guy was going to kill me for sure.*

Mark was so pissed that he looked to have tears in his eyes.

"I love her, Mark. I tried so hard to stay away after she moved in. I treated her like crap, and pretended that she meant nothing to me. I fought my feelings. We both did."

He looked over to Hope. "This is why you've been acting so weird? It's not because you're on drugs?"

She nodded. "We didn't want to tell you until my birthday, but Susan wouldn't leave Chance alone. I couldn't take it anymore. She's like a leech. Do you have any idea how it felt for me to watch her doing everything she could to be with him?"

He raised his brow and looked over at Buffy. "It explains a lot, that's for sure."

"I know you're upset. We both lied to you, but only because you gave us no other options. Chance and I are together, and I'm eighteen now. No matter how you feel, you can't stop us from being together." She was almost threatening him with it. I didn't know how he would react. "I won't let you kick him out of the pool house. Soon, we'll leave for college, and you won't be able to control us there either. Dad, I've spent the last couple of months trying my best to get back some kind of relationship with you. You've hurt me, worse than I'd ever wish on anyone, even Susan right now. You didn't trust me, and you put yourself before me, more times than I care to count. I'm telling you right now that Chance and I are going to be together, and if you want me to be a part of your life, you won't do anything to come between us. Like I said before, we're sorry for keeping it a secret. We knew it was wrong, but weren't willing to let anything stand in our way, including you."

The man shook his head, unable to come to grips with everything. "I think my biggest problem is that you two snuck around for months. This was all going on in my own house."

The caterers came in and interrupted us, inquiring as to when we'd be joining them. Buffy got rid of them quickly, without making a scene.

"Please say that you forgive us. Please, Dad. We're a family now. We have to be around each other."

"I need to talk to Chance alone." Was all he said.

I looked back and saw the two women that I loved the most in the world standing there with tears in their eyes. My sister was never going to forgive us for this. They walked out slowly, following a very confused Susan.

Mark headed over and closed the door behind them.

"Sit down," he ordered.

I did as he said and peered below at the floor, unable to accept that this could be the end of our friendship, if there was ever one at all.

"Do you have any of those cigarettes on you?" He asked.

"I quit for Hope months ago," I admitted.

"Of course you did." He shook his head and almost smiled. "You've really put me in a bad place, Chance. I trusted you with my daughter, and you gave me your word. Now, after all of this time I've really gotten to know you and accepted you into my family, you do this. I appreciated how you're always there for Hope, but I thought you treated her like a sister. I knew that you cared, I just didn't understand how much. Why didn't you tell me that you'd been together? Why go along with some charade that you were strangers?" He ran his hands through his hair. "I love you like you're my own son, Chance. I know you couldn't have committed that crime in Pennsylvania. I may not have believed it at first, albeit I know now."

"Mark, I'm sorry. I don't know what to say. I should have told you. We were just afraid that you'd keep us apart. Plus you went out of your way to get me back into school, and then Hope decided she wanted to go. There was never a good time to tell you," I admitted.

"I probably would have sent you away if I found out. God knows I haven't been a good father, Chance. I've hurt my daughter, abandoned her, and lost her respect. After all this time I finally feel like we're getting somewhere. How am I supposed to handle this?" He was trying so hard to settle this, but after Hope's threats he knew it was out of his hands. "I should've known. I should've seen it."

"Keeping us apart wouldn't have changed how I feel about her. Please give me the opportunity to show you. Let us be together with your blessing. She's given me my life back, Mark. When I moved here, after losing so much, I just wanted to give up. Hope changed that. She changed me," I admitted.

"So, you're asking for my permission to date my daughter, after you've obviously been together for the past seven months?" He asked.

I took a deep breath. There was no turning back. I had waited so long for this. "Yes."

Mark didn't say anything. He just stood there looking at me. Just when I thought all hope was lost, he extended his hand to me. "Fine."

As shocking as it was, I made it a point to keep my smiles to a minimum. "Thank you."

"I'm doing this for my daughter, and my wife. Buffy would never forgive me if I sent you away."

That was the truth. My sister would have given him a hard time about it. Through thick and thin she always had my back.

"For what it's worth, I'm sorry I lied. I get that you're angry with us, probably mostly me. It's understandable. I'll prove to you that I can be someone she can count on."

"I'll hold you to that, Chance. She's my only daughter."

It was another promise that I intended to keep. "As much as I'd like to carry on this conversation, I think I've taken up enough of you wedding. It's time for you to get back to your bride."

Yes, I was trying to get out of being alone in a room with Mark. His kindness only went so far, and after he'd sent me away before, I didn't want to risk pissing him off.

Once I'd made it back into the reception area, I spotted Hope. On my way toward her, Susan stopped me. "So she's the girl? She's the one you've been seeing?"

I never took my eyes off of Hope when I answered. "Yep. She's the one."

I have no idea how Susan looked when she was speaking. My gaze was fixed on the most beautiful woman in the room. "I'm sorry for throwing myself on you. I assumed she was being a teenager."

"Thanks for that." I glanced at her for second. "If you'll excuse me, there's someone I need to attend to."

I couldn't wait to have her in my arms out in the open. In front of her father, and everyone else in the room, I marched right up to my girlfriend and planted a kiss on her lips. She was mine, and I wanted everyone to know it. This was the moment we'd been waiting for, and finally it was happening.

Hope pulled away and wiped the lip-gloss off of my mouth. "You made it out alive."

"Only because my girlfriend threatened her father."

"I did what had to be done. He'd just overreact anyway. Besides, we'll be living together soon enough at school."

"Are you ready to start the new chapter of our future?"

She smiled and rested her head on my chest. "I'm ready, as long as I'm with you."

I placed my lips against her forehead. "I was hoping you'd say that."

In that moment nothing else existed except for the two of us. We had so much to be thankful for.

"Now that we don't have to hide, I almost don't know what we'll do," she admitted.

"Well for starters, we need to talk your dad into helping us get an apartment within the next week, because I'm not spending a single night without you in my bed."

"We could even share a room to save on cost," she suggested.

We both laughed. "Yeah. I'm cool sharing my space

with you. I'll even promise to put the seat down."

"How mighty kind of you." She rest wrapped her arms tighter around me.

"I know it was yesterday, but happy birthday, baby. I hope you got everything you wanted."

"I did," she said as we swayed to the music.

I woke up on edge, considering that I'd waited for this moment since the day I'd been kicked out of my last college. To be able to play baseball again, in front of a stadium full of people was quite an achievement. For me, it was much more. This wasn't about becoming a famous ballplayer. It didn't have anything to do with chasing my dreams.

It was about freedom.

Two weeks ago I was visited by several FBI agents. You can imagine the panic of seeing them sitting on my couch waiting to interrogate me. The look on Hope's face made it even worse.

It took five minutes and one phone call to confirm that I'd been at practice, in front of forty-eight men, all day long. Once they knew my alibi was rock-solid, I was informed of another attack at Penn State. The murder was exactly the same as my friend's had been. This most recent victim was raped and left in a ravine, this time with a note stating that they would never catch the assailant.

The sheer relief of what was happening besieged me. I couldn't recall a time when I felt so free. Being as I was no longer considered a suspect in two murders, I even received an apology. Nothing could bring back my mother, from the stress that led to her death, but I prayed that she was looking down on me, proud of the new life I'd found.

I know she'd be proud of my sister. Buffy's new business was doing great. Her grand opening brought in a huge crowd, and I'd never in my life seen her this happy.

As for Hope and I, well after convincing Mark to help us get an apartment together, we settled into not having to hide our relationship. It wasn't difficult considering that we enjoyed being alone more often than out in public. As soon as courses began I was busy with baseball. I spent every weekend at the batting cages, or the gym. One thing I had on my side was the fact that I'd stayed in shape. Not playing ball for a year hadn't taken away my skillset. After the fourth practice I was back on track. Since I wasn't there on a scholarship, I had less stress, finding it easy to manage schoolwork with everything else on my plate. Hope struggled at first, but finally got into the groove of how things worked.

We thought everything was going to be smooth sailing, until my coach called me into his office. Apparently new guidelines were being incorporated. There was a chance that I'd have to live on campus at least during baseball season. I knew it applied when I was on a scholarship, albeit it hadn't been implemented on any of my paperwork. I'd been assured that in my case it wasn't necessary.

Still, my coach was adamant about making sure I

knew that it could be an issue. There were ways around me having to move into a dorm. Convincing Hope it was good idea wasn't without a little effort. I'd sat her down one night after practice. I think she could tell that something was wrong. "Hope, I've got something we need to discuss."

"Me too."

This caught me off guard. I wasn't expecting her to have something to tell. "You do? Is everything okay?"

She shrugged and looked down at her folded hands. I could tell something was bothering her. "Is it because I'm away all the time for baseball?" Even though it was important to me, nothing meant more than having her by my side.

"No. Not directly. I mean, I suppose it could be hard for me if you were gone, but I'd figure out how to deal with things on my own."

"I'm confused."

Hope reached over, taking my hands in hers. "Please don't freak out."

"I'm about to if you don't start talking. After everything we've been through, why would you think you need to handle everything on your own?"

"Because this is sort of my fault. Okay, it's all my fault," she corrected herself. "I should have remembered. I can't believe that it never crossed my mind. It's just that with school, and moving, I forgot all about it."

With our fingers intertwined, I squeezed, reminding her that whatever she was overreacting about we'd figure it out together. "Hope, talk to me."

"You're going to be so mad at me."

Had she cheated on me? Did she give some random guy in one of her classes her cell phone number? I couldn't figure out what it was, or what she could have forgotten.

Then, as her eyes widened, I realized what I was overlooking. It was at that very moment when I figured out what she had forgotten. It would not only impact our relationship, but both of our futures. "You didn't?"

She looked away, and I watched tears fall down her cheeks.

"Hope, look at me."

She refused.

"Seriously, look at me." I removed my hands from hers to avoid letting her feel how I'd begun to tremble. This wasn't something that I would have expected. We'd gotten carried away with our new life to even think that we'd overlooked something so important. She was blaming herself, but I was equally at fault. This didn't just fall on Hope and her carelessness.

"I can't. I don't want to see how upset you'll be." She began to sob. "I'm so sorry, Chance. I know you don't need this on your plate right now. After everything you've went through to get back into my dad's good graces, this is going to screw it all up."

"Would you shut up for a minute and let me talk?"

She wiped her eyes and nodded.

"I love you. No matter what happens, that's not going to change. Stop putting the burden all on yourself. I don't give a shit what Mark thinks. We're adults. We can deal with our own problems."

"So it's a problem?" She implied.

"No!" I shook my head. "I'm not saying that. You're putting words in my mouth."

"You're the one who said it."

I ran my hands through my hair, reminding myself that I was in desperate need of a shower. "Jesus, would you stop freaking out for a second? I'm trying here, but you're not making it easy."

"None of this is easy," she cried.

I slid off the couch, crouching down in front of her. My hands found her thighs and I kept them there, trying desperately to find the right words. "It's easy, because it's us, Hope."

Slowly, she lifted her gaze until our eyes met. A smile formed out of the corner of her lips. "I don't know what to do."

I looked around the room. "You're right. This place probably won't be big enough, so we're going to need at least a two bedroom apartment. I don't see us being able to get out of our lease, but by the time the baby's born we can start looking. I mean, at first they'll sleep in our room, but -."

She leaned forward and put her fingers over my mouth to prevent me from speaking. I watched more tears trickle down her cheeks. "You're not mad?"

Mad? How could I be mad? "A year ago I thought I had no future. Look at me now. I'm playing ball again. I'm back in school, and I have the most beautiful woman by my side. The fact that you're carrying my child would *not* make me mad. Hope, it's not going to be easy, and I'm certainly going to be traveling a lot, at least until the season is over, but it's temporary. It's only a few months out of the year. I'll be home with you when the baby is born, and we'll figure things out."

Hope interrupted, "Saying it out loud makes it real."

I wiped the wetness on her cheeks away with my thumbs. "So it's true?" I think I needed her to confirm, even though I already knew the answer.

"Yes. I'm pregnant. I forgot to take my pills. In fact, I

forgot to refill them. It's just that I'd needed to switch pharmacy's and it seriously slipped my mind."

I smiled, even though I was unsure how I felt about everything. "I'm not angry with you, Hope. We've been busy. I haven't asked you about it either. You're dad's going to be pissed, but he'll get over it. There's nothing he can do anyway."

"What if I can't stay in school? What will we do about money?"

"For now, I'll use my savings. After baseball ends I'll get a job and we'll save every penny. If I can't finish my senior year after the baby comes it will be there waiting for me."

"Are you sure you want this? There are other options." She looked down, as if she was ashamed to talk about it.

"That's not happening. If we need to move back into the pool house to save money we will. For now let's just focus on school. We'll get you in to see a doctor, and go from there."

"Okay," she whispered.

"We'll figure this out, Hope. I promise." I wasn't so much worried about the baby, as much as I was afraid to tell her that we might have to live apart. It wasn't going to go over well, and with this new surprise coming into play, I needed to make some serious decisions. Our futures were about to change again, but this time I'd be able to accept it.

Hope

He promised we'd be okay, but I wasn't too sure. Chance was living his dream again. This pregnancy could end that for the second time. It petrified me.

We tried not to talk much about it due to the fact that he was playing in his opening game. My father and Buffy had made the drive to watch him. After meeting up with them we headed into the stadium and found our seats.

The early spring weather was crisp. I stuck my hands into Chance's new WVA hoodie to keep warm. Chance was playing catch with a teammate, but stopped to wave at me when our eyes met. I threw him a smile back, feeling like I was the luckiest girl in the world.

Then I got my first taste of what it was like to be the girlfriend of a college baseball player.

A slew of girls, all looking to be my age, filling in the lower bleachers. They certainly weren't wearing ball caps and planning on cheering because they loved the sport. Chance followed his teammates over to the side as they mingled with this group. I felt bile rising to my throat, even when he backed away, and ignored the catcalls.

It was difficult, even with him winking at me, and waving. I knew I couldn't always be at the games, and soon I'd be fat. I worried that he'd be tempted by another, and I'd end up alone.

Jennifer Foor

I suppose my hormones were making me think the worst. In my defense my last boyfriend had cheated, so it was all I knew. Chance's faithfulness to me was reassuring, but one could only take so much before they broke down. There would be nights when he was on the road, and they'd tempt him.

I recalled him telling me about them before. I think I just never realized how obvious they were.

Aside from my ill feelings, Chance played a great game. He struck out once, but ended up hitting three RBI's. His fielding was impeccable, and I understood why the scouts wanted him on their team. He was beneficial in his position, and proved to be a solid addition.

After the game we went out to celebrate. I kept my cool around my father, worrying about the pregnancy, and now Chance's fan base. It wasn't until we went home that I revealed my concerns. We'd both showered and climbed into our bed. Chance was still hyped from the game, and I could feel his excitement radiating off of him. He nudged me with his lips, before pulling me on top of him. "We should celebrate, baby."

I straddled him, letting my fingers tickle his rock-hard chest. "I need to talk to you about something first, and you're going to be pissed at me."

"Don't worry about those women. They're pathetic, and I'm so over that. You've got nothing to be concerned about. I'm not on the lookout for a quick fuck."

Just hearing him reiterate his previous statement made me calm down. I let my head fall down over him. "I hated seeing them."

"Hope, what can any of them offer me that I don't already have? I get that college is new to you, but it's just school for me. I've hooked up with girls like that a couple times my freshman year, before I got a girlfriend. They're looking for one thing, and I wasn't falling for it. Compared to you, they're nothing."

"What about when I gain a thousand pounds?"

He began laughing. "A thousand? Damn, that's a good question. I don't think you'd be able to move around with a thousand pound baby inside of you."

I lightly smacked his chest. "Be serious. You know what I meant."

"I'll still want you, Hope. I'll always want you. Don't you get that by now? I defied your father, and have done nothing but prove my faithfulness. I love the game, but not all that comes with it. I know it's going to be hard for you at first, but you'll get used to it. I'll make you see that you have nothing to worry about. I promise. I have the only cheerleader I need right here with me."

"I'm sorry. I know you want to celebrate. I'm being a downer." I felt terrible about bringing it up, even though he didn't act annoyed.

"No biggie. So where were we?"

I reached down inside of his boxers and took him into my hand. "I think we were right here."

Chance leaned forward and sucked my bottom lip in between his. Our kissing intensified, and I soon forgot all about the sleazy broads at his game. Chance was mine, and he wasn't going anywhere. I was carrying his child, and soon everyone would know it. Although I'd never get pregnant to trap him into being with me, it did give me some comfort knowing how devoted he was to our baby and me.

We'd come so far, and had a lot to look forward to. I was scared, which could be expected, but knew we'd figure out a way to make it work. If I had to babysit children, or take online classes while caring for my own child, I'd do it. Our first years were going to be a struggle, albeit I wasn't going to give up. I'd found love, forgiveness, and a reason to want to strive to be better. That was enough to put a smile on my face, and ease my soul.

Chance pulled away from me and began cackling. "I just realized something."

"What?" His excitement alarmed me.

"We don't have to talk about baby names."

"This is random. What do you mean?"

"If it's a girl it's Faith. If it's a boy it's -."

I hushed him. "Don't even say it. We are not naming our kid Lucky."

He pulled me in for a kiss, in which I fought him. It made him more determined to get under my skin. "Little Lucky will be born with a golden glove on his hand. I bet his first word will be ball, and then daddy."

"You're ridiculous. It's not happening."

He nodded. "It is. You just wait."

I appreciated his banter, especially considering the way I'd been worried. This was the man I loved, and he was all mine.

The End

Hope and Chance have a lot going on. Look for a novella in 2015 featuring more from the couple.

If you enjoyed this book, please share a comment or review.
Let me know what you think of this book by contacting me at the following:

www.jenniferfoor.com

http://www.facebook.com/JenniferFoorAuthor
www.jennfoor@gmail.com
http://twitter.com/jennyfoor

www.jennyfoor.wordpress.com
http://www.goodreads.com/jennyfoor

Jennifer Foor lives on the Eastern Shore of Maryland with her husband and two children. She enjoys shooting pool, camping and catching up on cliché movies that were made in the eighties.